June 2023

Dear Reader,

I'm excited to put into your hands Maggie Thrash's adult debut.

We all as readers are looking for those uncommon books that crack open the world on the first page, ensnare us totally, and cause us to come out the other end seeing things anew. To say *Rainbow Black* is one of those rare transporting reading experiences – which I will! – somehow doesn't do justice to the vein of dark hilarity and punk energy that runs through it. This novel truly is both the "rainbow" and the "black."

The story of Lacey Bond's young life is both beautifully told and utterly harrowing. It's also deeply funny when you least expect it and most need it. Finally, like all great books, it's a mystery....

Thanks for your reading time.

Sincerely yours,

Noah Eaker

VP/Executive Editor

IN-HOUSE PRAISE

"*Rainbow Black* is a stunning piece of work. The novel grabs you and doesn't let go, taking you on a journey that covers the Satanic Panic of the 1990s, the failure of the criminal justice system and child protective services, and the coming-of-age of a remarkable girl who has been failed by every adult in her life and survived unbelievable trauma. Lacey Bond is a character I will hold in my heart for a long time."

—MEGAN LOONEY, senior marketing manager

"This is a special book—one that I couldn't put down, didn't want to end, and can't stop thinking about. The Satanic Panic caught my interest, but Lacey Bond found my heart. Her remarkable resilience will stay with me for a long time!"

—AMY BAKER, vice president and associate publisher

"Lacey Bond is an outsider, and *Rainbow Black* is her coming-of-age story amid tragic events starting with the arrest of her parents who are accused of horrible crimes during the Satanic Panic of the 1990s. It's also a love story. Maggie Thrash has a real talent for language and bringing her characters to vivid life. The novel is darkly funny and beautifully written. I highly recommend!"

—MARY BETH THOMAS, vice president and deputy director of sales, independent bookstores

"This story is epic, twisted and twisty, and the characters are utterly fresh while remaining completely relatable. *Rainbow Black* is the murder mystery/gay international fugitive love story I didn't know I needed: timely and timeless and unequivocally cool."

—EDIE ASTLEY, editorial assistant

RAINBOW BLACK

ALSO BY MAGGIE THRASH

Lost Soul, Be at Peace

Strange Lies

Strange Truth

Honor Girl

RAINBOW BLACK

A Novel

MAGGIE THRASH

HARPER ● PERENNIAL

NEW YORK ● LONDON ● TORONTO ● SYDNEY ● NEW DELHI ● AUCKLAND

HARPER PERENNIAL

HarperCollins books may be purchased for educational, business, or sales promotional use. For information, please email the Special Markets Department at SPsales@harpercollins.com.

FIRST EDITION

Designed by Jamie Lynn Kerner

Library of Congress Cataloging-in-Publication Data:

Names: Thrash, Maggie, author.
Title: Rainbow black: a novel / Maggie Thrash.
Description: First edition. | New York, NY: HarperPerennial, 2024.
Identifiers: LCCN 2023017698 | ISBN 9780063286870 (trade paperback) | ISBN 9780063286863 (ebook)
Subjects: LCSH: Moral panics—United States—Fiction. | United States—Moral conditions—Fiction. | LCGFT: Bildungsromans. | Thrillers (Fiction) | Novels.
Classification: LCC PS3620.H7966 R35 2024 | DDC 813/.6—dc23/eng/20230421
LC record available at https://lccn.loc.gov/2023017698

ISBN 978-0-06-328687-0

23 24 25 26 27 LBC 5 4 3 2 1

to Nico

I simply want to live; to cause no evil to anyone but myself.

—LEO TOLSTOY, ANNA KARENINA

PART ONE

I'M STILL HERE, LIKE ONE OF THOSE CHILD STARS who's been around forever, one who, five nervous breakdowns into her career, people are astonished to learn is only twenty-eight. Baked into every newspaper article and television segment about my blown identity is a sense of surprise that I hadn't been frozen in time, that my life continued after the Medusa's eye of the American news machine moved on and forgot me. In a decade I imagine they'll circle back and rediscover me again, and we'll revive this whole song and dance for a fresh audience.

God, I hope not. What more could there be to say? And yet, someone always seems to come up with something.

Reporters have been camped out on our street twenty-four hours a day, hoping to catch me or Gwen in a moment of candor, to ask the burning question on viewers' minds: Which one of us did it? Which of us actually pulled the trigger and killed that kid fourteen years ago?

This distinction is less legally important than you might think. We were both there, we both fled, we would both get charged with conspiracy to murder. But for normal people, people who haven't been to law school, whichever one of us made that tiny tug of her finger is the truly guilty party.

I am the obvious suspect, with my mirthless face and

dark suits, the crease in my trousers so sharp it could draw blood. But wouldn't it be thrilling if it turned out to be Gwen, the golden girl, the beauty to my beast, the supernova to my black hole? Wouldn't that be a great twist?

If I'm to give my best assessment of what happened, I would first need the right word. What's something that has the long odds of a miracle but is so colossally ruinous you'd never call it that? If I go through the whole thing from beginning to end, without mercy, overlooking nothing, will the right word become apparent?

It was "whatever," to quote the golden girl. And I guess that word is good enough to get started, to convey, right off the top, a sort of bewildered acceptance of forces that are senseless, like how a leaf in flight accepts the wind.

i

NEW HAMPSHIRE
1983

THE FIRST COURTROOM I EVER SAW WAS ON AN EPISODE OF *ONE Life to Live*. My older sister, Éclair, was a soap opera fanatic. *Days of Our Lives* was her favorite, but she watched them all. I was six at the time, and she was thirteen. For a long time our family didn't have a TV, because our parents were hippies and thought television was the harbinger of doom. "If you want to rot your brain, you can pay for it yourself someday," my mom said.

So one summer Éclair called her bluff and worked her ass off laying mulch for half the farmers in the county, quitting as soon as she had her $560. The TV she bought lived in her room like a devoted pet. I was permitted the special privilege of watching her shows with her only if I promised not to ask dumb questions ("Why did Tony give the diamond necklace to the island girl?" "What does 'blackmail' mean?"), which meant I had to fill in the blanks myself, creating an even more dizzying web of amnesia plotlines and secret agendas on top of the existing ones.

In the *One Life to Live* episode that's seared into my memory, Karen the tormented housewife is forced to testify as a witness, in defense of her best friend, Viki Lord Riley, who's been accused of murdering an evil tycoon. In the climactic scene, the merciless prosecutor rips Karen to shreds, exposing the truth that she was secretly a *prostitute*, a word that shocked the characters so much I could not even imagine what it meant.

What really confused me was why Karen was being attacked by the lawyer in the first place. Wasn't Viki Lord Riley the one on trial? Wasn't Karen just the witness?

"It doesn't matter who you are," Éclair explained. "The point is, if you have a secret, you're fucked."

It's still probably the wisest thing I've ever heard anyone say.

ii

1988

OUR PARENTS OWNED A DAY CARE THEY RAN FROM OUR HOME IN New Hampshire—a converted old barn with a bright rainbow painted on the roof. Rainbow Kids Care, it was called. We had a little goat farm with five goats (Donny, Lonny, Sunny, Spunky, and Trailblazer) and a view overlooking untouched forest, the trees skeletons in winter, ruby red in fall. The trees were home to the fairy people, according to my dad, who sat hidden in the branches and sprinkled fairy dust on our heads to keep us all safe and sound.

It was the 1980s, before those studies claiming that your kid would become a mentally ill delinquent if you didn't pick the right preschool. Before the promises of "Baby Einstein Academy" or "Stepping-Stone to Success Day Care." No one thought, when they handed over their two-through five-year-olds to my parents, that anything crucial was happening inside those two- through five-year-old brains. Keep the kids alive and reasonably happy until they could be picked up at the end of the day—that was the job. It was babysitting. Apple juice, graham crackers, finger painting, story time. I remember it all feeling pretty simple. Then again, every speck of my memory has been turned over, interrogated, and second-guessed to the point where I hardly know what I remember and what I don't.

The day after she graduated high school, Éclair put us all in the rear-view mirror and moved to Miami, about as far away from New Hampshire as a person could get while still technically being in America. Her dream was to be a backup dancer for Gloria Estefan, get "discovered," and be propelled to stardom. She soon had a whole life of her own—a wardrobe comprised entirely of leopard print, a boyfriend with a car phone and his own exercise videotape company called Bangin' Beach Bods—and her trips home were brief and infrequent.

Without her around, *Days of Our Lives* and *One Life to Live* lost their magic, and I stopped watching them. I'd gotten sort of nerdy and preferred books anyway. In the woods, there was an old shed kids called the "witch hut," and I practically lived there, reading and listening to my Walkman and doing nothing.

But what were you doing in the woods?

I was asked this a hundred times, years later, in the sterile white office of a police station.

Nothing. I was doing nothing.

Adults seem to forget that between the grind of childhood (art time, nap time, snack time) and the grind of teenagedom (soccer practice, homework, party), there is a brief, sweet set of years where no one cares what you do, and you roam free. How could I explain the idle magic of these afternoons without sounding insane? That I collected rocks and gave them names, that I imagined clouds had personalities, that I believed animals would talk to you if they trusted you. Walking, walking, walking, practically losing my identity as I followed a red fox for miles into the forest.

I took after my mother, who was always more interested in animals than in people. The two of us would discuss our animal neighbors endlessly, like a pair of ladies gossiping at the hairdresser, except instead of so-and-so got drunk and wrecked his truck or so-and-so is sleeping with the mailman, it was the black bear found a new patch of berries or the skunk's babies all had pure white tails. Occasionally my dad would interrupt us with some news from the real world:

"I'm bringing Dylan Fairbanks to stay for the week. His mom's been arrested again, and she's trying to make bail."

Mom would seem momentarily confused, as if trying to remember which animal of the forest Dylan Fairbanks was and why we would ever bring him in the house.

"...Oh, of course, put him in Éclair's room. How about I take them to the movies tonight? I need a little change of pace. Does Dylan like movies, Lacey?"

I shrugged. All I really knew about Dylan was that he loved NA-SCAR, or at least I assumed he did, because he wore the same thread-bare NASCAR T-shirt every day. Only much later would it occur to me that, quite possibly, it was the only shirt Dylan owned. I was too sheltered to understand all the things I took for granted, like clothes and a stable home life. And I was dying to know what bad thing Dylan's mom had done to wind up behind bars. Was she a bank robber? A Soviet spy? But I was too shy to ask Dylan, and my mom wouldn't tell.

We got to the Stardust drive-in movie theater as the sun was setting, and Mom spread a quilt on the grassy knoll up front, in the family-friendly area. I didn't see many kids as young as me and Dylan there. *Alien* was playing, and as soon as the movie started, it was clear that it wasn't meant for children—no talking animals or goofy sidekicks or precocious kid characters. The dark, industrial spaceship was ominous and unsettling, and when the alien finally appeared, it was so terrifying I stopped breathing. Part of me loved it; I had never been so thrilled in my life. But another part of me was already blaming my mother: *Why are you letting me watch this?*

At some point in the middle of the movie my mom leaned over and asked Dylan and me if we'd like popcorn and hot dogs. I thought she was joking. *Hot dogs?* Mom always said the body was a temple and the meat industry was the axis of evil.

"Ketchup and mustard? Ketchup and mustard? What do you like on your hot dogs?" She looked from Dylan to me, weirdly agitated. I shrugged, baffled. Then she trotted off into the darkness without waiting for an answer.

The movie was scaring me to death, and I kept glancing at Dylan to see if he was as terrified as I was. But he had the same dim look on his face as always. And when it was over, all he said was "If I met an alien, I would do a karate chop and its head would fall off."

Mom never came back with the popcorn and hot dogs. I looked around and felt a creepy disconnect from reality—was this still the movie? If I opened the car door, would I find her body torn apart and a slimy alien waiting to leap out at me?

The family-friendly area was emptying out. A caravan of minivans streamed through the front gate, leaving behind popcorn-littered turf and derelicts and people with nowhere else to be: a teenage gang kicking abandoned cups across the gravel lot, cherry Slurpee spills arcing like blood splatters; a trailer park couple drinking from a jar while a baby howled in their junky back seat; a too-thin man leaning against the chain-link fence, flashing a switchblade open and shut: *click, click, click.* I felt lost, though I hadn't moved an inch from the quilt where my mother had left us—it was everything around me that had changed. Even the group of hippies in their peace sign T-shirts seemed suddenly homeless and addled. They weren't holding hands or strumming guitars like in *Alice's Restaurant*; they were arguing viciously, pointing fingers at each other: *"Your fault!" "No, your fault!"* You heard a lot in those days about how the region was falling apart; this was the first time I'd ever seen it with my own eyes.

"Where's my mom?" I asked. Without waiting for Dylan to answer, I said, "Maybe we should wait in the car."

But the car was locked. I didn't know what to do. Should we stay put, or sneak into a dark corner and hide? I decided we should look for her. Sitting on the knoll was like asking to be kidnapped. It was the age of "stranger danger"; every kid at school knew someone who knew someone who'd gotten AIDS from a candy bar or been abducted and sold to the Amish.

"Look at those kiddies," I heard someone say. "They're on a hot date. Hey, kids! Kiddies! C'mere! Where your daddies at?"

Just like during the movie, I checked Dylan's face to see if he was scared, but he seemed totally unfazed. Maybe in his world it was normal for moms to randomly vanish. At the Snack Shack, a boy with yellow teeth was sweeping up. I wanted to ask if he'd seen my mom, but I was smart enough not to advertise that Dylan and I were alone.

"I think we should call 911," I said.

Dylan shook his head. "No, no. Call my neighbor."

"What? What are you talking about?"

"When I can't find my mom I'm supposed to call my neighbor."

I couldn't believe it. *Call 911* was drilled into the head of every kid I knew. My friend Sandy had once called 911 when she couldn't find her cat for ten minutes. I'd never met anyone who'd been told to call their *neighbor*.

"Well, who's your neighbor?" I asked.

"Hank."

"Who's Hank?"

"My neighbor."

I decided to call my dad and ask *him* if I should call 911. I don't remember how I found a dime for the pay phone. Maybe Dylan had one, or maybe I begged one from the yellow-toothed guy in the Snack Shack. In any case, I dropped the coin in the slot, pushed the grimy buttons, and waited for my dad to pick up.

"4431." To the bewilderment of most people, my dad always answered the phone with the last four digits of our number. He was a British expat, and that's how he'd grown up doing it in England.

"Daddy? I can't find Mom. She went to get us hot dogs and she never came back." There was a pause. I wondered if he hadn't heard me. "Daddy? Hello?"

"Lacey, listen to me. Don't move. Stay with Dylan and don't move an inch. I'll be there in ten minutes." He spoke urgently, with a no-nonsense tone I'd hardly ever heard in his voice before. It scared me.

"Should I call 911?"

"*No.*"

I looked at Dylan. What did he and my dad know that I didn't? What was the point of all those videos we'd watched in school about Mikey and Janie and Susie and their various emergencies if we weren't supposed to call 911? I hung up the phone.

"Hey, kiddies. You on a hot date? You gonna go all the way?"

It was one of the teenagers wearing sunglasses. I looked away, which was what we had learned in the Just Say No after-school program. Never make eye contact with someone on dope, because they might "wig out" and attack you.

I hid myself behind the phone booth. Nearby, Dylan had found a half-finished hot dog on a table and was eating it.

"Well, I'm glad you got your hot dog," I said.

"Me, too," Dylan agreed, his mouth full.

I was being sarcastic, I growled at him in my mind.

A monotone voice sounded over the drive-in speakers: "The Stardust will be closing soon, please make your way to the exit."

I felt a lump forming in my throat. *Don't cry, don't cry, don't cry.*

Finally I heard a crunch of gravel as my dad tore into the lot. He was driving the old VW bus that we hardly ever used because it always broke down. I ran up to him, Dylan padding after me.

Dad leapt out of the van. "Get in now," he barked at us, and we obeyed. Everything felt confused, and I didn't know what scared me most: aliens, hoodlums, missing moms, dope fiends, the man with the switchblade—they all mixed together in the darkness.

The windows of the bus were dirty, and we couldn't see what was happening outside in the gravel lot. I heard my dad yelling, "That's my wife! Move aside!"

I was shaking. My mother was lying there dead, I was sure. Strangely, all I could think about was how much I didn't want Dylan to see me cry.

A man shouted, "You dirty hippies, get outta here, you filthy pieces of shit, get a job, wear some shoes, this is America, you commie Jew trash, get the fuck outta my place of business!"

Then a gunshot. Dylan and I both heard it and shrieked.

The passenger door groaned open. Dad had Mom in his arms. She was alive—I could tell by the delicate way he placed her in the van, like a knight who'd rescued a princess from a dragon. Relief flooded me. Before I could open my mouth to ask what was happening, he said in a strangely calm voice:

"Don't be scared. Your mom fainted. It's just the bloody arse of a manager, shooting his gun in the air. Just trying to scare us. Everything's hunky-dory. Just a little silly drama."

In the weeks to come, he'd refuse to tell me a version of the story that I found satisfactory. So I had to make one up myself. Maybe the hippies had attacked my mother for buying a meat product, or maybe the man with the switchblade had tried to murder her because she resembled an ex-wife who had stolen his money and faked her own death.

My dad's explanation, repeated many times to me, was completely insufficient: "Your mother fainted. And the manager wasn't nice about it."

"But why was everyone yelling?"

"Because when people are confused, they yell."

"Why were they confused?"

"Because it was dark and no one could see what was happening."

"Which was what?"

"Which was exactly what I said. Your mother fainted, and the manager is a mean man who doesn't like freethinking people."

"But doesn't he know this is New Hampshire?" I asked. From a young age I'd taken our state motto, "Live Free or Die," very seriously.

My dad gave an exhausted smile. "I'm sure he does. And that, my sweet, is called irony."

The next morning my mother stayed in bed all day, listening to the Moody Blues on her record player and reading *The Feminine Mystique*.

Dad said she needed to rest and I shouldn't bother her. I was tiptoeing around the house, hoping I'd overhear something that might explain what had really happened.

"Lacey? Is that you? Will you pick me some violets from the yard? I need a little extra color today."

I picked the violets, put them in a jar, and brought them back to her. She patted the bed next to her. *Finally,* I thought, ready to hear the full story.

But I was quickly disappointed, as she proceeded to give a scattered speech about how brave I was to call my dad and look after Dylan until he got there, and how the path to womanhood was a song with a thousand beautiful verses.

"But what *happened*?" I whined.

Her tranquil smile went flat. "Lacey, life is an art, not a science. Facts don't exist. Just live in the moment."

While these pseudo-philosophical question-avoiding tactics worked on a ten-year-old, they would later do her incredible damage. You can't tell law enforcement officers, a judge, and a jury that facts don't exist.

I couldn't wait to tell Éclair what had happened. The story contained so many motifs from her beloved *Days of Our Lives*: a damsel, a hero, gunshots, fainting, an array of mysterious strangers. Once a month I was allowed a very expensive long-distance call with her in Miami.

But when I told her the story, her reaction was not at all what I'd hoped.

"Éclair, did you hear what I said? There was a gunshot. And Dad was carrying Mom and she was *unconscious*. And the manager was screaming every bad word I've ever heard."

There was a long pause. Finally Éclair said, "Lacey, I want you to promise me never to go to the Stardust again."

"Well, Daddy says the manager is a bigot and we won't be patronizing his establishment anyway."

"I'm sure that's what he says . . ."

I'd been waiting for days to talk to Éclair, and the tepidness of her response made my heart deflate like a day-old balloon. She was barely interested in any of my wild theories and kept repeating, "Just promise not to go there, okay?"

When I tried to discuss the incident with Dylan, still loafing at our house while his mom sat in jail, he didn't seem to grasp that anything unusual had happened. He told me, delightedly, "One time, at the mall, the police chased me and my mom, and I got to hide in a suitcase in the luggage department for five whole hours!"

With no other options, I begged my dad constantly, "Please, please, please tell me what happened."

One day it seemed like he was about to crack. We were in the study, an austere room full of books and framed prints of moths and butter-flies from the nineteenth century. "Lacey, come here," he said, gesturing to his knee. I hadn't sat in anyone's lap in ages, fancying myself basically an adult, and I hesitated.

"Come *here*," he repeated, and I obeyed. I was stiff and awkward at first; I'd grown tall for my age and didn't fit snugly in his arm the way I used to. But once I stopped resisting, I felt the heavy cloak of father and daughter settle around our shoulders, musty with age but warm as ever. It was a love story largely unwritten; I'd consumed enough Greek mythology to notice that when daughters appeared in the stories at all, it was usually to be married off, locked up, or killed by their dads.

My father struck a match and lit his old briar wood pipe. He smoked English Cavendish tobacco. I loved the smell of it and breathed in as much as I could.

"I know you think you're all grown up," he said, "but there are things you don't understand about the world."

"What things?"

"You don't need to know. All you need to know is that I'm here, and I'll protect you. I promise I will never let anything bad happen to you or your mother or Éclair. Do you believe me?"

I was unsure. Dad was a male preschool teacher, hardly anyone's idea of Superman. And yet, the way he'd shown up at the Stardust and saved us all had been nothing short of heroic. I weighed these things, making my decision, and if that seems precocious, I assure you it ended up being the same decision any ten-year-old would make: to choose to believe her parents would deliver on their promises.

"Yes," I said finally.

My dad rubbed the top of my head. "Good. Then stop this silly behavior. Go back to living your life."

And I knew then that the conversation was over, that I'd gotten all the information I was going to get. Life resumed, and it became clear that nothing like that night at the Stardust was going to happen again. My curiosity faded. But at odd times, trying to fall asleep during a full moon or walking home from the bus stop with a book in my hand, my mind would wander back, and long-sunk questions would bob to the surface: Where was my mom for the entire second half of the movie? Why had the manager shot the gun in the first place? It seemed like a fairly extreme way to inform people that the drive-in was closed. Was there something I'd forgotten, a piece of the puzzle lost at sea and disintegrating into the black water? I could almost feel it, floating just out of reach. *Something. Something. I remember. I remember.*

iii

1990

BY AGE THIRTEEN I WAS AS STEREOTYPICALLY NEW HAMPSHIRE as could be, like a cardboard cutout created by the tourist bureau (COME SEE OUR RUGGED WOMEN AND GIRLS!). I wore hiking boots to school, I had a sweatshirt sewn into my denim jacket, I knew how to tap for maple syrup, and I hated the government for vague reasons related to "freedom." Meanwhile Éclair increasingly resembled Debbie Gibson. She'd figured out from a young age that she had "it," that God-given quality that distinguishes cool girls from posers. At this point we were like a TV movie about a pop star and a farm girl playing long-lost sisters separated at birth.

The only thing we really had in common was that we both hated the day care. Every afternoon the house was full of little kids' annoying, high-pitched voices. My parents, far from control freaks, believed children should have ample space for "independent play." Which meant the kids were *everywhere*, like an infestation of gnomes: in the goat pen, in the garden, in the bathroom, in the kitchen, barging into my room demanding my attention ("Lacey, look at this!" "Lacey, look at me!"). Every couple years there was a whole new crop of them.

Éclair hardly ever left Miami anymore, as if her family (and the entire state of "New Crapshire") was a black hole to be avoided at all costs. Which was why I was astonished one night, in the summer of 1990, when she appeared in the doorway of the barn, dumped a five-piece set of jewel-pink Diane von Furstenberg luggage on the floor, and said,

"Bonjour, peasants. Your queen is here."

No one had told me she was coming. I'd gotten the sense, lately, that something was going on behind my back, something between my mom and dad that they didn't want to tell me. Now I wondered if they'd been planning Éclair's visit as a fun surprise. Except it didn't feel that way.

"God, Lacey," she said, appraising me. "You look like Lumberjack Skipper."

Mom was staring at Éclair's suitcases like they were the tesseract, objects whose very natures were beyond her comprehension.

"How much was this luggage? You didn't charge it, did you?"

"Calm down, it was a gift from Chaz."

"*Chaz* has lovely taste," my dad said, planting a kiss on Éclair's cheek. I was starting to notice little things about my parents' relationship, like how my dad always got to be the good guy, the one who appreciated fine luggage, while my mom was the one to point out that we knew nothing about this "Chaz" character, who had apparently spent thousands of dollars on Éclair. Everything was a gift from Chaz: her diamond earrings, her cartons of Yves Saint Laurent–brand cigarettes, her sparkling white sneakers, her neon zigzag mohair sweaters.

"Did he really give you all this stuff?" I asked Éclair later. She was unpacking in her room, her tatty posters of Bananarama and *The Phantom of the Opera* still tacked to the walls, her broken-down television in the corner, an abandoned pet that died waiting for its owner to return.

Éclair paused, assessing me. I don't think it was ever clear to Éclair where my loyalties lay—with her or with Mom. It was never 100 percent clear to me, either. Whenever I was with Éclair, our mother's flaws loomed large: she was weird and distant; she used nature metaphors to explain everything even when they made no sense. But the reverse happened when I was with my mother. Suddenly Éclair seemed to be the root of the problem. She was selfish and shallow, egotistical and wild. But even that was partly my mom's fault; she'd run away from home at age fourteen to go to Woodstock, where she met my dad and immedi-

16

ately got pregnant. Was it really that surprising that a Woodstock baby turned out to be wild?

"I promise I won't tell Mom," I pleaded.

At last she leaned in, unable to resist a captive audience. She lowered her voice confidentially. "Once a week I go to Versace at the Omni International Mall, and I pick up a package. I bring it to the Fontainebleau hotel, which is outrageous, Lacey, absolute dyno. I go up to the penthouse, and I meet a guy named Joachim and a couple of his friends."

"...And?"

"And nothing. I give Joachim the package, and we watch *Dallas*, and he gives me a foot massage."

"What's in the package?"

"I don't know, and I don't want to know."

"You never took a single look?"

"Nope."

I imagined wreaths of sparkling diamonds stolen from exiled Russian royalty. An array of delicate spotted eggs from an illegal rare bird trade, pink and orange and gleaming turquoise. A stack of brute gold bars from a Nazi bank, or letters from a Mob boss in hiding.

It disturbed me to think of this Joachim person touching Éclair; Dad had always rubbed her feet, sometimes even painting her toenails. It seemed like a sacred father-daughter thing that she was now allowing to be polluted.

"Is Joachim, like, your boyfriend?"

"No. *Chaz* is my boyfriend. Joachim is just a guy."

"How did you meet him?"

"At a party. Parties are where everybody meets everybody. Speaking of, didn't you just finish exams? You should be partying right now!"

I had, in fact, been invited to a party at Melissa Shears's house to celebrate graduating middle school, an accomplishment so unremarkable that even Bobby Hayes, renowned glue-sniffer, had managed to achieve it. I felt ambivalent about going, but now Éclair was adamant that I had to. I had a feeling she was trying to get me out of the house.

She drove me to Melissa's in Dad's pickup truck. Melissa lived in a brand-spanking-new development, Whispering Pines, that had polarized the town: either you were jealous of the people who got to live there or you thought it was the death knell of our special New England character. The houses were identical, with large front windows and two-car garages, flat green lawns relieved of any naturally occurring tree or bush or squirrel.

"This is so middle class," Éclair said in disgust, lowering her shield-style rainbow sunglasses, which were maybe normal in Miami but up here made her look like an alien.

"Middle class?" I said, surprised. I knew the development wasn't universally liked, but I thought it at least agreed upon that the homes were fancy. Plush carpeting, shiny brass doorknobs, "barbecue-ready" decks, and tile countertops. Brand-new side-by-side refrigerators with ice makers.

"When you visit me in Miami, I'll show you real class," Éclair said. "There's a club called Reflections where you can have a cocktail in a Jacuzzi. Right there in the middle of the club!"

When you visit me. It was the first time Éclair had floated the possibility of me being part of her new life, rather than locked in the past with the barn and the goats and our clog-wearing parents. I wanted her to come to Melissa's door with me so that everyone could see what a wild and cool person I was related to. But I couldn't think of a way to ask her without seeming like a baby. So I said goodbye, and she tore away in the truck as if middle-classness were contagious.

All of eighth grade had been invited. Melissa's parents greeted me and then led me down to the cellar. There was the usual racket of boys at the foosball table, an MC Hammer tape in the cassette player, tinny gunshots from *Duck Hunt* on the Nintendo, and the tinkling giggle of Twister-playing girls as they fell in a heap on top of Ricky Morris, the only boy in our grade brave enough to cross the gender divide at social

18

events.

I found my friends Ann, Marjorie, and Sandy, who were often embarrassing at parties, doing things like dressing in green, red, and blue like the three fairies from *Sleeping Beauty*. Our friendship was based on the fact that on Wednesdays we took a bus to Boost, the gifted program at the high school in Concord.

Sandy was being weird, avoiding eye contact with me and pointedly directing her conversation to only Ann and Marjorie. I didn't read too much into it—maybe she was in a bad mood or something.

Ann and Marjorie were engaged in a hushed conversation about whether there would be "kissing games" at the party. The prospect of kissing a boy did not fill me with the same cocktail of anticipation, exhilaration, and terror as it did my friends; it had been apparent for a while now that I was a lesbian. Éclair had been calling me a dyke since I was nine, and I'd endured many conversations with my mom and dad about the mystical nature of sexuality.

"Some people are special," Dad would try to explain before Mom cut him off.

"*Everyone* is special. But some people want different things in life, things that aren't shown on TV as much."

"What things?" I asked.

"To marry a woman instead of a man," my dad said.

"She's in middle school, Hugh. Don't co-opt her into the marriage-industrial complex."

I remember Mom saying unhelpful things like "Love is fluid and can take the shape of any vessel," and Dad's pipe bobbing as he nodded in agreement. He was ten years older than her, and the pipe might have made him seem older still. But with his Beatles hair and holey tweeds, he managed to seem more like a schoolboy puffing on his grandfather's pipe. Mom, too, was stuck in her youth, still dressing like it was 1969. Little treasures could always be found braided into her long blond hair: lilac buds, a tiny sparrow's skull, a brilliant red maple leaf. During her portion of the sex talk, she listed all the mammalian species known to engage in homosexual behavior: lions, giraffes, elephants, hyenas, bonobos, pole cats, wild marmots. I came away from the conversation understanding that while I was just as normal as a wild marmot, I shouldn't talk about it at school because other people wouldn't see it that way.

A small hubbub was brewing at the refreshments table, which held the snacks, the bowl of pink punch, and a stack of untouched party hats Melissa's parents didn't seem to realize we were too old for.

"Who ruined the cake? Who ruined the cake?" Melissa was demanding. Everyone, including me, crowded around the table excitedly. But the cake wasn't ruined at all, I saw with disappointment. A single piece had been neatly cut from one corner.

"Who cares?" I said. "It's just one piece."

"We were supposed to light the candles and blow them out *together*," Melissa whined. Her friends, out of loyalty, folded their arms and contributed a half-baked chorus of "Yeah, *together*," and the catchphrase from *Full House*: "How *rude*!"

"Who was it? Who did it?" Melissa said. "Everyone show your tongues right now!"

The cake's frosting was electric blue with CONGRATULATIONS 8TH GRADERS scrawled across it in green letters. The tongue of whoever had eaten the cake would certainly tell the tale. Rolling my eyes, I stuck my tongue out along with everyone else. Though it was embarrassing to be treated like a five-year-old at a party supposedly thrown to celebrate our maturity, it would have been more embarrassing to refuse and wear the badge of cake-eater for all of high school.

Melissa stomped across the room in her pink Keds to badger the boys playing Nintendo. "Stick out your tongue. Stick out your tongue." I wasn't expecting any of this to result in finding a culprit. But at the exact wrong moment, as the MC Hammer song faded out and the tape wound to its end with a foreboding *click*, Melissa's eyes landed on Dylan Fairbanks, who I hadn't even realized was there.

As soon as I saw him, I knew with 100 percent certainty that he was the cake-eater. He'd been caught stealing sixth graders' lunches during their recess period, and another time he'd stolen a granola bar and a can of Tab from a teacher's desk. Everyone said he was probably retarded and a kleptomaniac. That's what they said about his mom, too, who was always in and out of jail. At some point it had become common knowledge that Dylan's mom did drugs, which was "bad" and made Dylan "bad" by association. I didn't get it. I'd known Dylan's mom since I was two years old and Dylan first started at Rainbow Kids. She was nice, with a pretty smile and blond hair that flowed down the sides of her face like two branches of a caramel river. After the Stardust incident, when she got out of jail and picked up Dylan to take him back home, she'd pulled me aside and whispered, "I think you're smart and fantastic, Lacey. I'm glad you and Dylan are best friends." The comment had flattered me but also embarrassed me—we were far from *best friends*. Did Dylan think we were?

There was a moment when Dylan could have pulled it off, as far as the cake eating went. He could have stuck out his tongue like a lizard and grinned mischievously, like it was a funny prank, or flourished an imaginary cape and declared, *It was I who ate the cake! Bwahaha!* But Dylan was utterly incapable of social panache. His blue eyes swam with tears, which revealed he not only was the offender, but also a loser who was going to *cry* about it.

Don't cry, don't cry, I begged in my mind. I was painfully embarrassed for him and also annoyed at him for being so stupid. Had he never been to a party before? Could he not have waited thirty minutes till Melissa's mom came down and lit the candles? Maybe Dylan really was as dumb as people said. Because that's the thing about watching someone be humiliated: you don't blame the bully; you blame the victim for walking right into it.

For the love of god, don't cry.

"Stick out your tongue."

It was too excruciating to watch. I focused on the Nintendo screen, where a hapless duck flapped back and forth, practically begging to be killed.

There was a blur of a black NASCAR T-shirt as Dylan whizzed past me. He'd eaten the cake and gotten caught, and now he was running away—a triple crime. Someone changed the MC Hammer tape to Madonna, and the boys all went through the motions of groaning and pretending they hated Madonna so no one would think they were fags. The Twister game resumed, and it was accepted that Dylan should disappear and no one should go after him.

The party was boring. After about thirty minutes of shifting around, I snuck away and found an empty room with a television—a teenage boy's room, belonging to Melissa's older brother, Ronald. Posters of sports cars covered the walls amid cutouts of nearly naked *Sports Illustrated* swimsuit models with mustaches drawn on them in marker.

I had been sitting on the bed watching *Columbo* for twenty minutes when I heard a rustle in the closet. I froze.

"... Hello?"

The door cracked open and I saw a ghostly white hand. Then a head emerged from the closet, topped by a bowl of yellow hair.

"Lacey? I thought you were Melissa's brother."

"Dylan? Are you hiding in there?"

"Yes."

"Well, come out," I said. "You can watch *Columbo* with me."

He sat hesitantly on the edge of the bed. I wished he would relax so that I could relax.

On the TV, Columbo was confronting a rich murderer in a mansion. The villain sicced two ferocious Great Danes upon him, but at the last second, instead of ripping Columbo to shreds, the dogs smothered him in wet kisses. It turned out that Columbo had cleverly retrained the murderer's dogs behind their master's back. He was in control the whole time.

When the show was over, I flipped channels for something else to watch. I was getting a ride home with Ann, whose mom wasn't coming till 10:30.

"What shows do you like?"

"Mrs. Faveraux only lets us watch PBS."

I'd sort of forgotten about Dylan's situation. His mom was in prison, this time for a long time, and until she got out, he was living with twelve other kids in an old lady's house behind the church. Suddenly I saw the cake situation in a different light: Dylan wasn't a kleptomaniac; he was *hungry*. He didn't have enough to eat. I wanted to hug him and tell him I was sorry for thinking he was a moron and for letting Melissa treat him like dirt. But I didn't know how to begin to connect with someone in a real way like that, especially a boy. So we just kept watching TV.

"I'll look for a *TV Guide*," I said, because we couldn't figure out what we were watching. Some movie about a group of teenagers who find a mutant creature growing in a vat of nuclear waste under their high school. I was rummaging through the drawers of the desk when I saw a magazine with a barely clad model straddling a saxophone. Before I could think about what I was doing or whether Dylan would be embarrassed, I grabbed it.

"Oh my god!"

I'd seen porn before, but only my dad's. He kept a hidden collection, black-and-white pictures of 1950s-era women being spanked, gagged, or tied up in their retro lingerie: torpedo bras and garter belts and silk stockings, the women's faces all screwed up in hammy expressions of fear: *No, mister, please don't hurt me!* The men wore impeccable suits, and their faces were covered by masks. The photos had always scared me a little, but now they seemed corny and goofy compared with the anatomical explicitness of *Hustler*.

I flipped through the pages as Dylan looked over my shoulder. I knew it wasn't ladylike or whatever to look at porn in front of a boy—or at all—but I was too curious not to. And there was a strange freedom, I realized, to hanging out with a loser: it didn't matter what he thought of you.

"I don't like the men," Dylan said.

"I don't either," I agreed. Their penises were ugly and scary and seemed to tear the girls in half at the crotch.

"We should cut them out so it's just the girls," Dylan suggested.

"What do you mean, cut them out?"

He grabbed a pair of scissors from a pencil cup on the desk.

"But it's not our magazine."

Dylan looked at me blankly, and I wondered if maybe he was a little dim after all. No wonder he always got caught stealing. He opened to the page with the orgy foldout and started snipping around the shape of the muscle-bound cowboy. Then he crumpled up the excised man and threw him in the trash can. The picture looked much better: a pair of naked girls tangled in each other's arms, gazing dreamily at an empty space.

"Let me do one," I said, and Dylan handed me the scissors. I flipped to a bunch of girls in bed with a pair of sandy-haired men with fake tans. I chopped around their faces, bodies, and hulking johnsons until they had been annihilated, leaving the girls to their naked slumber party.

"What are you *doing*?"

An older boy stood in the doorway. Though his eyes were bulging and he looked like he might stab us to death, I wasn't afraid of him. Compared with the beefy he-men from the magazine, Melissa's brother seemed peewee and puny. His chin was bumpy with zits, and his tie-dye shirt hung almost to his knees. It was the trend that year, meant to be tough and hoodlumish. But it just made him seem like a little boy with an outsized idea of his own body.

Dylan had gone white as a ghost. Melissa's brother looked from us to the magazine and back. His mouth gaped open in an instinctive cry: "Mooooooooooom!"

Quickly, I stuffed the magazine out of sight and leapt up from the bed, hissing at him, "What are you going to tell her? That we messed up your *porn*?"

His mother called from downstairs. "What is it, Ronald?"

Ronald appeared to consider his options. Finally he said, "Nothing!" Then, turning to us, "Get out of my room!"

I scampered out, Dylan at my heels. We went outside and waited for the party to be over. I'd decided I didn't like Whispering Pines after all. The streetlamps were garish and made me feel oppressed and watched. It was sad to think of the trees that had been chopped down, the squirrels who'd been made homeless so that Melissa's obnoxious family could have all the "amenities" of life.

Dylan picked at the stubby blades of grass, all the same neighborhood regulation height. "That was amazing," he said quietly. *"Whaddaya gonna do? How stupid can you be?"*

I realized he was imitating me, making me sound like a streetwise cop or the leader of a much-feared girl gang.

"I wish I could think that fast. I have conversations, and I replay them in my head over and over, and a week later I'll finally think of something great I could have said."

It surprised me to imagine Dylan agonizing over his conversational abilities. It suggested a level of self-awareness I hadn't imagined he possessed. I could see where this was headed, and I didn't particularly like it: Dylan following me around like a runty junkyard dog, expecting me to save him from the Melissas and Ronalds of the world.

What I didn't know that night, and couldn't have known, was that it would be a long time before I saw Dylan again. In some ways, I would never see him again at all.

THINGS HAD BEEN DETERIORATING FOR A WHILE BEFORE I REAL-
ized something was truly wrong. My dad had been shielding me from
it, the drips and drops, the warning trickles, so that when it all crashed
down, it was such a flood I nearly drowned.

Éclair's visit stretched on with no explanation. She grumbled constantly about being bored and being so sick of the smell of patchouli she
might barf. When I said, "Go back to Miami if you're having such an
awful time," she just sighed and told me to leave her alone. She and my
parents were having a lot of arguments that seemed to center around
my mother and that ground to a halt the second I entered the room. I'd
catch Éclair muttering cryptic phrases like "sick freaks" and "psychotic
morons." "*Who*'s a psychotic moron?" I'd ask, but no one would tell me
anything.

One night I woke to the sound of my father yelling, "I don't bloody
know! I don't know what they're talking about!" My father hardly ever
raised his voice, and it made me feel shaken.

And then, all at once, the day care was over. It just stopped. No
more kids trailing after my parents and filling the house with their loud
voices. I'd always longed for peace and quiet, but now that I had it, it felt
weird and ominous. How were we going to make money now?

Into the sudden emptiness came a strange woman in a red car. She
came to the house three times, always excessively wiping her high-heeled
shoes on the welcome mat as if she were allergic to dirt. Each time she

came, my father sent me outside to carry out some suddenly urgent farm chore. Instead, I would sneak around the house to peek in the windows. I watched as the woman wandered from room to room, frowning at everything as if the place were a den of filth. She barely spoke to my parents, who seemed bizarrely helpless in the situation. I couldn't understand it. Why didn't they tell her to get the hell off their property?

Then, one afternoon in mid-June, my dad called the Episcopal church youth group and finagled an invitation for me to see *Ghost Dad* with them at the big movie theater in Salem.

"I never said I wanted to see *Ghost Dad*," I said, appalled. I was at the age where being mistaken for a kid who wanted to see a kids' movie was the greatest affront imaginable.

"You'll like it! It's . . . supernatural!" he insisted.

Neither Éclair nor my mother would look me in the eye. There was clearly some *adult* matter that the three of them wanted to attend to without me. I made no secret of my resentment, sighing and sulking, behaving just like the child they were treating me as.

Before I stormed out the door to meet the church bus, my dad stopped me and wrapped me in a tight, almost suffocating hug. It wasn't like his normal hugs, which were gentle and mostly defined by a shoulder squeeze. This hug had a desperate, possessive quality to it, and when he said, "I love you," his voice cracked. "I love you's" were not unheard of in our household, but they weren't especially common. I didn't expect to receive one every time I walked out the door.

"Dad, why is everyone being so weird?" I asked, my voice muffled by his chest.

"Put a jacket on," he said, mussing my hair. "It'll get chilly tonight."

And then he pushed me toward the door, more roughly than I was prepared for, causing me to trip over my feet.

Ghost Dad was exactly as terrible as I'd predicted. It was about Bill Cosby being turned into a ghost by a Satanic cabdriver. The physics were nonsensical; Bill Cosby had no material form and could walk through walls, yet at the same time he could somehow hold objects. It was so stupid, and I was so furiously annoyed, that I spent the second half of the movie in the arcade, reading a newspaper I found in a trash can.

"She thinks she's better than everyone else. But I've been to her house, and it's really weird. Her parents are, like, witches."

I froze, hunched behind a Teenage Mutant Ninja Turtles console. Two girls were at the concessions stand refilling their Cokes. I recognized one of them—she was a grade younger than me and had been a Rainbow Kid back in the day. Chelsea or Kelsey was her name.

My face went hot. Was that the common opinion of me? That I thought I was better than everyone? I just thought I was better than *Ghost Dad*. I didn't expect the whole youth group to take it personally.

On the way home, I rode self-consciously in the back of the van, wondering if everyone thought I was egotistical. I was certainly self-absorbed enough to focus only on that part of Chelsea's or Kelsey's comment, rather than the part about my parents being witches.

I was the last kid to be dropped off. The final stretch of road on the way to the barn was a one-lane dirt path. Miss Felicity, who was driving, pulled the van to the side as another car came the opposite way—a police car. Miss Felicity rolled her window down and waved her manicured hand; her husband was a deputy county sheriff, and she knew every cop in town.

"I wonder who that is. I didn't know they patrolled way out here. Oh, it's Stan Gardner. Hi, Stan!"

But Stan only nodded a grim nod and kept driving. A second cop car appeared, this one flashing its lights, turning the dark trees red and blue, red and blue.

Once both cars had passed, Miss Felicity pulled back onto the road. When we got to the barn, I said goodbye and watched the church van roll away. For the first time, I noticed the message painted on the back: LIFE IS SHORT, BUT HEAVEN IS FOREVER.

The porch light was on, and I saw Éclair in the hammock, smoking a cigarette.

"Did you see those cop cars?" I asked her.

"Yep."

"Where were they going?"

"Back to the sheriff's office, I imagine."

"What were they doing here?"

"Could you cool it with the twenty questions?"

"I only asked three."

Our cat, Taz, meowed to be let in. I opened the door and followed her into the kitchen, walking slowly, carefully, like a burglar. It didn't feel like my house. It felt hollow and vacant. Even Taz was anxious, circling my feet and ignoring the dinner I'd given her.

I didn't have to look for my parents to know they weren't there. There was no tinkle of music from my mother's record player, no trail of pipe smoke curling in the air. It wasn't just that they were physically gone; the house felt empty of their spirit. I'd hoped to make up for my earlier behavior by being extra nice to them. But where were they? A half glass of wine sat on the counter beside an unfinished sandwich. Maybe they were out stargazing.

I knew better than to pester Éclair. So I went to my room, Taz at my heels, and I went to sleep. I suppose it was a testament to my basic, inborn faith that nothing bad could ever happen to me or to anyone I loved, because my dad had promised it wouldn't. The night at the Stardust seemed like a lifetime ago, almost a dream, and it hadn't been enough to crack my essential belief that no matter what, I was safe.

When I woke up the next morning, the phone was ringing. I wondered why no one was picking up. I looked out my window to the porch where Éclair was still lying in the hammock. I could see her pretty feet hanging over the end, her gold anklet catching the light.

I went down to the kitchen. The wineglass and half sandwich hadn't been touched. "Scram," I said to the flies congregating around the plate. Then I picked up the phone. "4431."

29

"H-hello? Hello? Am I speaking to Éclair Bond?"

"No."

"Is this . . . is this the other daughter? Uh, Lakey Bond?"

"*Lakey?* Yeah, you're speaking to Lakey."

"It's a pleasure to meet you, uh, my name is Belinda Crater, I'm from the *Telegraph*. Do you have a statement about the, uh, let me just look at my notes. I honestly didn't expect you to pick up the phone . . ."

I dragged the phone as far as the cable would go and kicked the front door open.

"Éclair? There's some lady on the phone."

Éclair bounded out of the hammock and snatched the receiver from me. "Hello? This is Éclair Bond. . . . Yes, I *do* have a statement. I would like to state that I will hunt you down, shove this phone down your throat, and pull it out your cunt if you ever call this number again, *Belinda.* . . . Yes, you can consider that a threat! Please do!" Éclair thrust the phone at me. "Hang it up. Go on, hang it up."

"What's going on?" I asked her.

Éclair flopped back into the hammock. "I would love, *love*, a tequila sunrise right now. I would marry a tequila sunrise. No prenup, no bullshit. Just me and a tequila sunrise, for better or worse."

"You sound like Mom," I said.

"What? No, I don't! Mom's never had a tequila sunrise in her life."

I was too annoyed to articulate what I actually meant, which was that Éclair shared our mother's tendency to derail the most straightforward question with ditzy non sequiturs.

"Where are Mom and Dad?" I asked.

She groaned dramatically. I rolled my eyes and started pulling on my boots.

"Where are you going?" Éclair asked, suddenly on the alert.

"To take care of the goats. Someone has to feed them."

She hopped out of the hammock. "I'll do it."

"What? You hate them. And you don't know how to do it. You give them too many greens."

"I'm in charge, and if I say I'll do it, I'll do it! Just stay inside."

I gawked at her. "What is your problem?"

Her eyes darted to the side of the house, and I realized there was something there she didn't want me to see. I walked down the steps and around the side. Éclair watched me do it, her face stony.

A streak of white on the side of the barn caught my eye. A word scrawled in white spray paint:

PREVERT

I stared uncomprehendingly.

"It's supposed to be 'pervert,'" Éclair said, walking up behind me. "Welcome to Retardsville, USA."

"What is this? What's going on?"

Éclair burst out laughing. "You know what? I'm getting a camera. This is too fucking hysterical. This is supposed to scare me? I am *so sure*." She went inside and came back out with a yellow Kodak camera. "Smile, Lacey! I'm serious, smile!"

I managed a bewildered half smile.

"Okay, now get one of me. Chaz is going to wig. I've been telling him stories about all the hicks up here."

Éclair posed in front of the barn like it was a Madonna video. She puckered her lips and framed her face with her hands as if she were the center point of the universe. If I'd understood what was happening, I would have told her this was a bad idea, but I didn't, so I just snapped the picture, the word "prevert" hanging behind her like a billboard.

Three days later, that photo was on the front page of the *Nashua Telegraph* and, soon thereafter, the *Washington Post*. I never received a dime for it or even saw the original print. Whoever has it now, I hope they at least understand its significance, not as a historical document but as a work of art, capturing the essence of feminine star power.

V

MY MEMORY AT THIS POINT IS JUMBLED. I DON'T REMEMBER whether I talked to the police or the lawyer or the psychologist first. I remember Éclair seeming more beautiful than ever, like a vibrant bloom photosynthesizing all the gawking and staring at us into boundless life energy. Meanwhile I was wilting, dying, yearning to crawl underground and hide.

I do remember Éclair storming into D.J.'s Pharmacy & Mountain Goods, wearing her alien sunglasses, a tiny yellow skirt, and a leather jacket, gripping me by the hand and demanding to speak with whoever had developed her photos.

"This is *bogus*! Those photos were my personal *property*! This is America, and you'll be speaking to my *lawyer*."

The guy behind the photo-developing counter was scrawny and unshowered-looking. His mouth hung open as Éclair accosted him.

Mid-rant, her tone changed. "Wait, do I know you from somewhere? Timmy? Tommy?"

"Talmadge," he said, his face bright red. "From Piscataqua High School? We had homeroom together?"

"Of course! Tillmidge, how could you do this to me? You know I always had a crush on you. Half the reason I left for Miami is because you broke my heart!"

I could see the gears in Talmadge's mind frantically spinning as he tried to recall a single moment when he might have been in the position to break Éclair Bond's heart.

"And now I come home, thinking maybe, just *maybe*, we could finally go on a date, but it turns out you've *stabbed* me in the *back* and sold my personal photos to a newspaper! Whatever could have been between us, it's over, Tillmidge!"

Talmadge's lip trembled. "I'm—I'm sorry, Éclair. I'm so sorry."

I whispered to her, "Éclair, can we please leave? Everyone's staring at us."

Everyone was staring at us everywhere now: in the grocery store, in the police station, in the driveway just beyond the yellow DO NOT CROSS tape that the sheriff had set up along our property lines to deter photographers. The only place to escape was the forest, where the endless white birch trees stood like kind soldiers.

In the forest, life resumed—real life. Natural creatures in a theater of symbiosis honed over thousands of years. Tree, spider, bird, deer. I'd always envied animals, their souls' sense of purpose, of *destiny*. A fox is born knowing what it's meant to do. Its life is meaningful because it plays the role it was born to play. Unlike people, who flail cluelessly from cradle to grave, fucking everything up. I remember a quote from some old historian in the 1900s: "Chaos is the law of nature; Order is the dream of man." To me it has always seemed the opposite.

But soon, even the solace of the forest was taken away. I was clomping down a vague path—not a trail, just an unmarked route between the barn and the lake—when I heard the snap of a twig behind me.

"Hey, girl. You're that girl."

I whirled around. A wiry guy in a grease-splattered shirt was standing uphill from me, blocking the way back to the barn. I couldn't tell if he was a grown-up or one of those hardscrabble rural kids who look forty by the time they're fifteen. I started edging around him, but he blocked my path.

"You're that girl," he repeated. "The girl from the TV."

Every news program was playing the same clip of Éclair storming out of D.J.'s Pharmacy & Mountain Goods and hitting a reporter over the head with her purse, which had burst open and spilled out a dozen condoms in front of all the cameras. In the clip, I stood behind her like a dazed, flannel-wearing lobotomy patient. *Kill me now, just kill me.*

"Your mommy and daddy are pedophiles," he said. "Your mommy and daddy like Satan. They like turning good little boys into fags."

I started walking backward, slowly, which is the protocol for encountering a venomous snake. The guy leered at me. He had his mouth open, and I could see his gummy white tongue. He scratched his hand, a twitchy, pointless motion that made me feel sure he was on drugs.

I started running. The birch trees blurred past. The sound of my pounding feet and frantic breath drowned out everything else. Was he chasing me? I didn't know. I flew up the hill, and for the first time I was thankful to see the menagerie of news trucks and reporters loitering at the edge of our driveway.

"Can you help me?" I yelled.

The camera guys hoisted their bulky equipment, turning into machines like the Transformers of news broadcasting. The reporters rushed me, all speaking at once in a Babel of crazed voices.

"Lacey, over here—"

"Lacey, do you have a comment—"

"Lacey, were you a victim—"

"Lacey, is it true—"

"Lacey—"

"Lacey—"

"Lacey—"

It was just like the five-year-olds from Rainbow Kids who used to hound me. I scrambled up the porch steps, flung the door open, and locked it behind me. I crouched on the floor, hugging my knees in terror. I kept expecting to hear a banging at the door, a crash through the windows, for the entire house to cave in around me.

"Mooooooooom!" I shouted without thinking. That long, drawn-out syllable with a thousand meanings: *I'm bored, I'm hungry, I'm hurt, I'm scared, I'm confused, I'm alone. Whatever's wrong, fix it for me.*

But then I remembered she was gone.

"Éclair?" I called in a weaker voice.

No answer. She'd told me her schedule for the day—interviews with the police and with lawyers—but it was too much for me to remember. My mind lurched between the gaunt, twitchy guy in the forest and the rapacious reporters, who would probably let me get murdered if it meant catching it on video.

Seconds passed, then minutes. My panic morphed into despair. Taz padded up to me cautiously, then hunched next to me like I was a kitten needing warmth. To this day, I have never been more grateful for anyone's sympathy than I was for my cat's in that moment. I started crying—wretched, moaning tears that made me shake until I had to lie on the floor. No mom or dad to swoop in and make it better. I hadn't thought of myself as a kid for a long time, but suddenly my delusion that I was all grown up came crashing down. Straight A's and farmwork and a responsible attitude couldn't prepare any thirteen-year-old for this, for their life to break apart, crumbling against the wrecking ball of a single word: "pedophile."

How could anyone believe my parents were *that*? Pedophiles drove around in decrepit vans trying to lure little kids from playgrounds. And yet, we *had* a decrepit van, didn't we? It was sitting right outside in the yard.

Tears kept streaming down my face. I lay on the floor in numb silence, petting Taz's fur but not really feeling it. *Get up,* I told myself over and over. *Get up.*

When I finally dragged myself to my feet, I felt different. I wasn't going to cry again, I told myself. Of course I *would* cry again, many times, but in the moment it felt true enough. Some aspect of my soul had been reconfigured, or perhaps abandoned. My parents had drilled trust into me: trust my family, trust my heart, trust nature, trust karma, and everything will work out exactly as it's meant to. I felt stupid and set up, and stunned that they had lied.

MY PARENTS HAD BEEN CHARGED WITH MORE THAN THIRTY counts of child molestation and sexual abuse. The claims spanned almost two decades, with some former Rainbow Kids as old as eighteen coming forward. Because of the heinousness of the charges, bail had been denied, which meant my parents had to remain in jail until the trial. Since I was a minor, the state had issued a temporary no-contact order until it was determined whether I, too, was a victim of the alleged abuse. It was a stark yes-or-no question, and my answer was always the same: *"No."* But for some reason the process went on and on. I imagined my dad saying calming words like "Stay strong, Lacey darling, it's just a little case of mistaken identity," my mom complaining about the prison's negative vibrations and out-of-whack chi. Since Éclair was an adult, she was allowed to visit them whenever she pleased. I wanted her to go every day and pass secret messages back and forth like a spy. But Éclair never wanted to go at all unless the press was there to take her photograph. "Trust me, Lacey, you're not missing anything. It's just dank buildings full of sad fuckups," she told me, as if prison were a disappointing tourist attraction.

To get the no-contact order lifted, I had to undergo a psychiatric evaluation with a therapist. In a private office on Main Street, a middle-aged woman named Barbie showed me an anatomically correct doll with vacant black eyes and a thicket of curly yarn at the crotch. I felt extreme annoyance at the fact that the therapist went by Barbie. Was

I seriously expected to look at a naked doll with a vagina in front of a real-life Barbie?

"Did you ever touch your mother . . . here?" Barbie pointed between the doll's legs.

"Yeah."

She nodded gravely. "Thank you for your honesty. Can you tell me when that occurred?"

"When I was born."

Barbie frowned. She picked up the male doll and pointed to its puny stuffed penis. "Did you ever touch your father here?"

"No."

"Did he ever ask you to touch him?"

"No."

"Did you ever see your father's penis?"

"I mean, not on purpose."

"When did you see your father's penis."

"There wasn't, like, one specific time."

"So you saw your father's penis on multiple occasions."

"No!"

"Did your father ask you to drink the blood of a bat so you could stay up late and 'play night games' with him?"

"What? *No!*"

Barbie smiled an impatient, tight-lipped smile. "I think we should relax a little. Would you like to lie down?" She gestured toward a pink settee covered by what looked like a huge doily. Then she rummaged in a drawer and pulled out a Walkman and a tape. "Just lie down and relax. I've got New Kids on the Block!"

I stretched out awkwardly on the settee. An annoyingly bland song about a "funny feeling" that someone's girlfriend didn't love him anymore blasted in my ears. Barbie was saying something. I lifted the headphones to hear. "What?"

"Just relax and remember that you're in a safe space. You haven't done anything wrong. Close your eyes."

I didn't want to close my eyes. All this talk about touching was making me paranoid, and I was worried she might try to feel me up or something. But I did as she said, pretending to be relaxed but clenching my fists the whole time. Finally the song was over.

"Lacey? You can sit up now."

I ripped the headphones off, feeling woozy as I sat up too fast.

"Let's go back to your earliest memories. Do you remember anything . . . strange? Anything that makes you feel funny?"

"No." I rubbed my temples.

Barbie gave another of her tight smiles. Then she said, "You know who I think you'd really like? My friend Angelica. Let me go grab her."

I was expecting Barbie to return with another atrocious doll. But Angelica was an actual person, a woman in her early thirties with shiny copper hair. She wore a short paisley dress with a lace collar, looking like a model for a sewing pattern. She waited till Barbie had shut the door and the two of us were alone before she spoke.

"I'm sorry about that. Barbie's specialty is children. She doesn't have much experience with teens. You don't need these, do you?" She dangled the dolls by the very tips of their feet, like they were toxic waste.

"No, definitely not," I said, relieved.

"Okay. So, here's the deal. I'm not on anybody's side. I'm just here to figure out the truth. I know this is a really hard time for you and that you're being pulled in a couple directions. I'm so sorry you're going through this. Just so you know, we're taping this. Is that all right?" She nodded toward a camcorder stationed in the corner on a tripod.

"Um . . . I guess," I said.

"It's really not a big deal. It's more for your benefit than mine."

I didn't ask what she meant by that.

"So, your parents. Do you have a close relationship with them?"

"Yeah."

"Is there one parent you're particularly close to?"

"Um, I guess my dad."

Angelica jotted that down in her notebook. "Why is that?"

"He's easy to talk to. He's a people person. My mom's, like, more weird. She's like me, I guess."

"You think of yourself as weird?"

"I don't want to be, but . . ." I thought about *Ghost Dad* and the girls who had called me egotistical.

"I don't think you're weird," Angelica said. "To me, you seem very mature and intelligent."

"Thank you." I felt my cheeks going hot, and I hoped it wasn't too obvious that I was already obsessively in love with her.

I had six sessions with Angelica MacDonald. She wore a different jewel-colored cardigan to each one. One of the sweaters, a blue one, must have shrunk in the dryer, because it was tighter than the others, the fabric stretched torturously across her chest. I tried to concentrate on her questions, but all I could think about was how I wanted to pounce on her and . . . *something*. I wasn't well acquainted enough with lesbian sex acts to know exactly what I wanted to do. But every time she sipped her Tab or crossed her legs, I could hardly bear it.

My raging lust for her was screwed up by the fact that 90 percent of our conversations were about the sexual abuse of preschoolers. I wished we could talk about Paris or our favorite books or the difference between dusk and twilight. It was a perverse, confusing time for me. I was so horny I wanted to die, while simultaneously being subjected to the idea of *my parents* carrying out the most bizarre and sickening sexual scenarios imaginable:

"If I told you that your father made five-year-olds wear purple capes and simulate oral sex with each other, then dipped his penis in the blood of an owl and made the children lick it off, what would be your reaction?"

My reaction was to sit there like a mute, unable to summon the slightest response. My mind rejected everything Angelica said, instead focusing on the place where her knees met, where I could almost see up her skirt.

"If I told you your mother brought children as young as two into the goat shed and touched all their orifices, how would you react? How do these allegations make you feel?"

A lock of her hair had settled into the crevice of her collarbone, like a mermaid's tail resting in a pool.

"I wonder if your brain is trying to protect you. It's a gift, in a way. Your brain is like, *This hurts! I'm gonna bury it deep, deep down so I can't feel it anymore.* It's called memory suppression. The memory is still *there*, causing subconscious damage. Is there anything in your past that feels . . . confusing? If you work with me, we can pull that memory out."

Her face was so earnest and pretty. I said, "There was this one time . . ."

Angelica leaned forward. "Tell me, Lacey."

"There was this one night at the Stardust—the drive-in? And my mom disappeared. And I had to call my dad, and . . ."

"And what? You can tell me."

"And I don't know. But it was . . . confusing."

"Do you know a girl named Sandy Goodwin?" Angelica asked.

"Yeah. I've known her forever."

Sandy hadn't changed much since we were kids. She was still the quiet, slightly dorky girl who brought homemade valentines to school every year instead of the store-bought ones.

"I'm only telling you this because you'll find out soon enough. She's one of the victims who's come forward. I worked with her, and we extracted some very painful memories about her time at Rainbow Kids, about ten years ago. She says your father took pictures of her naked, wearing only a crown made of sticks. And your mother drew the sign of the devil on her chest."

"What's the sign of the devil?" I asked.

"Oh, um, that's a good question, actually." Angelica stood up and went over to a file cabinet. As she bent over, I yearned to press my entire face against her ass. I couldn't not want it, even though wanting it made

41

me feel lecherous and pervy. She flipped through some papers, then sat back down. "I don't have that specific information in my notes, it seems. Maybe you could tell me what it is."

"Me? How would I know?"

"Because Sandy says you were there."

I stared at her. Surely I'd heard her incorrectly. "There? *Where?*"

"Sandy and I retrieved her memories in under four sessions. And with you, it should be even faster, because you're a lot more intelligent than her." She covered her mouth: *Oops!* "Don't tell Sandy I said that."

"I won't," I promised.

"That's why I love talking to you," Angelica said. "You're so smart."

"Thank you."

"I want you to reach backward into your mind, Lacey. The goat shed. Is Sandy there with you? Close your eyes and concentrate."

I closed my eyes. But all I could think about was how it would feel to sigh Angelica's name while tangled in her sweaty cotton sheets: *Angelicaaaa...*

At home, everything was in chaos. The police had sealed the house for twenty hours while they searched every corner and crevice. When we were finally allowed back inside, it looked like a tornado wreckage site: the contents of drawers and cupboards dumped on the floor, piles of books and dishes and trash everywhere. All my mother's New Agey paraphernalia had been boxed up as "evidence": her candles, crystals, bottles of herbs; all her nature and animal husbandry books, which had taken on witchy meanings ("Why did your mother have so many goats? Are you aware that, historically, goats represent Satan?").

Detectives were searching for the photographs Sandy claimed existed, along with other pieces of evidence mentioned in the victims' various depositions: the deer antlers my father allegedly wore while spanking two four-year-old girls with a leather strap and chanting "Hail Satan"; the jars full of various kinds of animal blood ("Over a hundred different animals," a boy named Chucky testified); the red velvet blanket a ten-year-old named Justin accused my mother of throwing over them like a fort while she molested him. Much of the testimony involved this velvet blanket fort, which the kids all called the "red cave." A five-year-old named Tiffany claimed that inside the red cave my parents had forced her to "pretend to make a baby" with a boy named Carl, also five, while my parents watched and touched each other's privates. In half these stories, I was present.

"Did Lacey hurt you, too?" the attorney asked each child.

"No. She was tied to a chair in the corner. She was crying."

More than two hundred children had filtered in and out of Rainbow Kids over the years. To me, they all blurred together.

"How can you not remember Travis?" the prosecuting attorney demanded, showing me a picture of a kid who claimed that, at age three, my parents had made him drink "gross white slime" and crushed a live squirrel's head with a meat pulverizer.

"I don't know. There were a lot of kids at a lot of times."

"Well, he remembers you."

The prosecutor was a curly-haired woman named Zora Grange. I'd seen her before. She was the lady with the red car who'd been so careful not to muss up her high-heeled shoes. I understood now that all those times she'd walked through our house, she had been deciding whether pursue charges.

At first she was nice to me. She gave me Capri Suns and Hershey bars and smiled a lot. "I'm just a mom!" she said about a hundred times. "Don't let all this lawyer stuff fool you. I've got three kids. You need a snack, Lacey? The second you need anything, you let me know, and I'll take my lawyer hat off and put my mom hat on."

I was susceptible to any woman paying attention to me—a powerful double whammy of sapphism and longing for my mother. So I accepted her Hershey bars, tried to remember Travis and Kenny and Tiffany and Blakely and all the other names on her list, and refrained from screaming when she called my parents "bad, bad people."

She had a framed picture of Joan of Arc on the wall of her office. "Joan's my hero," she told me when she caught me looking at it.

"You're on a first-name basis?" I said, a quip I'd probably picked up from *Moonlighting* or some other show Éclair watched.

Mrs. Grange laughed, but her eyes were icy. "I suppose I am. God spoke to me, is what I mean. Just like Joan. He told me to fight for children who stand alone. Children in the shadows, children who have been abused and stepped on and manipulated."

She looked at me expectantly, like I was supposed to burst into applause.

"Okay," I said.

"I know this is very, very hard, but I have a story that might help you. I once locked up a criminal who'd been trafficking drugs into the state. Sent him to prison for thirty years. This guy, he was a real piece of work. Had this dog he'd beat the hell out of. A black Lab mix, pitiful thing. That dog had been starved, made to live in its own filth. We sent animal control to go get it, clean him up, give him a new lease on life, you know? But this dog would not leave the house. Can you imagine? Years of being cooped up in that hell, and the dog would not move. They tried treats, big juicy steaks; they tried leaving the door wide open, hoping he might venture out on his own. The dog would not budge. That miserable existence was all he knew, and he was too scared to leave. In the end, they had to shoot him.... So, what I'm trying to tell you, Lacey, is don't be scared to come out of the house. Don't end up like that poor dog. You're safe now. We're here to help."

She dabbed at her eye with a Kleenex, having moved herself to tears.

"That never happened," I said. I knew how animal control worked. They used nets and tranquilizer darts.

"Excuse me, young lady? Why would I lie about such a thing?"

"I don't know, but that story never happened, so you should stop telling it."

I didn't see Mrs. Grange's "mom hat" again.

THE PRESS ADORED ÉCLAIR. THE DRAMA WHIRLED AROUND HER like an insane solar system in which she was the spellbinding star. We had our pick of lawyers. On top of the mess left by the police, the entryway to our house overflowed with letters from law firms all over the country offering their services. With one exception, they gave the same free advice: "If anyone asks you anything, your answer is 'no comment.'"

The exception was an Aaron Feingold from Los Angeles, who promised that after he won our parents' trial, he'd get Éclair a record deal. He said he was personal friends with Björn Ulvaeus and that Björn was looking for new talent, now that ABBA was officially never getting back together. The fact that Éclair's voice was about as melodic as a screech owl's didn't seem to be an issue. According to Aaron, it was all about "the face."

"We get your face in front of as many cameras as possible," was the strategy he proposed. "Look at that face! That's the most popular girl in school. That's not the daughter of some fuckin' crazy cult sex offenders!"

It concerned me that Aaron's primary goal seemed to be to make Éclair famous, not to win our parents' trial. Éclair assured me it was all part of a shrewd legal strategy. Aaron was "a real Jew" (her words) and he knew what he was doing. He even claimed he'd once finagled a verdict of "not guilty" for a man who'd been caught *on camera* stabbing his wife thirty times in the chest.

Before I knew it, Aaron had practically moved into our house. At first I was incredibly relieved—an adult in charge again. And he seemed like an *actual* adult: He was old. He had thinning gray hair. He wore boxy three-piece suits and was always poring over stacks of important-looking papers.

But Aaron didn't seem to have much experience with kids. He cursed constantly and expected *us* to nanny *him* instead of the other way around. "Lacey, could you iron my pants?" "Lacey, grab me the Yellow Pages." "Lacey, wake me up in precisely two hours. Thanks, kid!"

I felt alarmed that Aaron never asked me to leave the room when he discussed the case with Éclair. Did he not understand that I was thirteen? That he was supposed to tell me everything would be okay and I should go upstairs and do my summer reading and not worry about it?

"This Satan shit is happening all over the country," Aaron said loudly in the kitchen. We were eating pizza. It was a beautiful night—the sky rosy and gold as the sun set; fat, dreamy clouds floating over the mountains—but we couldn't go outside without being photographed by reporters. The house was a disaster, and all I wanted was to escape, but there was nowhere to go.

Aaron was making pink-and-orange tequila sunrises at the sink with tequila from a fancy gold bottle he'd had shipped from L.A. He set down a tray of three, one for each of us. I looked at mine, depressed. The colors seemed fake and flat compared to the vibrant sky outside.

"It's all falling apart, though. Everywhere. No one can find any evidence. The McMartin trial? It's going tits up as we speak. The judge is dismissing half the charges."

The McMartins were a family in California. Before being charged with more than three hundred counts of child sexual abuse, they'd run a preschool not unlike Rainbow Kids. Everyone from trashy talk show hosts to serious newscasters were repeating claims about a Satanic conspiracy infiltrating America's day-care system.

"Tits up is good, right?" Éclair asked, sipping her drink and sighing like it was liquid heaven.

Aaron shook his head. "Good for them, bad for us. Do you know how much money was spent trying to prove those old ladies molested those kids? *Fifteen million dollars.* For fifteen million dollars, the American people want a head on a stake. Anyone's head. Just put one motherfuckin' Satanist in prison so the American people can go to sleep at night knowing it wasn't all one big ass-fuck."

I'd assumed Aaron had made my tequila sunrise "virgin." But as we slurped down our third round, my brain felt loopy and I couldn't focus on what anyone was saying. I stared out the window, where the sky had turned from pink to violet.

Then I heard my own voice: "Crest . . . oh . . . man . . . see."

Éclair snorted a laugh. "What did you just say?"

"Crest-oh-man-see, Crest-oh-man-see," I repeated.

"Oh my god, Lacey is totally buggin'!"

I was too drunk to explain I was quoting a line from my favorite book, *Witch Week*, by Diana Wynne Jones. In the book, five teen witches—in a world where witchcraft is punished by death—summon the enchanter Crestomanci by calling his name three times. Crestomanci appears and saves the day by transporting them all to a parallel universe. I imagined a parallel universe where Éclair and I were drinking chamomile tea with our dad, not tequila sunrises with Aaron Feingold, and in my intoxicated state, a tiny part of me believed the spell might actually work. If people could believe my parents were perverted servants of Satan, why couldn't I believe that a fictional wizard might solve all my problems?

I excused myself and went up to my room, nearly killing myself on the stairs when I tripped over Taz. Everything was spinning. I careened into the bathroom, knowing I was going to throw up and also knowing that I'd have to clean it up myself if I didn't make it to the toilet. No dad to fetch a bucket, no mom to sit beside me until it was over, to scrub up the mess with her home-mixed organic cleaning products, which had been taken by the police as evidence of "potion-making."

I heaved up tequila sunrise. The orangey-pink swill floated in the toilet bowl like it expected me to drink it again. The thought made me hurl once more. Then I flushed the toilet and brushed my teeth. I could hear Éclair and Aaron laughing about something—probably me. I crawled into bed, my head spinning. It was barely nine o'clock. The first stars were just starting to appear in the dark sky. For a second I felt like I could touch them, rearrange the constellations. But then my fingers hit the window.

Crestomanci, Crestomanci, Crestomanci.

viii

"HAVE YOU EVER BEEN HYPNOTIZED, LACEY?"

I was in Angelica's office. It was our fifth meeting. Barbie had just knocked on the door and offered us blueberry muffins, which Angelica refused, rolling her eyes at me like we were two cool teens whose dotty aunt kept barging in on our sleepover. These little displays of intimacy enthralled me.

"Like David Copperfield?" I asked.

She laughed. "Well, I won't make you walk like a duck or pretend you're from the moon. Hypnotism isn't just for entertainment. It's a powerful therapeutic tool. I put you into a light sleep, and then we can explore any secrets that might be buried in your mind."

"I don't have any secrets."

"I spoke to a friend of yours who said the two of you witnessed your mother having sex in the forest with an orgy of people whose faces were covered in blood. The memory was repressed until I used hypnotherapy to unlock it."

"What friend? Who said that? Sandy?"

"When I hypnotize you, you can find out for yourself. You won't remember anything when you wake up, but you'll be able to see what happened." She pointed toward the camera, its red light like a tiny demonic eye. "Does that sound good?"

It did not sound good. The last thing I wanted was for Angelica to go rooting around in my brain and discover all my lascivious fantasies about her.

"I don't know," I said. "I don't think I want to."

"Why not? Don't you trust me?"

I didn't answer.

"I have to say . . . I'm disappointed, Lacey."

"Maybe later, okay?"

The next day, my parents were indicted by a grand jury, which meant the trial was definitely going forward. It also meant that Angelica had to give the tapes of our sessions to Mrs. Grange, who had to give them to Aaron, who sat in our living room watching them on the brand-new TV and VCR Éclair had bought. Supposedly Aaron had rented office space on Main Street, but he seemed to prefer sitting in our house all day, screaming at the recording of Angelica.

"She said *no*, you fucking whore!" He threw balled-up pieces of trash at the screen as Angelica continued to pressure me. It was weird seeing myself on-screen. I looked blank and dim-witted, like a farm-hand being asked to do calculus.

"How long can they drag out this psychiatric evaluation?" Éclair asked from the kitchen, where she was making a tray of cocktail wee-nies.

"As long as they want, unless I can come up with a valid reason why Lacey needs a different psychologist."

"I like Angelica," I protested weakly.

Éclair made a V with her fingers and wagged her tongue between them lewdly. Éclair loved making fun of me for being a dyke and seized on any chance to embarrass me.

"Shut up!" I said, face reddening.

"You know what I want?" Aaron banged on. "That cassette tape they made you listen to. What was it called? Kids in a Gang?"

"New Kids on the Block?"

"I bet they put subliminal messages on that tape. 'Your parents mo-lested you. Your parents molested you.'"

Meanwhile Éclair was saying, "I'm pretty sure wanting to eat out your psychologist is a valid reason to get a different one."

"Oh my god! No, I don't!"

"Yes, you do. I can tell by the way you say her stupid name. *Angelica* this, *Angelica* that."

Aaron looked up, interested. "Is that so, Lacey? Hmm. Hmm."

I couldn't believe this stranger was sitting in *my* house eating *my* mom's frozen vegetarian pot pie mulling *my* private feelings for *my* psychologist. But I felt utterly powerless to assert myself. My parents had made me feel like I was in control of my life, though I was starting to realize they'd been tricking me the whole time. When they said, "Lacey, would you like to take a bath at six thirty, seven, or eight o'clock?" it was just a way of making me take a bath.

Aaron subpoenaed the New Kids on the Block tape and made us listen to the song "Funny Feeling" backward. It was a trick he'd learned from Parents Against Subliminal Seduction, a group dedicated to spreading awareness that Led Zeppelin albums contained Satanic messages when played backward.

"Hear it? Hear it? Tell me you're hearing this!" Aaron bellowed. And there actually was a small part where it kind of somewhat sounded like they were singing, *Mommy bad, listen to Barbie.*

"How would Barbie have gotten the New Kids on the Block to record a subliminal message for her?" I asked.

"It's recorded on top of the original track," Aaron insisted, turning the tape over again.

I didn't say anything; Aaron was the adult, and I was the kid, and I was terrified that if I made him mad, he would abandon us. Half the times he left the house, I was certain he'd never come back. So I learned to use his fancy coffeemaker. I delivered his meals to the study he'd taken over, using my dad's pens and listening to his old gramophone and even smoking his pipe. ("I musta been English in a past life! Lord Feingold, whaddaya think of that?") He didn't adore me the way he adored Éclair, but he seemed mildly fond of me. One time he even rubbed my head like I was a lovable mutt who'd followed him home. *Please keep me,* I was thinking.

During my sixth and final session with Angelica, the air was stuffy because the windows were all closed. "They just repainted them," she explained, "and they're all wet." For days I would shiver every time I remembered the way I glimpsed her tongue when she said the word "wet."

"I'm going to miss you, Lacey," she told me.

"Are you going somewhere?"

"This is probably our last session, I'm afraid."

"It is?"

"I'm an advocate for the victims in this case, and unless you reveal to me that you are also a victim, I can't help you anymore. Mr. Feingold has threatened to sue me for intentional infliction of emotional distress if I don't wrap up my evaluation today."

"Huh," I said.

"Do I make you feel emotionally distressed?" she asked.

"Umm . . ." My distress was mainly physical, an agony between my legs that I was powerless to subdue. But it was also emotional—the stress of holding it inside, of no release.

"Mr. Feingold can't pursue a lawsuit on your behalf without your consent. I would really like to keep exploring your memories, Lacey. Especially that night at . . ." She flipped through her notes. "The Starlight?"

"The Stardust."

"I believe that something terrible happened that night. I can help you remember. I think it's a mistake to discontinue these sessions. Do you want to keep seeing me?"

A thousand times, yes.

"I know you want to be loyal to your parents," Angelica said. "But if they're part of something evil, something Satanic . . ."

"I don't believe in Satan," I said firmly.

She laughed. "Of course not. Neither do I. But I do believe in *Sa-*

tanists. Do you see the distinction? My only agenda here is the truth.... You look skeptical."

"Aaron said the therapist in the McMartin case got a book deal. He said you're just copying her so you can be famous."

Angelica was speechless for a second. "That's—that's ridiculous. I hope you don't believe that. Mr. Feingold is not protecting you, Lacey. He just wants to win your parents' case. Your sister's not protecting you, either. She's protecting herself. Who is looking out for *you*? Who's putting *you* first? If you could just give me something, *anything*, I could have the judge order more sessions. We could see each other as much as we wanted."

"I . . . um . . ." My mind was at war with itself. One part was scrambling to devise a true statement damning enough to keep me in Angelica's office indefinitely: *My father owned pornographic images of people wearing masks. Once when I knocked over a wooden box full of a strange powder, my mother became furious and slapped me. Sometimes when I got headaches, she gave me a strong-smelling tea that made me fall asleep.* The other part of my brain was trying to warn me that pleasing Angelica might feel good for a moment, but I'd feel like shit later when Éclair and Aaron learned what I'd done.

As if reading my mind, Angelica said, "You don't have to go home. Maybe you can even stay with me in my apartment until we find a safe place for you to live during the trial."

My eyes swam with visions of living with Angelica: her in a skimpy, see-through nightgown making me breakfast; the two of us bumping into each other in a narrow hallway in the night, falling on the floor, and making beautiful love, whatever that meant between two women, which I was dying to find out.

I opened my mouth. I had almost decided what to say when Angelica said, "You can have your own lawyer, Lacey. I know Mrs. Grange will be happy to represent you."

The mention of Mrs. Grange broke the spell, and in the race to control my actions, my brain finally sprinted ahead of my vagina. My mouth shut. Angelica tried to backpedal, but the window of opportunity had closed. I was shaking my head vehemently, as if trying to make up for my earlier waffling.

"I don't have anything I can say."

"You can't say it, but could you write it down?" She stood up and fished around in the desk for a pad of paper and a pen. As she leaned over to hand them to me, I glimpsed her white bra and the curve of her breast.

I looked down at the paper. "I don't think so."

"Whatever's deep inside you, whatever secret is holding you back, just write it down, Lacey. Write it down."

"I don't—I can't—"

"Just think for a moment. Concentrate, then write it down. Write it down, Lacey. Write it down."

And then I snapped.

"Leave me alone!" I screamed. I hurled the pad and pen onto the floor. "Just leave me the fuck alone, will you? *Leave me alone leave me alone leave me alone!*"

I will never forget the look on Angelica's face. Startled but radiant. Triumphant.

"Let it out, Lacey, let it all out." She stood up and came over to me, attempting to gather me into a hug.

I screamed—*screamed*. I pushed her away, and she toppled onto a glass table, which shattered. From the wreckage she looked up at me, and I saw a flash of anger on her face. Her hands were seeping blood. Our reaction was identical: we looked at each other, then we looked at the camera in the corner, its little red eye all-seeing.

I spent the next fifteen hours crying and contemplating suicide. I was so mortified I wanted to die, even without Aaron's assessment that I'd just "scored a home run for the other team." He said he took 85 percent of the blame, but that still left 15 percent for me.

"I don't see what the big deal is," Éclair said. "That slut goaded her. If it had been me, I would've pushed her out the window."

We were on the big velvet couch in the living room, and she was crimping my hair, which was Éclair's way of being maternal and which made me look even more like Lumberjack Skipper.

"The problem is that Angelica MacDonald may now claim that Lacey's extreme, violent reaction to being touched is evidence that she was molested."

A snowdrift of balled-up Kleenex was accumulating on the floor. I couldn't stop crying. I'd always been an emotionally guarded kid, never prone to tantrums. Yet here I was, one minute attacking a psychologist, the next sobbing in front of a lawyer while eating an entire frozen tiramisu.

Later, alone in my room, I lay awake thinking about how badly I'd fucked it up with Angelica. How could I have shoved her like that? What was wrong with me? *My life is over,* I thought. I still had no real conception of how bad it could actually get.

ÉCLAIR AND I STARTED WATCHING *DAYS OF OUR LIVES* AGAIN. AT the beginning of the summer, Éclair's main source of entertainment had been long-distance calls from Chaz in Miami. But as the weeks wore on, the phone stopped ringing. The house was a wreck and we had no money. The press was inhabiting our driveway, meals were erratic, and I'd received a letter from teen Bible camp suggesting I not bother showing up ("In this time of distress, we understand if you feel it is more appropriate to remain at home this summer. God's love to you!"). But every day at 1:00 P.M., we turned to NBC and escaped for an hour to a world that was just as psychotic as ours, yet somehow much more wonderful.

It was the summer of the "Cruise of Deception," a story line that would go down in *Days* history as one of the greatest of all time. The vengeful Ernesto Toscano has gathered his enemies on a yacht called *The Loretta* in the middle of the Mediterranean Sea to terrorize them with magic tricks. Isabella is being poisoned by Ernesto as revenge for killing her half sister, Marina. The sexual tension between Jack and Jennifer culminates in passionate lovemaking inside an island cave after *The Loretta* is shipwrecked. It was the wildest summer of *Days* ever; at one point a beloved character is dropped into a vat of acid.

My conversations with Éclair became increasingly insane as we dissected the show's goings-on in the same breath as the predicaments of our parents' case:

"Isabella is obviously in love with Roman, which never would have happened if Marina hadn't been so damn obsessed with the Toscana family treasure. Did Aaron tell you that Sandy's going to testify in court? Why is she stabbing you in the back? Weren't you two friends?"

"We were never that good of friends. I don't think Jack and Jennifer will last. You can't have a stable relationship with a guy who kidnapped you on your wedding day."

"Oh, by the way, if you see some random men lurking around, they're digging up the old well to try and find the tunnel where those kids say Dad *sodomized* them."

"But Jennifer doesn't have a diaphragm!"

"Yes, she does! She just put it in!"

Jennifer had spent an entire episode persuading Jack to make love to her in the cave, and Jack was about to give in when he pulled back in alarm and exclaimed, "Jennifer! You don't have a diaphragm!"

"Yes, I do," Jennifer told him. "I just put it in."

It made Éclair and me laugh whenever we thought about it, so we quoted it whenever the mood in the house became intolerable (which was about once an hour). Aaron would ask us some appalling question ("Do you remember a girl named Lydia Beach? She says she witnessed your father having sex with a tree. Like really going at it"), and Éclair or I would exclaim, "But Jennifer doesn't have a diaphragm!" and the other would shriek with laughter. Éclair's coping mechanism was to act like it was all a joke, so I coped by imitating her.

Until one afternoon when Aaron pulled me aside for a "private chat."

"Listen, Lace, I need you to not encourage Éclair's . . . *daffy* side so much."

"Her daffy side?"

"Come on, we love Éclair, but we both know she's cuckoo for Cocoa Puffs. You're my rock, Lace. Quiet, smart, level-headed kid. I need you to understand, we are on very thin ice. It's pure luck that none of the

Rainbow brigade have accused Éclair of being involved. Pure luck. One kid points a finger at her, says, *Éclair wore a witch's hat while the cow flew over the moon*, and we're done. There goes my prom queen. No offense, but I can't win this just with you. I need my rock *and* my rock star."

"It's not *luck*," I argued. "No one's accused Éclair of anything because she didn't do anything."

Aaron gave me a weird look. He appeared to consider his next words very carefully. Finally he said, "Lacey, your parents didn't do anything, either. You understand that, right? These accusations are all lies. Unless . . . Lacey, is there something you need to tell me?"

". . . No?"

"Because if there's anything you need to get off your chest, I am the person to tell it to. You don't tell your sister, or some cop, or some busty Jezebel headshrinker. I am the only person you can trust with your secrets. Do you understand?"

Every day was tenser than the last. On TV, *The Loretta* hurtled toward disaster. Like Ernesto's captives, I was trapped in my house, shut against an ocean of press and townspeople whose rabid curiosity mingled and overlapped with their hostility. It was hard to tell who hated us, who was merely obsessed with us, and whether there was much of a difference. It started to feel like *Days of Our Lives* was our real life, and the other twenty-three hours were a strange drama we were being forced to watch.

One plot point on *Days* particularly obsessed me. Earlier in the season, Isabella had been held against her will in an insane asylum while Marina hunted for the Toscana family treasure. Later, Marina's dead body was discovered in a hotel room. Astonishingly, *Isabella* had killed her and *blocked the incident* from her memory.

To a normal person, the fact that this was a plot device on a soap opera would have been a discrediting factor. But the way the logic of my life was going, it made it all the more potentially real.

"Did the cops talk to you about repressed memories?" I asked Éclair one afternoon as the closing credits of *Days* rolled over the hourglass.

"I dunno. Maybe," Éclair said, her voice muffled by a pillow she'd shoved over her face. She became suicidally depressed for about twenty minutes at the end of our daily dose of *Days*.

"I mean, is it a real thing?"

"I guess. If we're lucky we'll repress the memory of this entire summer and never have to think about it again."

"That would be so cool," I said. "Think about it. We could tape *Days of Our Lives* on the VCR and watch it, and then repress the memory and watch it again. The same episode over and over, each time for the first time, forever."

"Ugh, that makes my brain hurt," Éclair groaned.

"Angelica wanted to hypnotize me. Did your psychologist try anything like that?"

Because Éclair was legally an adult, she'd had a different psychologist, and her sessions—only two—had been voluntary. I was learning that unless you break the law, there's very little society can force an adult to do. Once I was eighteen, I vowed that I would be just like Éclair, whom no one dared boss around—not our parents, not Aaron, not even the reporters, who sometimes squeaked apologies to her when she yelled at them from the porch.

Éclair pulled the pillow off her face. "As if I'd let some skank put me in a trance and read my mind. Thank god you didn't let her, either. She probably just wanted to feel you up."

"That's exactly what I thought! But she acted like hypnotism was totally normal. She wanted to take me back to the night at the Stardust and recover my memories."

"What night at the Stardust?"

"You know, where Mom disappeared, and then she was unconscious and the manager screamed at Dad? Angelica thinks I saw something that night that I suppressed . . ." My voice trailed off as I watched Éclair's face change. "What?" I demanded. "What?! Tell me!"

"What does *Angelica* think you saw?" Éclair always pronounced Angelica's name as if it were made up, which was ironic considering that Éclair's name actually was.

"I have no idea," I said. "But something *did* happen that night. Remember when I called you in Miami and told you that Mom fainted?"

Éclair got up and opened the window blinds. I heard a mild hubbub outside as the reporters noticed she was there. She stuck out her tongue and gave them the bird. Then she giggled and leaned out the window. "Hey, Pauley! Pauley! Eat shit and die!"

"You know their names?" I asked.

I heard a faraway man's voice shouting, "Marry me, Croissant!"

"I'll marry you if you lose that fugly mustache!" Éclair yanked the blinds shut again and flopped back on the bed. Then she said to me, "Hey, about that night at the Stardust. I think you're old enough that you need to know something about Mom. You're not a kid anymore. You have to understand something."

"Understand what?"

Éclair lay on her back as if she were talking to Sting, who gazed down at her smolderingly from a poster tacked to the ceiling. "Mom is a heroin addict."

"What?"

"She's a junkie. She gets clean, but then she always fucks up again. Dad talked to all their old Deadhead friends from the seventies, so none of them would deal to her anymore. So she'd go to the drive-in and buy from teenagers. She probably shot up and had a mild OD, and that's why you couldn't find her, and that's why she was unconscious, and that's why the manager was having a cow and shooting his gun at everybody."

The grim simplicity of this explanation was in some ways more disturbing than a sex-and-blood cult in the woods. Yet the clues were all there: the money Dad gave her that sometimes disappeared (hence my birthday party in second grade, where, instead of a cake, she made my whole class split a bag of M&Ms); the golden glow of her complexion that went dark at times, as if sucked out by a vampire; her dislike of Dylan's mom, who was a druggie too and probably knew her secret.

An old memory, fuzzy with age, snapped into focus just like Angelica said it would. I was five years old and had accidentally broken an old Victorian lamp, the kind with a glass shade and little dangling prisms. Instead of getting angry, my mother just stared at the sparkling rainbows scattered amid the mess of broken glass.

"Do you know how rainbows work?" she asked me, then said, "The sun is white light, but it isn't really white. It's all the colors combined. And they travel together, like a family. But when they hit the glass, they break apart, and all their colors show."

She'd been so transfixed by the prisms that she hadn't noticed I'd stepped on a piece of glass and was bleeding.

I didn't know what to say. Finally I asked Éclair, "How did you find out? Did Dad tell you?"

"No, I figured it out myself. People think I'm such a dumb blonde.... You go about life completely wrong, Lacey. You want everyone to know what a smart little shit you are. But people *hate* smart people, don't you realize that? I figured that out when I was ten years old. If you actually had a brain in your head, you'd figure it out, too."

I ignored her lecture, still struggling to put the pieces together about Mom.

"Why can't we just explain it to people?" I asked. "Mom's not Satanic, she just has a problem."

Éclair scowled. "What good would that do? *Rest assured, parents of New Hampshire, you didn't leave your children in the care of Satanists, just a heroin addict.* It would only make everything worse."

It turned out the prosecution already knew about the heroin, plus a lot of other stuff, and it did make everything worse. But it's hard to say whether that was the particular crack in the glass that caused it to shatter. It could have been a hundred things—including, most likely, me.

X

IN AUGUST THE NO-CONTACT ORDER WAS LIFTED. MRS. GRANGE couldn't keep claiming I was a victim without my testimony or any evidence, so I was finally permitted to visit my parents at their respective detention centers. I was dying to see their faces, to hear their voices, to be reassured that we were still a family. My dad was the one I wanted to see first, with his special Princess Diana–ish ability to make everything feel better with just a hug and a smile.

The facility was precisely as horrible as I'd imagined: a drab cement building, security guards who looked right through you. I was so nervous I felt ill, and in a semiconscious effort to sabotage the whole thing, I wore "farmer jeans" (overalls), though they were strictly prohibited by the dress code. The blank-faced guard didn't seem to notice or care. Not even Éclair's tiny miniskirt (also against the dress code) sparked his interest, which depressed me utterly. Only a man truly beaten down by life could fail to worship at the altar of Éclair's legs.

Apathetically, he signed us in and escorted us through the metal detectors into the visitation area, which resembled an office break room from hell. The taupe paint on the walls smelled fresh, yet was somehow already covered in mysterious stains. The vending machine was, according to a rather threatening sign, BROKEN, DON'T INSERT CHANGE OR ELSE. We were led to a table far away from the other prisoners—all skinny, twitchy, mean-looking men—at the very edge of the room. I later learned this was because during Éclair's last visitation, a fellow prisoner had tried to stab my dad with a toothbrush sharpened to a lethal point.

Our state boasted one of the lowest violent crime rates in the country, which unfortunately meant the system was ill-equipped to deal with the surge of glory-seeking inmates bent on stabbing the infamous Satanist pedophile. After the toothbrush incident, my father had been placed in solitary confinement for his own protection. He and Éclair both thrived on the energy of other people, like vampires. Without it, they starved. I could see the abject hunger on his face as soon as he appeared. It struck me, with a kind of horror, that he might no longer be able to comfort me, that perhaps it was *my* job to comfort *him*.

I looked at Éclair for some kind of cue, but she was busy making sure Dad saw her new snakeskin cowboy boots.

"Aren't they divine?" she gushed.

Dad only glanced at them, his eyes fixed instead on me. "Lacey, my darling," he said. For a second he seemed to forget his handcuffs, opening his arms to me. But then he remembered and set his wrists down on the table carefully, to minimize the clatter of metal.

The other prisoners were gawking at us. An old man with squinty eyes, another with cheeks so hollow you could fit a plum in each one. A skin-and-bones, weasely young guy ignoring his haggard-looking girlfriend and infant child to stare at the local Satan family.

"Lacey, hello? Look at Dad," Éclair scolded me.

"Sorry, sorry. Hi, Dad."

I don't know what I expected would happen when I saw him. Perhaps all the stories about the "deranged priest of Satan" had wormed into the crevices of my mind. Perhaps I feared that when he smiled, I would see a demonic smile; that when he touched me, it would be lewd, inappropriate. But it was the same smile, the same touch. He was the same man. Thinner, sadder, but the same. *I* had changed. I felt awkward and stilted. I couldn't remember how to be myself.

"You look well," I forced myself to say, sounding overly formal.

"No, I don't." He sighed. "I look awful. I'm bollocks at wearing a mask. That's what's so damned ironic about all this, you know? I'm actually a terrible liar!"

He started laughing, and I wondered if he'd snapped. I'd heard people went insane in solitary confinement. Then I realized he wasn't laughing, he was crying. I couldn't hold my tears back any longer, and within seconds, I was crying, too.

"Oh god," Éclair mumbled. "Can't you two keep it together for five seconds?"

I heard the weaselly man across the room mutter, "Faggot cunt."

Éclair whipped around in her chair. "Hey, you! Are you retarded? A 'faggot cunt' would be a gay man vagina. Does that make any kind of sense to you?"

"Speak only to your family member," the guard's voice boomed.

"He's the faggot, you're the cunt."

"Powell, stop it, goddamn it," the weasel's girlfriend snapped at him. Their baby had started crying—a long, ceaseless newborn wail.

"Kid-fucker," the weasel spat.

"I dare you to say that again," Éclair growled at him.

"Kid-fucker. Kid-fucker. Kid-fucker. Kid-fucker."

In a flash of neon, Éclair leapt up from her chair, flew across the room, and smacked her hot-pink purse across his head. The girlfriend shrieked, and the baby howled even louder. The weasel seemed stunned, but the next second he growled and lunged at Éclair. She hopped away from him like a little girl avoiding the spray of the sprinklers, and he tripped on his shackled feet.

The door of the room crashed open, and several guards rushed in, one going for Éclair and one for the weasel. A third went for me, yanking me up by my overall straps like I was a toddler.

"Dad! Dad!" I screamed, losing my self-conscious sense of constraint. It was the first time we'd seen each other in months, and they were trying to separate us. I reached frantically for him, the tip of my finger just barely grazing the back of his hand—sickly pale, not the swarthy brown I knew—before I was wrenched away.

"Please don't take her," my father pleaded, his tone anguished but still civilized. He was the only one in the room not screaming.

"You'll pay for that, cunt!" the weasel yelled at Éclair.

"No, *you'll* pay for that," Éclair shouted back, barely seeming to notice the guard hauling her out of the room. "This bag is Chanel! I'll sue the shit out of you! This is America!"

The guards dumped Éclair and me outside the wire fence like sacks of garbage. "And don't come back," one of them actually said, as if we were little kids being expelled from the neighborhood tree house.

Éclair whipped out her pack of Yves Saint Laurent cigarettes and lit one up.

"That was quite a picnic," she said, exhaling smoke.

"Don't make this a joke," I said, my voice cracking. I was so furious I could barely speak.

"Give me a break, Lace."

"Do you understand what you just did? Because of you, we can't see him anymore!" I was fighting tears. I wanted to kick the wire gate until my foot was a blood-spurting stump.

"Because of *me*? It was that rat-faced tweaker's fault! I couldn't let him say that about Daddy and get away with it."

"Don't act like it's some family honor thing! You didn't do it for him, you did it for yourself, because you're a selfish, obnoxious psycho!" Her attitude had been driving me crazy all summer, and it felt good to let it out and scream at her.

"Like you're any better, *Lacey*." She spat my name like it contained a map of all my sins. "You were ready to sell this whole family out for a glimpse of that redheaded whore's fire-snatch."

"I was not!"

"I saw those tapes. You were this close to turning on us." She threw her half-smoked cigarette on the ground, even though there was a garbage can mere feet away. Angrily, I picked up the butt and threw it in the trash.

"Well, I didn't, did I? Because unlike you, I have the ability to think before I act. You just lost us Dad! He needs us, and you screwed it all up because you can't control yourself."

"No one can *control* anything!" Éclair screamed. "That's your fucking delusion! It doesn't matter what you do or don't do. Life rains shit on you either way! So I'm going to be *me*. Deal with it or fuck off!"

She lit another cigarette, but her hand was trembling. An angry red flush had bloomed across her cheeks, visible even beneath her makeup.

"I'm waiting in the truck," I said. I couldn't stand to look at her.

In the past when Éclair and I had fought, I'd had my father to vent to. He'd make me a cup of tea and flatter me with a lot of praise about how I was such a steady, levelheaded kid and how much he relied on me. But it wasn't fair. We couldn't all be Éclairs or the world would be in chaos. How did I get stuck being the "levelheaded kid" while Éclair got to be an asshole?

That night in my room I started penning a fiery letter to him:

> *Dear Dad,*
> *What a catastrophe! I hate Éclair with all my being. I wish she'd drop dead of lung cancer from her fancy cigarettes. I will never forgive her in a thousand years. All she cares about is whether the photographers get her good side. I say who cares, because her heart is ugly. I hate her I hate her I hate her I hate her—*

I imagined him reading it, sitting alone in solitary confinement, already miserable and now even more so because his children were wrecks. I tore the paper to pieces and started a new letter, one with the words I knew he needed to hear:

Dear Dad,

    I wish our visit had been longer. Éclair and I are fine. I hope you're not worried about us. If there is any upside to all this, it's that we can come together as a family. Éclair and I are the closest we've ever been. She is taking very good care of everything. She even learned how to make dinner. We are visiting Mom soon, and we'll tell her hello from you. We all love you very much and hope you're okay. We love you, we love you, we love you.

Lacey (and Taz) (and Éclair)

Desperate for someone to unload my actual feelings upon, I found myself loitering around Aaron, hoping he'd offer a penny for my thoughts. But he was too embroiled in his work to notice me.

One night I overheard Éclair asking him, "Can't you do something about the stupid visitors' list? Can't you sue them and get us back on?"

"Sometimes when you make your bed, you gotta lie in it, baby," Aaron said.

Why do I have to lie in it, too?

The next day Éclair and I drove in stony silence to the women's detention facility in Goffstown, which was even tinier than the men's, with capacity for only a hundred inmates. The small, nondescript brick building could have been a school or a library except for the barbed wire fences surrounding it.

Bizarrely, my mom wasn't even the most famous prisoner inside. Pamela Ann Smart was there, a pretty schoolteacher who'd allegedly conspired to murder her husband with her fifteen-year-old lover and his three teenage friends. The tabloids were playing it up, predictably: "Something in the Water in New Hampshire?" "Granite State Beauties Can't Keep Their Hands off Kids!"

If Dad had looked tired, Mom looked positively *ill*. Her hair was limp and straggly, and the dull red jumpsuit brought out an unflattering, jaundiced tone in her complexion.

"Have you met Pamela?" Éclair demanded the second we sat down. The visitors' room was empty except for us and a glazed-over guard doing the *People* magazine crossword puzzle.

Mom rolled her eyes at Éclair, then thumped her head on the table. Éclair was the only one who brought out this side of her: a teenage petulance that was a reminder she'd been just a teenager herself when Éclair was born.

"Tell me!" Éclair insisted.

"Yes, all right? I've met her," Mom said with a sigh.

"Do you think she did it?"

"Yes, I do."

"Oh my *god*," Éclair gushed. I could already see the headlines forming: "SHE DID IT,' Satanist Says of Close Friend Pamela Ann Smart."

"How are you doing?" I asked Mom, changing the subject.

"I'm all right. There's a little pond outside, a lovely pair of ducks. Everyone feeds them, so they're absolutely ruined. Terrible, really. But still nice to see."

My mother's vast, beautiful forest realm had been reduced to a man-made pond occupied by two ducks overstuffed with human scraps. And yet she still managed to love them. I felt utterly sad.

"The baby skunks are all grown up," I said. "I think one of them is living under the house."

"That's nice," Mom said vaguely.

"You two and your skunks! Can't we talk about something more interesting?" Éclair whined.

Mom twitched in an odd way, and I wondered if it was because she was craving heroin. I didn't know enough about drugs to understand that twitching was associated with meth.

The idea of her using any drugs still chilled me to the bone. If the Reagan years taught children anything, it was that only low-life, disgusting people did drugs; good people would "just say no." But looking at my mother, it seemed like the Reagans must have been wrong. She wasn't low-life or disgusting. She was my mom. I couldn't understand it.

"How's Hughie?" Mom asked, and Éclair shrunk a little in her metal chair.

"We wouldn't know," I said, "because Éclair got us kicked off the visitors' list."

Éclair shot me a ferocious glare. It was the first time our eyes had met in days.

"What? How?"

"She attacked an inmate with her purse."

Éclair folded her arms and wouldn't look at either of us.

"Éclair, for god's sake. Are you *trying* to sabotage us?"

"Me? *Me?* Aaron says *I'm* the only thing we've got going, between Daddy the bumbling fag and you the fucking weird heroin addict!"

Mom blanched and glanced at me, embarrassed. Apparently that was how it was going to be: I'd rat out Éclair, and she'd rat out Mom, and we'd all drag one another down while the world applauded our demise. Who even needed a trial?

"You should be thanking me for saving your ass," Éclair went on. "The press loves me. Aaron says I'm a media princess."

"I think the word is 'whore,'" Mom said flatly.

My mouth fell open. I'd never heard my mother say anything that harsh before. I waited for Éclair to spit out one of her eviscerating comebacks, but she just blinked in shock. Before I knew it, she was crying. The last time I'd seen Éclair cry, she'd been thirteen and Mom had said she wasn't old enough to go to Boston to see Lisa Lisa & Cult Jam. Those tears had been mostly fake. These were real, streaming down her face in rivulets that shone under the dingy fluorescent lights.

"No one appreciates me!" she sobbed.

In the corner, the guard looked up from her *People* magazine, but apparently decided we weren't as interesting as Patrick Swayze's biceps.

"You guys, stop," I pleaded. It was so obvious to me why they didn't get along: they shared the same mean streak, which they unleashed mercilessly upon each other while my father and I stood by, sipping tea and waiting for the hurricane to pass.

"What about the famous *Chaz*?" Mom spat. "Doesn't he appreciate you anymore? Or has he stopped calling?"

"Fuck you! He calls every day!" Éclair insisted.

Mom turned to me, expecting me to call Éclair out on this obvious lie. But as I looked between them, I felt my allegiances unexpectedly shifting. Éclair had wiped off her mask of makeup with the scratchy "courtesy" tissues on the table, and for the first time in months I could see her actual face: the red tip of her nose, the freckles peppered across her cheeks, her eyes suddenly vulnerable without their armor of liner and purple shadow.

"Let's just . . . be calm," I implored them both.

"I'm out there fighting for you guys every single day," Éclair said. Her voice was low and quaking, a voice I'd never heard before. "While Dad twiddles his dick and you stare at ducks and Lacey has wet dreams about her therapist and the whole world goes to hell, I'm out there putting *my face* on this bullshit. Strangers come up to me just to say they wish I'd been aborted. And lately I'm kind of starting to agree with them!"

"Don't say things like that," Mom said sternly. "The universe can hear you. Life is a gift."

"Yeah, real spectacular gift, Mom. Thanks from the bottom of my heart. From one whore to another."

Chains clanged as Mom stood up, leaned across the table, and whacked her cuffed wrists across Éclair's face.

"Ah!" Éclair gasped, touching her cheek. Her fingers came away bloody. My heart stopped in my chest. I'd never seen my mother do anything so . . . *vicious*. It stunned me.

The guard leapt up from her chair, her magazine fluttering to the floor. She grabbed Mom by the arms, shouting, "Whoa, whoa, whoa. Sit your ass down, inmate. This visit is over. You two, out." She nodded toward the door where we'd come in.

"Mom," I called after her, but my voice was tired and resigned.

Mom didn't struggle as the guard escorted her away. She didn't look back at us or say a word. I turned around, expecting to see a rage-filled Éclair gnashing her teeth and shouting, *Go to hell!* But she looked as numb as I felt. A trail of red blood ran down her cheek like a stroke of calligraphy.

"Come on." I tugged her arm, but she didn't move.

"Everyone hates me," she said, barely audible.

"I don't."

"Yes, you do. Even the cat hates me. She won't come near me, have you noticed that?"

"Taz hates everyone but me and Mom. Don't take it personally. Come on. Let's go home."

She started crying again, making a high-pitched sound like a baby wolf trying to howl. "Everyone—hates—me!" she gasped between sobs. I felt tears starting to prick my own eyes. I put my arm around her shoulders.

"I don't. And Mom doesn't, either. She just flew off the handle. You know how that is, you do it yourself all the time. Give her a break."

I didn't know if I was saying the right thing. Were you supposed to give a parent a break when it came to violence? All I knew was that I was exhausted. I couldn't negotiate any more of this unhinged emotion.

"Come on, let's go home," I said. "We'll stop by the store and pick up some Oreos, and I'll make that revolting pie you like."

She sniffed and looked up at me. "Really?"

"Sure. Come on."

We walked slowly out of the prison, Éclair leaning on me like she was an eccentric old lady and I, her loyal caretaker. *This is how we'll be,* I thought, as if we were practicing for a distant future. Our parents gone, the two of us, having shared a small, strange life, strolling together toward the end.

THE TRIAL COMMENCED IN SEPTEMBER. AARON WAS OPTIMISTIC about the jury. In a county comprising approximately five black people, he'd managed to get two of them in the jury box.

"Blacks will be more sympathetic," he insisted. "They're always getting accused of shit they didn't do. Angelica MacDonald represents every white bitch who ever cried rape because a black man looked at her sideways. They'll hate her."

Debate raged about whether I should wear a dress to the opening statements. According to Aaron, male jurors would find my "sexless tomboy thing" appealing, but female jurors would find it threatening. Éclair said we should both be ourselves, and anyone who didn't like it could "eat a dick." When Aaron bought me a pink Laura Ashley dress with puffy sleeves and a daisy pattern, we all agreed it somehow made me look *more* like a boy—a miserable, cross-dressing boy who'd been kidnapped by Mennonites. In the end I wore a pair of jeans and a button-down shirt that Aaron picked out from the Gap. I looked like a teen convict applying for a job at the mall.

My parents were also unrecognizable, like lobotomized, yacht-club versions of themselves. Dad wore a beige suit with a pocket square, and Mom wore her hair in a ponytail with a puffy pink bow—an actual *bow*. Aaron's strategy was to play them up as "classy." People had always been charmed by my father's accent and by his quintessentially British surname ("Bond, James Bond"), but now the newspapers were seizing upon his foreignness in the worst possible way, casting him as some sort of Dracula-esque, vaguely gay villain who'd been banished from England for being too lazy and perverted. A photo of him from Cambridge, lounging on a settee and holding a damningly effeminate cigarette holder, had made the rounds. The photos of my mother were all from her childhood on a cattle ranch in Indiana—a pretty blonde surrounded by a crew of strapping, rough-and-tumble brothers. The story told itself: heartland darling wooed away from the bosom of American family values by a sinister European.

Éclair and Aaron made half-baked attempts to keep me away from the newspapers, but neither of them had the parental drive necessary to control a thirteen-year-old's appetite for traumatic reading material. I compulsively consumed everything I could get my hands on in a state of numb self-hatred, the way I imagine men with porn addictions do.

I was allowed to hug my parents briefly before the proceedings— awkward, one-sided hugs because their wrists were in handcuffs. My father looked uncomfortable in his suit; in fact, he looked scared to death. My mother and Éclair avoided each other's eyes. I wished we could have a moment together as a family to smooth things out. It seemed like bad luck to go into the trial divided.

I surveyed the jury: seven men, six women. All white except for the two men whom Aaron called our "black guardian angels." Five of the jurors were elderly, which Aaron said was bad because "those old fuckers will believe anything they hear."

One juror intrigued me. She was about Éclair's age and wore a pale green suit with white tennis shoes. By the end of the opening statements, I would consider myself to be passionately in love with her. I never knew her name, but I'll always remember that she was Juror Number Five. I checked her reactions throughout the opening arguments: her slight wince when Mrs. Grange said words like "sodomize" or "oral stimulation," her furrowed brow when Aaron gestured toward my parents and called them "scapegoats."

"Cut it out with staring at the jurors," Aaron chastised me during the lunch break. "They'll think it's cute at first, but then they'll start to hate you. It makes them feel oppressed."

I was starting to feel oppressed, too, by the way the entire trial seemed to be about how things looked, as opposed to what the facts were. When I expressed this to Aaron, he said, "Welcome to life."

Mrs. Grange went first in the opening statements. I didn't want to hear what she had to say, but Aaron said it was important that Éclair and I be present. So I sat with clenched fists while she spoke for forty-five minutes. My dad was a pedophile, and my mom, his heroin-addicted sex slave; together they forced children to perform grotesque sex acts in the name of Satan. "These acts are unspeakable," she said, "but we must speak them. We must speak up for the children who have no voice."

Only one time during her opening argument did Mrs. Grange seem to refer to Éclair and me. It was indirect, brief, almost missable: "Through manipulation and abuse, the Bonds mentally warped children into keeping their atrocious secrets. During this trial, you will hear the testimony of over thirty children who have recovered memories of horrific abuse. Some children, we can only deduce, are so traumatized that their memories have yet to surface." She was planting the seed early on that we weren't to be trusted—especially me, since I was allegedly present for the acts in half the victims' taped testimony. If I said I wasn't there, it's because I didn't remember. Couldn't remember. Refused to remember.

When Mrs. Grange finally stopped talking and sat down, I noticed my clenched fingernails had punctured skin and my palms were bleeding.

Then it was Aaron's turn. He argued that the American small town was suffering and the people needed someone to blame. More women in the workforce meant more children spending their formative years in the care of veritable strangers, creating misplaced resentment toward day-care providers. He said the fast-paced hedonism of the recent decade ("the greedy eighties") was causing a backlash of religious zealotry and desperation to believe Satan was the root of all human problems. Add a dash of twenty-four-hour TV programming and the decline of journalistic standards, and *boom*: here we were. Aaron was basically calling our whole region a bunch of pissed-off and ignorant hicks, which I didn't imagine the jurors would appreciate, especially coming from a California Jew.

Éclair wore her loudest yellow sweater and a miniskirt covered in cartoons of bananas wearing sunglasses, which matched her banana-yellow sneakers and dangling banana earrings. Sitting next to her in the courtroom was like sitting next to Supergirl. I pictured her pulling a fiery comet out of her Chanel purse and hurling it at anyone who tried to mess with us. I pictured the whole courthouse going down in flames—Mrs. Grange's head on fire, the reporters' cameras melting—and Éclair and me abandoning this burning planet and flying into space.

xii

AT SCHOOL I DIDN'T HAVE ÉCLAIR TO HIDE BEHIND. MY PLAN FOR survival was to glide through the halls as invisibly as possible, like a ghost carrying the shame of a family curse. This might have worked if our high school hadn't been recently consolidated. Everyone in my class avoided me like I was radioactive, especially Ann, Marjorie, and Sandy. I was grateful, because being ignored was better than the alternative. But the school districts had been shuffled around to save the crumbling system, and as a result, our school had absorbed the trailer parks and row houses behind the old mill, which were notorious drug dens. There had always been troubled kids at my school—kids with parents out of work, kids who drank—but the new influx was different. Twitchier, angrier, more eager to drag everyone else into their misery.

At first Autumn seemed harmless; she wore bell-bottoms and blue eyeshadow, a style choice Éclair would have called "tragically out." She found me in the bathroom during lunch one day (the cafeteria was a land mine I no longer attempted to maneuver) and handed me a Mountain Dew from the soda machine, cracking one open for herself.

"Thanks," I said. I was so unused to kind gestures, the act astounded me.

"This school sucks," Autumn said, perfecting her blue eyeshadow in the dirty mirror.

"Worse than your old school?"

"Way worse. At Northview there were, like, two teachers, and one was an old lady, and we ran them, not the other way around. You know the Dominos?"

I nodded. This was what everyone was calling the new kids, which made them sound like a tough gang but actually came from the fact that they all seemed to have after-school jobs delivering pizza for the Domino's on the bad side of town.

"They're cool. No one will mess with you if you're friends with them. But if you're not . . . maybe *they'll* mess with you." Her tone was so over-the-top ominous I assumed she was joking.

"Oooooooh. Spooky."

"You think I'm kidding? They'll kill you. They'll kill your whole family."

A weird chill ran down my arms. Autumn snapped her eye shadow compact closed, said, "You can pay me back for the soda later," and clomped out of the bathroom on her platform clogs.

The next day I brought fifty cents and gave it to Autumn in the hallway between classes.

"It was actually sixty cents," she said.

"Oh, sorry. I'll give you a dime tomorrow."

The next day, when I tried to give her the dime, she said, "I said sixty cents, not ten cents."

"I gave you fifty cents yesterday."

"No, you didn't. Are you trying to cheat me?"

The next day I brought two quarters and a dime. She accepted them, and I thought it was over. But the day after, she said, "Remember to pay me back for that Mountain Dew. It was seventy cents." I'd already given her $1.10. I thought maybe she was a speed freak. We'd learned in health class how speed causes brain damage and memory loss. A few days later she reminded me, again, that I owed her for the Mountain Dew, saying, "It was a dollar."

Meanwhile, the Dominos haunted my steps, dogging me between classes and saying my name all the time: "Hey, Lacey. Hey, Lacey. Hey,

Lacey." Often, Autumn was with them, either harassing me for the dollar she continued to insist I owed her or pouting that I wouldn't go to the movies or smoke skunk weed, as if we were lifelong friends and she was hurt by my sudden neglect.

"I have to go to court" was my usual excuse. So she and the Dominos started asking to come with me. They wanted to be on TV. A guy named Ty, who had a Grim Reaper neck tattoo, kept telling everyone I was his girlfriend. Twice he felt me up on the pretext of hugging me, hugs I'd tried to fight off.

"Leave her alone, man. She's a muffin-eater," his friend with a skull tattoo snapped at him, planting a seed of hope that he might be my ally. But two seconds later he held me by the shoulders and forced me to stand still while Ty kissed my cheek—a dainty peck, like a kindergartener kissing his make-believe bride in a playground wedding, and somehow more humiliating than if he'd just shoved his tongue down my throat.

Mr. Hantz, the guidance counselor, had been bugging me since the first day of school to come see him. I was sure he just wanted the inside scoop on the trial so he could get a book deal like everybody else. But I thought there was a chance he could get the Dominos off my back, so I finally made an appointment.

"So you're saying you owe them a dollar, these pizza delivery boys," he said when I told him the story. He was young and good-looking with eager eyes; I knew all the girls called him Mr. Hantzsome.

"No, I mean, I owed Autumn fifty cents, but . . ." I kept being distracted by a poster of Bill Cosby reading a book to a bunch of children. Every time I thought of the movie *Ghost Dad*, I wanted to throw up. Half the Greek myths were about fools who offended the gods with the crime of hubris: Icarus, Cassiopeia, Niobe. Deep down I'd started to wonder if my arrogance about *Ghost Dad* had caused this whole thing. It sounded insane, but the universe *was* insane, as far as I could tell.

"Lacey, is it possible you came to my office to discuss a different subject? It's hard at your age to ask for help. Everything you say here is confidential."

"I know you want to talk about the trial. Everybody wants to talk about the trial. But I just want these kids to stop harassing me. I've paid back their money and they know it. They're messing with my head."

"Well, don't let them. Stand up for yourself."

"But they're eleventh graders. And there's, like, five of them. Why can't they just leave me alone?"

"Unfortunately, that's life, Lacey. People make other people suffer. And they don't stop until you make *them* suffer."

I blinked at him. I'd never heard such Machiavellian advice before.

Mr. Hantz seemed to realize he'd said something unbecoming the office of guidance counselor. "My advice? Take the mature point of view. Be honest with these new kids about your feelings. Let them see your humanity. Maybe they'll let you see theirs."

That Friday the Dominos cornered me while I was outside waiting for the bus and trying to study algebra, a subject so unrelated to my life I wanted to light my textbook on fire and scream into the void.

"Hey, Lacey."

I looked up. It was Ty, Autumn, Skull Tattoo, and a guy and girl with matching dyed black hair who were always making out in public.

"Hey, girl, come get ice cream sundaes with us," Ty demanded. "Ice cream sundaes" was the Dominos' clever code for huffing whipped cream canisters.

"No thanks."

"Get in the car," Ty said, jerking his chin toward his junky brown Pinto, which was parked in a spot reserved for teachers. "You can sit on my lap."

"I said no thanks."

He sat down next to me on the bench and slung his arm around my shoulders. When I tried to squirm away, he crushed me tighter.

My blood was boiling. I hated him. I hated his premature forehead wrinkles and his foul pizza breath and his shitty tattoo and the way he littered cigarette butts even though there were posters all over school about how they were nonbiodegradable. I hated the way he constantly mocked me for being a muffin-eater while still expecting to get in my pants. Searing hatred, burbling hatred, hot flowing lava of hatred.

"Get away from me."

"What'd you say? You want a kiss?"

"I said get away from me!" I shrieked. I leapt up and whacked him across the jaw with my algebra book.

"Holy crap!" I heard Autumn yell.

I kept hitting. I bashed his face until blood sprayed from his nose and mouth. He didn't make a sound or fight back. Too stunned, I guess. His face was spurting blood, which made me happy on a level so profound I barely comprehended it. And then I felt dizzy, and everything went black.

I came to in Mr. Hantz's office. Except it was extra disorienting because I wasn't lying down—I was sitting upright in a chair, and I seemed to be in the middle of a conversation.

". . . and I didn't know what else to do. He was trying to drag me into his car. He was threatening to rape me," I heard my own voice saying. Between the slats of the cheap plastic blinds, I could see an ambulance outside and a bloodied Ty being loaded onto a stretcher.

"Hopefully Ty won't press charges," Mr. Hantz said. "Between you and me, I doubt he will. He's had a number of run-ins with the law. He won't want trouble. I'm more worried about you, Lacey. Violence should never be the first resort. You should have yelled for help. I was sitting right here. And if these threats of Ty's were a pattern like you say, you should have reported it."

"I tried to. I reported it to you earlier this week." My mind raced to catch up to the present. Aaron was going to be *furious*.

"You mentioned that you owed Autumn money . . ." Mr. Hantz hedged.

"I said they were harassing me. I used that word, 'harassment.' And you did nothing. Maybe I should have my lawyer present right now."

I held eye contact. Mr. Hantz took a deep breath. "Okay, let's . . . let's just be calm. I'm on your side, Lacey. If Ty presses charges, I will be happy to write an affidavit stating that you were acting in self-defense."

"Thank you." How easy it was, to get what I wanted just by threatening legal action.

"So let's help you right now. You can't go outside looking like that."

He was right. My arms were covered in a spray of blood like I'd been disposing of a body with a chain saw. Mr. Hantz got up from his desk and walked over to the door, sticking his head into the hallway. "Hey, Melissa? Melissa, can you help me, please?" Then he turned back to me. "I can't go with you into the girls' room, but Melissa will help you get cleaned up."

Melissa gawked at me from the doorway. "Oh my *god*."

"Lacey needs help. She was attacked and defended herself very valiantly."

"Um . . . okay?"

"Melissa, you're an important leader in your class. I trust you to be mature and cool about this."

Melissa stood up straighter and batted her eyes. Mr. Hantz was everyone's teacher crush. I was sure Melissa was less interested in helping me than in impressing Mr. Hantzsome.

"Yes, Mr. Hantz. Come on, Lacey."

The girls' bathroom was empty except for us. Melissa rubbed wet paper towels over my arms, which smeared the blood and made it look even more grotesque. For a while we didn't speak. Then Melissa said, "It was that guy Ty, wasn't it?"

I nodded.

"He's so disgusting," she said. "I heard he jerks off in the pizza at Domino's, and they only found out because, like, ten kids got syphilis from it."

"Ewwwww!" I shrieked, and Melissa shrieked, too, and it was like we were in middle school again, laughing about the disgusting stuff they made us learn in health class. But then our shrieks subsided, and the awkward silence resumed. I couldn't help checking her out as she wiped my arms with a second round of wet paper towels. She'd gotten prettier over the summer. She was tan, and either her boobs had grown or she was wearing a Wonderbra. In eighth grade her makeup had looked slightly clownish; she looked better now, less artificial. I probably looked different to her, too, and not in a good way.

I glanced at myself in the mirror. A tired and hollow person looked back.

"I can't get the blood out of your shirt," Melissa said. "You can borrow the extra one I keep in my locker." She left the bathroom and returned with a hot-pink tank top with Mickey Mouse on it. "You can return it whenever. Just wash it first."

I put the shirt on and tossed my bloody one in the trash.

"You look pretty in pink," Melissa said, checking me out in the mirror. "You should wear it more often."

"So I can attract more attention from guys? No thanks."

"They're not all like Ty. Some guys are actually nice about it."

"Nice about what?"

"About sex."

I looked at her, astonished. "Who did you do it with?" I asked.

"David-Patrick Laramie."

"Wow." David-Patrick was a senior. Everyone knew him because he had a hyphenated name like a movie star and a brand-new Jeep Cherokee. Everyone else took the bus or drove pieces of junk. "Is he, like, your boyfriend now?"

"No. I mean, the whole boyfriend-girlfriend thing is pretty immature." I got the sense that these were David-Patrick's words. "It's more high school if I just do it with him and with some of his friends sometimes."

"You have sex with his friends, too?"

"Yeah, I mean, as a favor. They were jealous of him because they liked me, too, and David-Patrick said it would ruin the friendship if I didn't have sex with all of them. He's really sensitive about his friends. It's so cute."

"That sounds . . ." It sounded like he was taking advantage of her. But I'd witnessed Melissa's ability to turn on people in a split second, going from a basically normal person to a cruel bully if anyone threatened her most fundamental idea about herself, which was that her life was perfect and she was the perfect girl. ". . . cool," I said finally.

"Please don't be jealous. I'm so bored of every girl in our class being jealous and hating me. Ann and Marjorie and Sandy—" She shut her mouth.

"What?" I asked.

"Sorry, I didn't mean to mention Sandy. I know she's . . . whatever. Honestly, she's so self-centered these days. All she does is cry about that stupid trial. I wish you and me could be friends instead."

"Why can't we be friends?" I asked. I knew it was a stupid question, but apparently I was becoming a masochist.

"Because, Lacey"—she snorted a laugh—"Your parents are pedophiles!"

After that I started skipping school. It was easy to pull off; I just pretended to catch the bus in the morning, then waited in the goat shed until Éclair and Aaron left for court. There wasn't much press on our property anymore. Most of the vultures had migrated to the courthouse, where the action was better.

In the house alone, I'd awakened to the mind-numbing bliss of channel surfing. I'd click through our thirty channels over and over, the clips forming a sort of schizophrenic poetry: *So kiss a little longer—And the actual retail price is $849!—feeding you like family—Inside your refrigerator is the power to destroy odors—Remember when you wished you were an Oscar Mayer wiener?—They call them "raves," secret drug-fueled* parties—*Hi, welcome to the world*—*For those who thirst for something different*—*What ever happened to predictability?*

Taz stayed closer to me than usual. The shake-up in the house had discombobulated her. She meowed in my parents' empty room in the middle of the night, as if screaming, *Where are you? Where are you?* My mother had always been her favorite. Reluctantly, she now settled for me.

I hadn't returned Melissa's shirt and found myself wearing it around the house. It smelled like Melissa's peach perfume and made me feel oddly subversive, like when boys wore girls' clothes as a joke. I didn't understand the impulse at the time, this pathetic protest against my own life. I'd never had fantastic self-esteem, not like Éclair, who constantly quoted the L'Oréal commercial ("Because I'm worth it!"). But I'd at least possessed a basic respect for myself. I could milk the goats and mulch the vegetable garden and do homework without feeling like I was polluting all of life with my existence. Not anymore. The goats had become skittish around me, sensing my depression. The vegetable garden was a jungle of rot. My grades were plummeting. I was tired of feeling smarter than everyone, a feeling linked in my mind to *Ghost Dad* and my crime against the gods. So I escaped into *Full House* reruns and virgin tequila sunrises, sometimes not-so-virgin ones. Reading books had always been an escape for me, but they were an escape to *something*—a quest, a saga, another world. This was an escape to nothing.

One afternoon Éclair and Aaron came home unexpectedly at two thirty. I heard the door open and jumped up from the sofa.

"Lacey? What the hell are you doing here? And . . . what the hell are you wearing?"

I snatched my flannel and buttoned it up over the hot-pink Mickey Mouse tank. Through the window, I could see Aaron unloading a box of paperwork from the red Ferrari he had on lease. It was a ridiculous vehicle for our mountain roads, and we'd already had to help him push it out of a ditch twice.

"Don't tell Aaron I skipped school," I begged Éclair.

"God, Lacey. Are you developing some sort of daddy complex for Aaron? And are you *drinking*? Jesus! It's one thing to have a little cocktail to unwind. But you're not gonna be some thirteen-year-old alcoholic drinking alone in the middle of the day."

"I'm fourteen," I corrected her. My birthday had come and gone, unremarked upon by Éclair and everyone at school except for my homeroom teacher, who'd given me a birthday card that looked like it had been sitting in a drawer for twenty years. It showed a girl in a blue bonnet, holding a basket of flowers in front of a country cottage. The scene was so wholesome and bore so little resemblance to my life that I wanted to cry. My dad had called from the detention center, but the connection was cut off before we could even finish saying hello.

About ten days after the fact, an envelope arrived from my mom. Inside was a single pressed lilac bloom. I couldn't imagine where she'd gotten a lilac in the middle of November in a prison facility. If I'd been younger, I might have believed she'd grown it from her palm using the magic of Mother Earth. But the last five months had extinguished the final sparks of "childlike wonder" left within me.

"Whatever," Éclair said, snapping me back to the present. "No more booze for you. And happy birthday."

"Thanks."

Aaron barely noticed I was there. He was in a rage over a mishap with a witness, which was the reason court had recessed early. He locked himself in Dad's study and didn't come out for hours.

"His main witness was declared incompetent and removed from the witness list," Éclair explained.

"Incompetent?" I echoed. "How competent do you have to be? You just swear to tell the whole truth and nothing but the truth."

"Apparently this girl's a real nut bag, like clinically insane. Which doesn't that speak volumes? The only person Aaron could find who was willing to be on our side turned out to be a psychopath."

"Who was she?"

"I have no idea. And I don't recommend bugging Aaron about it."

The days were getting colder and darker as we hurtled toward winter. It annoyed me that the trial wasn't over, though Aaron had warned me that it could take months, even years. Still, I'd hoped it would be like *The Prisoner* or *Northern Exposure*, those weird series the networks aired in the summer to fill the void; that soon we'd be back to our regularly scheduled programming. It killed me to have to drag my coat out of the back of the closet; it was 41 degrees outside, and this shit show wasn't over yet?

On December 5, Angelica was called to the stand. I told Aaron I'd rather die than sit in attendance while she talked about me in front of my parents, the judge, Mrs. Grange, and a roomful of strangers. Aaron told me to lose the attitude. "You can't run away. Every time she says your name, the jury needs to see you. They need to remember that your side of the story is coming next." So I just stared at the backs of my parents' heads, noticing every time Dad tugged uncomfortably at his collar and how Mom's yuppie pink bow sagged as the day wore on.

It had been five months since my disastrous final meeting with Angelica. She seemed different. She was still pretty, but now her clothes looked corporate and expensive, and she'd gotten a perm with blond highlights, like Meg Ryan in *When Harry Met Sally*. She didn't make eye contact with me as she seated herself in the witness box and smoothed down the enormous ruffles of her salmon-colored blouse.

Mrs. Grange questioned her first, if you could call it that. It was more like a polite conversation about Angelica's credentials and her lifelong passion for abused children. At this, Éclair snorted loudly.

"Passion for *justice* for abused children," Angelica corrected herself.

My entire body was tense, waiting to hear my name. Finally it happened.

"You performed therapy on all twenty-nine of the victims, as well as the defendants' younger daughter, Lacey, who claims to have never witnessed or experienced any abuse. Given the flagrant nature of the pedophilic acts described by the victims, does that seem likely to you?"

"Objection. Speculation." Aaron's objections possessed the oomph factor of a bored kid in math class asking to go to the bathroom. It wasn't like the movies where the lawyer yells and pounds the table.

"Her professional opinion is very relevant, Your Honor," Mrs. Grange said.

"I'll allow it," said the judge. She was a diminutive, witchy old lady with the voice of someone who'd been chain-smoking since puberty. I liked her and imagined dumb scenarios where she invited me into her chambers and said things like: *I like you a lot, Lacey. You're gonna survive all this bullshit. I think my friends at Harvard Law School might enjoy hearing about you.*

In these ridiculous fantasies I got a law degree at age fourteen and astonished the world by returning to my hometown and freeing my parents in the most brilliant legal maneuvering since Clarence Darrow. At this point the fantasy fizzled; even in my wildest dreams, I couldn't imagine one second past "not guilty." No group hug, no popping a champagne bottle, no slow-motion reunion full of tears and joy. Though I was young enough to entertain the fantasy, I was old enough to understand that, even in the best-case scenario, none of us was ever going to be the same.

"I would characterize it as extremely unlikely," Angelica said. "These allegations span twelve years and occurred in almost every area of the Bonds' property. It is almost unimaginable that a child growing up in that environment wouldn't have seen something. Especially since several of the children reported seeing *her*. It's far more likely that Lacey buried the traumatic memories."

"You recovered buried memories from many of the other children, is that correct?"

"I did," Angelica said. "Several of the teenage victims had suppressed the memories of their trauma. Through focused therapy techniques, I was able to bring the truth to light."

"So why didn't these techniques work on Lacey? In your opinion?"

"Well, Lacey is under unique pressure, since the abusers are her parents. Her brain is working harder than the other children's to protect her from hurtful memories. Unlike the other children, she has nowhere else to go, nowhere to feel safe."

"Would you characterize Lacey Bond as 'desperate' to believe her parents' innocence?"

"I would use that word, yes."

Mrs. Grange picked up a videotape from the prosecution table. "I'd like to present evidence item D-4 to the jury." She popped the tape into the enormous TV set stationed next to the witness box. "This is a tape of your last therapy session with Lacey Bond, correct?"

"Yes," Angelica answered. She still hadn't looked at me. "I had hoped to continue our therapy but was unable to, due to concerns for my own safety. As you'll see."

Mrs. Grange played the tape. I averted my eyes. From the TV speakers, I heard the scream of a psychopathic, feral child and the shattering of glass. I glanced at the jurors and immediately regretted it. They looked scared. Of *me*. My crush on Juror Number Five felt more hopeless than ever. She could never love me now. No one could.

Mrs. Grange stopped the tape. "What could possibly have happened to provoke such a savage reaction?"

"She was on the verge of recovering a memory," Angelica said.

Without even looking up from his notes, Aaron interjected, "Objection. Speculation."

This time the judge said, "Sustained."

"Withdrawn," Mrs. Grange said. "The scene we just saw—I see a young person who will do anything to avoid facing the truth."

"Objection!" Aaron was starting to sound annoyed now. "Leading the witness."

"Sustained."

"Let me shift gears. Ms. MacDonald, in your time with Lacey, did she show any signs of abuse beyond the violent scene we just witnessed on tape?"

"Objection. That scene is not proof that Lacey was abused, only that she was very annoyed with Ms. MacDonald."

"Sustained. Mrs. Grange!"

"Apologies. I'll reword. Did Lacey show any signs of abuse?"

"Objection. Any signs Ms. MacDonald *interpreted* as signs of abuse."

"Sustained. And I'm getting tired of saying that word, Mrs. Grange."

Watching Mrs. Grange get snapped at by Judge Barclay was fast becoming the highlight of my life.

"Did Lacey show any signs that you interpreted as abuse."

"Yes, in fact," Angelica said. "It was quite obvious to me that Lacey was developing homosexual tendencies. When homosexuality appears at this young of an age, it's often the result of childhood abuse."

"Objection!" Now Aaron was getting riled up. "Is Ms. MacDonald an expert on homosexual psychology?"

"Overruled. But, Ms. MacDonald, please answer Mr. Feingold's question."

"Yes, a course in human sexuality was required to fulfill my master's degree from the University of New Hampshire. And I have an extensive personal library on the subject."

Judge Barclay did not look happy. Aaron had speculated that she was a closeted lesbian ("a miniature bull dyke" were his exact words). If it were true, Aaron said it was 99 percent terrible for us, because a homosexual—especially an old one like Judge Barclay—would be much harsher toward pedophiles because of built-up resentment from years of being lumped in with their gross deviance.

"But that one percent is *you*, Lacey," he'd intimated. "She'll like you. And that might be enough."

Mrs. Grange said, "No further questions," and sat down. Aaron stood and took his place in front of the witness stand.

"Ms. MacDonald, let me begin by thanking you for your dedication to the welfare of the children of New Hampshire." I wondered if he'd chosen the word "welfare" on purpose. It was a bad word in this part of the country, synonymous with taxes and the government's assault on independence and dignity.

"Thank you," Angelica said stiffly.

"I'd like to start by discussing your therapy techniques. Could you describe them to us?"

"Of course. It's all about gaining the trust of the child. My partner, Barbie Peters, and I, we may use dolls to represent the abuser, or allow the children to tell their stories through puppets."

"Like a puppet show?"

"Not exactly. I'll give the child a puppet, Mr. Froggie, for instance, and I'll ask Mr. Froggie questions instead of posing them directly to the child."

Aaron put a videotape on the TV set. "I'd like to present evidence item D-8."

It was a kid I recognized, Billy Hobart, about nine years old. He had red hair and freckles like a boy in a Norman Rockwell painting. On the tape, Angelica asked him if Mr. Hugh ever touched him in funny places. "No" was Billy's answer. Then Angelica gave him the frog puppet, saying, "Maybe Mr. Froggie can tell us a better answer." She asked Mr. Froggie the same question: "Did Mr. Hugh ever touch you in funny places, Mr. Frog?"

"Yes!" Billy answered in a croaky froggy voice. "He touched me on a volcano!"

"I mean on your *body*, silly frog," Angelica said. "Did he ever touch your wee-wee?"

"Yes!" Billy answered.

"Ewwww! Yucky," Angelica exclaimed.

"It was yucky!" Billy agreed.

Aaron turned off the tape. "I can see that you get different answers when you use the puppets. Is it possible that, when you ask a child to talk through a toy, they start to lose touch with reality? To my knowledge, a frog does not anatomically have a 'wee-wee.'"

There was a low chuckle in the courtroom, which surprised me. I'd assumed any attempt at humor in this environment would go over like a lead balloon. But I guess people were so desperate for some form of levity that even a joke about frog penises was welcome.

"I can see how you would make that mistake," Angelica said loudly, bringing the chuckling to an end. "But you don't understand child psychology. These children had been threatened, told that their families and pets would be killed if they told anyone what had happened to them. They don't feel safe in the real world. They feel safe in Mr. Froggie's world because the Bonds aren't there."

"In the tape you told Billy that with Mr. Froggie he would give a 'better' answer. Don't you feel that 'better' is a manipulative word? It implies that what he's saying isn't good enough."

"I want them to associate 'good' answers with telling the truth."

"In this courtroom, if I questioned you the way you questioned Billy on this tape, Mrs. Grange would object and say that I was 'leading the witness,' biasing your answers. Do you agree with that?"

"I agree that there are different rules for speaking to adults in a court of law than when speaking to a child who has been horrifically abused and needs help admitting it. Besides, we only used puppets and toys for the younger children. The older ones did not use puppets at all, and they told very similar stories of abuse."

"Ah, yes, with the older children you used different methods, didn't you?"

Angelica looked annoyed. "Yes."

"Evidence item D-4." Aaron put a different tape in the VCR. It was the tape of my final meeting with Angelica, rewound to the beginning. In the tape, Angelica said, "Gosh it's hot. Sorry the windows are all closed. They just painted them. Do you mind if I take this off?"

On the screen, I looked like a mute hick, watching while Angelica pulled her blue sweater over her head to reveal a tight, lacy white tank top that exposed her cleavage. Aaron paused the video on a moment that particularly emphasized her buxomness.

"Objection," Mrs. Grange said. "Could Mr. Feingold advance the video to a less salacious frame?"

"Thank you for making my point for me, Mrs. Grange. Your Honor, this is meant to show that Ms. MacDonald used inappropriate techniques to try and coax the answers she wanted out of Lacey Bond."

"Overruled," Judge Barclay said.

"Ms. MacDonald, you stated earlier that you had preconceived suspicions that Lacey was a homosexual. You know what? That word is so clinical. Can we just say 'lesbian'? It's not a dirty word."

Angelica glanced at the judge as if she would tell her what to do. But Judge Barclay was stony and silent.

"Of course," Angelica finally said. "'Lesbian' is certainly not a dirty word."

"You said earlier that being a lesbian was the result of childhood abuse. That's not a very nice characterization."

"I said when it appears in children as young as Lacey, it is *often* the result of early childhood abuse."

"In your professional opinion, what is an appropriate age to be a lesbian?"

Angelica made a grasping-at-straws gesture. "I suppose . . . eighteen. Twenty."

"And what is an appropriate age to be a heterosexual girl?"

"Objection. Relevance."

"We see your point, Mr. Feingold," Judge Barclay said. "Move it along."

Aaron nodded. "You knew Lacey was a lesbian, and yet you thought it was appropriate to remove your clothes in front of her."

For the first time, Angelica met my eyes. I was so mortified I wanted to grab Judge Barclay's gavel and knock myself unconscious. The way Angelica looked at me—coldly, with no feeling or recognition, like I was an ugly stranger—it almost caused my heart to stop beating.

"I was wearing a camisole," Angelica said. "It was perfectly appropriate."

"Hmm, Mrs. Grange didn't seem to think so five minutes ago."

"It was very hot, and our building doesn't have air-conditioning, and the windows were closed."

"Ah, yes, because they'd just been painted."

"That's correct."

"And yet, I couldn't find any record of your windows being painted on or around that date. I checked with the building manager, with three different hardware stores."

"We hired a local boy to do the work."

"I see. You and your partner, Barbie Peters, you rent your offices, correct? You don't own the property?"

"That's correct."

"Sooooo . . . Okay, I'm just trying to figure this out. Property maintenance is usually the jurisdiction of the building manager, not the tenants. Why would you hire someone to paint the windows instead of going through the building manager? Why pay for something you could get for free?"

"I . . . I don't remember."

"Hmm. Do you think I could get a better answer from Mr. Froggie?" There was a rumble of laugher, louder this time than the last.

"Objection. Badgering the witness."

"Get to your point, Mr. Feingold."

"You knew Lacey was a lesbian, and you manufactured an excuse to take your clothes off in front of her. Is that not true?"

"No. That is not true."

"Okay! Moving on, then. What was your primary focus in your sessions with Lacey Bond?"

"Going through her memories and trying to find weak spots."

"What is a 'weak spot'?"

"Any place where memories feel confusing, or muddled, or blank. It can indicate the site of a repressed trauma."

"Did you identify any 'weak spots' with Lacey?"

"Yes."

"Can you describe that weak spot?"

"There were many, but we focused on one in particular. A night at a drive-in movie theater, where Lacey had some confusion about the events that transpired. Her mother abandoned her for the entire movie and was later found unconscious."

"And what is your opinion of what happened that night?"

Angelica said, "I don't have opinions about the children I'm helping. I just want to hear the truth."

"How many times do you think you asked Lacey to focus on that night at the drive-in?"

"Um, I would say five or six? Maybe ten times? I definitely urged her to think about that night in every session. It seemed very important."

"Maybe ten times. Okay. Well, I went through the footage of all six sessions, and you asked Lacey a version of that question . . . one hundred and eleven times." Aaron paused, letting the number sink in. "One hundred and eleven times over the course of six one-hour sessions. That's approximately once every three minutes that you pressured her to come up with an answer that satisfied you about a night she could barely remember."

"Recovering memories takes a tremendous amount of focus," Angelica insisted. "Especially if the child is resistant."

"Uh-huh. If someone asked you the same question one hundred and eleven times and was never satisfied with your answer, is it conceivable that you might snap and have a violent reaction like Lacey did?"

"It's . . . conceivable. Any number of things are conceivable!"

"I would agree," Aaron said. "It's conceivable that the pressure you put on Lacey caused her to snap and react violently. It's conceivable that the pressure you put on the other children caused them to snap and recite the lies they felt you wanted to hear. You agree that those things are conceivable?"

"Conceivable? Yes. *Likely?* No. Children don't attack other people unless there's something deeply wrong. Children don't lie unless there's something deeply wrong."

"I'm no expert in child psychology, but I have three nephews, and they lie all the time. They told their mom that God spoke to them in a dream and told them they could have a puppy. And a Nintendo."

More laughs from the jury. Angelica's mauve-colored lips formed a tight line. "Children lie about puppies and Nintendos. They don't lie about rape."

The laughter stopped. Aaron said, "Thank you, Ms. MacDonald. No further questions."

It was always hard to tell who was winning. Aaron said the first 60 percent of the trial didn't matter anyway, because most people had the memory of a goldfish. He said all that mattered was the "final flourish," like in a stage magician's climactic illusion. I hoped Aaron had come up with a better final flourish than the subliminal messages on the New Kids on the Block tape, which he was still obsessed with.

In the end, though, it didn't matter. Aaron's tenure as our attorney came to an abrupt and unceremonious end on December 12. I was making coffee in the kitchen when I looked out the window and noticed the red Ferrari missing from the driveway.

"Hey, Éclair? Where's Aaron?"

"Hmm?" she said groggily. She was smearing on a thick coat of frosty pink lipstick, using the toaster as a mirror.

"Coffee first, then lipstick," I said, annoyed, handing her a mug. "How many times do I have to tell you?"

She batted my face vaguely with her manicured fingers, a gesture

95

that indicated she was too hungover or still drunk from the night before to deal with my nannying.

"Where's Aaron?" she asked, noticing the empty driveway.

"That's what I was just saying. You don't know?"

"No . . ." She seemed to wake up and started looking around. "Aaron? Aaron?" she called, but it was obvious he was gone.

"Maybe he had an early meeting," I suggested.

"Fuck," Éclair said.

"It's not a big deal," I said. "We'll just take the truck and meet him at the courthouse."

"We can't go in the truck! We'll look like dirty hillbillies! We *have* to go in the Ferrari!"

"Well, unless a Ferrari magically appears in the next five minutes, it's the truck or walk," I said.

Éclair's brow knitted together as she apparently seriously considered walking ten miles in the snow.

"Éclair, don't be an idiot. Let's just go."

At the courthouse, the melee of reporters seemed even more out of control than usual, and without Aaron to shove them away, the walk from the parking lot to the front doors was a claustrophobic press of humanity. I heard one of them shouting near my ear, "What are you going to do now?"

Aaron's area at the defense table was empty. No papers, no mug of coffee, no him. When Judge Barclay appeared, I could tell something was truly off. She was muttering to herself as she clomped up the steps to her high-backed leather chair. The jury hadn't been summoned, and their vacant seats filled the room with foreboding. The press had also been uninvited. Without the reporters' humming energy, the room felt as quiet and empty as a tomb. My parents, in their yuppie costumes, looked like brain-dead vacationers abandoned by their cruise director. Mrs. Grange and her fellow prosecutor were whispering words I couldn't hear.

Éclair and I exchanged nervous looks: *What is going on?*

"Guys, we are in a pickle, to say the least," Judge Barclay said. For a little old lady, her voice boomed like Charlton Heston's in *The Ten Commandments*. "It's come to my attention that Mr. Feingold has been practicing law without a license. He has never passed a bar exam in any state and is not legally qualified to be practicing law or trying this case. He has apparently fled the area rather than face my wrath, and I am at a loss for how to proceed."

"Your Honor," Mrs. Grange piped up, "if the defendants will simply waive the ineffectual counsel of Mr. Feingold, we would be happy to proceed with the trial as normal, with a new, court-appointed defense attorney. If I may cite the case of—"

"Did I ask for your opinion?" Judge Barclay snapped at her. I tried not to smile too widely.

"No, Your Honor. Apologies, Your Honor."

"After some consideration, I feel the only proper course of action is to grant the defense a mistrial."

I saw my dad clasp his hands and bring them to his forehead, something he did when he was relieved, like when the engine of the truck came to life after several bad starts or the snow stopped just before the roof of the shed was about to cave in. Mom was whispering to him, obviously confused as to whether a mistrial was good or bad.

"Your Honor, please!" Mrs. Grange said. "A mistrial disproportionately disadvantages the prosecution. For all we know, this situation was cooked up by Mr. Feingold to get precisely this result!"

Judge Barclay peered at Mrs. Grange from over her glasses. "And why would he do that? Out of the goodness of his heart? You'll pardon me if I'm not compelled by your theory. I am granting a mistrial. That's my final decision."

"But they haven't even requested a mistrial!" Mrs. Grange shouted, starting to sound hysterical.

Judge Barclay turned her gaze to my parents. "Mr. Bond? Mrs.

Bond? Would you like to request a mistrial?"

My dad seemed to have trouble speaking. "Uh—I—"

"If you would prefer to consult a lawyer, of course that is your right. But I don't recommend looking a gift horse in the mouth."

"No, Your Honor," my dad said. "We request a mistrial."

"I grant your request. The Bonds will remain in custody until your office formally declares that it will reprosecute."

"I assure you, we intend to reprosecute! For the sake of the children of our fine state—"

"Good for you. I hope you enjoy using our tax dollars to take these poor parents to the woodshed."

"Your Honor!" Mrs. Grange sputtered.

"If you want my advice, Mrs. Grange, let a dead dog lie. Court adjourned." She banged her gavel, stood up, and left.

Éclair turned to Mrs. Grange and spat, "Eat shit, hag!"

"Éclair, please, be gracious," Dad begged as he and Mom were escorted out the side door by the guards.

I followed Éclair into the lobby bathroom and watched her freshen up her makeup before going out to meet the crowd of reporters. Her electric-yellow sweater was so bright it made her chin glow. Splashes of deep magenta blush colored her temples, blurring into purple eyeshadow. It was a strange makeup style I'd seen in magazines; Éclair was probably the only person doing it in real life.

"Can you believe this?" she exclaimed, powdering her nose. "Lacey, what's wrong with you? Why do you have to be so relentlessly glum?"

"Aaron left us," I said. "He didn't even say goodbye."

I recalled my final interaction with him, an unremarkable exchange of "Good night" and "Good night." He'd been on the sofa watching *Dallas* and wearing a pair of dad's long johns, which stretched around his middle and bunched up at the ankles. He could have said goodbye then. Or just said anything. *I see a bright future for you. You're one in a million, kid.* For some reason everything I imagined him saying sounded like it came from a fortune cookie or a Judy Garland movie.

"It's a bummer, for sure." Éclair sighed, then pursed her lips at her reflection in the mirror. "But don't worry about it. We'll get another lawyer. A better lawyer! We're famous!"

"How can you say that? You love Aaron!"

"Honey . . ." She snapped her compact closed. A puff of powder filled the air like she'd done a magic trick. "You have to live your own life. If you get too attached to people, you're just setting yourself up to get fucked."

Outside on the courthouse steps, a swarm of press was waiting for Éclair like she was Eva Perón. "How do you feel?" "Do you see this as a victory?" On the other end, a secondary swarm hovered around Mrs. Grange, asking basically the same questions: "How do you feel?" "Do you see this as a failure?"

"This is absolutely a victory," Éclair stated, while, feet away, Mrs. Grange stated the opposite: "This is absolutely not a failure."

Everyone was so loud it took me a minute to realize someone was saying my name. "Lacey. Lacey. How do you feel? Do you have a statement?" She was a small Asian woman with a Channel 2 microphone, and she was the only person not looking at Éclair.

"I do have a statement," I told her, surprising myself.

All the microphones shifted like magnets to my face, and for a second I completely forgot what I'd been about to say. "Um . . . I . . . I think it's wrong that a great lawyer like Aaron isn't able to practice law just because he didn't take a stupid bar exam. I think he was doing a really good job, and this mistrial is the result of unnecessary government interference."

My statement landed with a thud. The reporters stared at me for a second, baffled.

Then something happened. Everyone was shouting at once. Someone had hurled something at Éclair's face. She was splattered in red. I thought it was blood, but no, it was ketchup. I blinked, and a second object—a ketchup-covered hot dog—sailed over the reporters' heads and smacked against Éclair's cheek.

"Whore!" I heard a male voice shouting.

Everyone looked around to see who he was.

"You come back here and say that to my face, you redneck coward piece of shit!" Éclair screamed, trying to wipe the ketchup off her face. But she just ended up smearing it around, making it look even more like blood.

"There he is!" someone yelled.

I saw a guy darting through the crowd, his coat too big for his rail-thin body. I caught a glimpse of the side of his face and felt sure, for a second, that I recognized him. Was it Ty? No, Ty's Grim Reaper neck tattoo was unmistakable. It was someone else, someone I was sure I'd seen before.

The crowd was pushing in. "Éclair, let's *go,*" I shouted. I grabbed her arm and dragged her through the throng of press, practically beating them away as Éclair continued to yell for the cameras. Finally we made it to the truck and roared out of the parking lot. Éclair lit a cigarette and started complaining about her sweater, which was ruined.

"What's obnoxious is that I actually have this exact sweater in red. But no, today I had to wear the yellow one."

"Éclair, shut up about your sweater! That was really scary," I said, checking the rearview mirror every two seconds to make sure no hot dog–flinging psychopaths were following us.

Éclair glanced at me. "Jesus, Lacey, you're white as a ghost."

"No one stopped him," I said. "A hundred people around us, and no one stopped him. They let him throw garbage at you, and then they let him get away."

"Really, I'm fine. It's whatever."

"Aaron would have stopped him."

"Ugh, Lacey, you always do this."

"Do what?"

"Romanticize people after they're gone."

xiii

IN THE DAYS THAT FOLLOWED, WEIRD PEOPLE IN RUMPLED, CHEAP suits approached to hand me pamphlets for Freedom Lawyers, an organization of people who believed in the right of any citizen to practice law without attending law school or taking the bar exam (they had a sister organization called Freedom Doctors). One of them even showed up at the house.

"We want to make you our official poster child," a man who introduced himself as Stanley told me as he shivered on our doorstep. "Might I come inside and tell you a bit about it?"

I shook my head. I was alone. Éclair was out lawyer shopping, which was proving more difficult than she'd predicted. No one was jumping to seize the disgraced Aaron Feingold's leftovers.

"I'm not supposed to let strangers in the house," I said.

"I'm not a stranger! I'm Stanley!" The man's smile was warm and cheery, but when I looked in his eyes, they were cold.

I shook my head again. "My sister wouldn't like it. Sorry."

"We're fighting for individual liberty," Stanley pressed. "Don't you want to break free from the chains of government regulation?"

"I don't want my face on any posters," I said. "I just want to be left alone."

Stanley didn't move. Was he really who he said he was? These "Freedom Lawyers" were all over town since my statement at the courthouse. Anyone could have picked up one of their pamphlets, figured out where we lived, and knocked on the door.

I was barely breathing. A long moment passed.

Then he said, "Well, of course I respect your freedom to be left in peace. Have a good day!" He tipped an imaginary hat, turned on his heel, and clomped down the steps. As soon as his car was gone, I picked up the phone and dialed the sheriff's office.

"Hi, this is Lacey Bond?" I hated how small and fearful my voice sounded.

The lady on the other end asked if I was having an emergency.

"No, but can you send an officer out to patrol our house or something? It's just me and my sister here right now. It doesn't feel very safe."

"I'm afraid we don't have the resources for that. You are perfectly within your rights to hire personal protection. I can refer you to an agency—"

"We don't have any money."

"I don't know what to tell you, Ms. Bond. We can send a cruiser twice a day if that would make you feel more comfortable."

"You people don't *want* to help! Well, guess what? It's your job! I don't care if you think your kid was molested!" I stopped. I could feel the operator's stony hostility oozing through the phone. "I mean . . . I didn't mean—"

"Is there anything else I can help you with today, Ms. Bond?"

". . . No."

"Then have a good day."

There was a *click* and the dial tone. I stared at the phone. Then I rummaged in the kitchen drawer and found the business card with the number for Aaron's portable phone, a device that had enthralled Éclair and me. It resembled a suitcase with a phone sticking out of it, like something out of *Inspector Gadget*.

But when I dialed the number, a recorded voice answered: "We're sorry, the number you have dialed is incorrect or has been disconnected."

I turned on the TV, just to feel less deathly alone. Sally Jessy Raphael was hosting a debate between Christians and witches. A woman with white hair and a foreign accent was trying to explain that she didn't, in fact, worship Satan: "I'm sorry I'm not evil enough for you, Sally! The truth is that witches worship *nature*! Nature is a force—"

A bald man, representing the Christians of America, interrupted her: "There are no morals in nature. An earthquake has no morals. You can't live in 'harmony' with an erupting volcano. I don't want to go back to the jungle. Mankind has been trying to *arise* from the natural order."

To which the witch responded, "No, no, no. If there is no jungle, there is no air. You can go around in your concrete structures, but there will be no air."

"You stupid, stupid hippie," I muttered. She thought she could just go on TV and explain that she was a nice person and everyone would understand. But no one wanted to believe her. For some reason, they wanted to believe in Satan. *They* were the Satanists.

I flipped through the channels, but it was like the entire world had checked into a mental institution. A violent fever dream of a commercial filled the screen: a giant anthropomorphic pitcher of Kool-Aid crashing through a cement wall like a wrecking ball before turning into a boom box playing loud, atonal music to see-through people with Kool-Aid running through their veins like blood.

"Jesus," I said to no one. No wonder half the Rainbow Kids were having psychotic delusions. I snapped the TV off but still felt tense and afraid, as if the Kool-Aid Man could come crashing through the wall at any moment and I'd die a bloodred Kool-Aid death.

I pictured myself six months in the future, locked in a bunker, every creak and squeak the portent of a murderous intruder. I wanted the house to feel safe again; I wanted my mother. I imagined the sadness on her face if she knew my mind was collapsing into such a paranoid spiral. *Fear is natural,* I was sure she would say. *Fear is good. Fear is the universe whispering in your ear: I want you to survive.*

I RETURNED TO SCHOOL IN TIME TO CATCH UP FOR EXAMS. THE Dominos more or less left me alone. I figured Ty wanted to erase any memory that he'd had his face bashed in by a freshman girl.

It was snowing a lot, which always sent everyone's rowdier tendencies into hibernation. In English class we were reading a book I actually liked, *The Wolves of Willoughby Chase*, about two orphans who flee their evil governess and are chased by wolves in the forest.

One day Mr. Hantz poked his head in. "Can I see Lacey for a moment?"

Everyone looked at me, and I immediately wondered which of my parents had died in jail. I felt a nauseating mix of panic and weird relief: if they were dead, it meant the world couldn't hurt them anymore.

Mr. Hantz led me into the empty hall and explained what was going on, which was that Melissa Shears had just tried to kill herself in the janitor's closet.

"What?"

"I need you to sit with her in my office while I wait for her parents to come. She needs a pal right now," he told me. Apparently in Mr. Hantz's mind, Melissa and I were very close friends.

Mr. Hantz shoved me into his office and left. I'd expected Melissa to be a blubbering, hysterical mess. But she just sat there, eating a Crunch bar and pressing a stack of paper towels against her left wrist. She looked at me like she couldn't remember who I was.

"Lacey? What are you doing here?"

"Mr. Hantz grabbed me out of class to hang out with you. Do you want me to leave?"

She shrugged. Her eyes were puffy and red. I wanted to ask her why she'd chosen a janitor's closet of all places to commit suicide. This was New Hampshire; we had some of the most beautiful views in America. She'd wanted to die surrounded by brown-stained mops and jugs of industrial bleach?

She lifted the paper towels to peek at her wrist. I could see three horizontal gashes like a set of red bracelets.

"That's the wrong way," I said.

"Excuse me?"

"You're supposed to cut *vertically*, along the vein." I rolled up the sleeve of my flannel shirt and pointed to my arm. "Look, see that long vein? That's where you have to cut. And really dig in."

Her nose wrinkled. "Oh my *god*. That is such a freaky thing to know, Lacey."

I rolled my eyes. "It's not. We had to kill one of our goats last year when it got a bad infection, and my mom taught me about arteries and stuff. If you really want to die, you should stab yourself in the jugular. That's what we did with the goat."

Melissa was gawking at me. The divide between us was half a century in the making: farm dweller versus suburbs dweller. To me, death was part of life, a thing to be accepted and respectfully managed; to Melissa it was abstract, shocking and unimaginable. Which was probably why her attempt to end her life had been so half-assed.

"Why the hell would you say stuff like that to me right now?" she sniffed.

"Sorry." I wanted to be more helpful. Melissa had been helpful to me when I'd beaten up Ty. I owed her. "Melissa, what happened? You can tell me. I won't say anything, I'll just listen."

I thought she would start crying again. Instead, she grabbed one of the couch cushions and screamed into it—an enraged, muffled roar. Then she took a deep breath and launched into a semicoherent monologue about how David-Patrick wouldn't take her to the Snowflake Dance because his mom was a chaperone and he didn't want them to meet, because his mom was old-fashioned and believed her marvelous son should only be with a girl who truly loved him.

"And I was like, 'I *do* love you!'" Melissa shrieked. "And he said that wasn't possible, because if I loved him I wouldn't have had sex with Kenny and Ray and Brandon and Brayden, and I was like, 'But you asked me to! I didn't even like it!' But he said if I truly loved him I would have said no and saved myself only for him. So I thought if I killed myself he would realize that I really did love him, and then he'd take me to the dance."

"W-wow," I managed. "Except how would you go to the dance if you were dead?"

She scowled at me. "He was supposed to find me before it got that far, obviously. Like in *Snow White*, when she's awakened with a kiss. I left a note in his locker to meet me, but the janitor found me first, that dumb, greasy spic."

I said nothing, though it seemed unfair to blame Juan the custodian when Melissa should have seen the major flaw in her plan: it hinged on David-Patrick caring enough to even read her note.

"Now my mom's going to freak out and probably send me to a lunatic asylum," she said, checking her wrist again. The bleeding seemed to have stopped. I didn't dare suggest that Melissa might benefit from a week of intensive therapy in a controlled environment, away from shitty boys who manipulated her into sex, then punished her for it. "And I *still* don't have a date for the dance tomorrow."

"Lots of people go stag," I said. "You should show up and look amazing and pretend you're having the time of your life. Tell everyone that you dumped him because his penis is the size of a twig and he doesn't know how to pleasure a woman." I didn't know much about boys, but I knew that penis size was very important.

Melissa's mouth was hanging open. "Lacey, that . . . is . . . brilliant. But what about Kenny and Ray and Brandon and Brayden? What if they hang around me at the dance and bug me for blow jobs?"

"I'll go with you, and if they annoy you, I'll beat the shit out of them."

Her eyes brightened. She was starting to look like the Melissa I knew: sharp, mean, and, above all, in control. "Let's do it. But will you please wear a dress? Don't embarrass me."

So I was going to go. And I was going to have to wear a dress.

The idea of being Melissa's bodyguard held a strange appeal. Everyone was afraid of me anyway. If playing Melissa's attack dog was my ticket to surviving high school—to having friends, even—wearing a dress seemed a small price to pay.

I allowed Éclair to take me shopping at the Pheasant Lane Mall. I think she'd been waiting for this since the moment I was born, the day she could drag me to Contempo Casuals and shove me into a velvet dress with poufy sleeves and have a lady inform me that my "color season" was autumn and I should wear more aubergine. The headline in the *Telegraph* the next day read "Satanists' Daughters Enjoy Shopping Spree," accompanied by a photo of Éclair posing like she was in a perfume ad.

The spell she had cast over the press never seemed to lose its power. They posted only the most flattering photos of her, with playful captions that evoked a sassy, all-American girl whose dazzling smile could outshine the shittiest of shit sandwiches. There was talk of a Lifetime movie in which Éclair would be played by Vanna White, who was trying to break into acting.

"Vanna is a piece of cardboard," Éclair complained while we split a Cinnabon in the food court. She put on a show with each bite, moaning and tossing her hair like she was having an orgasm.

"Please don't do that in public," I said.

"What? Can't I enjoy a freaking cinnamon roll? No one's looking at us," she said, which wasn't true. Everyone was looking. Everyone was always looking. "Anyway," she went on, "I think Kimberley Conrad should play me."

"The porn star?"

"She's not a *porn star*, she's a Playboy Bunny. There's a big difference."

"Bridget Fonda should play you. You look exactly like her."

"Do I?" she asked demurely, as if people hadn't been telling her that for years. One time Éclair had even convinced me that she *was* Bridget Fonda and was in the witness protection program as part of a complicated conspiracy involving an actress from *Pretty in Pink* who'd been murdered.

"Who should play me?" I asked.

She snorted on her Orange Julius. "Corey Feldman."

I swatted her. "He's a boy! I hate you."

"You love me."

This exchange was the closest Éclair and I ever came to saying "I love you" and "I love you, too." Later I would replay the words over and over in my mind: *I hate you. You love me.* Sometimes I'd insert Bridget Fonda and Corey Feldman into the roles of Éclair and me, which made the memory easier to bear.

The movie never got made, in the end; I guess events took a turn that was too macabre even for Lifetime.

Before leaving for the dance, Éclair made me pose for a photo. Since I had no date, friends, or family members to pose with, she shoved Taz into my arms. The cat wasn't happy about it and squirmed away at the exact second Éclair demanded, "Smile!" and pressed the button. The photo ended up in an evidence locker; it would be months before I saw it. When I did, I hardly recognized the girl in the velvet dress. I might have mistaken her for a normal teen on the verge of womanhood, the brown blur of fleeing cat giving her a spontaneous, even beautiful realism. In no way did she resemble me: a girl whose dismal life was about to get infinitely worse.

XV

THE SCHOOL PARKING LOT WAS CROWDED WITH CARS: PARENTS dropping off their kids, seniors circling the lot for spaces. Éclair pulled up to the front to let me out.

"You look so hot, Lacey."

"I do not. I feel like an idiot."

"You are *objectively* hot, Lacey, no matter how you feel. Your feelings are stupid and made up."

"That's not what Mom says. She says who you are comes from inside you, not from what other people see."

"That's stupid. If everyone sees you as hot, then you're hot. It's as simple as that."

"What if everyone sees you as a child molester?"

Éclair rolled her eyes. "That's different. You make everything so complicated, Lacey. Why are you afraid to be beautiful?"

I gave an embarrassed shrug. Éclair shoved me out of the car ("Go be hot and have fun" were her last words on the subject) and drove off, the truck's tires crunching on the salt brine.

The gym was unrecognizable—dimly lit and covered in glittering cutouts of snowflakes. People either ignored me or stared at me, two diametrically opposed yet equally effective modes of social ostracism. I teetered across the floor in my ridiculous high heels. Paula Abdul was playing, and a few girls were brave enough to bop around, but most everyone was loitering along the walls, not knowing what to do. I found myself wishing it was the 1940s, a time when everyone took dance lessons—foxtrot, cha-cha, waltz. Was there a word for feeling nostalgic for a time you'd never experienced?

I spotted Melissa, standing under a cluster of snowflake decorations with Ann, Marjorie, and Sandy. She was wearing a dress similar to mine: black velvet with a puffy, bright-colored skirt. The other girls looked less trendy, especially Sandy, who in her white frilly dress resembled a Madame Alexander doll. I was nervous about approaching the group—Sandy and I had gone out of our way to steer clear of each other since the trial started. I assumed Melissa would have at least warned her that I would be hanging out with them at the dance.

But as soon as I saw Sandy's face, I realized she'd had no idea. She froze and stared at me like I was holding a bomb.

"Hi," I said awkwardly over the music. "Step by Step," by New Kids on the Block, was playing. The sound of their peppy chipmunk voices made me feel nauseated.

Melissa looked me up and down. "Oh my god, you guys. It's trying to be a girl."

"I am a girl. And you told me to wear a dress."

"What is she talking about?" Ann said.

"Get away from me, lesbo," Melissa said. "I told you to stop following me."

I looked at Ann and Marjorie. "I'm not following her. She asked me to come."

"Why would I ask a girl to the dance? I'm not a raging dyke like *you*," Melissa spat. I was taller than her—much taller, thanks to my heels—but she made me feel as small as a cockroach. I glanced at her left wrist, which was covered in a thicket of bracelets to conceal her cuts.

"Nice bracelets, Melissa," I said, desperate to gain the upper hand. "Really stylish."

She shot me a cold look. Then she turned to her friends. "Lacey said if I didn't go to the dance with her, she'd kill me and then kill herself."

"Lacey!" Ann exclaimed.

"She's lying," I said dully. I could see what was happening and felt utterly foolish for not predicting it. I'd caught Melissa in a moment of vulnerability, and now she was punishing me.

Sandy growled, "*You're* the liar." Her hands were balled up in tight fists. She was trembling.

I ignored her and turned back to Melissa. "Melissa, if you didn't want to hang out with me, you could have just called. You don't need to re-create *Carrie* for me to get the message."

"Don't ignore me!" Sandy shrieked, and I was so startled I almost tripped on my high-heeled feet. People started looking at us. I could see the indictment in their eyes, directed at me and Sandy equally, the two freaks at the center of the "Satan trial" that had made our little hamlet synonymous with child abuse (the town sign reading YOU'RE GOING TO LOVE IT HERE! had recently been vandalized to read YOU'RE GO-ING TO GET RAPED HERE!).

"I'm—I'm sorry—" I stammered.

"Why can't you just tell the truth?! Why do you keep lying? Just tell the truth! Tell the truth!"

"God, Sandy, don't have a cow," Melissa snapped. "You're being em-barrassing!"

Sandy's pale gray eyes brimmed over with tears. I wanted to run away, but I felt frozen, like in a bad dream where your legs don't work.

"Tell the *truth*. Just tell the *truth*. You were there. He took pic-tures!"

"Then why didn't the police find any?"

"I don't know!" Sandy shouted. "But you were there! So just stop lying! Tell the truth!"

"I'm not lying! All *you people* are lying! You're in some conspiracy! You're all crazy!"

At the word "crazy," Sandy lunged at me, eyes wild. She started hit-ting me with her fists—pathetic, kiddie punches that felt like nothing—

111

still screaming, "Tell the truth, tell the truth!"

The song cut out mid-refrain, its inane rhyme hanging unfinished in the ether. A circle had formed around us.

"Fight!" someone shouted.

I heard the principal saying, "Hey! What's going on here!" which spawned an inevitable round of Mr. Belding's catchphrase from *Saved by the Bell*, "Hey-hey-hey, what is going *on* here?" I slipped into the crowd and darted out of the gym. I heard Melissa saying, "Nothing, Principal Webster. Sorry, Principal Webster," and then the music started again. I went to the girls' locker room and grabbed my coat. I fished a dime out of the pocket and dropped it into the pay phone in the hall. Éclair was going to be disappointed that I wanted to leave so soon. I was sure she'd been having visions of me being crowned Snowflake Princess or whatever popularity contest had been devised to ensure that no more than one girl had self-esteem at a time.

I got a busy signal. I called again five minutes later: still busy. Who the hell was she talking to? I wished I'd brought a book. I wished I hadn't come at all. I found a bench in the corner of the ill-lit hallway and sat there. Music drifted from the gym, each obnoxious song about the right stuff or bustin' a move bringing me three and a half minutes closer to the night being mercifully over.

When the dance ended at 9:30, I stepped outside and looked for the truck. It wasn't there. A gust of freezing air assaulted my legs through my sheer stockings. Why were girls' clothes so idiotic and impractical? My high heels had zero traction, and I nearly killed myself slipping on a sheet of ice as I headed back inside.

People were streaming out of the gym. I hid behind a doorway when I saw Melissa and Sandy leaving. Then I dropped another dime into the pay phone. Still a busy signal.

"What the hell, Éclair!" I hissed, hanging up with a slam. It was 9:45. Then 9:55. Then 10:00. Only the chaperones and Juan the custodian were left.

"Lacey? Is someone coming to get you?"

It was Mr. Hantz. I glared at him. In some ways, this entire thing was his fault. If he hadn't foisted Melissa on me, then presumed we were friends and foisted *me* on *her*, I would never have fallen into this social trap. For a guidance counselor, Mr. Hantz was severely clueless about girls.

"My sister should be coming . . ." I said, but I guess he heard the abandoned resignation in my tone.

"Do you need a ride? It's no problem."

"Sure."

Mr. Hantz drove a dad car, a brown AMC Eagle with wood panels. I climbed in, thankful that there was no one around to see us. I knew the tiniest spark could ignite a rumor that we were having a torrid student-teacher affair.

"What radio station do you like?" he asked. "Do you like Kate Bush?"

"I'm not sure," I said.

He pushed a tape into the tape player. We drove down the dark road, hemmed in by piles of snow on both sides.

"Your father's British, right?"

It seemed like a non sequitur until I realized he was asking because Kate Bush was British, too.

"Yeah."

"Have you ever been? To England?"

"No."

"I think you'd like it there. I spent a semester in London in college. Great music. Amazing punk scene."

"You were a *punk*?" I snorted, imagining nice Mr. Hantzsome with a flaming orange mohawk and a safety pin through his nose.

"I was a *tourist*," he said. "Anyway, I was just thinking about how big the world is. You might really thrive in a different environment, Lacey. I know you're only fourteen, but you don't have to stay here for-

113

ever. You can work toward a new life, make plans. Your sister moved to Miami, right?"

"I'm not like Éclair," I said. "I love New Hampshire."

Mr. Hantz's eyes met mine, and I could see that he felt sorry for me, like I was a battered woman who insisted she loved the husband who beat her. We spent the rest of the drive in silence, except for the Kate Bush tape and me occasionally giving directions: "Turn here. Up this hill. Watch out for that ditch."

As we pulled up to the barn, something seemed off. The front gate was open, which would have been normal in the old days, but ever since the insanity had started this summer, we'd kept it closed. The front door of the house was open, too—wide open, letting all the heat out.

"What the hell . . ." I said. "Why is the door open?"

"Stay in the car a sec," Mr. Hantz said to me.

He got out, and I could hear his footsteps crunching on the snow as he shouted, "Hello? Hello?"

I got out of the car.

"Lacey, get back in the car," he said to me, but I just stood there and watched him go up the front steps.

A small dark shape circled his feet. It was Taz, but she was walking oddly, with a limp. Mr. Hantz bent down to look at her, then recoiled.

"What's going on?" I yelled across the snow-covered yard.

"Don't move, Lacey!" Mr. Hantz shouted. "Stay right there!"

"What's wrong with Taz?"

Mr. Hantz stepped inside the house. I wobbled across the snow in my heels. As I reached the porch, Taz limped toward me—there was obviously something wrong with her paw. When I got closer, I could see what had caused Mr. Hantz to recoil: the whole left side of her face was matted with blood, and her eye was pinched closed.

"Oh my god! Taz!" My mind raced, trying to remember where my mom kept the number of the horse doctor we used sometimes instead of the vet in town. I prayed the police hadn't seized it as part of their evidence sweep. I ripped off my coat to make a little bed for Taz, unsure of what else to do. The freezing air hit my bare shoulders as I tried to coax her onto the coat. I didn't want to pick her up in case her bones were broken. I'd learned from my mother to never baby cats. "Cats can take care of themselves," she'd always say.

"Come here, Tazzie, come here, tough girl. What happened to you? Did a coyote try to eat you?"

Inside the house I heard Mr. Hantz talking to someone on the phone. It sounded like he was having trouble breathing. "Please— come—as fast as you can." I wondered how he'd found a phone number for a vet so quickly. He hung up the phone, and it sounded like he was hyperventilating.

"Mr. Hantz? Are you okay?"

I heard his footsteps thundering toward me. "Lacey! I told you—I told you . . ." His face was white as marble and his hands were shaking. His eyes darted from Taz bleeding in a ball on my coat to me. He took off his own coat and threw it over my bare shoulders. Then he mumbled something incomprehensible that sounded like "Wuhbarivhar" and collapsed. Just fell backward with a thud like a cut tree.

"Mr. Hantz? Mr. Hantz!" I shouted. I kicked him lightly with my foot, feeling furious. What kind of grown man fainted at the sight of blood? *Cat* blood, even? I dragged the coat inside with Taz lying limply on it. I tried to drag Mr. Hantz, but he was too heavy, so I just threw his coat on top of him and left him lying on the porch. I went inside and closed the door to stop any more heat from escaping.

"Éclair!" I shouted, with the same whiny, overly long emphasis on the vowel sound as a kid yelling for their mom. "Éclaaaaaair!"

There was no answer. And that's when I noticed how quiet it was. A hollow, cold quiet like the whole world had fallen to the bottom of a well. I stood still, training my ears for a sound—any sound. There was a *drip-drip-drip* coming from the living room.

I remember a white tingling nothingness in my hands. I remember red. Everywhere, red. On the floor, a tiny red paw print like a valentine. On the wall, a spray of blood in an elegant arc, a rainbow of only red. Red in a pool so dark it was nearly black. Flamboyant splatters of blood perfuming the air with the unmistakable odor of rusty pennies. The top of a head blown off, brain matter showing like a jaunty red cap. A throat slit open with blood spilling like a matching red scarf. To describe the scene completely would make me feel like a sad phone-sex operator forced to bring vampire fetishists to their climaxes of debauched bliss. I was still at an age where I questioned everything—why this, why that, why did the road curve one way instead of the other. Of all my questions, this one still feels the most reasonable to ask: Why did I have to see this? Why did Mr. Hantz fail me so utterly? Why am I alone in this red memory, this garish stain so dark it never fades?

PART TWO

I'VE ALWAYS ATTACHED MYSELF TO BEAUTY, AS IF ITS dazzling beams offered concealment, forcing anyone who might be looking for me to squint into its blinding glare. The few hellish weeks I spent thinking it was gone forever convinced me that I couldn't survive without it.

If there's one mistake Gwen and I made in all of this, it's that we stayed together, doubling the odds that both of us would be caught. It was my identity that got blown first; my picture, plastered across the tabloids and gossip websites, that led them directly to her. If Gwen had been somewhere else, some location unknown even to me, it's possible she never would have been found.

But it's difficult to picture this version of our lives, one in which we'd been wiser and gone our separate ways. Where would Gwen be now? Tahiti? The moon? She's always been one of those people for whom anything is possible.

Things really break down when I try to picture my own life in this scenario. No lipstick stains on my mugs, forever vexing my dish scrub. No blast of fragrance greeting me each evening after work, indicating Gwen's perfume obsession du jour (currently: Kingdom by Alexander McQueen). No magazines, sunglasses, and bottles of nail polish cluttering every surface. I try to imagine my own things filling the space in their stead, but I can't. I can only imagine it empty.

All thought experiments aside, the fact is we did stay together, and because of that, we both got caught. Between the vagaries of Canadian extradition laws and the nature of the crime we committed, our legal options are a mishmash.

Still, I can't bring myself to regret our choice, because how sick would it have been to part ways with beauty when it was so miraculous that it had returned to me at all?

NEW HAMPSHIRE
1990

THE WEEKS AFTER WERE DIM AND BLANK, LIKE THE FIRST MO-
ments after a blow to the head. The sun emerged weakly, never fully
brightening the sky, and set with a whimper by four thirty. I was sweaty
all the time. The group home in Concord where I now found myself
had piping-hot metal radiators that spat and hissed and maintained a
sauna-like temperature while snow poured from the black sky in icy
sheets. As my mind jolted between delirium and denial—*I know who
did it, Éclair. I know who killed you. Wait, what am I saying? You can't be
dead*—it was the temperature that made me feel truly out of my mind.
Where am I? Why the fuck is it so hot?

When I opened a window, the other girls complained and called
me insane. I'd already made a minor scene in the dinner hall when I'd
laughed at the food, thinking it was a joke. I don't know what I was
thinking—in what universe would a bunch of long-suffering cafeteria
ladies play pranks on orphans? Yet somehow that seemed more reasonable than the idea that I was expected to eat this garbage. Soggy French
fries, a pale hunk of fried fish, a glob of creamed corn that looked like
it'd been regurgitated. I was used to fresh baked bread with Marmite,
lumpy yogurt, and delicious Gravenstein apples. When I asked Trisha,
the hefty horse of a girl in charge, if there were any vegetables in the
kitchen, she said, "Oh, is this not good enough for you?"

"Not really," I said. "It's, like, nutritionally bereft."

"Well, you're, like, not in a position to complain," she snapped back, mocking the Valley girl cadence I'd unintentionally picked up from Éclair.

Éclair, Éclair, Éclair. Every time I thought about her, which was constantly, my throat closed up and I couldn't get enough air into my lungs. I was having an allergic reaction to my reality.

During the exchange with Trisha, the other kids gawked at me. Everyone already hated me, just like the girls in youth group who'd called me egotistical. It was the way I phrased things, like when I complained about the water pressure in the showers by saying, "You actually wash your hair with this leaky drizzle?" My words seemed to judge the girls who used the shower instead of the shower itself. I soon learned the right way to say it, which was "This shower fucking blows."

There was a Christmas tree in each of the dorm rooms: thin, gaunt pines plucked from the discount section of Home Depot, rejects no one else wanted, appropriately. Taz practically lived under the tree, hiding amid the branches and cheap paper ornaments, emerging smelling like pine sap when it was time to eat or when it was quiet enough that she felt safe exploring the room. She was the latest addition to the menagerie of pets at the group home: a green iguana, a tarantula, some tropical fish darting back and forth in a dingy tank, and a ditzy black-and-white terrier named, imaginatively, Oreo.

I felt catatonic 90 percent of the time, with the 10 percent being the waking nightmare of red splatters filling my vision, blinding me, making me wish I'd never left for that godforsaken dance so that at least I would be dead, too. I imagined red turning to black, horror turning to an inviting nothing. But then I would look into Taz's remaining eye and remember that I had to carry on. I could not step into that black abyss, because I was all she had now.

I'd worried at first that the other kids would find a one-eyed cat repulsive, but I soon realized that most of them had seen worse. They thought it was cute how much she liked the Christmas tree, but to me it seemed tragically sad. Taz, an outdoor cat accustomed to a wide, woodsy territory, was now reduced to a single pathetic twig of a tree enclosed by four walls. I felt guilty all the time; I wished I could speak the language of cats and explain to Taz that this was better than the alternatives: freezing to death alone in our abandoned house or languishing in a cage at the Humane Society, waiting for an adoption that would never come, because who would want a one-eyed cat formerly owned by notorious alleged pedophiles?

My world had shrunk to the size of a thirty-inch-wide army cot. Nothing about anything was explained to me anymore. Mrs. Grange was reprosecuting, but I had no idea when the new trial was supposed to start. The press seemed as stupefied as I was, unsure how to proceed now that their media princess had been taken away. Headlines like "Grim Turn in Satan Family Saga" expressed a kind of deflated inevitability. The fun was over.

I had no idea where Éclair was supposed to be buried, since neither of our parents was a New Hampshire native and we had no plot. Our eternal resting place as a family wasn't something my parents had intended to contemplate until they were old. And I couldn't ask them about it or speak to them at all, because the state's no-contact order had been reissued. It clamped down like a cold dead hand as a new story rushed to fill the void left by Éclair: *my parents* had killed her, using witchcraft and a Satanic hit man. The news outlets were tentative at first ("Parents to Blame in Shocking Murder?"), then self-assured ("They Stole Our Children—Then Murdered Their Own"). It was obvious to *me* who had killed Éclair: the guy on the courthouse steps who'd thrown the hot dogs at her and called her a whore. But nobody cared what I thought.

Graham, the psychiatrist who'd been assigned to assess me, liked to talk about my dreams and do word association exercises while I closed my eyes on a leather chaise longue.

"I'm going to say a word," he said, "and I want you to respond by saying several words that come to mind. Don't think about it too hard.

Just lie back and let your mind be free."

Unlike Angelica's office, which had been all fluffy pink pillows and kid-friendly furniture, Graham's office was dark and masculine. It reminded me of my dad's study. There was even a hint of pipe tobacco in the air. I wanted to ask Graham if he smoked British Cavendish, but I was afraid. I'd gotten attached to Aaron only to have him leave without even saying goodbye. I wasn't going to make that mistake again.

"'Home.'"

I took a breath and said, "Splatter. Ruined. Gone. Lost."

"Interesting . . ." I could hear Graham scribbling things down on his notepad. "Next word: 'mother.'"

"Umm . . ."

"Don't think about it. Just go."

"Strong. Tough. Sandalwood. Raccoon."

"'Father.'"

"Heart. Nice. Smoke. Nice. . . . Sorry, I said 'nice' twice."

"That's okay. 'Sister.'"

"Love. Gone. Life. Fire. Knight."

"'Night'? Like, 'nighttime'?"

"No, 'knight.' Like knight in shining armor."

"'Killer.'"

"Hot dog. Loser. Psychopath. Man."

"It seems like you feel very overwhelmed by the situation," Graham said.

"No shit, Sherlock."

"Fuck you, Watson."

I snorted a shocked laugh and raised myself up on my elbows to look at him.

He chuckled. "Sorry." He closed his notebook and dropped it in a drawer. "We've got ten minutes left, but you can head out early if you want. I'll see you on Thursday."

"Actually, can I just sit here for a minute?" I asked.

"Sure. Want a cup of coffee?"

"I would love that."

I sat in silence on the chaise longue, sipping pretty good coffee from a mug with the words FREUDIAN SIPS on it. I gazed at Graham's oil paintings of sailboats and tempestuous seas and allowed my mind to wade into an ocean of white noise, the combination of mental numbness and caffeine as intoxicating as a drug.

At the end of our next appointment Graham did the same thing, offering me a cup of coffee and letting me sit in silence for the last segment of the hour. It became our routine, and for ten minutes twice a week, I was able to feel, if not peace, then the next best thing, which was nothing.

The group home, called Germaine House (I later learned that Saint Germaine was the patron saint of abused children), had once been a Victorian hospital. The sinks were overly large, the hallways overly wide, the bedrooms long corridors able to fit ten narrow cots each. The room I slept in was over three-fourths vacant when I arrived. A lot of kids returned to their own homes for Christmas, I learned, and the others were sloughed off into foster homes.

Christmas at Germaine House was so gloomy that the previous year there had been no fewer than four suicide attempts. This fact was gleefully reported to me by Carly Beth, one of my new roommates (we were the "Monkey Room"), a short, cross-eyed girl with pink glasses and blond hair down to her butt. Carly Beth told me she'd been in and out of Germaine House for the last eighteen months. She read books constantly and seemed hyperintelligent. She wanted to be a veterinarian when she grew up.

"Me, too!" I exclaimed when she said this. "But not for pets or farm animals. For wild animals like tigers and dolphins."

"Like for a zoo?"

"No, in the wild. In the jungle and the ocean. Like, I would scuba dive until I found a hurt dolphin and then I'd fix it."

"I've read eighty-nine books about marine life. Name any sea creature and I'll tell you an amazing fact."

"Um . . . lobsters."

"Did you know that lobsters are practically immortal? They never die unless you kill them."

"What? Really?"

"A natural death of a lobster has never been witnessed. And they're smarter than human beings."

"Have you ever met a human being?" I said. "They're the dumbest animals in the world."

There were sixteen of us on Christmas Eve. Most of us stayed in our rooms, trying to ignore Hernanes, the Brazilian kid who screamed all day in the rec room. The staff had changed up because of the holiday, and they'd neglected to keep on anyone who spoke Portuguese, which meant no one could understand what he was saying.

"What's Hernanes's problem?" I asked Carly Beth.

"He's emotionally deranged," she said, not looking up from her book, *Misty of Chincoteague*.

Hernanes was annoying the shit out of me; what gave him the right to scream all day and inflict his misery on us? Later, after we learned that he had developed a kidney stone the size of a grape and his screams had been screams of excruciating pain, I felt bad. It would be twenty hours before Maria, the social worker who spoke Spanish and Portuguese, came back and rushed him to the doctor.

A lady wearing the gaudiest Christmas sweater I'd ever seen arrived with three boxes of donuts from Cousin's Bakery and called out in a tinkling voice, "Merry Christmas!" She was Mrs. Newcomb, and she was in charge of the reduced holiday staff. When she set down the donuts in the dinner room, everyone rushed to grab one. Soon everyone's fingers were sticky with icing and red and green sprinkles, and the room was alive with murmurings of "mmm."

I stared at my donut, fighting tears. I would have traded a thousand festive donuts for a single carrot stick or an apple or a bowl of steel-cut oatmeal. I hoped Mrs. Newcomb, with her grandmotherly attitude, would be more sympathetic to my dietary requests than the jaded and exhausted-seeming Trisha.

"Um, excuse me? Is there anything healthy?" I asked her.

"And who are you?" she asked, before immediately answering her own question. "Oh, you're the poor Satan girl. Did you get a donut, sweetie?"

"Um, that's what I was wondering, was if there was something healthier I could eat."

Mrs. Newcomb frowned. "Don't be spoiled, Lacey. Christmas is about thankfulness."

"Thanksgiving is about thankfulness," I said. "Christmas is about giving."

"Well, I just *gave* you these wonderful donuts. So eat up! Oh, and there's a package for you on the front hall table. Some detective found it at your house and sent it along."

The small box had clearly been opened, examined, and taped back up. Inside was a tatty-looking book, accompanied by a short note:

> *Hey kiddo,*
>
> *Don't listen to anything you hear about me. I'm getting this whole Charlie Foxtrot of a fuckshow ironed out. I can't say too much because the govt is probably reading my mail, but don't get too down in the dumps. The system is all smoke and mirrors. All I can say, for now, is that you-know-who is closer than you think, on a beach somewhere, laughing at us and drinking a tequila sunrise, "the sun gleaming bright on her sail" and all that.*
>
> *—A.F., Esq.*

Was Aaron trying to suggest that Éclair was still alive? Then who was the dead girl I'd seen with my own eyes? Bridget Fonda?

I picked up the book. It was a beat-up paperback with bad cover art, titled *I Saw Marilyn Monroe in 1980*. I read the synopsis on the back. The author was a former Hells Angel who'd met a woman claiming to be Norma Jeane Baker panhandling in Nebraska. According to him, the woman was obviously mentally ill, but she looked like Marilyn, was the right age, and told "a very convincing story" about how she'd faked her death to escape the pressures of Hollywood.

My emotions were a wasteland, and I had no energy to negotiate how this made me feel. On the one hand, it was kind of offensive and ludicrous to suggest that Éclair had not been murdered, that she wasn't gone forever. On the other, it was a gift: permission to go off into la-la land if I wanted to.

After the donuts, all of us, minus the screaming Hernanes, were herded into a freezing yellow bus and taken to a Christmas Eve service. The atmosphere of the church felt weirdly comforting to me. At the center of the chapel was an enormous, grotesque statue of Jesus being tortured to death on a cross. I felt appreciative of the very thing that had caused my mother to flee her strict Catholic upbringing: the portrayal of suffering as holy.

The night of the dance, Éclair had asked me why I was afraid to be beautiful. It was because the world destroyed beautiful things, I understood now. But was it possible that they could come back under a different name, like how Jesus returned as the Holy Ghost? Or how, according to Aaron's book, Marilyn Monroe went from Norma Jeane to Marilyn, then back to Norma Jeane?

When the collection plate went around, Mrs. Newcomb made us all stand up in our pew and face the congregation. I'd spent the last seven months specifically avoiding situations where people might stare at me, but I was hemmed in by Mrs. Newcomb on one side and a boy who smelled like rotten cabbage on the other, unable to flee. The church people, mostly elderly couples, looked at us with tremendous pity. That's when I realized the collection was for us; I was officially a charity case. I thought of my mom, who was so strict about never feeding the wild animals in the forest: "If you spoil them with handouts, they'll forget how to survive. They'll die." Was that what would happen to me now?

At the end of the service, the choir sang "Silent Night," a hymn about inner peace and the coming of a savior. I felt like I was being chewed alive by a pair of ragged jaws. Suddenly Hernanes's unceasing screaming didn't seem so irrational. What else was there to do but scream and scream until the universe acknowledged your pain, or you died, or you accepted that no one would ever truly hear you?

xvii

1991

MY CASEWORKER FROM CHILD SERVICES WAS YVONNE, A WOMAN in her forties with skin turned orangey bronze from too much sunless tanner. Her clothing choices seemed confused (I'd picked up enough about fashion from Éclair), as she attempted to blend the dated, boxy tweed jackets of Diane Keaton in *Baby Boom* with the current youth-obsessed fashions.

Her office was spartan and beige: beige walls, scratchy beige sofa, blond wooden desk with no personal items except for a family portrait of Yvonne with her husband and two sons, posed in front of a blue background, all of them staring serenely at a fixed spot just above the camera lens. The husband was the dorkiest man I'd ever beheld: beige turtleneck, huge glasses that took up half his face, and a feathered haircut like John Travolta's in *Welcome Back, Kotter.* The two sons were miniature versions of him. In the portrait, Yvonne beamed as though belonging to this trio of lame males was the proudest achievement of her life.

"We've contacted your mother's parents in Indiana," she told me. "They say space is pretty tight, and they already have a Korean from some Christian foreign exchange program. But they're working hard to come up with a way to accommodate you. You'd like that, wouldn't you?"

"Indiana?"

The idea filled me with horror. It wasn't lost on me that I was the same age my mother had been when she'd run away from home. I had an awful feeling that I was paying back the debt her freedom had accrued.

"It's a lovely farm, as I understand," Yvonne said. "Perfect for an outdoorsy type like you."

"It's a *cattle* farm," I said. When Yvonne looked at me with blank incomprehension, I explained, "It's not good. It destroys the land."

Yvonne sighed. "I'm sorry it's not your preference, but beggars can't be choosers. We're looking for your father's family as well, but they've been more difficult to contact. And the logistics of sending you abroad would be very complicated."

"I don't want to go to England. I want to stay here. You're acting like I'm an orphan. I *have* parents. I need to stay close to them, for the trial."

Yvonne drummed her fingernails on the desk—hot-pink press-ons that reminded me, achingly, of Éclair. "We don't even know if there's going to *be* a trial, Lacey. Have you been able to speak to your parents at all?"

I shook my head no.

"But you're still talking to that psychiatrist, Graham."

When I nodded, Yvonne checked a box on a piece of paper.

"And it's still your position that your parents never molested you. That nothing ever happened."

I nodded again. Check. Sometimes I imagined how Éclair would answer that question: *It's not my "position," you pumpkin-colored hag. It's the fucking truth.* But without her and Aaron, I didn't know what to think or say anymore. So I just tried to think and speak as little as possible.

"Here's some good news. I talked to Detective Brennan. He said the autopsy was conclusive and showed your sister was not raped."

My life had sunk to such depths that it was "good news" that while my sister had been shot in the head *and* had her throat slit, she had, fantastically, not been raped first.

"They think the killer might be impotent. . . . I'm sorry, is this too much information?"

What Yvonne was suggesting was that rape and murder went so intrinsically hand in hand that the only explanation was that the killer couldn't get his dick up. As if no one could imagine the purpose of killing a woman if you didn't at least try to rape her first. It was so casually, hideously sinister.

"They're looking into this Ty person, the one who threatened to kill your whole family."

"He didn't," I corrected her. "A girl named Autumn said . . . Whatever."

Lately it depleted my energy enormously to speak a complete sentence. I did whatever I could to avoid it.

"Apparently your sister was getting a lot of hate mail, some of it very violent. Did she ever show these letters to you?"

She hadn't.

"Well, you have a meeting with Detective Brennan on Friday. If he asks, tell him we're trying to place you in the Concord area so you can be available."

"Okay."

"As for your placement, I think I can get you a really nice situation. Since you're new to the system, you don't have a record. You haven't set anyone's car on fire, or stolen money, or done drugs, or stabbed anyone yet." She spoke as if these things were inevitable.

"You're very quiet," she went on. "And you're very attractive."

The comment caught me off guard. "Excuse me?"

"Has no one told you that before? Surely you're aware. Not in a girlie-girl way, obviously. But you're . . . *strapping.* I'm not trying to embarrass you. So much of my job is about getting to know a child and learning how to emphasize their desirable qualities and hide their undesirable ones. I don't normally speak this frankly with my charges, but you just seem so mature. So intelligent."

I felt the atmosphere of the room change, like an electric current had been switched on, snapping me awake. I looked at Yvonne as if for the first time: her pearly pink lips like the inside of a shell; the unprofessional way she chewed her pen, suddenly sexy; the crinkles at the corners of her eyes, suddenly alluring.

So intelligent.

It was exactly what Angelica used to say. But she'd been tricking me the whole time. After a day of sashaying her ass in front of me, she probably went home to a Bruce Willis–type hunk and fucked his brains out while laughing about the gross, desperate muffin-eater she had wrapped around her little finger.

And yet, while I was wary of Yvonne's compliments, something about her seemed different from Angelica, something I couldn't quite pinpoint. Maybe I was finally developing gaydar.

"I see you have farm experience. Are you comfortable being placed on a farm? Doing some work after school?"

"Yes."

"That's great. Very desirable. I bet you have some great biceps, huh? Take off that sweatshirt—if you're comfortable with that. So I can get a better idea of you."

I paused, not sure if she was serious. Then I pulled the sweatshirt over my head. Underneath I was wearing a sleeveless field hockey shirt from middle school. I watched Yvonne's face as her eyes glided up and down my arms.

She wants me.

It was mind-boggling, electrifying, slightly disgusting. My self-esteem was shitty enough that I felt sure if she wanted me, there must be something wrong with her—as if a grown woman ogling a fourteen-year-old wasn't enough of a tip-off.

Yvonne's office was well situated for an illicit liaison, stationed as it was at the end of a random corridor neighboring the vending machines, the clatter of coins and tumbling of Diet Cokes and Tabs masking the thudding of the desk against the wall.

I'd always harbored some anxiety about the mechanics of lesbian sex. What did women *do*? What did they put where? When did they know they were done? All those ignorant questions that mystified men secretly mystified me, too.

In practice, though, the only secret was that women were sexual machines capable of an incredible variety of acts—on desks, on floors, on cheap beige sofas, behind closed doors, right under the nose of society, with fingers, straddled thighs, lips, mouths. Yvonne was so fuckable I'd leap across the desk the second she gave me a certain look: a twitch of her lip, a languid stare that indicated we were moving on to the true reason for our meetings.

Sometimes in our frenzy the framed portrait of her family would tip over and fall off the desk. I saw the picture differently now. Instead of a proud wife and mother, she seemed like a hostage, smiling on the outside, screaming on the inside: *Get me the hell out of here!*

Each time I returned to Germaine House after one of these filthy interludes, I would collapse on my bed and cry silently for an hour (a talent I'd picked up after seeing a girl get punched in the ear for sniffling too much). The feverish highs of sex were followed by crippling lows, endured alone in the overly hot Monkey Room.

These were the moments when I missed Éclair so much I truly prayed for death. All I wanted was to talk to her. I wanted to tell her I wasn't a virgin anymore and to ask her if it was weird that I didn't feel any different. We'd never had frank discussions about sex, probably because of our age difference and my lack of interest in penises. But now that it was too late, I wanted to know everything. Whom had she done it with? Had she been in love? I had two conflicting fantasies: in one, Éclair was impressed that I'd become a woman and we chatted like adults; in the other, she screamed that I was just a kid, stormed into Yvonne's office, and hit her in the face with her purse.

I asked Graham if there was a version of the Oedipus complex for girls who were obsessed with their sisters. Yvonne's jewelry could have been plucked from Éclair's collection: gleaming lacquer earrings, gold herringbone chains, chunky pearl necklaces. Even their pseudo-sophisticated Eurotrash names were similar.

"There's the Electra complex," Graham said, barely containing his excitement that I'd had the first sexual event of my life. I tried to be as honest as possible, telling him I'd entered a sexual relationship with an older woman I'd met randomly. I didn't mention that this random woman was, in fact, my social worker. He went on: "The Electra complex is characterized by penis envy. The daughter subconsciously competes with her mother for her father's affection. It's rooted in fear of losing a father's love. Did your mother ever make you feel unloved as a child?"

"I mean, she was never super affectionate, but she always made me feel like I mattered."

"Do you still feel like you matter?"

"No. I think that after Éclair, everyone forgot that I exist. My parents probably forgot I exist, too."

He shook his head intensely. "Lacey, your parents could never forget you. They're waiting for this to be over. Try to have faith."

"Why are you on our side?" I asked abruptly. "Everyone else thinks we're Satanists."

He chuckled. "I'm immune to all that. Freud was a Jew, you know. His theories have nothing to do with Christian hysteria. Believe me, Lacey, nothing that you are feeling right now is weird or freakish or inappropriate. Many people experience a heightened sex drive during times of crisis. It's your body's way of relieving stress. Now tell me about this older woman. Where did you meet her?"

"The library," I lied. The Concord Public Library was the one place that Germaine House kids were allowed to go to unsupervised if we'd accumulated enough good behavior stickers during the week.

"What attracts you most about her?"

"She knows what she wants. She wears these ladylike businesswoman clothes, but then she rips them off and becomes an animal. We both become animals."

"Very normal, very natural," Graham assured me. "You want to break away from the world of people, because people have hurt you so much. So you escape into primal sexual behavior. Your lover, she's escaping something too. Her 'ladylike' world, perhaps . . . Are you in love with her?"

"No."

Love, as I understood it then, was what I'd felt with Angelica. A twisted lie, a fantasy. What I had with Yvonne was all too real. Her frosted mauve lipstick that looked like cotton candy but tasted like mud, the stretch marks and dimples of fat that betrayed the age of her rigorously athleticized "Go for the burn!" Jane Fonda body. The way she barely tried to conceal how ready she was for me to leave once she'd been satisfied. The way I felt when we were done. All too real.

xviii

"HEY, BITCH. YOU'RE IN MY BED."

I stirred awake, sweating in my flannel pajamas as usual. The sun was barely up, giving the room a cold violet glow. A girl with dyed black hair was staring down at me. She had a duffel bag slung over her shoulder and wore the smeared eyeliner and dark clothes of an ash person (the term "goth" hadn't reached our remote corner of America yet).

"Hmm? Excuse me?" I croaked.

"You're in my bed, *bitch*," the girl repeated, giving me a rough kick for emphasis. I rolled off the cot and landed with a thud on the hard tile floor.

"Ow!"

The girl ripped my sheets off the cot and threw them on top of me. I looked around and saw that the rest of the beds were being claimed by girls I'd never seen before. I gathered my sheets in a ball and moved to the empty bed next to Carly Beth, who had woken up in the hubbub and started reading a book, *Stormy, Misty's Foal*.

"Hey. Carly Beth. Who is that girl?"

"That's Natasha," she whispered. "She went to her dad's for Christmas, but I guess she's back now."

"Who are the rest of these people?" I pressed.

Carly Beth shrugged. "People come and go. Did you know that horses are practically immortal? They never die unless you kill them."

I gawked at her. "Are you kidding me right now?"

"Shut up, bitches!" Natasha shouted across the room. "I'm trying to sleep, goddamn it!"

In the dim light the newcomers all looked vaguely the same. I imagined this was how we'd seemed to the congregation at Christmas: a blob of stray children, all interchangeable and expecting handouts. I was never sure anymore when someone recognized me as the "Satan Daughter." The looks of disgust I received as Lacey Bond were similar to the looks of pity I received as an anonymous homeless child. I was realizing how close the two concepts were. The line between pity and disgust was very thin.

I felt too nervous to go back to sleep. Early morning had become my worst time, psychologically speaking. It was when I succumbed to the pulverizing weight of my thoughts: *Éclair is gone. I face this life alone. This ugly, ugly life.* Thoughts of blood consumed me. Time stopped having meaning, and minutes felt like hours. It disturbed me that my body could just *go on* while this was happening—heart still beating, lungs still breathing, all the basic biological functions going off without a hitch. That while my mind was breaking down, I could somehow still be a person.

"Get up, monkeys! Breakfast, then showers."

As I dragged myself out of bed, I saw something that almost made me scream: the hands of the new girls were red. *Red*, as though blood-stained. I wondered if my mind had snapped, if I'd become insane. Maybe I would see blood everywhere from now on.

The dining room was loud and crowded with the influx of new kids. I watched them wiping at their red hands with scratchy paper towels. The red was real, I decided; I wasn't hallucinating. The sight of it made me light-headed. Quietly, I asked Lori, who was gossipier than Carly Beth and seemed to know everything about everyone.

"It's from beets," she explained between loud slurps of radioactively orange juice. "Services broke up the Henderson farm. Apparently they've been using foster kids as free labor and basically kept them prisoner in the cellar canning beets."

Beets. My whole body relaxed. *Just beets.*

After breakfast we were all herded into the rec room. The tables and sofas and the Ping-Pong table had been pushed against the walls. Random boxes and pieces of detritus were scattered around like there'd been a small, localized tornado.

"Everybody stand in a big circle. That's right, come on in." The regular staff was back, which included Trisha and a very fat girl unfortunately named Patty, inspiring the nickname the Hamburger. She took so much abuse for her weight that it amazed me she didn't just quit her job and tell us all to go fuck ourselves. On the contrary, she seemed to genuinely care, buying us little personal items that weren't budgeted, like Topex zit cream and brand-name maxi pads instead of the generic ones that felt like diapers.

"Welcome back, guys," Patty said now. "Those of you who went home, I hope you had a super-duper Christmas. Those of you who are back from the beet farm, we're really sorry that was a bad situation. But we're happy to have you back, and we'll find you some better placements this year. 1991 is gonna be the best, you guys! I can feel it in my bones!"

"You can feel your bones through all that fat?" one of the guys snickered. Patty pretended not to hear.

"And we have a special new friend, so everyone say hi to Lacey over there."

I felt my cheeks flaming. I stared at a spot on the floor, unable to look anyone in the eye. Even though I hated Patty in that moment and wished a burning meteor would drop on her head, it occurred to me later that she'd done me an enormous kindness: she hadn't told them my last name.

"Trust," Patty said, dragging out the word like we were all hard of hearing. "What *is* trust? The dictionary defines it as 'the firm belief in the reliability of the truth, ability, or strength of someone or something.' Every single one of you is here because someone let you down. What's

important is that you don't lose your ability to trust others. Most people are really good in their hearts. Don't let some bad apples keep you from growing into the most beautiful apple in the world—an apple who can trust other apples, and have wonderful relationships, and grow into a beautiful apple tree."

It was the metaphor of someone who had never worked on an apple orchard. An apple didn't need to have wonderful relationships with other apples to grow. An apple tree sprouted from a solitary seed or was grafted from an existing tree, like a clone. There were no lessons to be learned from apples in regard to trust.

"So we're going to do a trust-building exercise today. As you can see, the room is a bit of a mess. You guys are going on a little obstacle course! Trisha, if you could tie the blindfolds, please. Those of you without blindfolds, your job is to safely lead your partner around the room."

I prayed my partner wouldn't be the scary, black-eyeshadowed Natasha. It didn't occur to me that *she* should be scared of *me*—hadn't I pushed Angelica into a glass table? Bashed Ty's face to a bloody pulp? And yet I still considered myself unequivocally nonviolent, like the men who go to their graves never seeing themselves as wife-beaters, merely burdened with unruly and irritating wives who continually provoked them.

Trisha divided the room and placed half of us, including me, in blindfolds made from cut-up T-shirts. The fabric was so thin I could make out the vague shapes of everyone in the room, and if I simply gazed downward, I could see the floor. I saw Patty's pink Keds coming toward me.

"Lacey? Here's your partner. Let Destiny guide you."

It took me a second to realize that Destiny was a girl. I could see her shoes: pearly blue jellies, the kind you could buy for ninety-nine cents at the dollar store.

"Hi," I said to Destiny, whose face was a dark blur through the blindfold.

"Hi," she said back. She touched my arm softly, like I was a cat who might run away. "Just, uh, step forward two steps. Don't trip on the chair."

"I can pretty much see everything."

"I know," Destiny whispered, "but it makes Patty happy."

It startled me when she said that, since it was rare at Germaine House for anyone to acknowledge that other people's feelings even existed.

Destiny pretended to guide me around the various obstacles. Everyone else was being loud and obnoxious, but Destiny's voice was calm and focused: "Step onto the box. Lift your foot. Higher, higher, got it." She seemed very ladylike, and I found myself flexing my biceps like a dumb jock, hoping maybe she'd notice. At the same time, I was rolling my eyes at myself. Probably only a desperate old closet case like Yvonne would ever find me desirable.

We were the first pair to successfully circle the room. I heard Patty clapping for us. "Great job, you two! Amazing!" Then she hurried away to deal with the boys, who were using the obstacle course as an excuse to injure each other.

I took the blindfold off and blinked in the sudden brightness. Then I looked at Destiny and almost screamed. Her face was so surprising I thought I was seeing things. I knew exactly who she was—and I knew her name wasn't Destiny. A vision of a blond bowl cut and a NASCAR T-shirt flashed in my memory. But before I could say anything, she raised a finger to her lips. *"Shhh."* Then she whispered, "Don't tell anyone."

xix

IT WAS A WHOLE DAY BEFORE I WAS ABLE TO SPEAK TO DYLAN PRI-
vately, though I kept a close eye on him—I say "him," for my mind had
instantly reverted to seeing Dylan as a "he." A he in a startlingly convincing, even pretty disguise, but a he nonetheless. I watched his face
obsessively, across the dining hall, in line for the bathrooms. Some moments I could clearly see the boy I'd known. Others, I was sure I never
would have guessed. Whenever I caught his eye, he blanched slightly. I
didn't think he was afraid I was going to tell anyone; he was just embarrassed to be caught being a girl. *Welcome to my life,* I thought.

I passed him a note during dinner: *Meet me tomorrow in non fic
Guinness World Records.*

The library was a hulking stone building that reminded me of a
bank vault. New Hampshire was very proud of its high literacy rate,
and the library seemed to reflect that, protecting the books within as
if they were man's greatest treasure. Of course, once you got inside, it
was mostly hobos escaping the cold and penny-pinching middle-aged
ladies reading plastic-bound issues of celebrity gossip magazines. When
the bus dropped us off, we all dispersed to various corners. I'd catch
Carly Beth in the travel section, poring over maps of Quebec and New
Brunswick, where she claimed she was going to run away to as soon as
the snow thawed. She described Canada as the land of milk and honey,
with a people vibrant and hardy from free health care, enlightened and
wise from free education.

"Canada has the highest suicide rate in the Western world," I'd informed her. It was one of those oft-cited "facts" circulated among Libertarians as proof that the welfare state robbed people of dignity and the will to live. The statistic was incorrect, it turned out. Canada's suicide rate was more or less comparable with the United States'. But by the time that information got to me, I had other, far surpassing grievances with the Canadian government.

The most deserted section of the library were the shelves devoted to all the volumes of *The Guinness Book of World Records*. I crouched between the stacks, waiting for Dylan. Five, then ten minutes went by. I wondered if I should have been more specific in my note. From what I recalled, Dylan wasn't the sharpest tool in the shed. Maybe he didn't even know what "non fic" meant.

Finally, he arrived, holding a colorful stack of Lang's Fairy Books.

"Hey," he said. He sat down next to me like a girl, keeping his knees together. He wore a long, floral skirt with a brown leather belt and a white blouse covered in ruffles. Éclair would have laughed, the style was so out of date. The *Little House on the Prairie* fad had come and gone. But I thought it looked lovely on Dylan, like he was a wholesome young bride from the 1870s.

"Hey," I said back.

Dylan grabbed one of the *World Records* books and started leafing through it. I realized it was totally possible that he thought I'd asked him here only to read about the world's biggest hamburger or the fastest hundred-meter dash over burning coals while holding an egg. Then he said, looking not at me but at a picture of the world's tallest dog, "I was really sad when I heard about Éclair. She was the prettiest person I'd ever seen."

Hearing Éclair's name sent me to a dark, reeling place, and my throat closed up.

"I think it's dangerous to be that pretty," I croaked. "You get too much attention, and then some psycho kills you."

"Ugly people get killed, too."

I thought about it. "I guess that's true."

"I stayed in Éclair's room once when my mom was in jail, remember that? Everything smelled like perfume."

"Vanna White's going to play her in a movie. But I think Bridget Fonda would be better. Vanna's a piece of cardboard."

"That's so cool. Jo from *The Facts of Life* should play you."

"I think she's too old now."

Dylan kept flipping through the *World Records* book. I tried to think of a delicate way to ask him what the hell he was doing passing himself off as a girl. I knew he was too shy to simply volunteer the information.

"So are you in disguise or something?" I asked abruptly.

"No," he said.

"Is it like on *M*A*S*H*? How Klinger tries to get out of the army by cross-dressing?"

"No."

"Hotter or colder: You're in the witness protection program."

"Colder."

"You're . . . posing as a rich man's long-lost daughter to steal his inheritance."

"Colder."

"You're impersonating your twin who supposedly died in the womb but was actually sold to the Russian mob."

"Colder."

I racked my *Days of Our Lives*–addled mind for another explanation. "I give up, just tell me."

"I can't. You won't believe me."

"Dylan, I swear I will! Have you heard about my life recently? I'd believe anything at this point."

Dylan chewed his lip. With his girlish facade, it was almost adorable. Then he declared, "Pinkie swear?"

142

"Pinkie swear."

Dylan extended his pinkie finger and hooked it with mine. He took a deep breath and said, "I'm dressed like a girl because I'm a girl."

I stared at him. Of all the crazy scenarios I'd concocted, this one had not occurred to me.

"So you were in disguise *before*?" I said, confused. "Why?"

"I've always been a girl. But everyone thought I was a boy because of the body I had."

"A *boy's* body," I clarified.

"But I was a girl the whole time. Secretly. Inside."

"But . . . how did you know that?"

"I just knew."

"Oh . . . Well, you sure look like a girl now."

"It's temporary." She sighed. "The medication will wear off soon. My mom got it for me, but now she's gone."

"Is she back in jail?"

"She's dead."

"Oh. I'm sorry." I didn't know what else to say. An image of Dylan's mom flashed in my mind—young and pretty, but a drug addict. Drained-looking. I wasn't ready to admit that my mother was a drug addict, too; that despite my froufrou British dad, Dylan and I were the same. Tragic, lost townies with druggie moms.

"When Services found me," Dylan said, "they listed me as a girl. So I just went along with it. No one knows. Trisha and Patty don't know. Glen, my caseworker, he doesn't know. They all think I'm Destiny. I even ripped up my birth certificate."

"That was smart. Wait, you said there's a medication you can take to be a girl?"

"It's an injection. It makes you less of a boy."

"Dylan—Destiny—" I corrected myself. "Sorry. God, why did you have to pick such a stupid name?"

"Destiny was my mom's name."

143

"Shit. I'm sorry." What was this *thing* in my soul that caused me to insult everyone all the time?

"You can call me Dylan as long as no one else is around."

"No, I mean, if you want to be Destiny—"

"I'm Dylan," she said firmly, "but a girl Dylan. Do you believe me?"

Looking back, I'm embarrassed by the way I studied her face and body like a detective with a magnifying glass, seeking clues of masculinity or femininity. In the years since, I've bumped up against enough queers of all types to understand the etiquette: when someone tells you who they are, they're not asking your permission. But that was a wisdom I didn't possess at the time, so I examined Dylan for proof. More than the superficial male/female checklist, I was looking for an energy, the special magic of my mother, of Éclair, of Angelica and Yvonne and Melissa. *Girlhood*.

"I believe you," I said. I wasn't sure if I was being 100 percent honest, but it seemed more important to say what Dylan needed to hear.

Dylan exhaled like she'd been holding her breath since the moment I removed my blindfold in the rec room. We didn't talk about the girl thing much after that. I think it made us both uncomfortable. But we became a pair, like two objects colliding in the coldness of space and traveling on together in fragments, bound by velocity and gravity. We waited for each other in the hall before going downstairs for meals (she was in the Bear Room) and sat together in the dining hall or the rec room to watch *MacGyver*, which was still Dylan's favorite show.

Lots of things about her were unchanged: her awkward way of hovering in a room like an ashamed dog waiting in dread; saying random, weird things like "I know that man died. I just know he died," and if you prodded her, you'd realize she was talking about a *Murder, She Wrote* episode from three days ago. But her personality seemed to benefit from its newly female context. By some strange magic, the qualities that had made Dylan a stupid-seeming boy made her a weirdly appealing girl. Of course, it wasn't magic at all; it was gendered conventions about what made girls and boys valuable. No longer "skinny" and "retarded," Dylan was now "delicate" and "innocent."

The first time I saw Dylan's new smile—her *girl's* smile—was when she saw Taz. Dylan hadn't seen Taz since she was a kitten, a clumsy ball of mottled fur, not at all the self-possessed, brooding feline she was now.

"Taz! Taz!" she exclaimed. She looked so happy I thought she might cry. I was only beginning to understand the power of the past, of artifacts that conjured a better era. Éclair still felt close enough that I could reach backward in time and touch her. I took for granted the junk that contained small traces of her: bottles of nail polish, her alien sunglasses, her LouLou Cacharel perfume. Objects from the past contain meaning only for those who accept the past is truly gone. I'd read *I Saw Marilyn Monroe in 1980* cover to cover multiple times by this point, and part of me hoped that through some twist of fate, Éclair might waltz through the door drinking a Diet Coke through a red Twizzler and say, *This place is a fucking dump! Let's make like a banana, kid.*

Dylan had a hundred questions about the farm and Rainbow Kids, which she stopped asking once she realized all the answers were depressing.

"How are the goats?" she wanted to know first. "Donny, Lonny, Sunny, Spunky, and Trailblazer?"

I was astonished that she remembered them all. Not even Éclair had remembered their names half the time.

"They were sold except for Spunky. The police left the gate open, and she wandered off during a snowstorm and froze to death."

Dylan frowned. "What about the pumpkin patch? That was so cool. It was like Halloweentown."

"The investigators dug it up. All the pumpkins rotted."

"Remember the sculpture garden we made? Is it still there?"

"No. It got vandalized."

"Do you still have that funny old VW bus?"

"Some kids bashed it in with a baseball bat." It would have been quicker for me to offer a blanket statement: *Everything you remember from our childhood is gone; it has been destroyed, abandoned, or mutilated.*

"Who's your caseworker?" she asked next, changing the subject.

"Yvonne." I felt my cheeks flush, as if by saying her name Dylan would psychically know that we were fucking.

"I don't like her," she said plainly.

"Why not?"

"I just don't."

We were sitting on her bed in the Bear Room one day while a group of eleven-year-olds nearby tried to play Monopoly. "This is stupid!" one of them screamed, kicking the board and sending colorful fake dollars flying. She stormed off, and the remaining girls silently picked up the mess, looking annoyed but not surprised. Whenever anyone tried to do a constructive activity at Germaine House, you knew someone at some point was going to ruin it.

Dylan reached under her bed and pulled out a half-eaten pack of peanut butter crackers. As she fished one out, the crinkle of the plastic wrapper drew the attention of everyone in the room.

"Can I have one?" one of the Monopoly girls asked in a tiny, hungry voice.

"No," Dylan said. "It's for me and Lacey."

She handed one of the crackers to me—a good one, not a crushed and crumbling one. And that's when I realized that I might, after everything, still possess the capacity to have a friend.

THINGS WITH YVONNE DETERIORATED QUICKLY. IT BEGAN ONE afternoon as thick flakes of snow pelted the window, making her office and the two of us inside it feel like a pornographic snow globe. When we were done, Yvonne began looking around for her bra. This part of the session was always awkward, because she had more clothes to put back on than me and hers were more complicated: tiny pearl buttons, hidden clasps, skirt over slip over stockings.

She was on the couch, still breathing heavily from the final climax, too exhausted to move. I sat at her desk to give her space (she was very clear that she didn't need me hanging on her for a single second after the deed was done). To be helpful, I tidied a stack of papers that had been sent into disarray. My name caught my eye, and I paused to admire Yvonne's beautiful, womanly handwriting.

Then I saw the other words she'd written. "Paranoid delusions" . . . "pathological liar" . . . "extreme psychological trauma" . . .

"Um, Yvonne? What is this?" I held up the piece of paper.

"Don't read that. It's my case report."

"Why does it say all this crazy stuff?"

"Well, honey, I'm meeting with you five times a week. That's not exactly normal. If my supervisor gets suspicious, I need an excuse for why you're getting so much extra attention."

"You can't write that I'm a pathological liar," I said, my voice rising in panic. "I have to testify in my parents' trial! There can't be any documents saying I'm a liar!"

She calmly put her shoes on. "Honey, these reports are confidential. No one sees them but me."

"What if you're subpoenaed?" I demanded. "You can*not* write this shit about me. This is my life!"

"What about *my* life?" Yvonne spat back. "I could go to jail for these little romps."

"Then maybe you shouldn't be doing it!"

"I'm not doing it all by myself, am I?" She folded her arms and gave me an unfeeling stare that chilled me to the bone.

I took a deep breath, trying not to become hysterical. "You can write anything you want. Write that I cry all the time. Write that I pee my pants. Write that I have a foot fetish. Just don't write that I'm a liar."

"Don't tell me how to do my job," Yvonne said. "Get out of my chair."

I was nearly in tears. "You have to write something else!"

She pointed toward the door. "Out. See you tomorrow."

"You're supposed to be helping me, not screwing me over! I'll tell everyone what we've been doing. I'll tell the police and they'll arrest you for child sex."

"Good thing for me I have all these documents detailing what a deranged liar you are," she said coolly. "Now get out."

I stood there, waiting for her to at least look at me like I was a real person—a person she'd been intensely intimate with, literally *naked* with. She didn't.

It was twenty minutes until Trisha was scheduled to pick me up in the van. I sat on a bench in the drafty lobby, flashing back agonizingly to the night of the Snowflake Dance, when I waited for Éclair, who would never arrive. I thought of storming back into Yvonne's office and screaming at her, *Why are you doing this to me? Why? Why? Why?* But deep down I knew. I had just learned a fundamental lesson about sex: sex makes people vulnerable, and for that they will punish you.

Yvonne transferred my case to Glen, a bland, sanguine man who wore mohair sweaters. I could tell from his overly avuncular attitude—all friendly smiles and pats on the back—that he'd read Yvonne's reports and thought I was hopeless. "Let's find you a family!" he exclaimed with such fake cheeriness I wanted to weep.

Yet another adult drawn into the tornado of my life was Jeannine, the court-appointed attorney brought in to replace Aaron. We met at the police station to talk with Detective Brennan, who was handling Éclair's murder investigation. I was already confused about the points at which her death and the case against my parents intersected, but Jeannine brushed off my questions: "Just leave it to the grown-ups, Lacey."

But I had changed. I was no longer the girl who fetched Aaron's coffee and acted on a basic faith that no matter what wrinkles life served up, the grown-ups would find a way to iron them out. Grown-ups were the source of the problems, it was starting to seem. I knew nothing about this Jeannine person except that she was twenty-six, which seemed alarmingly young, and that she hadn't chosen this case but been assigned it, like it was homework. She wore dowdy tweed skirts and nerdy eyeglasses, and buttoned her shirts all the way up to her neck.

"Are you ready?" she asked me before we went into the police station.

My mind revolted against reliving that blood-splattered night in any capacity. I wanted to run, to find some granite cliff to jump off. To be with Éclair, wherever it was that souls went.

"I don't want to talk to them," I said. "They never listen to me. They just ask a bunch of questions about Satan."

"Not this time," Jeannine assured me. "They've been looking for the guy who threw the hot dog. Detective Brennan thinks they found him."

I felt sick all the way to the station. On one level I was desperate to point my finger at the killer, say, *That's him*, and watch him get hauled away in handcuffs. But on another, I dreaded the moment when it truly sank in that locking him up wouldn't bring Éclair back.

Like Yvonne, Detective Brennan had a framed portrait of his family on his desk. Two freckled sons, a beaming wife. I wondered cynically if she, too, fucked fourteen-year-old girls behind her husband's back.

I was expecting a classic lineup like in the movies, but instead Detective Brennan spread five mug shots out on his desk. They looked virtually identical: same stringy build and tan skin, like five pieces of leather with greasy mullets stuck on top. One seemed familiar. He was younger than the others, practically a kid. I pointed to his photo.

"That one."

"You know that guy theyah?"

My heart was racing. "Yes. He stalked me in the woods, way back in June. He said he'd seen me on TV. He said, 'Your mommy and daddy like turning good little boys into fags.' He was really scary."

"What about these other men? Do you recognize any of them?"

"Um, I'm not sure."

"Did your sister ever talk about a guy named Joachim down in Miami?"

I didn't want to say. I knew it didn't matter anymore, but I'd promised Éclair I wouldn't tell. The promise felt sacred to me.

"Just tell the truth, Lacey," Jeannine pushed me. "There's no point covering for her now."

"Éclair hadn't heard from anybody in Miami in months," I said finally. "They were all fair-weather friends. That's all I know."

Detective Brennan started gathering up all the mug shots.

"What about that kid?" I pressed, pointing to his photo. "Are you going to arrest him? I know he's the guy. He killed her, I just know it."

"We'll keep you infahmed," he said vaguely. I got the feeling I wouldn't be hearing shit from Detective Brennan any time soon.

Jeannine drove me to her office on the other side of town. On the way I begged her to stop at the organic food store and buy me a bag of carrots, which I devoured like a starved rabbit. I felt her judgment as she watched me; I was acting exactly as weird as people had warned her I would be.

"I thought kids liked candy, not vegetables."

"My mom says candy is a drug," I said between chomps, and was hit for the first time with the irony of that statement coming from a heroin user.

Jeannine's office was covered in rows of Post-it notes. There was barely any room to walk, there were so many boxes of files. I sat down in a metal folding chair across from her desk.

"Just a couple things and then I'll drive you back to the home. I've gone over your parents' case, and we're not in the best shape, even with the restart from the mistrial."

"Did you listen to the New Kids on the Block tape?" I asked her. The "Funny Feeling" subliminal messages theory used to seem ridiculous to me, but now that Aaron was gone, I'd become painfully sentimental about it.

"Um, I did give it a listen," Jeannine said.

"Aaron said it would be the 'final flourish.' Do you know how to do that? A final flourish?"

"Hopefully it won't come to that. I've filed another motion for a mistrial. Ideally Judge Sanders will throw the whole thing out. He's a very experienced judge, but he's not a hard-ass like Barclay. He tends to let everything fly. So who knows which way he'll land."

"Can I see my parents soon?" I asked.

Jeannine frowned. "I'm working on that. It's inhumane to keep a child from her parents after a sibling is killed. But expect no sympathy from Zora Grange. I've encountered her in court before, and she's like a dog with a bone. She will never let go. If the trial is to go forward, we need more witnesses. I've been looking through Feingold's prep, and there's one person I was hoping you could enlighten me about. Are you familiar with a Dylan Fairbanks?"

"Yeah. I've known . . . *him* my whole life."

"He was going to testify that your parents were innocent. That to his knowledge they never drank raccoon blood or danced naked or molested anyone. He made a statement to . . . Angelica? The therapist? Originally he stated that he'd seen your mother having ritual sexual intercourse in the forest at a drive-in movie theater. Does that sound familiar?"

"Yes," I said. "Angelica told me someone said that. But she wouldn't tell me their name."

"Well, it was Dylan, but he recanted. Said the therapists had confused him, pressured him to say things that weren't true. When Mr. Feingold tried to bring him on to the defense, Mrs. Grange had the boy declared mentally incompetent."

The day Aaron had come home inconsolable because of some witness he'd lost . . . *It was Dylan*.

"I talked to one of Dylan's teachers, and she said Dylan was perfectly competent. Not a genius by any stretch, but not a liar and certainly not insane."

"He's not insane. But he, um, he has a thing. He thinks he's a girl. She thinks she's a girl."

"You mean . . . a transsexual?"

"She wears girls' clothes. She had medication that makes her less of a boy."

"I see. Well, that's *unusual*, but not psychotic by any means. All I need is a psychiatric professional to state that a person with gender identity disorder is capable of testifying in court."

"My psychiatrist Graham would testify. He thinks everything is normal! If you told him you wanted to have sex with your mom and a porcupine, he'd just say, *Perfectly normal. Perfectly natural*."

Jeannine nodded slowly. "Well . . . let's not say things like that publicly, shall we?"

Back at Germaine House I couldn't find Dylan anywhere—not in the Bear Room, the rec room, the bathroom, or the dining hall. I felt myself go into a familiar panic mode. Usually this happened when I couldn't find Taz. I checked on her about ten times a day, always paranoid that she was going to run away and abandon me.

"Where's Dylan?" I asked Trisha, hoping I didn't sound as frantic as I felt.

"Uh, she's at Services. She has the same caseworker as you—Glen. I think he has some leads for a placement."

"Oh . . . Will she be back in time for *MacGyver*?"

She scowled. "Do I look like the *TV Guide*?"

As the minute hand on the ugly brass clock in the rec room ticked toward the hour, I became increasingly nervous. I wanted to ask Trisha to call Glen's office and make sure everything was okay. But even if I could have explained my anxiety issues, I didn't think Trisha would care. At eight o'clock the show started with a man sinking into quicksand. Would MacGyver rescue him in time?

Finally Dylan appeared. She went straight to the nontattered end of the sofa in the rec room, which became vacant as the younger girls who had been sitting there moved to the floor. I wondered if Dylan even noticed. Beautiful people took it for granted that they would get whatever they wanted; Éclair had expected attention, freebies, and upgrades wherever she went. But what was it like to become beautiful in a short span of time, as Dylan had? How quickly did you forget what it was like to be a normal person, for whom the best seat did not magically become available whenever you walked into a room?

During the commercial break I whispered to Dylan, "You should have told me you tried to testify in my parents' trial."

On the TV, a soothing voice informed us, "Years ago, mothers who cared gave their children the one laxative specially made gentle for children!"

Dylan didn't look at me. For a second I thought she hadn't heard. Then I saw her face had gone white, her eyes had filled with tears. I'd seen this look before—the night of the stolen cake, which seemed like a thousand years ago. *Stick out your tongue.*

"Please don't cry," I whispered. "It's okay. I know they tricked you. We don't have to talk about it."

Silent tears streamed down her perfect face. She looked like a Tiny Tears doll ("You can feed her, change her, and wipe away her tears!"). I put my arm around her, and she sort of collapsed into me, burying her face in my shoulder.

"What's wrong with her?" Lori asked loudly.

"She's fine," I said. "She's just scared MacGyver won't find the bomb Scott planted on his odometer."

Dylan stopped crying, but her head remained in the crook of my neck, my arm around her shoulders. I felt embarrassed—not by her, but by myself. My pseudo-masculine posturing, the boy with his arm around the girl at the movies. Bobby and Judy: one shake, two straws. A tiny voice in my head warned me that I was touching a boy. *Yuck.*

And yet there was a feeling of rightness. She felt warmer than I remembered human touch being. The scent of the shampoo we all used, an industrial pink goo, smelled sweeter in her hair than anyone else's. The more time I spent with her, the more nervous I became that someone was going to kill her. Getting murdered was just the luck of the draw, as far as I could tell. All it came down to was your proximity to a psychopath.

So I weighed my options, going back and forth about whether I should cut her off completely before I got too attached or try to get as much love from her as possible while she lasted.

xxi

SCHOOL STARTED THE LAST WEEK OF JANUARY, A NEW SCHOOL for me, though I'd been there many times before. Concord High was where Melissa, Ann, Sandy, Marjorie, and I had bussed on Wednesdays for Boost, the gifted program. Every year Melissa had tried to flunk the admissions test because she didn't want boys to think she was a nerd. But as hard as she tried to be stupid, her intelligence was irrepressible. I suppose it took a level of sick genius to devise a suicide to get a boy to take you to a dance.

I dreaded the thought of seeing her. Some twisted economy was occurring between the two of us: first I'd owed her, then she'd owed me, now I owed her again—this time for my very life. If Melissa hadn't convinced me to go to that dance, I would have been butchered alongside Éclair. (Or would I? The thought that I could have prevented it, that I might have kept Éclair from opening the door or called the police in time . . . It was too painful to bear.)

To avoid her, I skipped class a lot, freezing my ass off behind the school with the smokers. Sometimes Dylan loitered with me, though she had no fear of Melissa.

"I've bumped into her in the bathroom about ten times," she told me. "She doesn't recognize me."

"That's crazy," I said. "I recognized you the second I saw you."

Dylan shrugged. "Melissa never knew me in the first place."

Occasionally Natasha would be there, smoking pungent cloves and reading *Interview with a Vampire*. She'd started being nicer to me after Lori informed her that my parents were famous Satanists. She wanted me to help her cast a spell on President Bush, to curse him for all eternity. Unable to resist the idea that someone might like me for the very reason everyone else despised me, I said sure.

We cast the spell in the girls' bathroom during the middle of fifth period.

"Turn off the lights and summon all the blackness of your soul into a spinning ball of energy behind your third eye chakra," I instructed her. "Breathe in and fan the flames of the curse inside you."

Of all the self-destructive things I'd done, this was probably the stupidest, the one I have no excuse for. The last thing my parents needed was for me to get caught improvising Satanic rituals with a local weirdo. But I had crossed over into that thoughtless, uncaring "fuck it" stage of life: in other words, I was a teenager.

I raised my arms. "We curse you for all eternity, George Bush. You promised not to raise taxes, but you lied! Read my lips: we curse you!"

"Mention Iran-Contra," Natasha said.

"We also curse you for Iran-Contra!"

"And for being a lame square," she added.

"You are a lame square, George Bush. May you lose reelection and choke on the taxes you stole from the American people! I summon the howling demons of hell and curse you! Now expel the curse from your heart chakra. *Aaaaaaoooo!*"

I howled and Natasha howled with me, the sound reverberating off the dirty tile floor. Then a teacher came in and threatened us with detentions, and Natasha and I scattered before she could take down our names.

At lunch I sat with Dylan in a dingy corner of the cafeteria, picking at an egg salad sandwich comprising mostly mayonnaise. My exploits had gotten around the entire school, and Dylan asked me in a hushed whisper, "Is it true you and Natasha summoned Satan in the girls' bathroom?"

"No. We just put a curse on George Bush."

"That's awesome. Can I come next time?"

"Sure, if you want to."

"Definitely."

She looked so pretty I wanted to lean across the table and kiss her. Not the ravenous, devouring kisses of Yvonne—a fairy-tale kiss, like a snowflake falling on a pure red rose. I was in the middle of this cheesy and slightly incestuous-feeling fantasy (this was *Dylan*, a person I'd known nearly as long as I'd known my sister) when she checked her pink Minnie Mouse watch and said, "I have to go. Glen's picking me up. I'm meeting my real dad for the first time."

"Wow. That's exciting." I'd never realized Dylan *had* a dad. I'd assumed he was dead or that his identity was a mystery.

"Not really. He's the worst person on the face of the planet, actually."

"Oh . . . How do you know that if you've never met him before?"

"I just do." She picked up her tray and her ratty backpack. "See you later."

As soon as she left, Natasha slid into the empty seat, slamming down her lunch tray.

"That bitch teacher found me and gave me a detention. Why do you hang out with that Podunk Barbie doll?" Her eyes followed the pink-and-blond vision that was Dylan. "She's such a normie."

The idea made me laugh. "She's not a normie on the inside. Trust me."

Natasha, unconvinced, stabbed at her soggy French fries with her fork. I think it unsettled her worldview to imagine that a girl could be weird while still preferring the color pink.

A cold, wet blob hit the side of my face. I heard laughter and a voice shouting, "Freaks!"

"What the fuck?" Natasha yelled. Runny creamed corn slid down her black hair. I touched my face, and my fingers came away with more corn.

I looked around and there she was: *Melissa*. I looked for Ann, Marjorie, and Sandy, but I didn't see them. The kids Melissa was with now seemed older, cooler, meaner. Boys with blond helmet hair and girls hanging on them like human accessories.

"Who the fuck is that shit-eating whore?" Natasha demanded.

"She's from my old school," I said. "She hates me."

Natasha stood up, her chair scraping loudly. She cracked her knuckles. "Well, she's about to get the crap kicked out of her."

"Stop," I said. "Let me deal with it."

Filled with strange confidence, I stood up and walked between the tables. Melissa and her charming new friends snickered at one another. I heard one of them say, "Oh my *gawd*."

"What?" Melissa demanded.

"I curse you," I said, looking straight into her eyes. She snorted and looked at her friends, like, *Can you believe this psycho?*

"Okay, freak," she said, and made a shooing gesture. "Run along now."

I didn't move. Melissa tried to keep laughing, but the color drained from her cheeks. When she glanced at her friends for backup, they wouldn't meet her eyes. The message was clear: *You started this; you're on your own.*

"I curse you," I repeated, leaning close to Melissa's face. She recoiled. "You will never know happiness. You will die a slow and painful death. As I will it, so shall it be. You are *cursed*!"

I flicked Melissa's forehead with the back of my hand, causing her to jump. Then I turned and walked away.

"Bitch," I heard her mutter.

That night there was a fight between three of the boys at Germaine House, and they broke the downstairs window. The house was suddenly drafty and cold, which pissed everyone off.

I'd noticed odd, gendered tendencies in the ways everyone expressed their rage. The boys picked fights, fists swinging at the slightest provocation. The girls, more sinisterly, sabotaged each other's possessions, stealing or destroying them and leaving the broken pieces on the owner's pillow as a message: *Nothing. Is. Safe.* Natasha was famous for ripping the heads off teddy bears and dropping precious photographs in the toilet. I was terrified that she might hurt Taz. Just because we'd done witchcraft together didn't mean I wasn't still on her list.

One night before lights out, there was a knock on the door. Trisha poked her head inside. "Lacey? You have a phone call downstairs from the prison. A guy who says he's your . . . goat husband?"

I blinked at her. "What?"

"He says he's a farmer."

"I have no idea who you're talking about."

"He asked for you by name. He says it's important. Come on, just go answer the phone, and if it's some creep, hang up."

I glanced at Natasha, who was staring at Taz with an evil expression on her face. I imagined returning from my phone call to find Taz's body hanging from the rafters and a message on the wall in blood: NOTHING. IS. SAFE.

"Lacey. Now."

I followed Trisha downstairs to her office (a closet, really, with room enough for a desk and a single chair). "I'll give you some privacy," she said, closing the door. I picked up the phone.

"Hello?"

I heard a jumble of voices and a sputtering sound on the other end of the line.

"Hello?" I said again. "Who is this?"

"Lacey, darling." It was my father.

"Dad? Oh my god. Dad!" I sat up so abruptly my chair banged against the desk.

"Are you alone?"

"Yes."

"Sorry for the confusion. Do you remember old Bill Swanson? He's in here, too, poor chap. Small world!"

I did remember Bill, an ancient man who was the local go-to guy for animal husbandry needs, and I realized what was going on. Dad couldn't call me himself because of the no-contact order, so he'd cooked up a scheme with Bill, which must have been extremely difficult to organize from solitary confinement.

"Are you still in that cell all by yourself?" I asked.

"Yes, unfortunately. But don't worry, I'm hanging in there. I'm writing a book of poems! I'm calling it *Wild Beasts and Gods*."

The title referred to my mother's favorite line from *Politics*, by Aristotle: "Whosoever is delighted in solitude is either a wild beast or a god."

"But enough about me," he said. "Are you all right?"

"I'm fine. I have the cat."

"And you're safe?"

"I'm safe." Tears pricked my eyes. "Is Mom okay? Have you heard from her?"

"She's fine. She's pushing through it. She's tough as nails. Don't you worry."

He sniffed. *Please don't cry,* I thought. If he started crying, I'd start crying, and I might not ever stop.

"I still don't believe it, if I'm being honest," he said. "I keep thinking it must be some terrible mix-up."

I felt a brief urge to tell him about *I Saw Marilyn Monroe in 1980,* how Marilyn had faked her own death to live among the Hells Angels, and maybe Éclair was still alive, too. I abandoned the thought two seconds after I had it. I knew the book was cuckoo.

"The cops are really close," I said. "They have the killer's photo. I think they'll arrest him soon. It's some crazy guy—the same guy who threw the hot dog at her."

"They know that for sure?"

"Well . . . *I'm* sure."

There was a pause, and suddenly I questioned whether I was as cuckoo as Aaron's book. Did serious murderers really throw food at their victims in public before killing them?

Dad was already brushing past my theory. "I blame myself. We didn't give Éclair enough discipline. We never taught her any boundaries. And she took such joy in provoking people."

The suggestion that Éclair was even the slightest bit to blame for what had happened startled me. Dad must have sensed my tension (even over the phone he was an emotional psychic), and he dropped it.

"How is it where you are? Are they treating you well?"

"It's fine, I guess . . ."

"Doesn't sound fine. Come now, Lacey. Tell me everything."

It was like sinking into a comfortable couch, like we were in his study again, the smoke from his pipe curling around us like a diaphanous shield.

"It's just that everyone's a stranger," I said. "These people could all be psychos. Just now, for example, I was afraid to leave the room because I thought this one girl might *murder* Taz. Which, now that I say it out loud, sounds completely paranoid and nuts. But it's like, I don't *know* this girl! I don't know anybody! I don't know what's insane to think and what isn't!"

"You have good instincts, Lacey. If you have a bad feeling about someone, you should listen to that."

"I don't know. I think my instincts are haywire. Just . . . too many new people. But oh my god, guess who's not new? Dylan Fairbanks! *Dylan* is here! Except he's, like, a girl now!"

"A girl?"

"Yeah, I mean, she looks exactly like a girl and . . . *feels* like a girl and everything."

"A transsexual?" he exclaimed, using the same word Jeannine had used. "How very beautiful. Our own Orlando. Everything changes, nothing stays the same, eh?"

"No, she's exactly the same," I said, "only a girl now. It's weird. Everything here is weird. They shovel the snow on the sidewalk *twice* a day!

Like, people think they can live in New Hampshire and somehow have their feet never touch snow in winter?"

Dad laughed, a sound I hadn't heard in ages. I thought my heart might explode.

"And that girl I was talking about, Natasha, she's sort of nice to me, but only because she thinks I'm a witch."

"This obsession people have with witchcraft right now . . . It says so much about our society," he said, his voice crackling from the poor connection.

"Like what? That we all need to check into an insane asylum?"

"You're not far off. I've been thinking about it a lot, for my poetry, you know. It's this suburban American grind. These modular, soulless homes. You turn the TV on, and some commercial explains that what you really need is a new dishwasher, or that your food lacks 'personality,' so you better go out and buy some of that orange crap, what's it called . . ."

"Cheez Whiz?"

"Cheez Whiz! But Cheez Whiz doesn't help. And yet everyone on TV seems happy, so *they* must have the secret. There's some *power* people believe they don't possess, do you see what I mean? That's why they hate us. Do you see?"

"Sort of," I said. He was speaking very quickly, and the connection wasn't great.

"I just keep thinking, *Witches, witches.* They're intrinsic to our society—Puritanism, the casting out of evil, purging, burning, blaming, purification. We don't see it anymore, with our modern eyes, but it's there, in the soul of America. They think *I'm* the evil corrupting their children, but it's their own homes! Their televisions! The land they poison with their bloody pesticides. For what? For lawns. *Lawns,* for god's sake! Do you see what I'm saying?"

"Uh-huh," I said, wishing we could talk about something else—anything else. I never wanted to hear the word "witches" again.

"It's really, rather, a blessing, a spiritual gift, this solitude, the apartness—quite ironic, truly, my own purification, unintended . . ."

His words danced around some meaning that was beyond me. The first half of our conversation had been the most normal I'd felt in months, but the feeling was quickly deteriorating.

"Dad? Dad. Just . . . slow down. What are you saying?"

I heard muffled voices on his end.

"Dad? Dad?"

A *click*, and the line went dead. I sat in the chair, praying he might call back. I stared at the dozen of framed pictures on the desk of Trisha and her dogs. She was smiling in every one, a smile I'd never seen in real life. Clearly she loved dogs more than children. Not that I could blame her.

Please call back. Please call back.

I waited and waited, but the phone didn't ring. A few tears fell down my cheek. I aggressively wiped them away. Then I trudged back upstairs, distantly relieved to find that Taz had not been murdered by Natasha. In the dark of night, I lay in bed reviewing every word of our conversation like a starving person gnawing a dry bone.

I wished we'd talked more about Éclair. Then again, what was there to say? Our family had said goodbye to countless animals over the years—feral barn cats, raccoons, at least twenty goats, the horse that contracted horse influenza—accepting with clarity and compassion that their lives were over. They were gone, and their absence made room for new animals, who would be nurtured and loved until they, too, died. There was no use fighting the cycle of life.

But that was a farmer's grief: constrained and sober and useless against the screaming, maudlin, drunk-as-balls pain that slammed me every time I thought of something I wanted to tell Éclair, then remembered she was gone. I could have made peace with it if she'd been struck by lightning or eaten by wild dogs. But I was coming to grasp a truth reserved only for a certain, miserable subsect of people: That murder is not the same as death. That human malice poisons the soil, and there would be no peace budding in the spring.

xxii

BY FEBRUARY, TAZ WAS GOING STIR-CRAZY. IT FELT LIKE WE'D been at Germaine House for an eternity, though it had only been two months. She'd started meowing at odd times, a throaty, repetitive *rr-rrow* that seemed to have no objective other than to inform everyone that she was unhappy.

I'd accumulated enough good behavior stickers that I was able to work out a deal with Trisha to let her go out onto the front porch once a day. This involved quite a bit of rigmarole—signing out, getting Patty to initial the sheet, signing back in, also with Patty's initials—all to stand in the 20-degree violet twilight for twenty minutes until Taz arrived at her daily realization that the world outside was foreign and freezing and hemmed in by snow, and there was nowhere else to go. Concord was hardly a bustling metropolis; to a person accustomed to cities, it would seem a quaint town. But to me, and to Taz, it was a bewildering place, noisy with snowplows, garish with streetlamps, full of concrete and cars, a confused mess of streets and parking lots. I didn't know how to live there, and neither did Taz. So inevitably she'd paw at the door, and I'd let her back in and sign the stupid sheet.

It was during one of these frigid porch sessions that Glen's tan Pontiac pulled up and ejected a glum-looking Dylan. Dylan's facial expressions were subtle, but I'd learned how to read them. She was rarely overtly sad, but when she was, I could detect it in her eyes, a light that went out and made her look like a beautiful cadaver. She clomped up the porch steps in her pink rubber rain boots and plunked down in one of the rocking chairs. Taz trotted up to her. Dylan dangled a limp hand. Her fingers poked out of a hole in her mitten.

"You okay?" I asked.

She didn't answer.

I dragged over a second rocking chair and positioned it directly across from her. Then I grabbed one of her feet and yanked off her pink boot.

"What are you doing?"

"These are the stupidest shoes I've ever seen. They don't have any insulation or traction. Your feet must be freezing, and it's a miracle you haven't slipped on the ice and cracked your skull."

I peeled off her dirty white sock and felt a lurch in my stomach, a faint repulsion. It was a boy's foot, long and bony. I hesitated. But then I looked in Dylan's eyes and got over it. I took off my gloves to rub some heat into her icy toes. Then I opened my coat and stuck the foot under my arm. I did the same thing to the other foot, warming it up and tucking it under my other arm.

"This is weird," Dylan said, and laughed, her legs bent like she was in one of those gynecologist chairs.

"You're weird," I said back. "You live in New Hampshire and you don't have snow boots."

Only later, of course, did it occur to me that she didn't have snow boots because she'd never been able to afford them.

The front door opened, and Trisha stuck her head out. "Destiny? You know the rules. You come back, you sign in immediately. What if you were sitting on this porch and a kidnapper crept up and grabbed you, and we wouldn't even know you were gone because you hadn't signed in?"

"If a kidnapper came, I'd kick him in the face," Dylan said, perfectly serious.

Trisha rolled her eyes. "Assume he was stronger than you."

"Then I'd eat Mayan seeds from the Amazon rain forest that make you invisible."

"Jesus, Destiny, just do as you're told. If you don't use the sign-in sheet, you'll be kidnapped and murdered. That's all I'm saying." Trisha went back inside and slammed the door.

I wondered if it was irresponsible of her to make the stakes so high. Germaine House was teeming with kids with anxiety and PTSD, and most of us already blamed ourselves for our shitty lots in life. I still harbored my belief that my parents would never have been arrested if I hadn't walked out of *Ghost Dad*. And hadn't I wished death on Éclair multiple times, not realizing the universe, as my mother would say, was listening? The last thing any of us needed was to be told that if we messed up one more stupid thing, we would literally be kidnapped and murdered.

Dylan was gazing vacantly at the snow. "What's wrong?" I asked.

"My dad's going to adopt me," she said. "I have to go live with him and my five brothers in Vermont."

"*Five* brothers? Wow. That could be . . . fun." I envisioned games of Capture the Flag, Dylan and a pack of boys running through sprinklers, riding bikes, pelting each other with snowballs in the winter, water balloons in the summer.

But I could tell from Dylan's face that she was envisioning something quite different.

"I've met them. It won't be fun."

I got the full story out of her in drips and drabs—a sentence here, a revelation there, large chunks filled in later by Glen, an incurable gossip who began every other sentence with the words "I shouldn't be telling you this, but . . ."

"Big football stud, now a car mechanic," Glen informed me in his office. "Nothing against car mechanics—those guys can be geniuses. But you know, sometimes they don't know how to treat a woman. A woman is not a carburetor, am I right?"

I nodded, though I kind of disagreed. I used to help my mom fix the pickup truck all the time, and I could easily come up with some eyeroll-inducing yet accurate metaphor about a woman's body in relation to gaskets and fluids and spark plugs. But Glen was one of those cheeseball guys who thought the secret to making a woman orgasm was to give her a dozen red roses.

"So, from what I gather, back in his football days, this guy used to, uh, *entitle himself* to a girl under the bleachers after every game. Sometimes it was consensual, sometimes it was . . . not. Destiny's mother was fourteen years old and pregnant, and her parents wanted her to marry this guy. *Demanded* she marry him. So she runs away from home, comes here, pretends she's eighteen, and gets a job at the pharmacy. Except this guy comes looking for her. She hides the kid, claims she had an abortion, says it's over and she never wants to see him again. And that should have been the end of the story. Do you mind if I eat this sandwich? I have to skip my lunch hour today."

"Go ahead."

"So life isn't easy. She starts doing pills. You know how it goes. She's arrested in 1987, again in '88. Say goodbye to that nice job at the pharmacy. She's a sweetheart, but she's absolutely broke and a drug addict. And here's where it just breaks your heart: she calls the guy. Admits she lied about the abortion and needs child support for their daughter. Meanwhile this guy's been impregnating girls left and right and has five kids living with him—one is even older than Destiny somehow, haven't figured that one out. Anyway, the guy sends her a paltry eighty-five bucks, which isn't enough to pay rent, but it's enough to get high. She can't find pills on the street, so she tries heroin and almost immediately ODs and dies. That eighty-five bucks killed her." Glen took a huge bite of his sandwich. "And what's worse is now the guy knows Destiny exists, so he's claiming his parental rights."

"But he's a rapist!" I practically shouted. "You can't send Destiny to go live with a rapist!"

"Unfortunately her mother never filed a police report. There's no evidence that it ever happened. Until this Mr. Roach guy is reported committing a crime, we don't have any grounds to deny him custody."

Roach. Dylan Fairbanks was now *Destiny Roach.*

"That's ridiculous," I said. "You're telling me Destiny has to go get abused by some rapist and *then* you'll help her?"

"I know, I know," Glen said. "It's eating me up! But there's nothing we can do about it. Her case isn't even my purview anymore. It's up to the State of Vermont."

That night I sat dejectedly on Dylan's bed while she packed her clothes into two beat-up suitcases. Snow pelted down outside, the last big snow of the winter, everyone was predicting. It was one of the rare nights when the room was quiet. As Dylan packed, I noticed that a lot of her blouses and skirts had little faded labels sewn into them: DESTINY FAIRBANKS.

"Were all these clothes your mom's?" I asked.

"Yeah. She always let me borrow them when I got home from school and on weekends and stuff. I guess they're mine now."

We were both fairly deadpan about death. I wasn't sure if Dylan had taken her cue from me or me from her, or whether it was a coincidence that we were both the type to suffer in silence. I wondered if that meant we'd be a bad couple. Communication was the key to relationship success, a fact I'd learned on *Oprah* and seen corroborated in my parents' marriage, which had managed to survive despite the staggering divorce rate for underage brides. When faced with conflict, my mother and I were the type to silently brood, while Éclair stomped around yelling indiscriminately. It was my father who always wanted to talk rationally and empathetically, to deal with the problem and work it out. I couldn't imagine our family functioning if none of us had been willing to be that person. Maybe, with Dylan, it would have to be me.

"You know what's weird?" I said. "Both our moms were pregnant by the time they were our age. And my mom has a drug problem, too."

Dylan paused mid-zip. "Really? I didn't know that. I always thought your mom was sort of perfect."

"So did I. But I guess everyone's, like, hiding a secret person inside."

"You're not," Dylan said.

I blinked, caught off guard. "Well, how would you know? Wouldn't it be a secret?"

"I just know."

And the way she looked at me, it felt true, like she could see under my skin somehow.

Then she said matter-of-factly, "If I were pregnant, I'd run to the Arctic Circle. No one would ever find me."

"You'd freeze your ass off."

"No, because I'd have an Inuit potion that would keep me warm even in the freezing cold."

"Oh. Okay."

She held up a small pencil case covered in stickers of unicorns and kittens and gazed at it mournfully. "This is my last injection. I won't be a girl for much longer. If my dad finds out . . ." She gave a little shudder.

"Surely you don't really need that stuff," I said. I was so used to girl Dylan that it was impossible for me to imagine the alternative. I tried to picture the Dylan from last summer—from Melissa's party—and it was confusing, because that person was both right in front of me and a distant, faint memory.

"Without it, my body will forget who I am," Dylan said. "And the timing is shit, because I'm fourteen now. That's when my mom said boys physically become men."

"When do girls physically become women?"

"Earlier. Twelve."

"So I'm a woman?"

"Yeah."

I wondered if Dylan could tell I wasn't a virgin. My mother had always made it seem like losing my virginity would feel like becoming a luminous fruit on the tree of knowledge. The reality was I felt like a lumpy apple someone had taken a bite out of and left on the ground to rot.

I tapped the pencil case. "But even when this runs out, you'll still be you no matter what, right?"

"My mom said all I really need is to believe in myself. She was kind of corny. Ugh." Dylan buried her face in a fuzzy pink scarf with a tiny DESTINY FAIRBANKS label hanging from a thread.

"I don't think that's corny," I said. "People treat me like I'm a boy all the time, I guess because I look like this and I don't wear lip gloss or whatever. I have to believe I'm a girl, too."

Dylan left the next morning. There was no kiss goodbye, though I'd imagined it plenty of times: Dylan running to me or me to her; the two of us stealing a moment of sublime privacy to express our undying devotion.

Moments like that required preparation, it turned out; life didn't just hand them out on a silver platter. Between the usual chaos of Germaine House and the dozen kids who started crying when Mr. Roach arrived (not because they were going to miss Dylan, but because they were bitterly jealous she was getting to leave), there was only time for a rather brusque hug and me telling Dylan, "Write me a letter. As soon as you can."

Mr. Roach was waiting impatiently for Dylan to get the hell in the truck so they could get the hell going. He looked too young to be a dad, more like a surly older brother. *You're a rapist,* I thought, hoping he would see the accusation in my eyes. But we were invisible to him, all us pathetic kids. From the porch, I watched Dylan tuck her long legs into the passenger side of the dirty truck. It was like watching an angel disappear into a pool of grime.

What I would miss most, I thought, standing there, was her different, superior reality, one in which the existence of Mayan seeds and Inuit potions was assumed. She was the one thing from my childhood that had *bloomed* rather than turned to ash. And I'd been dying to see her naked in a way I didn't allow myself to fully feel, partly because I was pretty sure she had a dick, a concept that flummoxed and repulsed me slightly, though not nearly as much as I repulsed myself: I wasn't good enough for her. I was a sad and ugly person. Meanwhile she was . . . perfect. Dick or no dick, I loved her. I *loved* her.

And now she was gone.

I went inside and ate a stale bagel with margarine. Even if it hadn't been totally flavorless, I wouldn't have been able to taste it. I felt numb, yet there was a prickling energy under my skin, a claustrophobic loneliness. At this point I'd heard all the depressing statistics about foster children: how only 50 percent ever graduate from high school and only 1 percent from college, how the chances of becoming homeless skyrocket. "Don't become a statistic," Patty was always yelling at us, as if it were our fault that we were 4.5 times more likely to contemplate suicide than the average kid. A poster on the kitchen wall showed a pretty teenage girl staring into a cracked mirror. FEEL LIKE YOUR LIFE IS IN PIECES? CALL NOW. WE CAN HELP. It was a suicide hotline, an 800 number displayed meaninglessly, considering we were all homeless and the only phone was locked in Trisha's office and fiercely guarded.

You got used to being on the receiving end of a certain kind of look: *Stop being a fuckup.* Why were a free bed, three free meals a day, and a free public school education not enough? What did we expect, a limousine service? An engraved invitation to a decent, normal life? And yet we languished. This is what happened when children were crippled by charity and raised to be takers, an opinion I continued to hold reflexively and without examination, despite the fact that the "taker" was now me.

If anything, my time at Germaine House only reinforced my half-baked ideas about the ineffectiveness of government handouts. The way we kids were shuffled around, coming and going as beds freed up and became available elsewhere, world-weary social workers just trying to keep a roof over our heads until we turned eighteen and were no longer the state's problem. The way Trisha and Patty treated us like babies, expecting nothing of us beyond refraining from killing ourselves with the bladeless craft scissors. The way I felt myself growing stupider and less capable every day, my dignity seeping away like a slow gas leak portending not an explosion but just . . . emptiness.

And yet, none of that should have been unsurvivable. With the addition of one single ingredient, one elusive step in the recipe, we could have blown those dreary statistics out of the water. The answer was both stupidly obvious and stupidly corny. It was the thing you can't give unless you already have it, the thing you can't accept if your heart is broken: love.

Of all the resources in low supply at that run-down home for run-down youths, it was the nonexistent stock of love that made us truly poor. With Dylan I'd managed to scrounge up a small, livable amount, but now even that had been taken away. And if such a thing as true love exists, then its absence is true loneliness—not the boredom of having no friends or no one to call in a strange new place, but the crushing, irreversibly retarding isolation of being a child whom no one cares about. They'd taken my parents, my sister, my home, my dignity. Now Dylan. *They* being the vague, all-encompassing forces of life: the government, newscasters, murderers, liars, lawyers, Mrs. Grange with her obnoxious Joan of Arc delusions, insisting to me a million times, "I *care* about you, Lacey," when I was certain that if she ever saw me begging on a street corner she wouldn't spare a motherfucking dime.

"Are you okay?"

I startled. Trisha was there, dumping a bunch of dirty paper plates into the trash. It was the thing that drove me craziest about Germaine House, how we always ate off paper plates. They were painfully wasteful—all those trees!—plus a taunting reminder that no one thought we were worth real dishes.

"No. I need to go with Destiny," I said.

"Go . . . where?" Trisha ripped off an excessively long piece of paper towel to wipe her hands clean.

"To Vermont."

"You're not allowed to leave the state. And besides, Mr. Roach isn't a certified foster parent."

"Yet he could be a certified rapist, and you'd still let Destiny ride off with him just because he's her 'real dad.' It's bullshit. She's going to get killed. I just know it!"

"Lacey, she's fine. You should be glad for her. Not everyone gets a happy ending in this world."

"You think she's *happy* to be carted off to go live with a stranger? No one even asked her what she wanted!"

"If kids got to do whatever they wanted, there'd be anarchy."

"Can you just give me her dad's address? I can go there myself. I know how to drive."

"You certainly cannot! You're fourteen years old!"

"Yeah, and you know what? I'd be perfectly fine if people like you stopped interfering in my life! You don't even know how to cook! You'd starve to death without a goddamn microwave! I could cook a better dinner than you!" Something was happening to me. My chest felt constricted, and my hands were trembling.

"You need to calm down. Give me that knife." She gestured toward the white plastic knife in my hand, the one I'd used to spread shitty margarine on my shitty bagel.

"You're seriously scared of a plastic knife," I said. "You seriously think I couldn't come up with a better way to kill you. I'm not a stupid person, in case you haven't noticed. I'm smart. A *toddler* could come up with a better way to kill you."

"Give it to me now."

I handed her the knife. She threw it in the trash. A perfectly reusable knife, now garbage.

"What is wrong with you?" she demanded, hands on her hips, the picture of an exasperated young mom.

"I'm just—saying—" There was a lump in my throat, and it was difficult to speak. "I need to go with Destiny, to make sure she's okay. She doesn't even have snow boots!"

And then I was crying. I'd managed to avoid crying in front of anyone for over two months, and here I was, bawling like a baby at the exact moment I was trying to prove that I was grown up enough to take care of myself and follow Dylan to Vermont. I snuck a peek at Trisha, expecting to see an annoying look of fake pity on her face. But she was stony cold, not even feigning compassion. My tears abruptly stopped.

"Don't think I don't know what you are," Trisha said.

My immediate thought was that she must have heard about me casting spells with Natasha, and she was accusing me of being a witch. But then she said, "You're *nasty*. You don't care that your parents are locked up and your sister's dead. You walk around here like it's nothing. But the second that white trash skank leaves, you're all boo-hoo, boo-hoo. I take care of you because it's my job, but I just want you to know, I think you're foul. And if I hear a single peep that anyone's spreading their legs in the Monkey Room, I'll send your ass straight to juvenile hall, where you can eat all the grade-D pussy you want. But as long as you're under this roof, you keep your nastiness to yourself."

It wasn't her words that shocked me (between Éclair and Aaron, I'd heard every crass word in the book), it was the way she said them—impassively, almost bored, like my sewer-level disgustingness was a long-established fact. Then she took a cold Tab from the refrigerator and walked out of the room.

I knew what Éclair would have done: grabbed the nearest heavy object and thrown it at Trisha's head. Or gone right for the jugular, verbally: *You're such an ugly cow, no wonder you need ten dogs to keep you warm at night!* But I just stood there, stunned. "Foul," she'd called me. *Foul.* I wished I could take a shower to wash the word off.

I almost started crying again. But instead I made a decision: never again would I ask anyone's permission for anything.

Trisha had a vulnerable point in her daily routine. Every night as she got ready to leave, she locked up her office and hung her cheap pleather bag on the doorknob for a second while she went to the front hall to put on her coat. Every night I watched her do this, waiting for the right moment to present itself.

Finally it arrived. A fight broke out on the porch between two boys, and Trisha busted out her moves (if anything impressed me about Trisha, it was her ability to wrestle enraged boys to the floor without breaking a nail). As she defused the fight, I darted to her office door, plunged my hand into her bag, and swiped her keys. Then I disappeared up the back stairwell and stayed hidden for the rest of the night. Through the walls I could hear her cursing and complaining ("Where in the hell are my keys?"). Eventually she got a ride home with Patty. I overheard her complaining the next day about what a "G-D headache" it had been getting into her house. But I didn't care about her house. What I wanted was her car.

The next day I snuck out of the library during our free time and went to the hardware store down the street. I'd invented an explanation for why I needed the key copied, but the old geezer who ran the place didn't care. He cut the key and handed it to me without a word. The whole process was so simple it confirmed my theory that life might not actually be that hard if everyone just minded their own damn business.

I left Trisha's original keys under the radiator for her to find the next time she vacuumed. The shiny new key I kept in my pocket at all times, a literal key to my escape, as soon as I could figure out where to go.

xxiii

IN MARCH, THE NO-CONTACT ORDER WAS FINALLY LIFTED, AS NO Satanic hit man had surfaced in the investigation into Éclair's murder. I was able to visit my mom but not my dad. Jeannine was still trying to get me back on the approved visitors list, a Kafkaesque task requiring documentation showing that I had visited my father without violent incident, documentation I couldn't acquire if I couldn't visit him in the first place.

Patty drove me to the women's detention center and spent the whole ride treating me to cheesy musings about mothers and daughters: "Remember that she needs you as much as you need her. She may be your mom now, but when you're older, she'll be your best friend."

"Why would you want your best friend to be your mom?" I asked. "She'll die before you and then you'll be alone. How crappy is that?"

Patty shut up and drove silently. I knew I'd hurt her feelings and I was glad. I'd meant to.

The visiting room was empty again. It smelled like stale coffee and stale humanity. I barely recognized my mother when I saw her. Her face was gaunt and pale, her dirty-blond hair more dirty than blond. She looked numb and totally beaten down. I realized I probably looked the same to her.

I noticed a bare-bones tattoo of a bird now covered half her neck.

"That's pretty," I said, though it was actually disturbing, like a half dragon, half swan drawn by a deranged child.

"Thanks."

"How are you?"

"Fine." She seemed to be in a stupor. I wondered if she'd gotten back on drugs somehow, but I was afraid to ask. After everything, she was still the mom and I was the kid.

"So . . . what's new?" It was such an asinine question I wanted to kill myself.

"Not much."

"How are you doing about . . . Éclair?"

"I've accepted it. That's all we can do. Have you accepted it?"

I could only shrug. "I don't think I know how to accept things anymore."

"I was so relieved when she came back home. You know she was a drug mule for some Cuban kingpin down in Miami."

It felt like a thousand years since Éclair had told me about the mysterious packages she carried between Versace and a guy named Joachim.

"How did you know that?" I asked. "Did she tell you?"

"No, I figured it out myself." She sounded like Éclair. *People think I'm such a dumb blonde.* "She could have gotten herself killed a dozen times doing that. When she came home, I thought, *Thank god, at least here she'll be safe.* I guess I was wrong. She should have stayed where she was."

She pushed a lock of limp hair out of her eyes, and I saw that her hand was shaking. She was in withdrawal, I was pretty sure. I was also pretty sure I'd seen her like this before. A host of memories came back to me—times Dad had told me Mom was sick and needed rest, me thinking nothing of it.

"How are those ducks?" I asked her. "In the pond?"

"They're gone. Some goddamn Canadian geese chased them away."

"Oh, that sucks. How's Pamela Ann Smart?"

"She's fine. We're fucking."

I snorted, shocked. "Are you—are you serious?"

"Where do you think you came from, Lacey? Your father? Did you think your father was a queer this whole time?"

"No . . . I don't know. But wait, really? You and Pamela?"

"No, I'm just joking."

I didn't know what to think. Since when was my mother ever "just joking"? She'd always been one of those relentlessly earnest people who never got jokes and never made them.

We sat in silence for a full minute. Finally I said, "I heard Dad's writing a book of poems."

"Mm-hmm."

"Did he tell you the title? *Wild Beasts and Gods*. It's your favorite quote."

"Mm-hmm."

"Have you read any?"

"Mm-hmm."

"Are they good?"

She shrugged—more of a twitch, really. I expected to hear another lifeless "mm-hmm," but instead she sighed and said, "They're incredibly beautiful. It makes me sad. Your dad never wanted to be a writer."

"Why not?"

"Because writers are miserable. He thought life was meant to be lived, not written about."

It made me uncomfortable, the way she talked about him as if he had died, as if we wouldn't all be in the same courtroom again once the retrial started. I changed the subject.

"Do you remember Dylan Fairbanks? He was at the group home, too. I guess his mom died. Except you'll never believe this: he's a girl now."

A look of slight interest passed over my mother's face. "Hmm?"

"She's a . . . transsexual." It was my first time using the word. Saying it made me feel very sophisticated and grown up.

"Why?" Mom asked with undisguised bafflement.

I shrugged. "I don't know. I guess that's just how she feels. And it happens in nature, doesn't it? Don't lizards have sex changes sometimes?"

"Lizards are *reptiles*," she said. "God, this world is fucking people up. Poor Dylan."

"I think it's okay," I tried to explain. "I think she's happier this way."

Mom looked at me like I was delusional. I felt frustrated that I couldn't seem to connect to her. In the past we'd always had the farm and the forest to talk about. Now what did we have?

"So . . . what do you think of Jeannine? She doesn't really have Aaron's panache, does she?"

Mom rubbed her temples, the chains of her metal cuffs clinking. "Could you just . . . stop asking me questions?"

"Okay. Sorry."

"It's giving me a headache. None of this bullshit is worth talking about."

"Okay."

We sat not talking for another minute. Then, abruptly, Mom stood up and said, "I have to go. This place is depressing."

Go where? I wanted to ask. Where else in the prison complex could possibly be *less* depressing? At least the visiting room had her daughter in it. Though I wasn't fooling myself that she was enjoying this visit. I wanted to snap at her, *Maybe it's not about you. Maybe I need this.*

"Simpson?" she called out, and a female guard materialized. My mother held up her cuffed hands for the guard to check.

"Wait—" I said. I stood up, but the guard motioned roughly for me to sit back down.

"See you in court," Mom said. And then she left, the metal door clanging behind her.

xxiv

I HAD A BAD FEELING ABOUT THE RETRIAL. NOT THE BLIND TERror I'd felt the first time around, more like a general black cloud of foreboding and doom. Everything felt wrong. The jury was a bunch of judgmental-looking, middle-aged farmers plus one Hispanic lady who kept clutching her gold cross necklace. My parents were looking extremely worse for wear, still in their preppy beige outfits, but lean and withered, like a couple of crackheads who'd stumbled into the Tweeds catalog. Judge Sanders was a famous bachelor who looked exactly like James Mason. It was too cruel that Éclair had died without knowing that the most handsome man in the state had been just a courtroom away.

Jeannine, to my shock, had undergone a makeover worthy of a before-and-after feature in *Glamour* magazine. Gone were her woolly plaid skirt and nerdy eyeglasses, replaced with a tight pencil skirt and contact lenses. Her hair was permed and her eyelashes were caked in mascara.

She mostly ignored me, keeping her eyes laser-focused on Judge Sanders as he strode into the courtroom. The makeover was for his benefit, I realized. She was trying to get a *date* out of this.

Midway through her opening statement, I felt mild panic set in. Jeannine wasn't making any of the interesting intellectual points Aaron had made during his opening statement, about women in the workplace and misplaced resentment toward caregivers and a desire to harken back to a simpler, more medieval time of good versus evil. She just kept harping on about how Mr. and Mrs. Bond could never have committed the crimes they were accused of because they "were passionate about children" and "loved children with every beat of their hearts." She was making my parents sound *obsessed* with children. All I could do was watch helplessly as she blathered on. I wanted smack-talking Aaron back, and grizzled, bewhiskered Judge Barclay and our "black guardian angels" and pretty Juror Number Five. Most of all I wanted Éclair sitting next to me in one of her outrageous neon outfits, whispering vicious insults about how Mrs. Grange looked like a hag.

The worst irony was that for once Mrs. Grange *didn't* look like a hag. She was *glowing*, and in exactly the specific way in which that word is so often used: she was pregnant. I was certain she'd deliberately gotten herself knocked up to boost her whole mother lioness routine. It was probably the first time her husband had gotten laid in years. She was at that awkward level of pregnancy where it could have been taken for unflattering weight gain or a goiter. But Mrs. Grange made sure no one made that mistake, referring to the "little one" growing inside her at least eight times during her opening statement.

The sound of her voice filled me with violent hatred. I imagined drop-kicking her "little one" into a volcano, the screaming infant engulfed by flames, a fantasy so barbaric it shocked me even as I indulged it. It was clear that I was starting to push the limits of my sanity. I decided I would tell Jeannine that I couldn't do this again, couldn't endure this charade, that it was hurting me, twisting me, fucking me up too much.

But at the end of the day, as my parents were being escorted away by the guard, my father turned and cast a look at me over his shoulder. When our eyes met, everything went calm, my pounding rage diffusing into stillness. He was still there—the world's last gentleman—under all the mud and grime that life had thrown at him.

Yet, while the recognition between us was powerful, I could feel it fading. My mother was already gone, seeming to register all people—including me—as a single threatening mass. Our family was shrinking, and it occurred to me that by the end of this I might be the only person my father had left. She was becoming feral.

XXV

SCHOOL WAS FUCKED.

I could no longer bring myself to care about algebra or the Revolutionary War or the structure of a generalized cell. The first few weeks of the semester I'd spent in a nerdy fervor, devouring textbooks and knocking my grades out of the park. It was an empty escape. But no one gushed over me the way the teachers had at my old school, where my report cards always read like glowing toasts ("a joy to teach," "a rare appetite for learning"). With my new teachers, who knew me only as the notorious Satan Daughter, I was the redheaded stepchild they wanted to see fail. Ultimately I gave them what they wanted.

Between classes, the halls were a war zone. Every time I spotted a skinny guy in a dirty shirt, I was certain it was Éclair's killer and that I was about to die.

It had been over *three months*, and still no one had been arrested or charged. I couldn't understand it. They had the hot dog–thrower's mug shot—why wasn't he in jail? Every day I stewed, brooded, and second-guessed myself, coming up with a wild range of other possible killers (it was the BTK Strangler; it was Jerry Falwell; it was Zora Grange and the entire DA's office) before circling back to my original conviction: it was *him*.

I'd heard nothing from Dylan, either, though this didn't surprise me. We'd entered and exited each other's lives many times before, never with any ceremony or promise of reunion. Perhaps she took it for granted that we would meet again. Or perhaps she lived in the moment, in that way so many people pretended to—poets, self-dubbed "free spirits," et cetera—thinking rarely of anything outside her immediate periphery.

Meanwhile I worried about her constantly and kept a mental list of things I wanted to talk to her about, from her thoughts on the latest episode of *MacGyver* to her opinion on whether mankind had a soul. I'd hoped that the trial would bring her back to New Hampshire, but in the end, Jeannine had decided it wasn't worth calling her in to testify.

"Mrs. Grange will just rip her to shreds, paint her as some kind of circus freak. The bearded lady, et cetera. She'll convince the jury that your parents' perversions are responsible for her gender disorder."

"But then you'll cross-examine Dylan and make Mrs. Grange look like a stupid fool," I argued. "I saw Aaron do it, and it was amazing."

"It's not the same situation. The mistrial put *us* in the power position. You don't take stupid risks when you have everything to lose."

"Aaron said big risk equals big reward."

"It's not worth exposing ourselves to that kind of attack. Dylan is a weak witness."

"Aaron said only losers allow their weakness to define them."

"I don't want to hear another one of Aaron's stupid, made-up aphorisms!" Jeannine snapped, throwing her pen down on the desk with such force that it made me jump. "Aaron was not a real lawyer! Do you understand that? He screwed you over, and then he abandoned you. You need to start respecting the fact that *I* am your lawyer now. *I* am going to win this case, because *I* went to law school and *I* know what I'm doing!"

"Okay! Sorry!" I sputtered, my cheeks flaming hot.

I stopped talking about Aaron but didn't stop silently judging her legal strategy, which involved teetering around the courtroom in tight skirts and daintily cross-examining witnesses like they were sharing a polite conversation over tea. She hardly ever offered objections, even though I'd learned from Aaron that objecting as often as possible was the best insurance for an appeal if the verdict went sideways. Her cloying nice-girl act was driving me insane. The jury was full of middle-aged men; maybe they'd want to fuck her, but they weren't going to respect her.

"He made me get naked. I felt like a sheep and he was a wolf. He looked like he wanted to eat me. He put a black velvet cape on my shoulders. Then he made me dance in a circle while he took pictures."

It was the day I'd dreaded more than any other, the day of Sandy Goodwin's testimony. Of all the alleged victims, Sandy was the only one I really knew, the only one I'd considered, at one point, a friend.

And something else was gnawing at me, too, a feeling that made me so uncomfortable I couldn't bear to think about it long enough to put words to it.

Sandy looked older. The reddish-brown hair that she'd always kept in braids was now a frizzy pouf encircling her head. It made me sad that she'd changed her look for the first time in her life only to get a hairstyle that was five years out of vogue. I imagined Éclair snorting with mean laughter: *She looks like an egg that rolled in pubes!*

Sandy's voice surprised me, too. The sharp edge of hysteria from the Snowflake Dance was gone. She sounded tired, almost drugged, like she'd told her sordid story so many times she could no longer summon the energy to care. I could tell from the tilt of my dad's head that he was staring at the floor. I wished he'd look up—look strong, look Sandy in the face, look all the liars in the face. My mother wasn't even there, her seat conspicuously empty. When I asked Jeannine where she was, she only whispered, "She had an accident. She's fine, don't worry. But she won't be coming in today. I'll explain later."

On the stand, Sandy finished her story in the same monotone voice she'd started in.

"That's *terrible*," Mrs. Grange intoned hammily, as if trying to make up for Sandy's shitty, emotionally dead performance. "Can you describe what happened next? I know this is very difficult."

"He put his dick in my mouth."

Mrs. Grange winced. I gathered that Sandy had been instructed to use a different word in prep.

"Were you scared?"

"Yes. He put it all the way in. I couldn't breathe."

"And how old were you?"

"I was four."

"The defense would like us to believe that you have invented these claims, that none of this is true. Do you have any reason for telling such a lie, Sandy?"

"No. I wish it was a lie."

When it was time for the cross-examination, Jeannine fluffed her hair and walked over to the witness box. She sashayed her ass for Judge Sanders, and I realized, with a start, that I hadn't sexually fantasized about Jeannine once. I wondered what made me immune to her, I who was horny for every woman who crossed my path. She was so . . . *domesticated*, I decided. She wanted to look good for men, unlike Éclair, who'd dressed to please herself. Jeannine completely missed the point of beauty, and that made her unbeautiful to me.

"So, Sandy," she began, "you were the very first victim to come forward in this case. Is that true?"

"Yes," Sandy answered.

"And what inspired you to do that after almost a decade of silence?"

"I was in therapy and it all started coming back to me."

"You're referring to your therapist, Angelica MacDonald."

"Yes."

"And why were you in therapy in the first place?"

"My parents were getting a divorce and I was really upset about it."

"I'm sorry to hear about that. Why were your parents getting divorced?"

"I don't know."

"Was your father ever abusive toward you or your mother?"

"No."

"Are you sure?"

"Yes."

"Think very hard before you answer."

Mrs. Grange stood up. "Objection. The witness has answered the question."

"Sustained," Judge Sanders said, causing Jeannine to blush.

"If I may present evidence item D-1 to the court," she squeaked. She pulled up the television set and popped in a videotape. It was Sandy from eighth grade, hair in braids, the slanting light from the window glancing off the same glass table I would destroy a few months later.

"And when did the 'bad things' start?" Angelica was asking in the grainy footage.

"When my mom got her job and she wasn't around as much."

"Have you been having any more of those nightmares lately? The ones where the scary man comes in the dark?"

"Yeah."

"Try to remember the dream. Can you see the man's face?"

"Yeah."

"Who is it?"

"It's . . ." Sandy paused for a long moment. Then she said, "Mr. Hugh."

"Who's Mr. Hugh?"

"A really bad man."

Jeannine stopped the tape. She turned back to Sandy and asked, "Why do you think Ms. MacDonald was so interested in your nightmares?"

"Objection. Speculation."

"Overruled," Judge Sanders said.

Jeannine smiled at Sandy, waiting for her to answer the question.

"Because . . . dreams are where repressed memories live? Because your mind can't control them there?" Everything Sandy said sounded sarcastic. I glanced at Mrs. Grange, whose jaw was clenched in annoyance.

"So when your mother started working, what year was that? 1980?"

"Yes."

"And with your mom out of the house, did that mean you were spending more time with your dad?"

"I guess."

"Was he working, too?"

"No. He'd gotten laid off. He was working odd jobs, like construction."

"Hmm." Jeannine lifted a finger to her chin thoughtfully. "You started going to Rainbow Kids in 1980, which was the same time that your father was having this crisis."

"Objection," Mrs. Grange piped up. "The witness never described it as a crisis."

"Sustained."

"Pardon me," Jeannine said. Then she turned back to Sandy. "I'm just wondering, is it possible that a *different* man was hurting you, and because of the timing, you substituted Hugh Bond for that man? To protect yourself from a more horrible truth?"

"Objection," Mrs. Grange said. "The witness is not an expert in psychology."

Jeannine argued, "I think the witness is qualified to speak about her own mind."

Judge Sanders paused, looking somehow even more handsome as his brow furrowed in thought.

"I'll allow it," he said. Then, to Sandy, "Please go ahead."

"Um, no?" Sandy said with an annoyed edge to her voice. At first I thought she was sassing the judge, but then I realized "no" was her answer to Jeannine's question.

"You don't sound certain."

"Well, I am."

"But it would be hard, wouldn't it, to admit that Hugh Bond wasn't the man who touched you. Because this trial has become such a big deal. Everyone would blame you, wouldn't they? They'd call you a liar."

"He did touch me," Sandy said. "So that's a stupid question."

"Sandy, is it possible that you need help telling the truth? Who was the scary man who came in the dark? Was it Hugh Bond, or was it your father? Tell the *real* truth."

"I *am* telling the truth! It was him!" She pointed across the courtroom to my father. Her hard expression cracked, and tears began streaming down her face. Her voice wobbled as she yelled, "He ruined my life! I see him in my mind and in my dreams. I can't be awake and I can't go to sleep. All my friends dumped me, no one likes me, I have no life, I have nothing, I wish I could die because of him!"

It hit me all at once then, the deeper reason that seeing Sandy made my skin crawl: we'd both been preyed upon. But in my limited understanding of what had happened between me and Yvonne, the fact that I'd had orgasms negated any argument that I'd been too young, that the power dynamic was fucked, or that I'd been miserable the whole time. It would be years and years before I truly thought of Yvonne as anything approaching a rapist. But as I watched Sandy cry, I felt a horrible twinge of a feeling: that I was looking into a mirror.

WE WERE HAVING ONE OF THOSE MUDDY GRAY SPRINGS THAT felt like an annoyingly hot winter, the temperatures rising into the fifties while the snow remained on the ground in a slushy brown layer.

One gloomy evening after a long day of school and court, I found three envelopes waiting for me on my cot. They were from Dylan. I checked the postmarks and found that one had been sent three weeks ago, another almost a month ago. I inhaled the envelopes to see if they smelled like Dylan, but they just smelled like old paper. Dylan had "boy" handwriting—not messy, necessarily, but challenging to read, the loops of the letters cramped and scratchy.

My parents had had a long-standing debate about whether the differences between boys and girls were created by society or nature. My father believed that if boys and girls were treated equally by society, they would perform equally in all areas. My mother believed boys and girls served different biological functions, just like in the animal kingdom, and that expecting them to perform "equally" was contrary to nature. Handwriting was a perfect example, according to her: "Girls have better handwriting because they have smaller hands and develop fine motor skills earlier, like the ability to hold a pen. Society didn't 'tell them' to be that way."

"Of course it did!" my dad would argue back. "Society tells girls to be neat and sweet and tidy, while boys get to run and climb and play outside!"

As I examined Dylan's *o*'s and *a*'s and *e*'s, I found myself in the middle, understanding both sides of the argument but feeling no particular eagerness to choose one, especially since Dylan hadn't asked for my opinion.

I picked up Taz and went outside onto the porch. The sun set murkily in the dim sky as I read:

> *Dear Lasie,*
>
> *How are you? I'm okay. Vermont is fine I gess. I get now why my dad was so excited to have a daughter—so he could have a live-in maid for free! I spend all day cooking and cleaning like Cinderella. I am so sick of boys I could throw up. Their crap is everywhere and everything smells like piss. My brothers are all named after cars and car parts: Dodge, Axel, Ford, Gauge, and Colt. Isn't that the dumbest thing you've ever heard?*
>
> *All the guys have different moms except Dodge and Ford, who have the same mom but she got cancer and died. Dodge is fifteen and he's definitely the worst one. The other guys are just kind of like a bunch of dumb puppies. I gess it's okay becuz at least I can cook whatever I want so I just make mac and cheese every night. Yum!*
>
> *You know how when you die in a dream you're supposed to wake up? I got shot in the heart in my dream the other night but I didn't wake up, I felt the whole thing. So I know how it feels and I wanted to tell you that it's not that bad. So I don't think Eclare probably had much pain. It just feels like your chest is a drum and the shot is a drumbeat. Do you believe in telepathy? I have to go becuz I have to clean the house before my dad comes home or he'll kill me.*
>
> > *Bye,*
> > *D*

Dear Lasey,

I don't know if you got my last letter but I was wondering if you have ever experienced telepathy. I was thinking about this time when I had a dream about my mom giving me a diamond ring and the next day she put a donut on my finger. And I was thinking about this movie I saw where the two best friends got matching tattoos and afterwards they could read each other's minds even across long distances. Then they grew up and one of the friends became a serial killer and the other became the detective who was trying to solve the murders, and they could still hear each other's thoughts. And then I realized it wasn't a movie, it was this idea I had when I was eleven. Do you remember that time when I drew a blue circle on your hand with a marker? That was why.

ANYWAY. Things here are really weird. Dodge freaks me out. He knows that I know you and he won't stop bugging me about it. I think he wants to be on TV. One time I saw him hold a gun to Axel's head and force him to say the Pledge of Allegiance. I was really scared but Axel said it was just a game they play. I said that was crazy!!! Dodge freaks me out becuz a lot of times when I am taking a shower I hear the door open and Dodge comes right in and I have to scream until my dad chases him out! I don't think he has seen YOU KNOW WHAT but its scary! The lock on the door is broken and when I asked my dad to fix it he got really mad and said, "I have five kids and none of them ever needed a lock," and I said, "Well I'm a girl and Dodge is being pervy," but he said Dodge just never had a sister before and doesn't know how to act. So I just stopped showering which meant I got pretty disgusting and everyone at school called me Stinky. But then this hippie teacher named Miss Lyla gave me a bottle of pachooli essenshal oil to cover up the smell so now everyone calls me Woodstock, which is better than Stinky.

I hope you write me back becuz I think about you every day and wonder how Taz is doing.

Bye,
D

In two letters I'd gotten more words out of Dylan than I had in our entire lives. I rummaged through my backpack, found a blue pen, and drew a thick O on the back of my left hand, like the tattoo in her story. I was already mentally penning an over-the-top response: *Dearest Dylan, My heart reaches out to you across the black abyss of life. My soul yearns for our reunion and withers every day without you.* But my heart and soul were brought to an abrupt halt by Dylan's third and final letter:

Dear Lasie,

I wish my dam dad never found out I exist. He's not that bad, he just drinks and I can't even tell the difference when he's drunk or not. But DODGE is freaking me out!!! He gets really crazy and starts hitting the dogs and yelling. And he gets the boys in a frenzy and they all restle on the ground and beat each other up. Dodge wants to join the Marines so he can kill Arabs but I don't think they let people that crazy be in the Armed Forses. But that's not even what's really bad. Whats bad is he says he knows my secret, you know what I'm talking about. He says hes going to tell Dad but so far I gess he's having too much fun torturing me. I'm going crazy!!! What am I going to do? I have to get away from him, Lasey. For now I have a system where I skip school so I can clean the house and cook dinner and put it in the frigerator, then when Dad and Dodge and the kids get home I'm out of there! I sleep in a barn I found way out on the neighbor's property. The only person whos seen me there is a down sindrome kid named

Charlie who lives with his grandma, who is the nicest kid I
have ever met. He is so sweet and brings me a peanut butter
sandwich and a glass of milk every day. I think he thinks I'm
a magical fairy like in a storybook. ANYWAY it's okay becuz
at least its getting warmer so I'm not freezing my butt off.
Maybe you could go to the police station and tell them Dodge
is a dog abuser. I am trying to train the dogs to kill him, like
in that episode of Columbo, but I don't know much about
dogs becuz I never had one. ANYWAY I miss you and wish
I was back there. Or maybe if you came here it would be kind
of fun if Dodge didn't ruin it.

> *Bye,*
> *D*

I grabbed Taz and went back inside and found Trisha. After an annoying back and forth about whether it was too late in the evening to make a phone call, Trisha left me alone and I dialed the number for Jeannine's home phone.

"Jeannine Fuller residence," she answered.

"It's me, Lacey. I have to talk to you." I described Dylan's letter to her, my voice shaking.

"Hang on, what?" she said. "You want to go to Vermont?"

"Her brother has a gun, and he knows she's a transsexual. He'll kill her!"

"Lacey, calm down. Do you know how statistically unlikely it is that *two* people in your life will be murdered? You're having an emotional reaction."

"So I'm just supposed to do nothing," I said incredulously.

"Show the letters to your caseworker. Maybe he can do something."

"I can't show Glen! What if he calls her dad and tells him that Dylan's a boy?"

"It sounds like it's going to come out anyway, if this Dodge kid already knows."

"So let's get her out of there!" I practically shrieked.

"Lacey, you have to let this go. It's not your problem. You need to focus on your parents right now. We're almost at the finish line. We're *so close*. The McMartins were acquitted, did you hear that? The whole Satan hysteria is starting to die down."

"But what about Dylan? She has to *live* with this guy."

"I'm sure he's just a typical asshole older brother. You wouldn't believe how mean my brothers were to me when I was a little girl. Try not to lose sleep over it. You need to get some rest before you testify. That's on Thursday, remember? I need you looking fresh and innocent."

That afternoon, I signed up for library time and followed Carly Beth to the travel section where she always hung out, plotting her grand escape from Germaine House to Canada. I found a large book of New England regional maps and opened to Vermont. It took me forever to find Dylan's town—the biblically and ominously named Canaan—because it was so tiny, just a speck in the upper right-hand corner of the state. I took out a notebook and charted a driving route from Concord to there, plus a backup route in case any of the mountain roads were defunct or misnamed.

"Hey, Carly Beth?"

"Yeah?" She didn't look up from her own map.

"How do you know that when you get to Canada they won't kick you out and send you back to America?"

"Because I'll pretend to be Canadian," she said, pushing her pink-rimmed glasses up the bridge of her nose.

"How?"

"It's easy. You just go to their social services and say you're from the cult."

"What cult?"

She reached in her pocket, pulled out a folded-up newspaper article, and handed it to me. The headline read "SQ Forces Break Up Quebec's

Earth Shine Cult."

I skimmed the article. The Earth Shine Harmony Collective claimed to be an organic, holistic retreat for artists and their families, but reports had been made to the government that children were being neglected and families were being prevented from leaving.

An estimated thirty-five children remain unaccounted for after the SQ investigation and subsequent raid of the Earth Shine group. Authorities are searching urgently. "It's a race against the clock," said Chief of Police Paul DuMont. "We're having a cold front and it's freezing out there. If we don't find them soon, we won't find them alive. Many of the parents are dead, and the ones who remain refuse to cooperate with the investigation. Kids are going to be lost if we can't get more accurate information."

The cult leader, the self-styled Romulus of Heaven, real name Richard Burke, ordered children as young as three to flee into the forest rather than face the authorities. The dead bodies of Burke and many adult members were found on the compound with evidence suggesting group suicide.

"He [Burke] told us the police would round us up and lock us in prison, where we would suffer a spiritual death," a source from inside the compound stated. "He told the children that the police would chop them into pieces. He said the outside world had gone to hell and we had to save ourselves."

I handed the article back to her. "You're sure they spoke English in this cult? Not French?"

Carly Beth narrowed her eyes at me, suspicious. "Why do you care?"

"I'm just curious. When do you plan to leave?"

She shrugged. "Soon."

"Like . . . how soon?"

"I don't know. I have a lot more research to do. I might decide to go to Cuba instead." She nudged a small stack of Cuba-related books with her elbow.

"How would you get to Cuba? There's a travel embargo."

"I'd go through Mexico."

"Okay, but why would you do that, when the Canadian border is right in our backyard and is basically unprotected?"

"Because I always wanted to live on the beach."

I looked at Carly Beth and realized she was never going to run away. She wasn't *planning*, she was *imagining*. It got her through the day.

The key to Trisha's car seemed to throb in my pocket, tempting me with its siren call: *Get out of here. Drive.* But I resisted because I was supposed to testify that week. The pressure felt crushing. I was the sole witness for the defense aside from Graham, who was being brought in only to assure the jury I was sane. Jeannine's order to "get some rest" was futile. I was so nervous I could barely sleep. I lay awake petting Taz mechanically and reciting my lines over and over in my mind: *My parents never molested me. I never witnessed or heard about anyone getting molested on my parents' property. This is all a witch hunt because my parents are different.*

Jeannine had prepped me with answers for all the aggressive questions she expected Mrs. Grange to ask, like *If your mother was able to hide her drug addiction from you, why don't you believe she could have been hiding other things, such as your father's pedophilia?* To which I was supposed to respond, *I interacted with the children at Rainbow Kids every single day. I had free rein to go wherever I wanted and talk to whomever I wanted. I never heard anything or saw anything.*

Then Mrs. Grange was supposed to ask, *But how can you know that your memories weren't repressed?* To which I would say, *Because I'm a strong person and my mind doesn't hide from the truth. I know the difference between right and wrong, and I know my parents are good people. I'm here today not just because I love them, but because I know in my heart that the claims against them are untrue.*

All I had to do was tell the truth and then, if possible, cry. Jurors loved crying children, and I was pretty sure I could deliver. I felt on the verge of tears more or less constantly.

By Thursday I was tense and exhausted, dread hanging on me like so much deadweight.

"You'll just have to do your best," Jeannine told me when she saw my haggard appearance. "If you ever get overwhelmed, look at your dad. He'll be right there, cheering you on."

"What about my mom?"

"She's, um . . . She's still, uh . . ."

"Where the hell is my mom?"

"Listen—" Jeannine said, but I cut her off.

"If you don't tell me where my mom is *right now*, I will scream! I swear to God, I will scream!"

"All right, all right, calm down. For god's sake. Your mom had a heroin overdose. No one's sure how she got the drugs, but that's what happened."

I felt my lip trembling. I could barely make my voice work. "Is she dead?"

"No! I told you, she's fine. She's been transferred temporarily to a prison with a drug treatment program. This is a *good thing*. She's getting *clean*. And she'll be back in court as soon as she can."

There wasn't any more time to argue. The doors opened, and we were swept inside the courtroom with the reporters and onlookers and everyone else. Graham took the stand first, swearing the oath, then leaning back in the witness chair as if he owned the place. He looked utterly at ease, bordering on smug (one newspaper would describe him as "the delighted Freudian").

"Lacey Bond is a very sane young woman. Shockingly sane, in my professional opinion," Graham said, prompted by Jeannine.

"What do you mean, 'shockingly'?" Jeannine asked.

"She has endured an incredible amount of trauma without being affected by the types of dysfunction common in children who experience these sorts of things."

"Dysfunction such as?"

"Increased violent tendencies, decreased ability to separate fantasy from reality—delusions, in other words—taking drugs, dropping out of school, deviant sexual behaviors. All in all, I'd say Lacey is handling this situation with tremendous maturity."

In my seat, I tried to sit up straight and look wise beyond my years so the jury could see with their own eyes the flattering portrait of me that Graham was painting.

"Interesting," Jeannine said. "Your report is very different from that of Yvonne Kramer, the social worker who was initially appointed to Lacey's case. Why do you think that is?"

"Well, Lacey's not perfect. She has some anger, understandably, and some issues with authority. She can behave impulsively sometimes. It's my professional opinion that Mrs. Kramer likely witnessed some of Lacey's . . . *imperfections* and exaggerated them in her reports."

"Why would Mrs. Kramer do that?"

"Objection," Mrs. Grange said, standing up. "Speculation."

"I'll allow it," Judge Sanders said. Then, to Graham, "You may answer the question."

Graham gave a sardonic laugh. "I'm not sure if you've noticed, but the Bond family is not particularly beloved around here. Because of the extreme media attention around the family, people have preconceived notions about Lacey. The 'Satan Daughter' and all that. I believe that Mrs. Kramer, consciously or unconsciously, had already decided that Lacey was a bad egg and was just looking for confirmation of that."

"But you yourself had no preconceived notions about Lacey Bond?"

"No, I did not. It's my job to be open-minded. And with an open mind, it's easy to see Lacey for who she really is: a very intelligent, grounded young woman who cares deeply about her family."

"Thank you, Dr. Schneider. No further questions."

Graham gave me a tiny wink, and I felt so moved I wanted to leap up and hug him.

Now it was Mrs. Grange's turn. "So you are a Freudian psychiatrist," she began.

"That's correct."

"And can you briefly explain to the jury what that means?"

"I practice psychoanalysis in the style of Sigmund Freud, who believed that much of human behavior could be explained by unconscious drives."

"Can you elaborate? Are these 'drives' often sexual in nature?"

"Often, but not always. Humans are very sexual beings, and yet most societies are sexually repressive in nature. This can cause intense and unhealthy conflict within the self."

"So you believe that people should just follow their sexual instincts no matter what?"

"Not at all," Graham said calmly. "But I do believe that people should not be made to feel guilty and ashamed for their sexual desires."

"No matter how . . . unconventional those desires might be?"

"Correct."

"Do you believe in the so-called Oedipus complex, Dr. Schneider?"

"I do."

"And could you explain that concept to the jury?"

"The Oedipus complex is a psychosexual phenomenon describing unconscious sexual desire of a male child for his mother."

Mrs. Grange frowned and looked down at her pregnant stomach. "You're saying you believe that when my baby is born—it's a boy, by the way!" She threw a beaming smile at the jury, and all around the courtroom people oohed and aahed as if we were at a baby shower. "That he will . . . have sexual desire for me? Pardon me if I find that idea a little disgusting."

"Why should it be disgusting?" Graham said. "Did you not create that baby with sex? Was *that* disgusting? Will that baby not suck on your naked breast? Is *that* disgusting? No, it's all perfectly natural. The creation of life *is* sexual. It's naive to believe that a child won't pick up on the flow of sexual energy surrounding his very existence."

I was starting to feel nervous. Several of the jury members had mildly repulsed looks on their faces. Graham possessed a certain easy charm, but that couldn't make up for the fact that Freudianism was just *weird*.

"And how would this Oedipus complex manifest in a female child? Like your patient Lacey Bond?"

Graham tented his fingers thoughtfully. "In the case of a female child, you might observe some penis envy. The child will likely identify with her mother and mimic her behaviors, motivated by an unconscious desire to replace the mother and arouse sexual desire in the father."

"That's . . . very interesting, Dr. Schneider," Mrs. Grange said. "So, just to be clear, it's according to *these* standards that you deem Lacey to be a perfectly normal young girl."

Graham gave a little chuckle. "I see what you're trying to do, Mrs. Grange. And yes, I'm aware that the classic Freudian theories may seem odd, even grotesque. Personally, I take a more individualistic approach to therapy. I believe all people are born with broad, unfocused sexual desires. Freud's theories can be a helpful road map in interpreting how these desires manifest in a person's life, but they are by no means law."

"Thank you, Dr. Schneider. This has been very illuminating."

Graham smiled. "I'm happy to lend my perspective."

When he left the courtroom, he gave me a second little wink as he passed by. I tried to smile back, but I felt sick. It was my turn to testify, and adrenaline was pumping through me like ten cups of coffee on an empty stomach.

Jeannine walked me to the witness box, where I took the oath on the Bible, a book that meant so little to me it may as well have been an old cereal box. I tried to answer her softball questions as naturally as possible, but my voice sounded stilted and shaky.

"Do you love your parents, Lacey?"

"Y-yes. Very much."

"I grew up in a very close family, too. And not a rich one, either. Half the money I make, I send home to my mom and dad so they can get by. I think I'd do anything for my parents. Is that how you feel? That you'd do anything for them?"

"No."

"No?" Jeannine exclaimed in feigned surprise. We had rehearsed this bit of theater about a hundred times. "You wouldn't?"

"I wouldn't lie for them. I would tell the truth even if it hurt them." I looked across the courtroom at my father, who was sitting alone at the defense table. He gave me a tiny nod. *Good girl,* he seemed to be saying. I'd spent so many weeks sitting behind him, gazing at the back of his head. It was the first time in a long time that I could really look at him. I saw the deepened crags in his face, the tense set of his jaw. Everything about him was thinner, like he was slowly caving in on himself. His eyes were dull and tired, but I could perceive a faint, surviving glint there, the last remnant of his old sparkle. It was enough.

"So you would admit it if your father or mother ever molested you? If you even felt the slightest uncertainty?"

"Yes," I said. "I would admit it. Because love isn't really love if it's based on a lie."

"That's very astute, Lacey."

"Thank you."

"Do you have any memory of either of your parents ever touching you inappropriately?"

"No."

"Did you ever see them molesting other children?"

"No."

"Have you ever dreamt that you were being molested?"

"No."

"Did you ever witness your parents worshipping Satan?"

"No."

"If there was anything you could say to your parents right now, what would it be?"

"I would say . . ." I glanced at my father, but it felt too intense to meet his eyes, so I looked away. "Please stay strong, because I really love you, and I need you, and I believe in you, and I want all this craziness to stop."

And then I was crying, too.

"Thank you for your honesty and your bravery, Lacey," Jeannine said. "No further questions."

Jeannine sat down. I wiped my eyes on the sleeve of my shirt as Mrs. Grange stood up to commence her cross-examination. The sight of her filled me with such sickening hatred I could barely look at her. Jeannine had taught me a trick: "When you speak to her, look right above her nose. Don't look her in the eyes." As if she were a mythical Gorgon whose gaze would turn me to stone.

"This whole process must be very upsetting for you," she said.

"Yes, it is," I said, looking at the spot between her eyes, where she had a pair of wrinkles.

"I'm very sorry for that. Do you need a moment, or are you okay to continue?"

"I'm fine."

"All right. Let's start with your psychiatrist, Dr. Schneider. He had a very interesting list of 'dysfunctions' that he claimed you did not exhibit. Do you remember that?"

"Yes. It was fifteen minutes ago."

At the defense table, Jeannine gave me a sharp look: *Cut it out.* She'd given me an unambiguous order to be polite to Mrs. Grange and to not allow myself to be baited by her.

"Let's go through them one by one, shall we?" Mrs. Grange was saying. "'Increased violent tendencies.' That's a biggie. Was Mr. Schneider not aware that you beat a student at your school so severely that he had to be hospitalized?"

I swallowed, horrified. I glanced at my father, who looked shocked. He was obviously hearing this for the first time. Carefully, I said, "Graham knew that I'd acted in self-defense. Because the boy was sexually harassing me."

Mrs. Grange gave me a dubious look. "Really?" It was a small word, but the implication was big and clear: I was too ugly for anyone to want to sexually harass me.

"Yes, really."

"Moving on. 'Decreased ability to separate fantasy from reality.' Hmm, that's a complicated one. Do you feel that, because of the traumatic nature of recent events, you have a decreased ability to separate fantasy from reality?"

"No," I said.

"And yet, you were seen casting a spell on a fellow student in the middle of the cafeteria at your school. Is that not true?"

Jeannine's face had gone white. Her eyes bulged, and she gave me a look as if she wanted to scream at me, *What the hell is she talking about, Lacey?*

"Yes, that's true. But—"

"You were witnessed, in public, cursing a fellow student *to hell* and telling her she would 'die a slow and painful death.' Do you deny that?"

"I don't deny it. But I didn't mean it. She was just this girl who'd been bullying me."

"And your response was to summon the powers of Satan and wish death upon her."

"No! I mean, sort of, but I didn't mean it. I was just tired of feeling powerless. So . . . I guess I was acting out. I regret doing it. It was really stupid and I'm sorry."

"Do you believe in Satan, Lacey?"

"No, I don't. I was just playing around."

"So you think Satanism is funny."

"No, I don't. I am the last person who would think Satanism was funny. Satanism has ruined my life."

Mrs. Grange nodded. "So you *do* agree that your parents are Satanists and that their Satanism ruined your life."

"No, I do not," I said, trying with all my might to remain calm. "I only meant that the *idea* of Satanism has ruined my life. The *idea* that there are Satanic people in America doing rituals and hurting people and crap. This witch hunt has ruined my life and my parents' lives. They never deserved any of this."

"Ah, okay. Thanks for clarifying that. Moving on to the next 'dysfunction' on Dr. Schneider's list: drug use and dropping out of school. Have you engaged in either of these behaviors?"

"No."

"And yet your grades are anything but stellar. I see you are flunking three of your classes right now. What were the words Dr. Schneider used to describe you? 'Very intelligent'? Your grades don't reflect that."

"Objection," Jeannine said. "Ms. Bond's academic performance is not on trial."

"Dr. Schneider opened the door for this line of inquiry," Mrs. Grange insisted.

"Objection overruled," Judge Sanders said.

Mrs. Grange focused in on me again. I continued to stare at the spot between her eyes, where an oily sheen had begun to form. "Your grades seem to have fallen precipitously."

"That's true. But I haven't dropped out of school. And I've never done drugs. Not ever."

"And yet you have over twenty absences since the semester started. Isn't that a lot of absences?"

"Yes, but all of those absences I've spent here in this courtroom, supporting my parents."

Across the room, Jeannine gave me a nod of approval: *Good answer.*

"Let's see, what's next. 'Deviant sexual behavior.' Mr. Schneider seemed confident that you have not engaged in such behavior."

"No, I have not."

"And yet you are a lesbian."

My cheeks went red hot. I looked from Jeannine to my dad to the judge, praying one of them would somehow save me from this humiliation. I squirmed in my seat. "I—I—"

"Objection," Jeannine said finally. "Being a lesbian is perfectly normal. It is not 'deviant,' nor is it this court's business."

"Experts in sexuality are not in agreement about whether homosexuality is 'perfectly normal,'" Mrs. Grange said. It was an argument she wouldn't have dared to whip out in front of Judge Barclay, but apparently she felt no compunction about doing it in Judge Sanders's territory.

"Homosexuality was removed from the *DSM-V* in 1973," Jeannine shot back. "It is no longer considered a disorder."

"It *is* a disorder if the person does not wish to be homosexual," Mrs. Grange insisted. "It's called 'ego-dystonic homosexuality.' The defense may feel free to look it up."

"Ladies, ladies," Judge Sanders said with the ease of a man accustomed to breaking up fights between women. "The solution seems clear. Let's ask Ms. Bond if she wishes to be a lesbian, and then we can proceed from there."

Jeannine gaped at him, seeming too baffled to argue.

Mrs. Grange said, "Of course, Your Honor. A very wise decision." Then she looked at me and asked, "Ms. Bond, is it your wish to be a . . . lesbian?" She uttered the word "lesbian" like it was "shit-eater" or "crack whore."

"Yes," I said.

"Just for the record, could you state that in a full sentence?"

"It is my wish to be a lesbian."

"So even if it were possible, you wouldn't choose to be heterosexual?"

I gritted my teeth. "I would not choose to be heterosexual."

"So you enjoy being a lesbian. You enjoy behaving this way."

"Objection," Jeannine exclaimed. "Badgering the witness."

"Move it along, Mrs. Grange," Judge Sanders instructed.

"A young, proud lesbian. Kudos for your bravery," Mrs. Grange said.

It was abundantly clear that this entire thing had been a trap. Not only was I a lesbian—that strange, genetically anomalous, family-unit-threatening category of woman—but I wasn't even the right kind: modest and apologetic, trying hard *not* to be. I glanced at my father, bracing myself, expecting to see my humiliation mirrored in his face. To my surprise, he smiled and gave me a tiny thumbs-up. And then I felt guilty for being surprised. What had happened to me to make me so shocked to find support anywhere, even so obvious a place as my own father's eyes?

"You say you were never molested," Mrs. Grange said, "and you say you would never lie. But what if you didn't know you were lying because the memories were repressed?"

"I know because I'm a good person." *Strong person!* I screamed at myself. I couldn't believe I was messing up my lines. "A strong person, I mean, and my mind doesn't have to protect me from the truth."

"I see," Mrs. Grange said. "Have you ever experienced blackouts, Lacey? Periods of time that you couldn't account for? Lost memories?"

I opened my mouth, then shut it.

"You seem to be hesitating," Mrs. Grange said, seizing upon the gleaming gold nugget of my uncertainty. "Trying to remember what you can't remember?"

"One time something like that happened," I admitted.

An ecstatic look flashed across Mrs. Grange's face. "Can you describe that time for us?"

"It had nothing to do with my parents. It was during the situation you referred to where the student was hospitalized."

"You mean the situation where you *beat* a student to the point where he *had* to be hospitalized."

"Because he was sexually harassing me."

"Yes, so you say. And you say you blacked out during that time?"

"Just right at the end. For a couple minutes, that's all."

"And why do you think that happened?"

"Um, I don't know. I think it was just really intense, and my brain couldn't deal with it." I couldn't bear to look at Jeannine, who I was sure was wishing an anvil would fall on my head.

"Interesting . . ." Mrs. Grange put her finger to her chin. "In your opinion, do you think it would be a 'really intense' experience to be molested by a parent?"

"No," I said. "I wouldn't use those words."

"What words would you use?"

"I have no idea what words I would use, because I have never experienced that."

"Why should we believe you?"

The bluntness of the question caught me off guard, and I accidentally looked into Mrs. Grange's eyes. They bore into me, challenging me; they held no glimmer of empathy.

"Why . . . should . . . we . . . believe . . . you?" she repeated, enunciating each word like I was hard of hearing.

"Because I'm not a liar," I said.

"That's not what Yvonne Kramer said about you. In fact, she labeled you a 'compulsive liar.' Do you know what that means? It means someone who lies so much that they can't control it anymore. Lying becomes their de facto way of dealing with the world."

"Well, she was wrong. And anyway, she's a social worker, not a licensed psychiatrist. So her word shouldn't count more than Dr. Schneider's."

"Of course you're right," Mrs. Grange conceded. "But I'm just wondering, why would she write that about you? Do you have any thoughts on why she would do that?"

"Objection, speculation," Jeannine interrupted.

"I allowed it before, I'll allow it again. Please answer the question."

"I can't say."

"Why can't you say? Because your father will hurt you?"

"*No!* Because you won't believe me. You'll say I'm a liar and make me sound crazy."

"Only you have the power to make yourself sound crazy, Lacey."

I said nothing, my jaw clenched shut, as if opening it even a tiny amount would release a deluge of words I would regret.

"Permission to treat the witness as hostile?" Mrs. Grange asked Judge Sanders.

"Permission granted."

"Mrs. Kramer reported that you are a liar because you *are* a liar, is that not correct? You lied to protect your parents, and you've been lying ever since."

I shook my head. "No."

"What strikes you as more likely, Ms. Bond? That over thirty children are lying about their abuse, or that *one* child is lying? That *you* are lying? When thirty children come forward and say they were molested, we have to believe them. We have to believe the children."

"Then why don't you believe Dylan Fairbanks?" I snapped.

"Excuse me? Who is Dylan Fairbanks?"

"Don't pretend you don't know what I'm talking about! When Dylan told you she was a girl, you had her pronounced legally incompetent! Why didn't you believe *her*? Why didn't you believe what *she* said?"

Mrs. Grange shot the jury an embarrassed look. "I . . . I honestly have no idea what you are talking about, Lacey."

"You're the liar! You're lying *right now!*" I pounded my fist on the witness box, and Mrs. Grange jumped back, startled. It was the first genuine emotion I'd ever seen on her face: *fear.* Fear of *me.* I saw Jean-

209

nine shaking her head at me furiously, but I couldn't make myself shut up.

"Ms. Bond, I have to ask you to calm down—"

"Shut up!" I hissed like a cornered cat. "I don't want to hear your shrill voice one more time! I don't want to see your monstrous face! *You* are Satan! I hate you and I hope you starve to death, alone and despised. I curse you and I curse your unborn child with all the fires of hell! I curse you, you evil fucking witch! I curse you!"

And then I felt a tingling sensation all over my body. Yellow and black spots filled my vision. The next thing I knew, I was standing in the ladies' bathroom hunched over the sink. I blinked in the bright light. The sun was making its first appearance in weeks, streaming through a mottled glass window and reflecting off the marble floor. My brain felt foggy and dim.

"Get out! Get the hell out!" Jeannine was shrieking at someone. In the reflection of the mirror, I saw two ladies scurrying away as Jeannine chased them out the door. Then she turned. Tears had reduced her makeup to a ghastly, melting mask. She walked slowly toward me, her eyes bulging with fury.

"You little cunt," she growled. I'd never heard her use language like that before, and it chilled me to the bone. "Do you understand what you just did? I told you not to let that bitch bait you. I told you to keep your shit together. You screwed us, Lacey! You screwed us!"

I felt myself snap to alertness, my defensive instincts taking over. "It's not my fault!" I shot back. "How could you let her talk to me like that? Aaron would *never* have let that happen! He would *never* have left me to wriggle on the hook like a fucking worm the way you did!"

"He *did* leave you!" Jeannine screamed. "He left you, Lacey! Get it through your skull! He was a scam artist! He was a nobody! And you are an unmanageable child who just cost us everything. Your parents are *done*, Lacey! Done! Are you not understanding me?"

She slapped me. Not a hard slap—the kind of slap you give to snap someone out of a drunken stupor. When I didn't say anything, she slapped me again, this time hard enough to leave a hand-shaped mark that flashed white before turning red.

I couldn't stand the sight of my reflection in the mirror. I started to cry. Then Jeannine was crying, too, and the whole thing felt unbearably high school, a catfight in the girls' room, followed by tears. Jeannine bent over the sink and put her head in her hands.

"I'm so sorry," she said, sniffing and grabbing a handful of paper towels to wipe away her smeared mascara. "That was incredibly unprofessional. I just . . ."

She sat down on the wooden bench next to the sinks.

"It's fine," I said, mortified, wanting it all to be over.

"I love him," she gasped.

"Yeah, I know. I'm sorry I made you look bad. But I'm sure Judge Sanders won't hold it against you personally."

She looked up at me in confusion. "Judge Sanders?"

"Isn't that . . . ?"

She covered her face in embarrassment. "Oh god. I didn't want you to find out like this."

"I really don't care," I said. But then something clicked inside my brain. "Wait. Oh god . . ."

"Your father, Lacey. I love him. I'm in love with him."

Her shining eyes met mine, seeking something—understanding? Catharsis? But my mind had gone blank. I had nothing to give her.

"This *so* isn't me," she blubbered. "I'm a professional! I'm not a homewrecker! I've always believed in *rules*. But love has no rules. That's what your father taught me. I was sleepwalking through life, and he woke me up. He's the most wonderful man in the world, and now he'll be in prison for thirty years!" She started bawling uncontrollably, her shoulders shaking as she wept. I felt compassion pricking at my heart, the basic human urge to comfort a person in distress. And yet I couldn't move; the idea of going near her repulsed me.

"But . . . but . . . you're a *child*," I said finally.

Jeannine blinked and dabbed at her tear-stained face, attempting to compose herself. "Listen, I know this is profoundly awkward and terrible timing. But I will never, ever try to replace your mother—"

"Oh my god. Stop. Stop. Stop." I couldn't stop saying "stop." I felt like a glitching robot. Jeannine stood up, threatening to hug me. I recoiled, backing away from her outstretched arms. I tripped on my own foot, and as I fell, she dove upon me like an eagle, scooping me back up into her arms.

"Stop. Stop. Stop . . ." I kept saying, but the word grew weaker with every repetition until it fell away. Jeannine pressed me against her, not letting go, and I surrendered, my body sort of collapsing. I was aware that Jeannine was loving this too much. *I really had a breakthrough with the daughter,* I imagined her gushing to her friends over glasses of white zinfandel, leaving aside the part where she called me a cunt. She stroked my hair, a deeply maternal action that immediately contradicted what she'd just said about never trying to replace my mother.

I still couldn't believe it. Dad's poetry book, *Wild Beasts and Gods*, flashed through my mind. He'd stolen my mother's favorite quote, all while cheating on her with a twenty-six-year-old? Despite Jeannine's pencil skirts and law degree, the scenario reeked of a too-tawdry cliché: Dad fucking the babysitter.

"All right, sweetie," she said, patting me on the back before gently pulling away. "We gotta get back in there."

I shook my head. "No, I can't. I can't face them."

The truth was I couldn't face *him*. He could have his ludicrous affair with Jeannine, but he couldn't expect me to look him in the eye ever again.

I couldn't explain it, but I had a harsh double standard about my parents: my mother could do heroin, get a neck tattoo, have a jailhouse fling with a convicted killer, do *anything*, it seemed, and it would barely disturb my concept of her—perhaps because I viewed my mother as a version of myself, with all my flaws and unsuitableness for human society. Meanwhile my father had remained godlike in my eyes, the sum of man's potential to be noble and good. The reality that he was just a man was too much to bear.

It seemed I had reached my threshold for pain. I was, suddenly, done. I could stay here and wait for my entire environment to be bull-dozed to rubble, or I could leave the nest now while I still had the will to live.

"You can't just go," Jeannine was pleading. "They'll think you were taken away in a straitjacket or something! It'll look so much better if you come back and sit nicely. Come on. I'm sorry I was such a bitch earlier."

I shook my head again. "I'm, like, dying inside, Jeannine. I can't do this anymore. Take care of my dad, okay? And my mom, too. Don't screw her over just because you're screwing my dad."

I started walking away, but Jeannine grabbed my arm.

"Hang on. You're not going to do anything crazy are you? Jump off a bridge or something?"

"No, Jeannine," I said in the exact tone of an annoyed teenager: *No, Mom.*

"Promise me you're not going to kill yourself."

"God, Jeannine. Yes, I promise."

She narrowed her eyes, skeptical. "Okay. Fine. How are you getting back to Germaine House?"

"I'll take the bus."

I considered saying something else, something profound and mean-ingful, something she could pass on to my parents to tell them that, though my heart was broken, it still contained love for them and always would. But I had no words. So I left, walking out into the last of the melting snow, and it would be years before I saw any of their faces again.

TITLE TK

MAJOR OVERHAULS TO ONE'S IDENTITY ARE QUEER RITES OF PAS-
sage. Cut your hair off or grow it long. Throw out your entire wardrobe.
Samantha becomes Sam, Phil becomes Phillipa. Or a person cuts the
thread completely, as Gwen and I did, choosing names that contain no
remnants whatsoever of the people we used to be.

These rites are equally common among criminals, but when they
do it, they're viewed differently, aren't they? They aren't defining themselves. They are hiding something. They are lying.

Standing, as I do, at the intersection of these two groups, I can tell
you unequivocally that it's all the same. No one person's identity redux
is more honest or sacred than another's. Each is what it is: survival.

The press has made short work of obliterating Jo Scottish, hollow-
ing out that identity and dumping its contents back into the ill-fitting
container that is Lacey Bond. Gwen, by some magic, or by sheer force
of personality, has managed to win her arm wrestle with the past. The
media outlets obligingly refer to her as "the model Gwen," rarely using
her former name. It's as if we're two spies whose home government has
collapsed: one of us is getting sent back to the ruins, while the other
is left abroad on her never-to-be-completed mission, her fake identity
becoming real.

While the issue of whether I'm going to spend the rest of my life in
prison is gnawed over like a bone by packs of lawyers, immigration offi-
cials, and FBI agents, I'm trying to enjoy the little things: a glass of wine,
Gwen's company, the sight of Montreal's glittering skyline reflecting on
the river. But enjoyment doesn't really happen when you're trying.

At that point, it's probably too late.

XXVII

1991

BEFORE I GO ON, IT'S IMPORTANT FOR ME TO SAY UNAMBIGUOUSLY that when I left the courthouse that day, it wasn't with the intention of killing anyone. Not a conscious intention, anyway.

I got back to Germaine House around 4:00 P.M., explaining to Patty that I was sick and wanted to go to bed. I'm sure I looked ghastly enough that the story was easy to believe. It wasn't a lie, really. I *was* sick, my spirit hanging by a frayed thread.

In the morning I was ravenous. I ate a full plate of shitty instant eggs while listening to Natasha's daily monologue about how people were sheep and deserved to be herded off the edge of a cliff. I felt strangely fond of her, in that haze of pre-nostalgia that comes when you know you're never going to see someone again.

I was nervous about my plan to steal Trisha's car. It involved taking Taz for her outdoor time during breakfast, something I feared would invite suspicion. I couldn't bring my suitcase without attracting attention, so I filled my school bag with pairs of socks (no piece of clothing mattered more than socks, as any experienced hiker would tell you). I went back and forth over *I Saw Marilyn Monroe in 1980*. I kept putting it in the bag, taking it out, then putting it back. It felt like being asked to declare, once and for all, whether I renounced any possibility that Éclair might still be alive.

I left it in the bag and zipped it up.

"I'm visiting my dad today in prison," I lied to Patty. "I'm supposed to take the bus downtown and meet Jeannine, who will drive me the rest of the way."

Patty shook her head, flipping through her papers on her ever-present clipboard. "It's not on your schedule."

"She just got me off the no-visitation list. Please, Patty? Please, please!" I scrunched up my face like I was about to cry.

She sighed. "Fine. I'm walking you to the bus stop, though, to make sure you're not kidnapped."

On the way, Patty rambled unbearably about how daughters have a special place in their daddies' hearts, and how great it was that I was still willing to visit my father and forgive him even after everything he'd done.

"He didn't do anything," I said, the words coming automatically. My heart wasn't in them anymore.

"Oh, of course. Innocent until proven guilty. That's the American way!"

When the bus arrived, I hopped on while Patty waited on the curb, waving cheerfully. I felt a surge of guilt. My disappearance was going to upset her, not because she cared about me in any specific way, but because I was a child and every child was precious in the eyes of the Lord, at least according to a T-shirt she often wore.

I got off the bus at the very next stop, crossed the street, and caught the first bus back to Germaine House. During breakfast, I'd left Taz hidden in her carrying case among a little thicket of trees down the street. I'd taped a note to the lid in case her yowling attracted a passerby: *Please leave this cat where she is, the owner will return shortly.* I dreaded coming back and finding the cage gone, scooped up by some meddling Good Samaritan who'd take her to the pound and seal her doom. Thankfully the carrying case was right where I'd left it, Taz meowing inside and clawing at the metal door like a wild beast.

"I'm sorry!" I said to her. "Just calm down. We're getting out of here, I promise."

Trisha's car was parked on the street, a bit away from the house. For a second I stood behind a tree, paralyzed with fear. I reminded myself that her office was on the opposite side of the house, and I would be fine as long as she didn't have some daytime habit I was unaware of, like gazing out the front window daydreaming about a world where orphans were simply put to death. Taking a deep breath, I unlocked the car, shoved Taz in the passenger side, and hurled myself into the driver's seat. The car felt small and claustrophobic compared with the pickup truck I'd learned to drive in. My mother believed that all children should know how to drive as soon as they were tall enough, even though it was against the law.

Would my mother cry when she found out I'd left her? I knew my father would, a thought I pushed aside. My mother, on the other hand—no. It was like the summer we took in a baby squirrel and nursed it through infancy. I'd thought of him as a pet, named him Nutty. But one day Nutty left his little house made of newspaper and sticks, and he never came back. When I cried, my mother said, "There's nothing to cry about. It's a good thing. Nutty can really live now."

XXVIII

VERMONT
1991

CONCORD WAS SMALL ENOUGH THAT WITHIN TEN MINUTES I had exited the town limits. I was gone. The roads were clear and glistening with melted snow. At some point Taz stopped her furious meowing, only giving me an occasional sulky *rrrow*.

I took the 114 instead of US-3 even though it wasn't as direct; it seemed smart to get off the New Hampshire roads as soon as possible. I missed the WELCOME TO VERMONT sign, but there were subtle indications that I wasn't in New Hampshire anymore, the rough edges of the land softening to lolling green dairy pastures.

The town of Canaan (THE CAN-DO TOWN, boasted an old sign with peeling paint) was so dinky I passed through it without realizing and had to double back. I couldn't find the road I was looking for and spent about twenty minutes circling around like an idiot until an old man asked me where I was trying to go. "Tim Roach the mechanic's house?" I said, a slip that I would end up regretting intensely later.

The old man pointed the way ("Keep north, past Beecher Falls, don't accidentally drive into Canada now"), and once I found the right road, it was obvious which was the Roach residence: a run-down ranch house, its huge overgrown lawn scattered with the remains of about a half dozen cars. As I drove past, I saw a pack of skinny boys, one barely three years old, all wrestling on the ground. The boy who seemed to be the eldest sat on the hood of one of the dilapidated cars, laughing and waving around a revolver. Even from a distance, his face gave me chills.

He looked maniacal.

I parked Trisha's car about a quarter mile down the muddy road, then grabbed Taz's case and set off in search of the barn Dylan had described in her letter. The trees in the forest were the same as home, just distributed differently: fewer oaks and hemlocks, more maples, birches, and firs. Vermont and New Hampshire fit together like puzzle pieces, each seeing the other as upside down. Vermonters thought our side was full of incoherent Neanderthals; we thought their side was full of crusty beatniks on drugs. I was thankful that the ground was damp enough to mute the sound of my footsteps. The last thing I needed was for some lunatic Vermonter on an acid flashback to shoot me for trespassing.

"Who're you? Hi."

I whirled around, almost knocking into a tree branch. A small boy was standing there. He wore thick glasses hooked around little ears that poked out like a bat's. He looked at me with blank curiosity.

"Hi," I said. "Are you . . . Is your name Charlie?"

"Yes'm, Charlie, I have one hundred books. What's in there?" He pointed at Taz's carrying case.

"It's a cat."

"Can I see?"

"Sure."

He walked up to the cage and peered inside. "Hi, kitty, kitty, kitty."

His presence was making me nervous. I was about to tell Charlie to go home when I had an idea.

"Hey, Charlie? Have you seen a princess hiding in the woods here? A beautiful princess with blond hair?"

He nodded.

"Can you show me where she is?"

He shook his head. "I'm not supposed to tell anyone. It's a secret. Can I pet the kitty?"

"If you tell me where she is, you can pet the kitty," I said.

"Nah-uh," he said, shaking his head again. "Not supposed to."

"I promise it's all right to tell me. Cross my heart and hope to die."

Charlie's eyes followed my hand as I mimed a small X over my heart.

"That's the princess tattoo," he said. At first I gave a patronizing nod. Then I realized he was talking about the blue ring I'd drawn on my left hand.

"Yes!" I exclaimed. "That's her tattoo. It means I'm her friend. So can you show me where she is?"

Charlie appeared to think for a second. Then he said, "Okay," and I followed him into the woods.

As the chirp of early spring frogs filled my ears, I realized how long it had been since I'd been outside, *truly* outside. The air smelled delicious and damp. Taz began to claw at the cage door of her case, as excited as I was by the concert of nature after four months indoors.

The birch trees gave way to a small meadow. At its center stood an old red barn.

"The princess is in there?" I asked.

Charlie nodded. He walked with me to the barn door. A bright, angled shaft of light shone down from an enormous hole in the roof, illuminating a sleeping bag encircled by an assortment of odd articles: a pile of feathers, dirty plates and candy bar wrappers, a pink rabbit's foot. And in the middle of the mess, there she was, bent over some kind of sewing project, her blond hair reflecting the light so brightly it formed a sort of halo around her head.

For a second, she just stared at me. Then she said, "Wow. This is just like a dream I had. And then we rode to another world on flying dogs."

"Hi," I said. I felt frozen. In my fantasies I'd imagined striding over to her, taking her in my arms, and kissing her like the famous V-J Day photo from *Life* magazine. But in those fantasies, I hadn't been awkwardly holding a cat carrier while being stared at by a child with Down syndrome. I closed the barn door behind me and put Taz's case down. As I opened the cage door, she bolted out.

"Tazzie, Tazzie, Tazzieeeeee . . ." Dylan cooed. Her voice was different—lower-pitched. I wondered if it was a side effect of her special medication lapsing. It still sounded pretty to me, almost more so because it was unique, neither boy nor girl but some rare note between the two.

My heart raced as I anticipated a hug: Dylan's arms around my body, the warmth of her cheek against mine, her hair brushing against my face. But she pivoted at the last second to Charlie.

"Charlie, you're a superstar! You brought me Lacey!" She squeezed him warmly and kissed his cheek. I felt oddly jealous—not of Charlie, but of Dylan's ability to be comfortable around people who were different.

Up close, I drank in the sight of her with some relief. I'd harbored a low-grade fear that, due to the lack of steady medication, I'd find her transformed into a hideous *male*. But here she was in front of me, real and the same as ever, though also different. She was dirty, for one thing, her hair greasy and knotted. Instead of one of her fluffy floral skirts, she wore cuffed jeans and a sweatshirt.

As she pulled away from Charlie, I caught a whiff of her. She *smelled*. Not the powdery, girlie scent of her Love's Baby Soft perfume, but the pungent smell of a boys' locker room—dirty feet and sweat—masked only partially by a heavy, woodsy musk (the patchouli oil her teacher had given her, I presumed).

And yet I didn't care at all. She was still her.

"Sorry I look like this," she said. "I had to start wearing pants because that pervert Dodge kept trying to stick his hand up my skirt."

"I think you look great. You look like me. Sorry, that sounded egotistical."

"Sorry my voice sounds weird."

"Sorry I didn't write back—"

"Can I play with the cat please?" Charlie interrupted.

"Sure," Dylan and I said in unison, and Charlie went off to follow Taz as she sniffed at every corner and crevice of the barn. I noticed how quiet it was: no cars whooshing past outside, no TV blaring *Full House* with its slightly sinister theme song (*Everywhere you look!*).

"I'm so glad you're here," Dylan said to me, smiling. "How long can you stay?"

"Not long, I don't think. We both should leave ASAP. I have a car. We can go anywhere."

Dylan shook her head. "Oh, I can't leave."

"Why not?"

"I haven't finished my pit. Come on, I'll show you."

Dylan told Charlie to stay with Taz and make sure she didn't run away. Then we walked together to the far edge of the clearing, where there was a large hole in the dirt about four feet deep. A shovel leaned against a nearby tree.

"When it's deep enough, I'm going to cover it with a fake layer of grass."

"Why?"

"So Dodge will fall in it and die."

I searched her eyes for a telltale glint that she was joking. But she looked as earnest and transparent as ever.

"Well . . ." I said carefully. "I was just thinking we would drive away and never come back. That way, Dodge won't matter anymore."

Dylan shook her head. "You don't understand him. It would be his new obsession, to find me. He'd follow us to the ends of the earth. He'd love it! He has nothing else in his life. That's why we have to throw him in the pit. I've been sewing the fake grass to put on top. It's almost finished. We just have to dig it a little deeper."

I pictured him begging for mercy while we stared down at him in the pit. *You picked the wrong girls to mess with,* I imagined us saying, like movie characters. It filled me with such giddy excitement that I had to stop and remind myself the "pit" was barely four feet deep.

"Dylan, this isn't going to work," I said.

She looked at me quizzically, reminding me of a fox I'd known as a child. It used to give me that same look whenever we encountered each other in the forest.

"The pit would have to be twenty, *thirty* feet deep to really trap him," I explained.

"Well . . . we could put a wolf in the pit, and then the wolf would eat him."

"How would we get a wolf in the pit?"

"First we'd put a sheep in the pit."

"Okay, Dylan, just . . . just answer me this question: Do you really think he'll be able to find us?"

"Yes."

"How can you be so sure?"

"Because he's done it before. He found me and my mom in New Hampshire last summer, before I even knew he existed. That's how he found out my secret. He *saw* me. He's known for *months*. If I try to run, I just know he'll find me again."

I stared into the pit, deciding. The alternatives looming before me hinged upon the very question I'd been secretly asking myself ever since Dylan reentered my life: Did I trust her? Furthermore, did I believe the way she saw the world?

"All right," I said finally. "If you say so, then I trust you. I'll kill him myself, and then we'll be done with it."

The fact that I spoke of *murder* like it was a mildly difficult chore should tell you everything you need to know about my headspace at the time. I wasn't weighing the magnitude of what I was saying or the potential consequences. What I was thinking of, strangely, was Mr. Hantz and the words he'd let slip back in the fall: "People make other people suffer. And they don't stop until you make *them* suffer."

"But how, Lacey?" Dylan said. "He has a gun, and he's scary. I had this other idea about tying him to a runaway horse—"

"I'll take the gun and shoot him in the head. It shouldn't be that hard. You said he likes to get drunk?"

Dylan nodded.

"Where?"

"Just around the house."

"Where's your dad? Doesn't he care?"

"He goes out with his girlfriend on weekends. They go bowling and get wasted, and then he stays at her place."

"Okay, good. Look, I need you to make sure Dodge gets really drunk tonight. Drink with him, just make sure your bottle only has water in it. Can you do that?"

Dylan nodded.

"I'll wait outside, and you can come get me when he's totally passed out. And then I'll come inside and . . . kill him." The words sounded completely absurd. "Okay?"

"Okay."

The plan was decided. I felt surprisingly calm, in the same way I imagined bulimics felt calm when they decided to purge a meal, an act that, as Mr. Hantz had explained to us on Eating Disorder Awareness Day, wasn't about being thin at all but about being in control.

We walked back to the barn. Taz had managed to climb halfway up the wall and find a perch to survey things with her single sharp eye.

"Kittie, kittie, kittie, hi, kittie," Charlie was singing to her.

All of a sudden I realized that my plan to run away in a stolen car was as childish as Dylan's death pit, especially if I was going to throw *premeditated murder* into the mix.

"Shit, hang on, we can't do this," I said, collapsing on Dylan's dirty, too-small Masters of the Universe sleeping bag.

"What's wrong?" Dylan asked.

"An old man in town saw me driving Trisha's car. We'll have to dump it in the woods somewhere. There's no way we can drive it out of here if we're going to . . ." *Kill Dodge* was the unfinished part of the sentence, but I didn't dare say it in Charlie's earshot.

"We can take one of my dad's cars," Dylan suggested.

I shook my head. "We can't take any car that could be traced back here. We'll have to escape through the forest."

"But . . . but . . ." Dylan said. She looked at Taz, who was giving Charlie's outstretched finger an experimental nudge with her nose. "How will we carry Taz that far?"

"We can't," I said. I buried my face in Dylan's dirty pillow, muffling my voice. "There's nothing we can do. I can't take her to a shelter because she's too feral. But she's not wild enough to survive if I leave her in the woods. She doesn't fit in anywhere. She's doomed."

This final obstacle—what to do with my cat, my poor fucking cat whose favorite person, my mother, had simply disappeared, who'd been uprooted and forced to live in a dingy room with me and fifteen strangers, who'd traveled 160 miles to a barn that wasn't *our* barn, to whom I could never explain why we *still* weren't home, because home was an abstract concept now, a feeling that was lost rather than an actual place to which we could never return—it felt like a stumbling block from a universe that knew I needed just one last *fuck you* to give up and die.

"You know what I think you should do?" I heard Dylan say.

"What?" I asked tiredly.

"I think Charlie should have Taz. He's such a sweetie. Look at him."

I lifted my head from the pillow. Taz was rubbing her cheek against Charlie's hand, a gesture she rarely made toward strangers, especially not males. She preferred female company. ("All cats are lesbians," my sister used to say. "Even the boys.")

"Charlie?" Dylan called out. "If we gave that kitty to you, could you take care of it?"

"Yes!" he exclaimed, pumping his fist in the air. "I can do it! I can take care of the kitty! I'll name him Garfield!"

I felt a lump forming in my throat. Could I really leave Taz, my last remaining family member, with a child I'd known for five minutes who intended to call her Garfield?

"She can't live alone in this barn," I told Dylan. "She needs to live in his house."

"Charlie?" Dylan said. "Let's go ask Grandma if you can keep Garfield, okay?"

I picked Taz up and held her. There were so many things I wanted to say: *Farewell, Taz. You are an old soul, and I hope we meet again in another world. Without you I would have jumped in front of a bus by now. Thank you for saving my life.* But I knew that if I uttered a single word I would burst into tears. I tried gently putting her back in the carrying case, but she struggled and scratched me, and I had to shove her in roughly, marring the romance of our last moments together.

We walked through the woods to Charlie's grandmother's house, a creepy, old two-story Victorian. I passed the cat carrier to Charlie, who lugged it up the porch steps and disappeared inside. Minutes went by. I gazed around the front yard, which was strewn with toys, chunky plastic kid versions of grown-up things: a Little Tikes lawn mower, a barbecue grill, a tiny car accompanied by a pornographically named Happy Pumper gas pump—all these so-called toys whose true purpose was to inculcate societal norms into children by making pumping gas seem like the height of fun. Their falsely bright presence in this somber, backwoods hollow felt more than a little off. I wanted to run inside the house and yell, *Never mind! Give her back!*

Dylan stood next to me, picking at her hot-pink nail polish in a way that reminded me painfully of Éclair. Soon Charlie came lumbering back out and set Taz's case on the porch, exclaiming, "Grammy says I can keep Garfield if I take care of him and stop asking for a Nintendo!"

Taz meowed in her case. I kneeled on the porch steps and opened the cage door.

"Come on out, Taz. You live here now."

She poked her head out, then trotted onto the porch, sniffing yet another new set of surroundings.

Dylan bent down to talk to Charlie just like Snow White in the Disney World commercial. "I have to tell you a secret, Charlie. Garfield is a fairy cat from my fairy kingdom. And now that he has a special home, I have to go back to my castle."

The huge grin on Charlie's face drooped and disappeared. "Where is that?"

"In the sky."

"When are you coming back?"

"I can't come back. But I'll miss you."

Charlie started crying, and I couldn't stand it anymore—my eyes brimmed with tears, blurring my vision such that my very last memory of Taz is of an indistinct brown-and-black blob.

"Bye, Taz. Your name is Garfield now," I managed to say, my voice choked.

Why is this so hard? I wondered. Both Glen and Graham had given me versions of a speech about how the most traumatic aspect of a family member's sudden death is being robbed of the chance to say goodbye. And yet this goodbye felt like the most brutal thing I had ever endured. I suddenly understood why people took off in the night: goodbyes are far harder for the people saying them than the people hearing them. All I knew was that I never wanted to go through this ever again.

"We have to go now," Dylan said, giving Charlie a kiss on the cheek. "I'll tell the king in the sky about your awesome deed! Take good care of our cat! Goodbye!"

With that, she grabbed my hand, and together we ran into the woods, not looking back. And to this day, whenever ugliness is all that reflects back at me in a mirror, I try to imagine myself through Charlie's eyes that April evening: the squire of the beautiful barn princess, worthy enough to ascend to her castle in the sky, connected to her not through tragic things—orphanhood, loss, death—but by gently intertwined fingers, by the glow of golden sunlight that touched both our shoulders, by the promise of a better world awaiting us above the clouds.

XXIX

THE SUN WENT DOWN AS I LURKED BEHIND THE DOGHOUSE. IT started to get cold. I was worried that the dogs—two enormous brown Great Danes—would growl and attack, but they just sniffed me and nudged my hand to pet their heads. I wondered if this meant I wasn't actually going to kill Dodge, that I was just pretending. Dogs could sense danger; if I were really a killer, wouldn't they try to ward me off?

Screams emitted periodically from the house. At first every yelp, shout, and screech made me jump up in alarm and look through the window with the hunting binoculars Dylan had given me. But every time it was the boys wrestling, or the little toddler shrieking because someone had grabbed his toy, or Dodge yelling orders and swinging his pistol around. The scene resembled a bunch of hyped-up monkeys from a sociological experiment about anarchy. Dylan stepped gingerly around them like a ballerina turned maid: *pas de chat* to pick up a knocked-over lamp, *allongé* to return the milk to the fridge, *échappé sauté* to avoid being pinched on the butt by Dodge.

He was obsessed with her, that much was apparent. He watched her every move from the corner of his eye and said something to her over and over. After a while I realized it was "Look at this." He was constantly performing stupid feats: lighting a paper napkin on fire, throwing a knife at the wall, crushing a beer can with his fist. I kept having the creepy feeling that he looked familiar to me. Then I remembered, with a bit of repulsion, that he and Dylan shared DNA, so the person he probably reminded me of was her.

The hours wore on, reaching 1:00 A.M., then 2:00. The smaller boys dropped like flies, falling asleep on the sofa or the floor. Dylan picked them up one by one and dragged them to bed like various-sized sacks of flour.

At last it was just her and Dodge in the kitchen. She offered him a huge vodka bottle, which he swigged like a cherry Squeezit. He was already drunk, stumbling around and swaying. Occasionally he rubbed his crotch in a way he seemed to think was stealthy. When Dylan's back was turned, he reached out and grabbed her sweatshirt, yanking her closer. *What is wrong with you?* I was close to screaming. *That's your sister!*

In a deft, elastic maneuver, Dylan disappeared into the sweatshirt, allowing it to fall off her inside out. Dodge stared at it, confused. Then out of nowhere he whipped his gun up, pointing it at Dylan's face. I was about to scream, but Dylan was completely unfazed, rolling her eyes as if this happened all the time. Through the window, I could hear her voice dully reciting a warped-sounding version of the Pledge of Allegiance: "I pledge allegiance to the *fag*..."

Dodge laughed drunkenly, took another enormous swig of vodka, teetered perilously, then fell to the floor like a downed tree.

Dylan just stood there, waiting to see if he would get up. Then she bent down, picked up his gun, and walked out the back door. The dogs came out excitedly when they heard her footsteps.

"Hey, Rascal, hey, Renegade," she said, petting them with one hand. The gun—a double-action revolver—gleamed in the moonlight.

"He's passed out cold?"

"Pretty sure."

"And the other boys are asleep?"

"Yeah. The little one wakes up sometimes, but I gave him cold medicine. He should be out like a light." She held out the gun. "Do you want this?"

"I guess so," I said, taking it. I'd held a rifle and a shotgun before, but never a handgun. I was awed by the difference: a rifle felt like holding a weapon, but within seconds of holding the handgun, it felt like part of me, an extension of my hand. I raised it up and held it against the cold white moon. It was . . . *pretty*. I'd never thought of guns as female before, but I did now, to such a perverse extent that I wondered if shooting someone would inspire the feeling of transformation losing my virginity had promised but not delivered.

The gun was seducing me. I tried to snap out of it, like an ancient sailor mid–Siren song. Why was I doing this again? Something to do with him following Dylan to the ends of the earth.

It scared me how quickly this reason had receded to the edges of my mind. Maybe I didn't need a reason. Maybe I just wanted to kill someone. Someone needed to die, because Éclair had died. I needed to kill someone, because someone had killed Éclair. Kill, kill, kill, kill. Die, die, die, die.

Dylan led the way to the house, opening the back door quietly. I followed, my mind about 99 percent gone. Beside the TV, I saw a pile of videotapes with messy, handwritten labels: *Satanists on Geraldo. Fags on Geraldo. Teen Satanist on Dateline.* A shudder ran through me. Aaron had talked about suing the TV stations for spreading paranoia about Satanic conspiracies. "Someone's going to get killed over this shit," he'd said.

"Shit, where's Dodge?" Dylan whispered. "He was lying right there." She pointed to a spot on the floor.

Then we heard a sizzling sound coming from the kitchen.

"Hey, bitch! Make me an omelet!" a boy's voice shouted.

We went to the kitchen, me holding the gun behind my back. Dodge was standing over a frying pan of eggs, his eyes bleary and unfocused. He thrust a dirty spatula toward Dylan. Then his eyes snapped to me.

"Who the fuck—"

I stopped breathing.

He recognized me, and I recognized him. Up close, his ugliness was unmistakable. It wasn't his gauntness or the way his wide pink lips were chapped raw. It emanated from within. I'd seen his face before—three times. The guy who'd followed me in the woods. The guy who threw the hot dog at Éclair. The guy in the photograph at the police station—it was *him*.

"You're that girl," he said to me, eyes wide.

"I know who you are," I said back. All the feeling had left my body. I felt dimly astonished that I could stand there and form a sentence.

"You don't know shit." Dodge patted around his belt. He was looking for his gun. "Where'd I put that tham ding . . ."

Dylan looked at me in alarm: *What's going on?* I could only shrug. I felt stupefied.

Dylan waved her arms, getting Dodge's attention off me. "Hey, Dodge, let's do shots!"

She grabbed three shot glasses and set them on the table, each with a different Derby-winning horse painted on them: PINK STAR, MAJESTIC PRINCE, CANNONADE. She poured some Old Crow bourbon into each one.

"You make my fuckin' omelet," he ordered her. Then, to me, "*We'll* do shots." He downed two and handed me the other one. I took a tiny sip.

"Fuck you, drink it!" he shouted. And so I threw it back, the smoky cheap liquor creating an instant buzz in my head. I hadn't eaten all day, I realized.

I asked Dylan, "Can you cook me one of those, too?"

"You boys," she teased tonelessly. "You eat like horses."

"She's not a boy, idiot," Dodge slurred. "Hey, wheresmy gun."

Dylan swooped in with the omelets, distracting him. I set the gun out of sight on the seat of my chair. Dylan poured herself a bowl of Cookie Crisp and sat down with us at the table. Dodge devoured his food, momentarily forgetting our existence. Then he looked up at me.

"Roo you rawnt ro row ry?" he asked, his mouth stuffed with egg, oily with cheap corn oil instead of butter.

"Huh?" I said.

"He asked if you want to know why," Dylan interpreted.

"Oh. Why what?"

"Ry I rill er."

"Why he . . . killed her." Dylan's face turned white as she realized he was talking about Éclair. She looked at me in disbelief—he was bullshitting, right? I shook my head gravely. No, he was not bullshitting.

Why? I said, turning back to Dodge. "Because you're a psychopath. You don't need a reason."

Dodge opened his mouth wide and let the yellow mush of egg fall onto his plate with a disgusting plop. He licked his thin lips. "You fucking whore cunt whore bitch! Did your dad make you gay, too, you whore-licking cunt? Destiny's a fag. *He* wants to suck my sick."

"No, I don't," Dylan said calmly. "I'm a lesbian, like Lacey."

"You're fucked up," Dodge said. He was rubbing himself again. Under the table I wrapped my fingers around the gun.

"Those witches fucked you up and made you gay. When we got that letter from your whore mom, I sneaked to New Hampshire and I found you. I thought I was getting a sister, but I saw what a fag you were. My own brother, a fuckin' faggot. And I knew it was those witches that done it. So I said to mysleff—myself—I said Dodge will make the buttfuckers die, starting with the loudmouth whore with her nose in the air. I wanted to see if she was a man, too." Disappointment crossed his face. "She wasn't."

My hand, the one holding the gun, started shaking. Up until that moment I'd been bluffing, daring myself to be capable of murder. I wasn't bluffing anymore.

Hatred was boiling over. I hadn't felt this much pure, unadulterated rage since I beat in Ty's face with my algebra book. It was a bear hug of hatred, crushing me with a promise of sweet release. This would all be over soon, it said. I would do this for Éclair. We would do it together. She would be with me one last time, and after that, nothing mattered.

"Kill 'em all. Because Dodge is godge. Godge! Doddie is God. Fuck it. You know what I mean. Butt-fucker."

Abruptly, his head tipped forward and he started snoring.

"Dodge?" I said.

He didn't move. I snapped my fingers a couple times. Nothing.

"Give me a rag and a pair of dish gloves," I instructed Dylan. "Let's move fast before he wakes up again."

Dylan handed me a pair of yellow rubber gloves, and I pulled them on. The plastic, combined with my nervousness, immediately caused my palms to sweat. I focused on staying calm, taking the rag and rubbing every last crevice of the gun until I was sure all traces of my fingerprints were gone. Then I approached Dodge and removed the plate of eggs. He didn't wake up.

"Wait," I said. "The gunshot will wake the boys, and they'll all come running out. We have to get him outside. Will you go open the door?"

Dylan nodded.

I shoved the gun into my belt and gave Dodge a light slap. "Dodge? Hello?" He groaned quietly but didn't move. "Okay, grab his other arm."

Dylan and I heaved him from the chair, his body slithering onto the floor like a dead snake. We dragged him through the living room, bumping into various pieces of furniture, and out to the backyard. He wasn't as heavy as I'd expected. He was a violent murderer, yet still a skinny fifteen-year-old who couldn't hold his liquor.

As we neared the woods, he started muttering a string of words that sounded like "Where my gun? Suck my dick." Was the rubber from the dish gloves leaving suspicious chafe marks on his arm? I needed a flashlight, but I was too nervous to wait for Dylan to run back inside and get one. I couldn't believe how poorly I'd thought this whole thing out.

Panting, I propped him up against a tree.

"The fuck . . ."

"He was supposed to be unconscious," I said. "Damn it."

"You could kick him in the head," Dylan suggested.

"That would look too suspicious. It's fine, I'll do it quickly." I wriggled behind Dodge and started arranging his arms. He smelled filthy, but with a faint whiff of bubblegum shampoo, the kind made for babies. I faltered, caught off guard. Every atom of my being was telling me this was a bad idea.

"Kill 'em fuckers . . ."

I put the gun in Dodge's right hand, knowing that if he snapped awake, he could turn it on me in a second. My heart was pounding, and I wondered if Dodge could feel it through my chest. I held him from behind like we were in a Lamaze class. *Breathe in, breathe out.* With the bulky dish gloves, it was more difficult than I'd expected to get Dodge's finger around the trigger.

"Shit," I said. "His brain's gonna explode all over my face. I can't do it like this." I wriggled out from behind Dodge. His body thumped against the tree and slumped over. I propped him up again and crouched beside him, putting the gun back in his hand and trying to point it under his jaw. Dodge started to squirm. He waved his hand, knocking the gun from my fingers.

"Damn it," I said, patting the dark ground. Where was Éclair now? The bear hug I'd felt in the kitchen had faded away, leaving me cold and bewildered at myself. *If I don't find this damn gun in three seconds, I'm walking away. Three . . . two . . .*

I found it.

"Hey. Heyyyyy. Hey, wazz goin on. Get offa me."

"Lacey, quick," Dylan said.

"I'm trying."

"Yourse gay. You cunt—"

"Shut up," I hissed. "Those are the last words you'll ever say."

My hand felt tingly and numb. I couldn't feel the gun anymore.

Then the shot cracked out, startling me even though I'd known it was coming. I heard a ringing in my ears that made me wonder if I'd shot myself. My vision was going black. I felt myself falling, but I didn't hit the ground.

When I snapped back to alertness I was standing. Looking down, I saw the lump next to the tree.

"Did I do it?" I asked Dylan.

She stood over the lump like a moonlit ghost. She nodded slowly.

"He's faking," I whispered. I was sure of it. I stared at the lump, waiting for it to move. Any second now, he would leap up and attack me.

I heard Dylan say, "I don't think so, Lacey."

The smell hit my nose. I knew that smell. That terrible, sickening smell.

My memory ends there, a tablet fizzing in water, the feeling of sinking into a dream or perhaps rising out of one, like a deep-sea diver who's lost sight of the boat and can no longer distinguish up from down.

And after this spasm of oblivion that felt like a single flowing moment but that I later calculated to have been twenty-four days—the green buds of the birch trees now slender yellow bells—I thought I was home. The sun was shining and I was staring at a point in the distance where two hills met, a view that resembled almost exactly the one from Éclair's bedroom, which she rarely looked at and had at one point covered with a neon poster of a pink Corvette flanked by palm trees.

As I stared, a loud truck whooshed past, startling me; I was at a gas station.

"Close your eyes."

Dylan's voice. I did as she said and felt her damp fingertips smear something across my cheek.

"Now look."

I opened my eyes. Dylan held up an old-ladyish mother-of-pearl powder compact. In the tiny circle of glass, I barely recognized the face reflected back at me. My skin was tan and gleaming—the skin I'd taken for granted and never thought of as pretty before hardship stole it away. Now here it was again, sandy brown, painted not with blood but with a sweet, childlike hieroglyph: a rainbow. Blue, red, yellow, and green fused together in an arc that curved across my cheek. The sight of it was so unexpected I instantly became choked with tears.

"Don't cry!" Dylan exclaimed. "You'll smear it. Actually, wait—do. It'll look more natural. Beautiful."

Of the many doors I'd assumed were shut to me forever, some oversight had left beauty ajar. And so, through that door, after a violent and bloody second birth, I emerged into a new life with no more than an infant's idea of where I was or the person I would become.

PART
THREE

XXX

MONTREAL, QUEBEC
2005

I LOST MY COPY OF *I SAW MARILYN MONROE IN 1980* LONG AGO, among the yellow birches and slippery elms of the Canadian border, or in the disorder of one of the many shelters and abandoned buildings that contained me at various points. But I remember one passage with vivid acuity. In a diner called the Pony Express, the woman claiming to be Norma Jeane Baker says to the Hells Angel, "I had to do what I did. They were going to kill me, slowly. They were never going to let me live."

We have arrived, at last, in Canada. The past is behind us, if not holistically, then at least chronologically.

It's my final summer working as a law clerk for one of Quebec's most famous judges, Justice Etienne Pierre Montagne. Two books were written about him and his influence during la Révolution tranquille in the 1960s, a time when Quebec was transforming from a brutal, dog-eat-dog agrarian society into a modern, bilingual, Technicolor butterfly.

Huge swaths of the province remained in black and white, however, like the little town of Lac-Froid, a speck on the map notable to no one until a massive lawsuit entangled every person living there. An iron ore company employed most of the villagers. The main street featured little more than a school, a grocery store, a café where the wife of the snowplow driver sold cups of plain coffee brewed in a Mr. Coffee, plus a church and a porn shop, situated across from each other in mutual disparagement.

In 2005, when my story resumes, six children of Lac-Froid were attacked in the woods by a pack of wolves. The sole survivor was a girl named Marie-Laure, who climbed up a tree and watched in horror while her friends were mauled and eaten. A day later she was discovered, still in the tree. The forest floor was littered with bloodied children's clothes, the half-masticated head of a boy she'd known well staring up at her from its lifeless, gaping eye.

Lac-Froid's city council, with the support of the Northcore mining company, immediately devised a plan to eradicate the wolves. But the wolves were eastern reds and legally protected under le loi concernant les espèces vulnérables. Several environmental organizations sued to halt the eradication plan. The case garnered national attention, enflaming four major groups: the villagers; the wildlife conservationists; the mining company, which faced legal action for placing its workers' families in unsafe conditions; and, finally, the logging company, which had destroyed the wolves' habitat in the first place, pushing the pack into Lac-Froid's area of the province.

Justice Montagne was so liberal he'd earned himself the nickname Père Noël, but the Lac-Froid case wasn't clear-cut in its political orientation. To side with the bereaved villagers was to benefit the mining corporation, which of course wanted the wolves eradicated so it could get back to business. But to side with the conservationists would send a callous message about the worth of working-class children.

All things being normal, the Lac-Froid case would never have involved me. Traditionally in Quebec, a clerk spent one or two years with a judge before moving on to a law firm. I'd been with Montagne for *five* years. People wondered what the hell was wrong with me. It was almost unheard of for a promising young lawyer to settle for career law clerk status. But this was what I'd chosen, putting me in the path of the Lac-Froid case and everything that followed.

It was late July, and Montagne and I were having cigars in the library portion of his chambers. The building had been nonsmoking for decades, but we cracked the windows and did it anyway. I'd taught

Montagne to say "I don't give a fuck" in English, a phrase he enjoyed whipping out to shock his old Quebecois colleagues. "Ma rebelle," he called me affectionately and with such frequency that around the court-house it had almost become my professional designation. "La petite re-belle du justice," I'd heard myself referred to on more than one occasion, or "Montagne's little rebel" among the Anglophones.

French was now my primary language. It had even become the lan-guage of my thoughts, especially when I was at work. Hopefully the French words that I inject here will serve as mellifluous reminders that while Montreal is a mere fifty miles from the border of New Hamp-shire, it is a foreign land into which I had disappeared as thoroughly as if it were an unmapped village in the jungles of Borneo.

"Mais alors, les enfants," Montagne said that evening, exhaling a thick plume of smoke in the direction of the open window.

"Oui, oui, the children," I replied brusquely. "But what about les loups? Are you going to castrate the only law that protects them? What, we'll only protect 'nice' wolves? Vegetarian wolves? I'm sorry about the children, but they shouldn't have been playing in the woods."

"The villagers will sue the provincial government if any more of their children die."

"They should sue the logging company," I argued. "Reckless endan-germent. The loggers should be responsible for trapping and relocating the wolf communities whose habitats they decimate."

"Wolf communities!" Montagne laughed. "Je suis désolé, but a 'community' of wolves has eaten all your children!"

We both laughed. I took a final puff of my cigar and stamped it out in the chunky Lalique ashtray.

"Are you leaving so early?" Montagne said, disappointed. "Fierté, I suppose. Pride?"

He nodded to the office across the street, where an enormous rain-bow flag had materialized overnight. Spontaneous shows of gay pride were erupting all over the city in the wake of Parliament's passage of the

Civil Marriage Act, which brought same-sex marriage from the realm of the individual provinces to federally mandated law.

"Non, reéllement," I said. "I have a busy evening. Gwen and I are trying couples counseling, and then I have two different parties I'm supposed to attend."

"Couples counseling?" Montagne asked, delighted.

"We had a wretched fight last week. Over whether to get a cat, of all things."

"Well, I'm sure therapy is very fashionable. Gwen's idea, I suppose?"

"Mine, actually."

He gave an approving nod. "Good. Love needs tending. You can't just stick it in the ground like a potato and hope for the best. Your generation understands that."

I waved away his praise. "It'll probably be a disaster. I'm heading to the Auberge afterward to get blitzed. You should join me. C'est une soirée pour le mouvement."

I'd RSVP'd weeks ago for an event for the Quebec independence movement, a group in which I'd become, improbably, a rather prestigious figure. This was a testament not to my personal eminence but to the quality of the people still loyal to a cause that had hemorrhaged support after two failed referendums in as many decades. An FLQ member who'd recently tried to firebomb Second Cup Coffee over its English-language signage had received only six months in prison—the sentencing equivalent of a jaded, indifferent sigh.

"Le mouvement," Montagne said, amused, shaking his head. "I couldn't possibly be seen at such a gathering. Absurde. What if my photo is taken next to a terrorist?"

I rolled my eyes. "There won't be any *terrorists*. And they'd treat you like a king. You'd be the toast of the event."

"What good is a toast if your glass is full of horrid Sainte-Croix wine?"

I opened my leather bag and pulled out a bottle of 2000 Le Pin. It was a Bordeaux in the French "garage" style, which had recently become all the rage among collectors. Bottles were being hoarded and traded and locked in cellars. The one in my hands was comparatively low-end, valued at $600. Montagne's eyes lit up when he saw it.

"I sign your paycheck," he said. "I know you can't afford that."

"Gwen bought it for me."

"And she doesn't want to drink it with you?"

"You know Gwen. It's all grape juice to her."

"D'accord, you win. Just let me call Patrice. I was supposed to go to her little place for dinner."

Patrice was his daughter, her "little place" a brick manse in Summit Park. She was a housewife to an investor from Toronto, whose flailing business ventures were supported by his father-in-law's wealth. They had three children, all boys named in some fashion after their grandfather: Etienne, Pierre, and, most horribly, *Monty*.

I could hear Patrice complaining to Montagne over the phone: "You shouldn't be drinking with that camionneuse. You know it interferes with your medication!"

Patrice despised me, a fact Montagne pretended not to comprehend. Her nickname for me, la camionneuse, essentially meant "truck driver."

I whispered, "I'll see you at the Auberge around eight?"

Montagne mouthed back, *À bientôt!* as I strode out the door.

The office, couples therapy, then back-to-back social engagements—I was the very picture of a yuppie. And far busier than I could have imagined as a child, with my books and my walks in the woods. Too busy to wonder what my parents might be doing at any given moment. Were they still in prison? Were they still *alive*?

Years had passed since I'd allowed myself to look backward. Behind my yuppie mask was a sweaty gambler determined to stay in the game and recoup her losses despite an extremely bad starting hand. In retrospect, that evening with Montagne was the night I should have cashed out and fled.

IT WAS A BEAUTIFUL EVENING, THE TEMPERATURE A PERFECT 23 degrees Celsius. I went along Vieux-Port toward the therapist's address in Old Town. From the cobbled streets and gabled roofs to the scent of frankincense and myrrh lingering around the creepy Gothic Revival basilica, this part of Montreal evoked all the quaintness—and dark-ness—of Catholic Europe.

Across the river stood a hulking grain elevator complex, built in the early twentieth century to stockpile imports from the great Canadian West. The complex was still operational when I first arrived in Canada, but in 1996 it had been abandoned. Every window was now broken, and the concrete was covered in massive rust stains resembling blood. It felt strange to be old enough to have witnessed such decay.

"Ex-cuzay moy?" A loud, broad-faced Australian woman was trying to get my attention. "Kuh voy frappay—"

"English, English," I said.

She held up a camera. "Can I get a picture?"

"Sure." I sighed, resigned to playing vacation photographer.

The woman handed her camera to her friend, and to my horror, I realized she wanted a picture with *me*. She liked my tailored suit and silk tie—I was a real Montreal power lesbian. The tourists were getting more invasive every year, but being asked to pose for a photo like it was Epcot and I was a background performer? That was a new one.

I covered my face with my bag. "No, no, I don't take pictures."

"Well, sorry."

Then I noticed, out of the corner of my eye, a small, bald man half hidden by the sandwich board of a patisserie. He had a camera, too, pointed directly at me. When I opened my mouth to ask who the hell he was and what he thought he was doing, he abruptly lowered the camera and disappeared around a corner.

Behind me, the Australian woman was hoisting her bulky backpack and muttering about how she thought Canadians were supposed to be *nice*. I walked away, deeper into Old Town, looking over my shoulder several times. I didn't see the bald man again.

Gwen was waiting for me, leaning anachronistically against a three-hundred-year-old stone-and-brick wall. Quebec's colonial settlers would have burned her at the stake if they'd gotten a load of her outfit: a slip dress of sheer rags encircled by a low-slung leather belt, tossed over a pair of camouflage cargo pants and topped with a fuzzy fedora that looked like it had been made from a carpet.

She peered at my face. "You look weird. What's wrong?"

"Nothing, that's just my face," I said back. "Are you ready?"

"I guess so. Why are we doing this again? You should hate therapists after what they did to you."

"There was a Freudian I liked. He tried to help me."

"Is this person a Freudian?"

"No, Freudians are hard to find these days. They went out of style."

Gwen fished a pebble out of her hot-pink mesh slipper, grimacing. "I just don't see what purpose this can have, since we can barely say anything."

"You'd be surprised how much you can say. I do it with Montagne all the time. Just tell the emotional truth without revealing any hard facts. No names. Nothing about America. And nothing about . . ."

"Obviously, Jo. I'm not an imbecile."

She picked at her nail polish, destroying it as usual. Fashion trends aside, in fourteen years she was almost entirely unchanged. The most daring aspect of our disguises was that they barely disguised us at all. We'd crossed a border drawn in the dirt and called ourselves new names. That was it. Identity was cheap, it turned out.

The therapist was an Anglophone from Nova Scotia named Chana. She looked like somebody's hippie lesbian aunt with her frizzy hair and flowing patchwork dress. Her office decor was fifteen years out of style, preserved, coincidentally, from the same era in which I'd last been to therapy. A queasy feeling of déjà vu crept over me.

We'd barely gotten past the introductory stage when Gwen announced, "Jo's afraid to live because her sister died. That's why she won't let us get a cat."

"For god's sake, Gwen," I sputtered.

I had to admire her—if I was going to make her do this thing, she was going to give me hell by actually *doing* it.

Before Chana could ask Gwen to elaborate, I said, "It has nothing to do with my sister. I just think pet ownership is masochistic. You get the thing, even though you know it's going to die, and then you have to get another one to replace the first one, and it goes on and on. Besides, indoor cats are unnatural."

"The cat can roam around the neighborhood if it wants," Gwen said.

"So it can get hit by a car?"

"Shit lives and dies, Jo. You just have to embrace it. My mother died, but it didn't make me afraid to live."

"Your mother died of an overdose. My sister was *murdered*. It's a little different."

A keen glint appeared in Chana's eyes. She sat forward. "They're both very traumatic experiences," she said. "What makes them feel different to you, Jo?"

I shrugged self-consciously. "I don't know . . . One was an accident. The other was an act of malice. Malice begets evil and more malice. It spreads like a disease. It makes people's souls rot off, like syphilis."

It was a speech worthy of a Puritan clergyman. Awkward silence ensued. Gwen stared at the carpet. Chana looked concerned.

"But anyway," I backtracked, "it has nothing to do with getting a cat."

Chana nodded thoughtfully. "You both must know the cat represents some deeper issue, or you wouldn't have sought therapy. The cat has to do with *something*, do you agree?"

"Jo fucked an old lady," Gwen volunteered cheerfully. "Maybe it has to do with that."

"Gwen!"

I smacked her shoulder, though I was happy to segue into the more banal territory of my infidelity. Three years before, I'd almost had an affair with a lawyer from Morton & Bell, an achingly sensual woman named Diane. She was a Catherine Deneuve type in her late fifties, seemingly designed by the devil to tempt me. She was experienced and professional, and she had amazing legs; most irresistibly of all, she was a stone-cold bitch. We'd shared one torrid, disgusting fuck in the library of her law firm after hours in 2002, during which barely any of our clothes had come off before we'd both climaxed and she was putting her shoes back on and I was feeling like a piece of trash carried through the streets by a cold and taunting wind.

"It happened one time," I explained to Chana, "and I admitted it immediately, and Gwen forgave me."

Chana seemed skeptical. "Forgiveness is easy. Building back trust can be harder."

"I don't care about *Diane*." Gwen spat the name. "Jo can do whatever she wants."

"I don't *want* to cheat on you. I keep trying to explain that. It's not a matter of my freedom being curtailed."

"Then I don't get it," Gwen said, picking at her nail polish again. "I don't want things I don't want. If I want something, it's because I want it, not because I *don't* want it."

Chana made a *let's cool down* gesture. "I'm curious what Jo would like to contribute to this process. Is there anything in particular you want to address, Jo?"

No, I thought. If Gwen's goal was to make me regret this, she'd succeeded.

I took a breath. "I guess my main concern is Gwen's . . . stash."

Chana seemed to brace herself for the expected drug problem.

"My *stash*?" Gwen echoed. "What stash?"

"The bridal magazines I found hidden in the closet."

She blushed furiously. "Oh my *god.* I like the fashion, Jo. I only hid them so you wouldn't freak out."

Chana turned to me. "Does marriage make you uncomfortable, Jo?"

"Yes. I don't like that kind of attention, and I don't need the government's stamp of approval to be in a relationship."

I wasn't prepared to admit that, in fact, I had a deep-seated phobia that if we ever got married, Gwen would be murdered. In my mind, the second we said *I do,* some psychopath would leap out of the wedding cake and shoot her in the head. I didn't know how this superstition had formed, exactly, but it had been there for years.

Chana clocked my body language, the way I'd crunched in on myself at the mention of bridal magazines. I tried to casually straighten out.

Meanwhile Gwen was chirping away. "Jo hates the government, yet she works for the government. Try to make sense out of *that.*"

I tapped my foot in agitation. "If this is going to be an inquisition into all my failures, we'll be here all day."

"I didn't say you were a *failure.* I just said it didn't make sense."

Chana intervened. "I think Gwen is trying to say that while life may be nonsensical, that shouldn't prevent either of you from living it to the fullest. Which, in Gwen's case, may well involve adopting a cat."

I sighed. "Cats are all well and good in the abstract, but which one of us will be taking it to the vet in the end, when things get very, very concrete? Because I guarantee it's not going to be Gwen. It's going to be *me*."

Chana held up a hand. "Why do you say that? What makes you feel so sure that Gwen can't take on that responsibility? Was there some event in the relationship," she asked slowly, "where you had to do a distressing thing that Gwen couldn't or wouldn't do?"

Gwen's face turned white as a sheet. My throat went dry.

Chana stared at me, then at Gwen, waiting for one of us to answer. My mind spun, thinking about murder statistics. How many girls' sisters got murdered each year? Was there any way Chana could link me to a *particular* murdered sister? Why hadn't Gwen said brother, or cousin, or friend?

Bone-chilling terror gripped me: it didn't matter what Gwen had said; somehow this woman already knew. It was written on my face that I was a murderer. She'd known it from the second I walked in the door, and now she was going to call the FBI.

Gwen clutched her purse, preparing to bolt.

I shook my head slightly. We needed to stay.

The next fifteen minutes were torture. We responded to Chana's prompts in monosyllables. Gwen invented a disagreement over money that took up some time. After we'd led the conversation away from the "event in the relationship," Gwen stood up and said, "Jo, we have to go to that thing."

I stood up, too. "Yes, I'm sorry, we do need to go."

Startled, Chana urged us to stay and take advantage of our full scheduled hour. I couldn't say what her expression looked like, since I was avoiding her eyes, but Gwen and I reiterated our regrets, gathered our things, and walked out the door.

xxxii

NEITHER OF US SPOKE UNTIL WE WERE ON THE OTHER SIDE OF Old Town.

"Jesus Christ," I said, looking over my shoulder for the hundredth time. "I'm sorry. That was a horrible idea. I never should have suggested it."

Gwen took off her fuzzy hat, then put it back on. "Whatever, it's fine."

"I'm sorry," I repeated. "Are you rattled? Don't be scared. Nothing's going to happen. It's not against the law to abandon therapy."

"Let's not talk about it." Her face was still bone white, and she kept her eyes fixed on the ground.

It was almost time for my separatist event. We'd joked about what a stupid idea it was to schedule therapy right before we attended *two* parties, but it didn't seem so funny now.

"This is ridiculous," I said. "Let's just go home."

Gwen rolled her eyes. "I'm sure you told Montagne, and if we don't show up, he'll assume we're fighting, and he'll hate me."

"I'll make an excuse for you, and you can go straight to your thing in the Village—"

"Stop babying me! It's fine. It's whatever. Let's just go."

We walked to the hotel Auberge du Vieux-Port in a silence broken only by a distant police siren, which made us jump like frightened cats.

At the hotel, we took the elevator up to the terrasse and parted immediately, as if by electrostatic repulsion. Alone, my panic dissipated into embarrassment. We'd overreacted and made the situation more dramatic than it needed to be.

I needed a drink.

On my way to the bar, I spotted Monsieur Cloutier in his yellow plaid suit, trying to convince everyone he had an "in" with Celine Dion and could get her to perform a free concert for the movement. All the old die-hards like Cloutier held an enduring delusion that Celine secretly supported the independence agenda and would reveal herself in our hour of greatest need.

"Well, well, well," he said, sidling up to me. "I heard the rumors of your influence over le justice. How marvelous to see it with my own eyes!"

He nodded toward Montagne, who was singing along merrily with the folk duo, a gray-haired husband and wife in Acadian dress wielding a violin and a pair of clackety wooden spoons.

"You make me sound like Rasputin," I said. "If you'll excuse me, Monsieur Cloutier, I desperately need a drink."

I begged off but was immediately stopped by a lawyer friend of mine, Alexandrine Sauveterre. "Félicitations, Jo!" she gushed. When I looked confused, she said, "On the Civil Marriage Act!"

"Ah, merci," I said.

"You look glum! Is Gwen expecting a marriage proposal? Ah, yes, you gays will have the same problems as the rest of us now!"

I glanced around for Gwen, regretting the way I'd let her stalk off. I hated losing sight of her in public places. One of these days, I just knew, her vanishing would end with me gulping down coffee in an interrogation room and sobbing, *I don't know what happened, I turned around and she was gone!* And some unimpressed cop would automatically mark me as the prime suspect in her murder. After all, more than 60 percent of the time, the husband did it.

By the time I made it to the bar, I was ready to stab the cork of my

$600 Le Pin with a key and swig it straight from the bottle.

"Excusez-moi," I said to the young man behind the counter. I pulled the wine out of my bag and handed it to him discreetly, along with a fat tip. "Do not serve this to anyone but me and my companion there." I pointed to Montagne.

"Pas de problem," he said amenably, whipping out two wineglasses.

Again I looked for Gwen, then told myself to stop obsessing. She was probably crouched behind a trash can somewhere, smoking pot with a cater-waiter.

Montagne found me, preceded by the scent of his woodsy cologne.

"Ah, there you are, ma rebelle. Where is the beautiful Gwen? Oh dear. I gather from your face therapy did not go well."

I heaved a shrug.

"My poor Jo. Is one of those glasses is for me?" He took a sip, a look of ecstasy coming over his face. "C'est incroyable! Heavenly. No, not heavenly. This wine is too sinful for God!"

He raised the glass to the crowd of people, and everyone cheered raucously, thinking he was praising the Sainte-Croix wine being served, which was made from Quebec's notoriously bad grapes. Montagne was promptly carried off by a wave of admirers, and I was alone again.

"Jo Scottish?" said a voice behind me. I turned and saw a stocky, well-dressed man in his forties.

"Oui? Puis-je vous aider?"

"Oh, I don't speak French, unfortunately," he said, seeming embarrassed.

"You're at a separatist party and you don't speak French?"

"Is the pot calling the kettle black, Ms. *Scottish*?"

My surname was the result of a paperwork snafu fourteen years ago, when a caseworker at the ministère randomly labeled me "Scottish" because of my accent, which didn't sound Canadian to her but didn't sound American, either. (My whole life, I'd had my own weird accent, a blend of posh Brit with nasal and working-class New Englander.)

Somehow, through a long trail of confusing forms, "Scottish" had become my surname.

"Yes, my name is very *amusant*," I said, not politely.

"So you're an Anglophone, eh? Your English has no accent. Not a French-Canadian one, anyway."

"I was born in the Eastern Townships."

"An Anglo separatist? Fascinating. Why are you on their side, if I may ask?"

"I'm on the side of anyone who wants to be free."

"How noble. May I get you another drink? Oh, but you have your own bottle, don't you? Was that a Le Pin I saw? *Wow.* How do you afford such luxuries on a law clerk's salary, if I may ask?"

I gawked at him. Had this man been watching me? "You may *not* ask. And it was a gift from my girlfriend."

"Now that's a keeper! Where is the lucky lady? She didn't want to share such a special bottle with you?"

"She doesn't enjoy wine," I said.

"A gal after my own heart. Give me a Bud Light any day!" The man's laugh had a sneering falseness to it. Instinct warned me to get away from him.

"It was nice to meet you—" I started, but he cut me off.

"But we didn't meet! My name is Harold Boil."

I couldn't believe a man named Harold *Boil* had the gall to make fun of *my* name. I shook his hand limply, then made a move to walk away.

But he wouldn't let go.

"Perhaps we could chat more later," he said.

"I'm afraid I'm leaving soon. Meeting some people in the Gay Village." I immediately wished I hadn't said where I was going.

"Oh yeah, congratulations on the marriage thing! That's really great. My brother's gay, too. Great guy." He yawned theatrically. "You know what? I'm tired! I think I'm going to head home and hit the hay.

Pleasure to meet you, Jo Scottish! Enjoy that wine!"

And with that, he set his glass on the bar and left.

"Who was that?"

I jumped. It was Gwen, the dome of the Bonsecours Market casting an alien-like halo around her head.

"I don't know," I said, realizing I hadn't gleaned a single fact about the man, such as how he knew my name. "Where have you been?"

She shrugged. "Nowhere."

Across the terrasse, Montagne was gazing in a melancholy way at the folk singers, who were singing "Le retour du soldat." It was an old song about a soldier who returns from war to find that his wife, having heard a false report of his death, has married another man.

The atmosphere of the party had changed. I overheard a man saying, "I'm just so exhausted. The fight never ends—and for what? America is swallowing the world. What difference if we go down screaming 'arrête' or 'stop'?"

The exuberance of these parties often downshifted into depression after a few drinks. Quebec's motto, after all, was "Je me souviens"—"I remember"—words that might be spoken exultantly at the beginning of an evening and bitterly by the end.

xxxiii

WE HAD ONE MORE PARTY TO GO TO: DINNER AT A FANCY NEW restaurant arranged by Gwen's Norwegian manager, Bjorn, for his top models. At least no one would expect me to participate in the conversation. My job was to show up, choose good wine for the table, and observe all the characters in the tableau so that when Gwen complained about everyone later, I would know whom she was talking about and be able to offer opinions. Gwen hated feeling like she was complaining to a wall.

The Gay Village was mobbed, inviting a dissociative fantasy I sometimes entered into, in which I guided an invisible Éclair on a tour: *That's the Cinéma L'Amour, where they show X-rated movies. Oh, that club has two-dollar tequila sunrises, you'd love it there.* Too often, I disoriented myself—why was Éclair visiting *me* in a glamorous city and not the other way around? Wasn't I supposed to be on a farm somewhere? And what was Éclair's deal in this scenario? Had she emerged from a cryogenic deep freeze, or had she aged fourteen years? Were my parents around somewhere, too? The fantasy fizzled out if I thought about it too hard.

When we arrived at the patioed restaurant, there was the usual five full minutes of everyone kissing each other and complimenting one another's clothes. Bjorn's absurdly handsome blond boyfriend, Zach, was there, along with three models whose names I couldn't remember, a style blogger, and a finance guy straight out of *American Psycho* who wanted to use Gwen's face to promote some internet Ponzi scheme. I'd told Bjorn multiple times that I didn't want Gwen associating with such sleazebags, to which Bjorn had replied, "Then who's left to work with? It's *fashion*, Jo. Just relax and watch the money pour in."

Gwen did seem to be on the cusp of a serious career. She'd made $20,000 last month during a two-week trip to Milan. I'd told her to stick it in a savings account, not quite believing it was real. I didn't know whether my vague denial had more to do with my incomprehension of the fashion industry or my fear that if Gwen didn't need me to pay the rent and put a roof over her head, she would run away.

The conversation at the table had already turned to sex (I always got social whiplash moving between the culture of lawyers, who never discussed sex, and that of "creatives," who discussed nothing but). Apparently American Psycho was on a quest to find a model who was "actually good in bed."

"No such thing, bro," Zach declared. He was a New York transplant, a fact that put me on edge, as if I might blurt out some obscure American detail from my childhood—New Hampshire's granite formations or the Pizza Hut BOOK IT! reading program—and be recognized. Freud would have called it a subconscious death wish.

"Like you would know what makes a woman good in bed, you homo!" Bjorn teased Zach.

"Hey! I banged *two* girls in college—"

"Don't gross us out with your bisexual stories, Zach. Models suck in bed, that's just a fact of life."

American Psycho nodded toward Gwen. "This one could be the exception that proves the rule."

"You'll never know, will you?" she said flatly.

"Easy," I whispered to her. I was "protective," people said. It was "cute." But the impulse wasn't cute, it was sickening terror, rising up like bile whenever Gwen provoked a man. It was an unwanted image of a red-splattered room with its gleeful, homicidal message: *I told that loudmouth whore to shut up.*

American Psycho was unamused. "I think I'm entitled to know. Money is sex, sex is money. I don't want an ice queen representing my site. I mean, I'm not saying I have to sample the goods myself. I'll take her boyfriend's word for it." He squinted at me. "Wait, are you a man or a girl?"

Next to me, Gwen slouched as if trying to disappear under the table. Bjorn laughed uneasily. "I'd leave Jo out of it if I were you, mate. Assuming you'd like to keep your face intact."

American Psycho snorted, and Zach immediately inserted himself. "No, seriously, bro," he said. "Take Bjorn's advice: don't mess with these bitches. They may look tame, but they're from the streets."

From the streets. The phrase mortified me reflexively, though it needn't have. The world had changed, a much-hyped new millennium had dawned, and the twentieth-century obsession with class and pedigree was over. Now it was de rigeur to be "self-made," from "humble beginnings." Far from ruining a person, a stint of poverty—homelessness, even—was valuable currency in the emerging fashion of *authenticity.* Zach probably thought he was complimenting us.

"It's what makes Gwen perfect for your investment group," Bjorn cooed. "Edgy rags to sexy riches. You can see it all, right in her face."

Across the street, I saw a tourist family having their picture taken with a rainbow-bedecked gay couple. I imagined them going home to Melbourne or Dallas and showing the photo to their friends: *We went to Montreal and met the queers! They're just like us! They just want to get married!* The dangling treat of tolerance had lured us from rank bars on the fringes of society to the squeaky-clean shopping districts, where we, too, could purchase glittering blood diamonds from De Beers and sink our assets into Ponzi schemes and adopt a Chinese baby or have our eggs fertilized in a doctor's office to form family units, that precious bread and butter of consumer-driven society.

Bjorn had redirected the conversation, telling a story about the trip to Milan. ". . . Bianchi was overseeing the shoot personally, and here comes Gwen, forty-five minutes late, as usual." He shot Gwen a pretend glare. "And she's carrying this ugly-as-balls crochet bucket bag from, like, 1994, and naturally Bianchi is like, 'Who the hell is this girl? Explain this hideous purse to me!' So then Gwen opens the bag, pulls out a six-pack of *Pabst fucking Blue Ribbon*, and says, 'It wouldn't fit in my Fendi.'"

The table exploded in laughter.

"'It wouldn't fit in my Fendi'!" Bjorn roared. "I still don't understand how she even found PBR in Europe! Anyway, Bianchi starts cracking up, and then we're all cracking up, and fast-forward, I get a call from Bianchi's people—he's designing a bag to fit Gwen's fucking *beer*! 'The Gwen,' he's calling it!"

With a flourish, Bjorn produced a stack of Polaroid pictures of a boxy leather bag. It looked pretty ugly to me—too shiny, with too many buckles and accents. But then, I found the world-famous Birkin ugly as well.

While everyone clamored over the photos, American Psycho eyed Gwen like she was a seventy-five-dollar steak. A powerful urge to break his nose with a wine bottle surged through me. The thought of his expensive clothes covered in blood was intoxicating. I could almost smell the iron, my imagination was so graphically vivid.

I stood abruptly.

"I'm going to the bar," I said to Gwen, and she nodded.

Inside, the restaurant was quieter and less crowded. Winter was cruel in Montreal, and we'd all be driven indoors soon enough.

"Un whisky, s'il vous plaît," I said to the bartender. "Rye."

I always got good service in restaurants; with my dark suits and slicked-back hair, I presented as richer than I was. The whiskey arrived immediately and I downed it.

"Jo? Hey, Jo Scottish! Wow! What are the odds?"

I whirled around, whiskey in hand, and saw the squat figure of Mr. Boil, standing in the doorway of the restaurant.

"Are you following me?" I demanded.

"No, no! Just a happy coincidence, that's all. Hey, *gar-son*! How about a martini over here!"

The martini materialized quickly—far too quickly, it seemed. I was drunker than I'd realized. Mr. Boil launched into a stream of chatter, of which I caught only half, like a car weaving in and out of radio signal.

". . . I'm a relationships guy, you know? I was put on this earth to connect people. Like me and you! We're *connected*. I've been watching the Lac-Froid case closely."

At the mention of Lac-Froid, I felt the hairs on the back of my neck stand up. "Sir, who *are* you?"

"Me? I'm just a guy who likes to keep up with current events! You know, if you ask me, old Montagne's verdicts have taken a pretty weird turn since you arrived on the scene, eh? I couldn't believe my ears when I heard that he ruled in favor of a gun manufacturer last year. That was your handiwork, I presume. You know, I think you've got a great gig, Ms. Scottish. Why be a lawyer when you can be the judge? Kick up your feet, whisper verdicts into an old man's ear. Tell you the truth, I think Canada's gotten a little pussified, you know what I mean? Père Noël my ass. It's a country, not a charity."

I needed an escape route, fast. I tried to get the bartender's attention, but he was at the other end of the room, shaking cocktails for a husband and wife who looked like they'd wandered into the Gay Village by mistake.

". . . you know? You devote your whole life to raising a kid, and *BAM*!" Mr. Boil smacked the bar, startling me. "It's all over. Bad enough thinking about those kids. Guts chewed out, literally eaten alive. But you know what kills me? The parents. You raise a kid, put all this energy into it, and what happens? Wolf food."

Finally I caught the bartender's eye. "Excusez-moi? Cet homme, il me harcèle."

Mr. Boil tried to avert the conflict, holding up his hands and saying jovially, "Hey, hey, it's all cool, man!" but there was no question whose side the bartender was going to take.

"Sir, pay your bill and get out," the bartender ordered, like in the Old West. Mr. Boil slapped a twenty on the bar.

"Fine. You make a shitty martini anyway." He started walking away.

"If I see your face again, I'm calling the police!" I shouted after him. Mr. Boil didn't look back at me.

"Je suis très désolé," the bartender said apologetically once he was gone.

"Ça va, ça va," I assured him. I paid for my whiskey and went back out to the patio, where the crowd seemed to have only grown gayer and louder and more explosively colorful.

"I need to leave," I whispered in Gwen's ear. "Stay if you want, but I'm going."

She looked at her plate. "The food just got here . . . Well, whatever." She dumped her French onion pie into a napkin and shoved it in her purse.

"Whoa!" Zach yelled. "Did you see that? She's like a homeless lady!"

Bjorn whacked Zach hard in the chest.

"Bye, everyone," Gwen said. It was one of my favorite things about her: when she was ready to go, she was ready to go.

"Why are you leaving?" American Psycho whined. "Don't be lame."

He reached after her and caught her wrist. My whole body went rigid.

"Don't fucking touch her, you piece of shit," I snarled, giving his chest a hard shove.

Instantly he was on his feet. I heard the scrape of chairs and a glass shattering as the table rocked violently. A vein throbbed at the center of American Psycho's perfectly symmetrical forehead.

"I'll pulverize you, you skinny dyke."

"Don't touch her, don't talk to her, don't *look* at her."

Bjorn leapt between us. "Whoa, whoa, everybody cool it!"

All around us, people were staring. Gwen plunked down at the table with a sigh. I almost expected her to take out some knitting while she waited for me to finish being a total nutjob.

Oh god, I thought, mortified. I knew, on some level, that my threat perception was blunted. Too many fistfights with addled assholes on "the streets." Too many run-ins with crazy people who were sometimes bluffing, sometimes not. I'd clawed my way back to the civilized world, only to find the ordeal had made me completely unfit to live there.

I turned to Bjorn, my hand still twitching. "I'm . . . I'm sorry, okay? Just get this guy out of my face. We're leaving."

Within minutes, Gwen and I were in a cab. She stared out the window, the excess of rainbows dropping away as we sped from the Village.

"That was a fifteen-thousand-dollar gig you just flushed down the toilet," she said.

"I don't want you working with that guy. I don't like him."

"You don't like anyone."

We'd lived in the same drafty attic apartment for six years, never upgrading even as our paychecks increased. It had a sharp, peaked roof and unfinished floors (we'd had to cover the entire place in carpets like a Bedouin tent, we got so many splinters). The kitchen was cramped, but we had a bed with a box spring and a real headboard. After years of sleeping on mattresses thrown on the floor, I considered the headboard a symbol of domestic stability and success.

Neither of us had any desire to address the calamitous therapy session or my blow-up at American Psycho. We were steps away from becoming one of those couples who avoid speaking to each other because *every single subject* is so loaded that even the most basic conversation can result in catastrophe. They never get divorced, those couples. They just gradually lower their standards for an acceptable level of human connection until one of them dies.

Gwen checked her voice mails. "It's Bjorn," she groaned. "That guy still wants me. He doubled the offer."

It didn't surprise me. For a certain type of douchebag, knowing he couldn't have something was the entire point of wanting it.

"But I don't think I'm gonna do it. The internet is for losers. Who wants their face on a *website*?"

I didn't want Gwen's face on *anything*. The peril of her becoming famous was so obvious it felt absurd to have to point it out. *One more job, then she has to stop*—so I'd told myself about her last five jobs.

Gwen fished the onion pie out of her purse and tossed it in the microwave.

"Want to hear something funny? Bjorn says no one wants to buy a bag from an old bag. So they're going to tell everyone I'm twenty-four."

"Ha."

Our two fields promoted opposite values: beauty and experience. Twenty-eight was useless in either direction—too old to be the fresh new thing, too young to be accomplished. According to our passports and papers, we were thirty-one. Canada was barely better than America at managing homeless youths; I'd figured that out as soon as we crossed the border. The best way to survive was to cheat ahead, to disappear as quickly as possible into university and adulthood.

"It's a total waste," Gwen said, licking her buttery fingers, "since you don't even like younger women. I can't wait to be a mean old hag. Then you'll finally love me."

I rolled my eyes. *Diane* was fucking child's play, we both knew. Our real issue was buried under layers of Dianes and cats and bullshit: How much of our love was *love*, as opposed to the chokehold of our secrets?

Now I understand that all lovers face this question at a certain point, that marriage is, at the end of the day, a pact between two people who agree to see the absolute worst of each other and continue on at risk of mutually assured annihilation. But at the age of twenty-eight I was still enough of a child to think my problems unique.

XXXIV

I PLAYED A SICK GAME ON THE METRO SOMETIMES: WHO IS THE Worst Person on This Train? Most days it was me; the premeditated murder of a minor was a tough sin to beat. But occasionally I imagined some evil in my fellow passengers that rivaled even mine. That man with the mustache and the leather briefcase? He was a serial rapist. The woman in pink scrubs reading Mary Higgins Clark? She'd killed a family of three in a drunk-driving incident and fled the scene.

By Hollywood standards I hadn't done anything wrong, I told myself sometimes. How many bad guys had Magnum, P.I., killed in the course of the show? Fifty? A hundred? I couldn't recall him ever struggling with his conscience.

Recently, *The Crow* had come out on DVD. Gwen loved it and watched it all the time. But I'd been disturbed by its premise: that revenge-seeking was mystical and imbued one with supernatural powers. Maybe Gwen thought I'd been guided by a magical bird when I shot her brother point-blank in the face. It was about as sensical as my actual reasons, which at this point felt hazy. Had I thought killing Dodge would bring Éclair back? Had I been under the impression that "he started it" was exculpatory in a court of law?

As time passed, I'd sort of retconned the whole thing in my mind, placing outsized emphasis on what Gwen had said, that Dodge would follow her to the ends of the earth. *That* had been my single, pure motive: to protect Gwen. Because surely I hadn't been so pointlessly barbaric as to commit murder for no legitimate reason.

When I got to the office, I checked Montagne's email account (he was easily flummoxed by computers and had given me his password long ago), followed by my own. At the top of my inbox was a message from Patrice.

From: pmtribble@yahoo.com
To: joscottish@casuperiorcourts.gov

Subject: HOW DARE YOU

I am simply irate. I simply cannot believe you took my father to a separatist gathering last night. What goes through your brain? I simply want to know. Do you wake up in the morning and think, "I wonder how I can dismantle a fine man's legacy today. I wonder what I can do to humiliate and degrade a fine man in his final years"? If I find out that you have taken my father to another such embarrassing event, I will be speaking to Chief Justice Durant about having you removed from your position.

Patrice Montagne Tribble

I deleted the message without replying. It wasn't the first time Patrice had threatened to go to the chief justice with her complaints. But any action on Durant's part would open them all up to a lawsuit. The tables had turned for the gays, especially up here in Canada. We could have whatever we wanted—the job, the wife, the house, the kids—and anyone who got in our way could expect a lawsuit up the ass. It was a pretty unromantic state of affairs, considering that the whole basis of our group was supposedly love.

I crossed the foyer into Montagne's office, giving the door a polite rap with my knuckles.

"Did you tell Patrice about the party last night?" I asked. It wasn't like him to rat me out.

Montagne was staring out the window. The pages of the newspaper he'd been reading were littered across the carpet.

"Monsieur?"

I went to his desk and hovered my hand over the cup of Earl Grey tea on the coaster. It had gone cold. I looked at Montagne. His expression had taken on a foggy quality, which I had come to see as a sign that we were in for a hard day. His mental lapses, at one time infrequent, were now an almost weekly occurrence.

"Shall we cancel the morning?" I suggested, keeping a light tone. "I can work it out with Narimane."

Narimane was Montagne's sharp-as-a-tack secretary, whom I'd come to rely on intensely. Together, we kept the office running and managed Montagne's increasingly unpredictable acuity.

"Hmm?" Montagne's eyes flickered to alertness. "Non, I'm quite all right."

I studied him. "Can you tell me the testimony we'll be hearing today?"

He shot me an annoyed look. "The ecological expert, as you know perfectly well. Why are you quizzing me like a child?"

"Bien, bien," I said, picking up the mess of newspapers from the floor.

The ecological expert was an American named Ron Winston from the Environmental Defense Fund. He was young, clean-cut, and handsome, defying the stereotype of the crunchy old tree-hugger. He had been called by Mr. O'Day, the attorney for Protecteurs de Prédateurs, the organization that had filed the suit against Lac-Froid.

"The defense has stated that the wolves in question have no value and pose an imminent threat to the community of Lac-Froid," began Mr. O'Day. "Do you agree with that assessment?"

"I do not," Mr. Winston said. "Wolves and other large predators provide incredible value to ecosystems."

"How is that?"

"Here's an example. In 1995, a pack of wolves was released into Yellowstone National Park. The effects of this were nothing short of miraculous. The wolves kept the deer population in check, and as a result, we saw increases in insect and bird populations. A species of beaver that had been extinct in the area returned. The rabbit and mice populations increased, which in turn increased the population of foxes, badgers, weasels, even bald eagles."

"So, a bunch more animals," Mr. O'Day summed up. "That's nice, I'm sure, but how does this help the citizens of Lac-Froid, who have lost their children?"

"The loss of life at Lac-Froid is tragic and horrible," Mr. Winston said. "But strong, stable ecosystems benefit *everyone*. The balance of predator and prey benefits *everyone*."

"So you do not believe that the solution is to eradicate the wolves."

"I do not. That would be a reaction, not a solution. The problem is not the wolves. The problem is the unchecked way that humans interfere with ecosystems."

Mr. O'Day switched the slide on the projector. "If I may turn the court's attention to exhibit—"

"I was just thinking..." Montagne said out of nowhere.

Everyone froze, as if an unseen viewer with a remote control had pressed "pause." Even Samantha, the court reporter, seemed frozen. I gave her a little nod. *Keep typing.*

"When I was a young boy in Saint-Michel-de-Bellechasse," he said, with the air of a man on his deathbed revealing a long-held secret, "my elder brother and I would ice-skate on the lake. One day the ice cracked, and I fell in. Frigid cold water, cold as death. Terrible, icy pain. My brother, Jacques ... he saved me. He grabbed my hand and pulled me out. It's only because of him that I am alive. But when he needed saving, over there in Sicily, I wasn't there. He drowned, you know. His ship was attacked by a Nazi submarine. He took my place . . . in the cold depths of the water."

The whole room waited in tense silence. I cleared my throat loudly, which seemed to get Montagne's attention. He looked out at the courtroom as though a cloud had passed, and suddenly he could see us again.

Mr. O'Day took the cue to say, "Thank you, Monsieur le juge, for that very moving anecdote."

Montagne nodded, seemingly confused as to how we had arrived at this juncture. "Bien, bien. Please go ahead with the exhibit."

The rest of the day proceeded normally. Back at the office, I asked Narimane to get me a copy of the court transcript.

"Just the 'anecdote,'" I said. "Samantha will know what that means."

I studied it in my office, looking for anything that either side could declare prejudicial or that could be red-flagged in an appeal.

It was not my first introduction to Montagne's older brother. Montagne had told me recently (with an air of great secrecy, as if it could ruin him) that after Jacques's death, he'd lied about his age in order to enlist in the Royal Navy and kill Nazis in his brother's honor. But then the war ended, and that was that. He'd told me this story wistfully, as if fate had robbed him of something. I'd replied only, "Sounds like you were lucky."

At the end of the day, I found Montagne in our usual spot in the library, unwrapping a pair of Romeo y Julietas and cranking the window open. I knew better than to mention the incident in the courtroom; depending on his state of mind, it would either embarrass or further confuse him.

I struck a match and lit both cigars at once, a trick that always made Montagne laugh and call me a gangster. Suppressing a cough, I handed him one.

"Did you read that memo from HR?" I asked him.

"I did. I suppose you'll be rethinking your birthday gift to me."

I always gave Montagne a bottle of Madrigal cologne by Molinard, a woody scent that had been around since 1935. But a memo was being circulated that, starting in 2006, no perfumes, deodorants, or scented lotions were to be used, as a person with a perfume allergy was going to be working in the building.

"I think it's ridiculous," I said. "How many people come in and out of this building? Hundreds every day? And we all have to bend over backward to accommodate a single person's dysfunction?"

"Oh, be generous," Montagne said. "What would you have this woman do? Live as a recluse in a cave?"

"If a person isn't equipped for normal life, they shouldn't be part of it," I said. "No one ever went out of their way for me, that's for damn sure."

"And don't you wish they had?" Montagne said. "Don't you wish the world had been kinder to a young orphan?"

Montagne knew the gist of the hardscrabble story Gwen and I told—that we were among the many youths abandoned by a cult leader in the early nineties (the "Lost Children," as the papers called them).

"I don't make wishes," I said. "I live in the world."

"But the world is what we make it, non?"

I exhaled a long plume of smoke. Montagne seemed so completely himself. It was hard to believe that mere hours before he'd committed such a blunder in his own courtroom.

"You know what your problem is, ma rebelle?" He gave me a wry, appraising look. "You don't see your life as charmed."

I heard myself scoff. "Charmed?"

"Yes, quite charmed," he said. "Lucky."

"Lucky?" I echoed. "Surely you're joking. We were on the streets, you know. We had nothing."

"And look at you now! Smoking a fine cigar in illustrious company, if I do say so."

"I wouldn't call that *luck*, monsieur. I put myself through school. I worked like a dog. I got here through my own intelligence—"

"Ahh," he interrupted me. "But where did that intelligence come from? You didn't spring from the ground like a turnip, did you? Like any person, you came from your parents, whoever they were."

My face must have changed, because Montagne became apologetic.

"Je suis désolé, I don't mean to tread on a sensitive area. I'm only saying, some people aren't as lucky as you, to be born with such a great mind. You think people choose to be stupid?"

"Yes," I said. "I absolutely do."

Montagne laughed. It was his privilege to be generous, I thought, to always believe that in his darkest hour the hand of life would reach into the waters and pull him to safety. If that same hand reached for me, I would probably kick it away, certain it meant to drag me further down.

It was also his privilege to see me as damaged but essentially innocent. Sometimes I imagined confessing everything to him. In my fantasy, he would touch my face with his aristocratic hand and say, *Ma rebelle, don't trouble yourself. I already knew.*

But if he did know me—the real me, the girl who'd killed a boy in cold blood, run away, and brought the stink of it into this office—he'd have no choice but to call the authorities. And while we waited for them to arrive (assuming I didn't run for it), I doubted he'd care to look me in the eye, much less touch my face.

XXXV

THAT EVENING, THE APARTMENT WAS COMPLETELY CLEAN WHEN I came home, and a glass of wine sat waiting for me on the dining room table next to that day's issue of *Le Devoir*. I looked around in surprise. Gwen hated housework and was easily oppressed by domestic chores—no doubt an unhealed wound from her "Cinderella" days in Vermont. I assumed this was her way of telling me she forgave me for the therapy debacle and my near brawl with American Psycho.

"This wine is good," I told her, taking a long sip. "What bottle did you open?"

Gwen shrugged. "I don't know. Someone left it at the door downstairs."

She handed it over, and my eyes widened as I took in the crimson capsule, the immaculate off-white label with its elegant cursive print. It was a 1982 Le Pin Pomerol Bordeaux.

"Oh my god. Oh my god!" I set the bottle on the table and backed away from it like it was a bomb.

"What? Is it poisoned?" Gwen's face had gone white. "Oh my god. Give me some. I won't let you die alone."

I wanted to laugh, but I was too flabbergasted. "Gwen, this is, like, a ten-thousand-dollar bottle of wine."

Gwen snorted a laugh, then stopped. "Wait, you're joking, right?"

I was laughing, too, out of shock. "Tell me you didn't buy this for me, Gwen. It's too much!"

"I didn't!" she insisted. "It was downstairs with the mail! It had a little note around the neck." She went to the kitchen and brought it back.

To Jo Scottish, with my most sincere wishes.—H.B.

"Who's H.B.?" Gwen asked. "I figured it was one of your law people."

"Oh, shit. He's a guy who's trying to bribe me. He's from the mining company. And we opened it, which means we can't give it back."

Gwen had the quickest tear ducts of anyone I'd ever met. Her eyes could go from crystal clear to brimming over in less than a second.

"I'm so sorry," she squeaked.

"It's all right. It's fine. I'll deal with it." I put my arm around her, trying to seem calm while internally panicking. *Shit. Shit. Shit.*

She squirmed away. "You don't have to downplay it, Jo. If it's a problem, just let me help."

I held up my hands. "Fine, what do you propose?"

"I'll buy a new bottle. I have the money."

I shook my head. "You can't find this in a store. We'd have to wait for a bottle to pop up at a wine auction, probably in London or Hong Kong. It could be months. *Years.* And this has to be handled now."

"Why don't I just write him a check for ten thousand dollars, then?"

I shook my head again. "That would look like we bought the wine in a private sale. It would still seem like a favor and fuck up the case."

"We should just explain that it was an accident," Gwen said. "I'll back you up."

I thought about it. The truth could prove technically sufficient, but I had a reputation—fair or not—for being a snake. I couldn't think of anything snakier than enjoying the fruits of a bribe while shielding my ass from the consequences.

"I think," I said slowly, "tomorrow I'll recork it and send it back. I do feel bad for whoever winds up with it in the end, but half these collectors are posers anyway. They won't know the difference."

"But how will you make it look unopened?"

"I'll go to Jean-Luc at the Cosmopolitan."

"You trust him?"

"No. He's a crook. But that's how I know he'll do it."

Gwen took a deep breath. "And you're not mad at me?"

"No, I'm not mad. Come on, we may as well drink it."

As I poured two glasses—carefully, so as not to spill a single drop on the label—Gwen shook her head.

"Don't waste it, Jo. It all tastes the same to me."

I pressed the glass into her hand. "This wine stuff, it's just a mindset. Honestly, most expert sommeliers can't even tell the difference in blind taste tests. Wine is about the *experience*. It's about enjoying something because it's rare. I say we drink it and have sex."

Gwen laughed, blushing. I was rarely, if ever, so blunt in my proposals. We had the sex life of a middle-aged couple; sex was an *event*, not a routine occurrence. This was partly normal and marital in nature, but partly something else. How do you make love to someone who watched you kill a person? I had no recollection of our first time; it was blacked out by the ink stain of my memory loss. And in the years since, I'd never figured out a way to ask Gwen how she was capable of loving a murderer without suggesting there was something wrong with her.

On the surface I had my force field of rationales (it was justified; the system had failed me; society was better off without Dodge Roach in it). Underneath, though, there were doubts. Had I enjoyed it too much? Had obliterating a human face and leaving the body on the ground like trash brought me too much pleasure? Any pleasure at all constituted too much in my view. The line between carnal ecstasy and carnal violence seemed so thin and poorly demarcated it took some amount of conviction for me to want to go there at all.

Getting drunk helped.

The wine was extreme—a bomb of dark fruits ripened to the point of obscenity. It exploded over the tongue, leaving a long, velvety finish. Gwen could typically drink me under the table, but tonight she was flushed and falling over after two glasses.

"You know how people have their song?" she said, her lips stained purple.

"What people?"

"Couples."

"Oh, sure."

"We don't have a song, but we have a movie. You know what it is?"

"What?"

"*Alien*."

I burst into drunken laughter. "Why?"

"Because it was our first date."

Jesus, I thought. If our first date had happened when we were ten, that meant we'd been in a relationship for *eighteen years*. In terms of genre, I'd always put my life in the bleak drama category, but it occurred to me now that it quite possibly belonged in *romance*. We were a love story, Gwen and me, the kind that earned free bottles of champagne at cheesy restaurants and powered a weary world's tenderly (desperately) held belief in soul mates. Hadn't we made it through bad luck and horror, death, the streets? Weren't we sipping one of the rarest French wines in existence? It didn't get more romantic than this.

"You know what I think?" I said, swirling my glass drunkenly. "I think you orchestrated this whole thing to put me in a mind to propose to you."

Gwen's face went stony. "Here we go," she said bitterly. "You always think I'm *manipulating* you."

"Whoa. I was just joking—"

"In every jest is a bit of truth."

It wasn't too late to backpedal and get the romance back on track. But instead, I doubled down.

"Just admit it," I said. "You want to get married."

I could barely say the words without the image of a blood-splattered wedding dress assaulting my mind. Even talking about it felt like inviting an ancient curse.

"Admit it? *Admit it?*" Gwen repeated. "You make it sound like some dark secret. So what if I want to get married? Why shouldn't I? I want to pick out colors and have a ridiculously huge cake and all that shit. Every other girl gets to do it."

I shook my head. "You don't know what you're asking. You don't understand what could happen."

She blinked. "What's that supposed to mean? What the fuck could happen?"

I was hardly about to tell her that a murderer could jump out of the wedding cake and unload bullets into her brain. Jesus, what was wrong with me?

So I ignored the question, pointing at her drunkenly and saying, "You started it, with those blue ballpoint circles! I don't even *remember* them, but you said it happened!"

"I have no clue what you're talking about right now." Gwen stalked to the kitchen to grab a bag of Old Dutch ketchup chips.

"Don't eat those, you'll spoil your palate."

"Don't tell me what to do." She ripped the bag open. "Why are you even in this relationship, Jo? You obviously aren't attracted to me, and you think I'm some manipulative bitch—"

"Gwen. Stop. I'm *extremely* attracted to you. I don't know if you've noticed, but I'm a pretty despicable person. I'm shallow. I don't have morals. If I thought you were ugly, I would leave you."

I hated, *hated*, the words coming out of my mouth. They were awful and untrue. Gwen could never be ugly to me, no matter how she looked. But this whole thing had veered into catastrophe so quickly I felt scrambled and dim-witted.

Gwen glowered. "Wow, that makes me feel better."

I set my wineglass down so hard I was surprised it didn't shatter. "What do I have to do to convince you that I love you, Gwen? I killed someone for you!"

They were the words we never said out loud. I'd deployed them purely to get a reaction, but Gwen just rolled her eyes.

"What?!" I demanded. "I did!"

"Whatever you want to tell yourself, Jo, I don't care. But you did it for yourself. You did it for Éclair. We both know that." Her face was defiant, contradicting the way she clutched the bag of chips like it was a life preserver.

"You think I *wanted* to do that? You think I enjoyed it? That's sick, Gwen. I can't get married to someone who thinks I'm a bloodthirsty killer."

"I never said that!" she hissed. "Don't put words in my mouth! And anyway, according to you, I'm a horrible, manipulative mastermind, so I guess we're a match made in heaven."

I rubbed my face. "Gwen, for god's sake. All I do is try to keep you out of harm's way, and all you do is roll your eyes and act like I'm trying to ruin your life."

She immediately started rolling her eyes again. "I'm sorry, but it's actually not helpful to me that you think everyone we meet is a psycho killer. It actually stresses me out. A lot!"

"It's hardly Zen meditation for me, either! But if I'd been more vigilant—"

Gwen cut me off. "Jo, you have to stop driving yourself insane. There's *nothing* you could have done to save Éclair. You'd just be dead, too."

"That's not true! I killed him, didn't I?" Remembering the neighbors, I lowered my voice to a barely contained whisper. "If I hadn't left her alone in the house that night, I could have done it *then* instead of four months later, when it was completely pointless!"

Gwen shook her head intensely. "No, you couldn't have. I don't know how to say this right, but you only killed him because he killed her first. It was like . . . a superpower that got unleashed."

"Oh my god." I realized I was trembling. "If you say one more word about superpowers—"

"I *just said* I didn't know how to say it right. God, I fucking hate you sometimes! You don't listen to me!"

"All right, Gwen, I'm listening. Tell me more about what a super-hero I am for shooting a teenager who was too blackout drunk to sit up straight."

Gwen screamed—a throaty, bestial *growl* of a scream. Then she burst into tears and ran into the bedroom, slamming the door behind her.

Fuck. All my pent-up, resentful energy went whooshing out of me like air from a punctured tire.

"Gwen?" I called, my voice five octaves higher. "Gwen, I'm sorry. Please come out. I'm so sorry. I'm just drunk and freaking out. It's that fucking therapist's fault. Don't jump out the window. Don't do anything extreme. Please, Gwen."

I heard her heave a sigh on the other side of the door. "I'm lying in bed with a pillow on my face. I'm not doing anything extreme. Leave me alone, Jo."

I listened at the door but heard only silence. Wiping the tears from my eyes before they could multiply, I staggered over to the bottle of Le Pin on the dining room table. A sip's worth of wine had pooled at the bottom. Doing a quick mental calculation, at $10,000 a bottle, I valued the sip at $300.

I poured it down the sink.

XXXVI

THE NEXT MORNING I WOKE UP ON THE SOFA, DESPISING THE CLI-
ché of it. A miserable rain drizzled down outside, and I had a headache.
I disliked being hungover as much as the next person, but I couldn't
deny it held a kind of masochistic relish, like inhaling the scent of a
loved one's old sweater. Hangovers and Éclair were inexorably linked in
my mind. As a kid, I hadn't understood why she wore sunglasses at 9:00
A.M. or needed all the blinds to be closed, but I got it now.

The empty Le Pin stood by the sink, evidence of the awful turn the
night had taken. A picture of how it should have been flashed through
my mind: the bottle's final sip savored, our affections passionately re-
newed, a different version of myself who wouldn't have ruined it all.

I cracked open the bedroom door to make sure Gwen was there.
She was out like a light, tangled in the sheets. Gwen could sleep like the
dead, an ability I envied. I didn't expect her to be up for hours.

I was not looking forward to dealing with Jean-Luc at the Cosmopolitan. His story was a strange one: in the early '90s, he'd gone to
prison for assaulting a customer who'd accused him of selling a fake
Colgin rare vintage. When he returned, his shop was on the brink of
ruin. But in a bizarre deus ex machina, the 1995 "Soup Nazi" episode
of *Seinfeld* aired, and somehow Jean-Luc became locally known as the
"Wine Nazi." Overnight he went from a man accused of fraud to a man
of such unassailable expertise that he'd earned the right to be irascible.
As a person who had shed her own ugly past, I was acutely aware when

other people did it, like a spy recognizing other spies in the front lines of battle.

The little bell tinkled as I opened the door to the shop.

"Salut, Jo!" David, Jean-Luc's assistant, was always bright and eager, as if to counteract the notorious crankiness of his boss.

"Salut, David."

"And did you enjoy the Le Pin?"

I froze. Was it written on my forehead or something? Then I realized he was talking about the 2000, not the 1982.

"Very much," I said.

"I had so much fun helping Gwen pick it out. We may make a wine lover out of her yet!"

"Don't count on it," I said. Especially not after last night.

As if on cue, Jean-Luc thundered out of the back room. He was a thick-set, mean-faced old man with a bushy mustache and a big nose, the very picture of a French asshole.

"Jean-Luc, may I speak with you privately?" I asked him.

He gave me an unhospitable glare.

"It's a delicate matter." I opened my bag and allowed him a peek of the Le Pin. He squinted at it, then at me.

"Come on." He led me to his office, a cramped space piled with disorganized stacks of paper and various editions of *The World Atlas of Wine*. He closed the door and sat behind his desk, gesturing to a metal folding chair.

"I need help," I said, sitting. "I need to give this bottle a new lease on life." I set the empty Le Pin on the desk.

"How dare you suggest I could possibly help you in that regard," he said flatly. He picked up the bottle and turned it over in his hands. "You know what happened to the last person to suggest my wines were inauthentic."

"I do," I replied, "which is why I have a gun."

He barked a harsh, scornful laugh. "This is Canada! No one has a gun."

I lifted my suit jacket, revealing an ugly, plastic-looking Glock holstered under my arm. I'd bought it years ago, illegally, back when Gwen was getting hormones off the streets. This had involved expeditions into the city's seediest corners, places where people regularly got killed. I was incredibly relieved when Gwen met a trans photographer who hooked her up with a reputable doctor. I should have thrown the gun in the river at that point, but I hadn't.

Jean-Luc stopped laughing. He picked up the empty bottle. "You are asking me to pollute the market. I have too much respect for wine to ever do this. Besides, how can I know this is not, eh, how do you call it, the trapment? You are a lawyer, yes?"

"Yes, I'm a lawyer. And lawyers never do their own dirty work, which is how you can be sure this is not entrapment."

Jean-Luc continued to appraise me.

"I'll give you one thousand dollars."

He scoffed. "You insult me."

"I'm not selling it," I assured him. "I'm just rectifying a mistake. No one's making any money on this deal except for you. I'll go as high as fifteen hundred, and that's it."

"Fine. You brought the cork and the capsule? I need to copy them."

"Yes." I fished both out of the bag and handed them over.

"You come back on Monday. Money now. All of it."

I handed him the cash.

Outside, the rain had stopped, but the mood was still gloomy. I was about to duck down the stairs to the metro station when a person caught my eye. He was bald and mouselike and held a camera pointed in my direction. It was the same man I'd caught watching me in Old Town, I was sure of it.

The second our eyes met, he lowered the camera and started walking in the other direction.

"Hey!" I shouted. "Hey!"

I dashed across the street, half hearing a car screech to a halt and honk behind me. I thought I'd lost the man, but then I saw his bald head turn the corner of a narrow alleyway. I bolted after him and seized him by the collar of his jacket.

"Pourquoi tu me suis?"

I pushed him hard against the brick wall. He was much smaller than me, quite diminutive for a man. A large bag hung from his shoulder, so large I was surprised he didn't tip over from its weight. He was panting and saying frantically in a voice that sounded American, "No français! English! I'm a tourist! Take my wallet, just don't hurt me."

"I'm not mugging you," I snapped at him. "*You* were following *me*!"

"I—I—just take the money!"

I pinned him to the wall with one hand. With the other I fumbled with the zipper of his bag and reached into it. It contained at least four camera lenses.

"You're not a tourist," I said. "Tourists don't carry telephoto lenses."

"I'm a birder!" he explained breathlessly. "I photograph migrations. Take the lenses. They're worth more than the camera!"

"You're lying," I hissed. "It's *July*. It's not migration season. Tell me why you're following me."

"You—you have me confused with someone. I swear I don't know who you are."

"Then why did you run?" I demanded.

"Because you chased me! Because you're crazy! Help! Somebody, help!"

A man walking past the alleyway stopped tentatively. "*Ça va?*" he called, squinting at us.

"She's harassing me!" the bald man yelled. "Help!"

"Should I call the police?" the man in the street called out. *So fucking Canadian,* I thought. Always asking for permission.

"We're fine!" I yelled. Then I turned to the bald man. "If I see your face again, I will hunt you down. Stay away from me."

I gave him a final shove against the wall and stalked out of the alley-way, not looking back. The first cab I spotted, I jumped in and told the driver to take me to my neighborhood.

"The long way," I said. "Through the park."

The whole ride I looked out the back window, scanning every car. I had the driver drop me four blocks from the apartment and waited until he was long gone before I walked home. My heart had been racing for thirty minutes, as if I were on some faddish, anxiety-induced cardio-vascular regimen.

As I opened the apartment door, I heard the TV flicker off. Gwen was awake. I set the gun down on the kitchen counter and tried to catch my breath. Had I just assaulted a stranger in an alleyway? Which was more likely, that I was being stalked by a tiny bald man, or that I'd fi-nally, truly snapped?

Gwen spoke before I could say anything. "Can we not be in a fight, please?"

"Fine with me," I answered.

She sighed with profound relief, as if everything were resolved and not merely shoved under the rug. We'd done this routine before, and the amazing part was that both of us would feel genuinely shocked the next time the same fight leapt out at us with no warning, baring the same ugly teeth.

She spied the Glock on the counter and smiled, as if the sight of the weapon brought back memories of dear and treasured times.

"Aw, Gunnie!" she exclaimed. "I haven't seen Ol' Gunnie in ages."

It alarmed me the way she did this, romanticizing our years on the streets, speaking of them fondly ("Remember the funny crack whore who set my hair on fire?" "Remember Scar Face, that snuggly old dog?" "Remember when we couldn't find Karl and everyone said he train-hopped to Vancouver, but he was just tripping balls two blocks from the warehouse and couldn't remember his own name?").

I remembered things differently: gritty, grainy, black and white. The freezing cold; the time I got caught stealing a GED prep book and was almost arrested, which would have been the end of the story right there; being hungry, lost; trying to hang on to Gwen's hand; trying to study in the noisy chaos of some children's shelter; the scary pimps who'd follow Gwen for blocks, taunting her, "You wanna be a girl? Be a girl and suck some dick. I'll make you rich, baby." Compulsively appraising the physicality of everyone I met: Could I take that guy? Could I take *that* guy? All the mentally ill people with the same, delusional story: "And I wanted to be free, so here I am, living the dream!" The dream of trash and drugs and listlessness and days that blurred together as society rendered you invisible and hopeless and powerless to regain control of your existence. I didn't know why it was so clear to me and not to Gwen. But some days I half expected to come home and find a note from her on the countertop: *I got sick of you and decided to go back to the streets.*

ON MONDAY, I FILED TWO REPORTS DETAILING THE SEPARATE IN-
stances of harassment. I recounted everything exactly as it had occurred
with two critical exceptions: I did not mention that the bottle of Le Pin
had been opened, nor did I mention that in the confrontation in the
alley, I had been carrying an illegal firearm.

I watched Montagne's face as he read them over carefully at his
desk.

"So two men have followed you," he summed up. "The first one,
this Harold Boil, mentioned Northcore specifically."

"Yes."

"And you still have the bottle he gave you?"

"It's at my apartment, yes," I lied.

"But this second man claimed he did not know you."

"Correct."

"D'accord." He looked up from the report, and I saw a teasing
sparkle in his eye. "You're telling me you had a 1982 Le Pin in your
apartment all weekend and you didn't even touch it? Mon dieu. You're
a better man than I."

After court I went straight to the Cosmopolitan, looking over my
shoulder every five seconds. When David saw me, he waved me over and
pulled a cylindrical container out from under the table. I popped the
top off, holding my breath and praying to an unspecified deity that I
hadn't forked over $1,500 for nothing.

"Ça va?" David asked.

I exhaled with relief. "C'est beau." The bottle looked as though it had never been opened. Fresh cork, gleaming crimson capsule. I turned it over in my hands. The work was flawless.

"That's an incredible acquisition," David said, eyeing the label. He tried to seem nonchalant, but he was practically bouncing with excitement.

"I'm just babysitting it, unfortunately. I have to give it up tomorrow."

"How terrible," David said, sounding genuinely upset. "To be near such beauty and never taste it."

I laughed falsely. "I know. It's like some medieval morality test."

I tucked the container under my arm and hopped on the metro. *Thank god,* I thought, grateful to have it over and done with.

Then, halfway home, my ears pricked like a dog hearing a high-pitched whistle.

Someone on the train had uttered a set of syllables that made my whole body go rigid. It was just a word, one that had never suited me, evoking a frilly, delicate girl; a doily; chastity; a wedding gown.

Maybe someone on the train was speaking English and describing a dress, I told myself. It had happened before—one of Gwen's people dropping the word in regard to a piece of fabric, causing my heart to momentarily stop. No matter how many years passed, I couldn't suppress my primitive response to those syllables, that name I no longer considered my own but, infuriatingly, remained lodged inside me, waiting to be called upon.

"Lacey?"

The second time I heard it, I was certain.

"I can't believe it's you," the man said. An attractive man, his face boyish despite his age, which was at least forty-five.

I looked away, shaking my head. I couldn't speak. The train car lurched around a corner, making me briefly lose my balance.

"Don't you recognize me? It's me, Kevin."

"I—I don't know anyone named Kevin."

"Kevin Hantz, from Concord High School. I know you know me. Talk to me. I can't believe how crazy this is, running into you!"

"I don't admit to knowing who you are," I said, my heart pounding. "But if you meet me in forty-five minutes, I will speak to you."

He nodded eagerly. "Sure. Meet you where?"

"Poutineville," I said. It was the first place I could think of where I would never normally go. I explained to him what train to take and how to find the restaurant from the station.

"Of course, I'll be there—"

"Please stop talking to me right now and go to the other end of the car. When I leave, don't follow me. Wait and take the next train."

He opened his mouth, then thought better of it. He went to the other end of the car as I'd instructed and sat down in an empty seat next to a woman carrying a bucket full of cut flowers. I looked around the car—for what, I didn't know. Some sign that either of us was being followed?

The train stopped, and I got off with the flood of passengers. Once I was on the platform, a creepy feeling came over me, a calm numbness I now understand to be a sign of disassociation.

Perhaps you imagine me, in this moment, feverishly plotting what I would say to this man, how I would explain myself and my fourteen-year disappearance, how I would convince him to tell no one that he'd seen me. Perhaps you even imagine I was thinking of killing him. But in reality my mind was as dully indifferent as any commuter changing trains, perhaps realizing she'd left her briefcase at the office or deciding to catch that after-work drink after all.

The hostess seated me at a booth next to the window. I sat in a stupor for nearly a minute before I realized someone on the street might recognize me. I asked the waitress to reseat me near the back, ordered a glass of wine, then thought better of it and changed my order to black coffee. I knew I was acting shady; the waitress probably thought I was on cocaine. I was accustomed to the waiters at good restaurants downtown—always men, always handsome, witty, and gracious, expert at turning a simple dinner order into an extravaganza of wine, small plates, dessert, coffee, and port.

Poutineville was no such place. It was Poutineville. Ugly red vinyl booths, a television over the bar playing a soccer game, French-language covers of dated pop songs on the speakers (I'd heard the French versions of Rolling Stones songs so many times I'd forgotten what the originals even sounded like). Merely glancing at the menu made me ill: poutine with hot dogs, poutine with beef, poutine with nacho cheese, "Pizzapoutine," and, finally, "the biggest poutine in town," the Heart Attack: fifteen pounds of poutine, bacon, gravy, and fries, enough to feed an old-school Quebecois family of twelve. My love of Quebec had never managed to translate into love for its most famous dish. The slop too closely resembled the bowls of fatty gruel served up at soup kitchens, the grayish half food, half garbage Gwen and I had dug out of dumpsters when we couldn't find anything else.

Why had I chosen this godforsaken restaurant? The numb calm from the metro station lifted, revealing the panic underneath. Mr. Hantz was going to call the FBI. He was going to blackmail me. And worse than either of those things, he was going to make me think about my parents, those distant dramatis personae I couldn't stand to remember existed, the pain being too much—worse than the pain of thinking about Éclair, because I had deserted them while they were still alive.

I was gearing up to leave when he appeared.

"Lacey, hi." Mr. Hantz slid into the opposite side of the booth. "I wasn't sure you would actually show up. Thank you so much for meeting me."

"Call me Jo," I said reflexively. "My name is Jo."

"Just call me Jo-oh," he sang back. It was a Sinéad O'Connor song from 1987. I remembered my father listening to that album, Éclair com-

plaining that it sounded "like a boring funeral."

Two seconds in and already this conversation was too much.

"I'm glad you picked this place," Mr. Hantz said. "I'm dying to try poutine, but my wife's a real health nut. That's why I was on the train. We're on vacation, and she sent me out to find a macrobiotic grocer. We're only here six days, but god forbid we go without spelt." He gave a small eyeroll, looking over the menu excitedly, like we were old friends trying out a much buzzed-about restaurant rather than two estranged people in what amounted, in my mind, to a hostage situation.

"So you're married now?" I asked.

"Yes! And we've got two kids, a girl and a boy. Want to see them?"

I nodded, though in truth I did not. He pulled a pair of photos out of his wallet, and I tried to make the expected response. "Very beautiful."

"And look at you! You look amazing, Lacey. Sorry—*Jo*. I hardly recognized you. You must be doing well."

"I'm a . . . lawyer," I said. I hated how my voice sounded. I was certain Mr. Hantz would laugh. Me, a lawyer? I was a loathsome child pretending to be grown-up. Tears pricked at my eyes, and I found myself yearning for death in a way I hadn't since I was fourteen years old.

"That's amazing," Mr. Hantz said. I searched his face for some sign that he was being cruel or sarcastic but saw none.

"Are you still a guidance counselor?"

"Yes. Not in New Hampshire, though. I'm at a boarding school in Massachusetts. My wife's the Latin teacher. It's a beautiful school."

"That's nice," I said, and there was an awkward silence. He seemed different—less cool somehow. Still good-looking, but not the same Mr. Hantzsome who'd lived in London during the punk era. The Sinéad O'Connor reference he'd made earlier would have struck me as edgy back in the day; now it seemed kind of dorky. A joke a guidance counselor would make.

And yet, he terrified me. Every time he made the smallest motion,

I was certain he was producing a cell phone to call Interpol. *I found the long-lost Satan Daughter. She's been hiding out in the land of poutine the whole time.*

The waitress appeared, and Mr. Hantz hemmed and hawed over several of the menu options.

"They all taste the same," I said.

The waitress glared at me as if I'd personally insulted her.

"I'll have the Montrealer," he decided finally, pointing at the menu in case the waitress didn't speak English.

"Rien pour moi," I said, shaking my head. The waitress left, and I stared into my empty coffee cup, wishing I'd asked for a refill but fearing more caffeine would only increase my anxiety. As I was considering this, the mug toppled over with a clatter. I picked it up, knocking over the salt and pepper shakers in the process.

"Whoa, okay," Mr. Hantz said. "You can relax. Take a deep breath."

I hesitated, then did as he said.

"There you go. Drink some water. Do you want to order a beer or something?"

"Wine," I said. "But the waitress hates me. Waitresses always hate me."

"I wonder why you think that," Mr. Hantz said, getting her attention again. "A glass of wine for my friend? Jo, red or white?"

"Rouge," I answered. "Merci." I couldn't believe this man was ordering for me—in English—in *my* country where I actually spoke the language.

The wine came and I took a boorish gulp. Then I set the glass down.

"Are you going to call the police?" I asked, my voice barely a whisper. I stared at the table, too afraid to look him in the eye.

"What? No. Lacey—*Jo*, look at me."

I looked at him, but my eyes immediately flickered away.

"Listen to me. I always felt that I let you down that night, that I should have been a stronger man. You know what I'm talking about.

That night . . . that night I drove you home from the dance."

I took another gulp of wine, commanding myself not to cry. Across the restaurant, I heard a family laughing.

"I owe you," he was saying. "I will do anything for you."

It was a strange choice of words, almost amorous. I didn't know what to say.

He reached into his pocket and pulled out a pen. "I cheated on my wife last year with the mom of a student. This is her information." He scratched out a name and number on a paper napkin and pushed it across the table. "It's nothing compared to . . . to the way you have to trust me right now. But this would ruin my life. I'm giving it to you because I trust you. Can you trust me?"

I was crying, tears streaming silently down my cheeks, the way I'd learned to do at Germaine House and never unlearned.

"I can't," I said, shaking my head.

"You can," he said back. "We shared something, you and I, something so horrible we will always be connected."

I forced myself to look in his eyes, which were also gleaming with tears.

And I realized that for the last fourteen years, Mr. Hantz had never stopped thinking about me. All that blood. I'd never gotten over it; why should I assume he had? Not even Gwen understood the sheer level of mental strength I had to exert every single day to keep those images at bay. She was lucky that when we'd done away with Dodge, it had been too dark to see the blood.

How strange that this random man should understand the most vulnerable, shaken part of me.

"Okay," I said, because the other words, "I trust you," were too impossible. I wiped the tears from my face with a napkin.

"Does anyone else know that you're here?"

I shook my head.

"Do your parents know?"

I shook my head again.

"Have you heard what's happening with the case? It's been in the newspapers."

"I don't read American papers. My whole life is French now. In 1991 I read about the guilty verdict, and that was the last I ever heard about any of it."

The waitress appeared with an immense plate of poutine and set it down in front of Mr. Hantz.

"Merci," Mr. Hantz said. "Smells delicious!" He looked over his shoulder to make sure she was out of earshot before continuing: "A judge is reviewing the entire case. Sandy Goodwin came forward to recant her testimony. I guess she couldn't live with the lie anymore. It was her *father* who abused her. I can't imagine the bravery it must have taken to tell the truth after all this time. The guilt she must have felt, the shame . . . Anyway, after she came forward, a bunch of the other accusers followed suit. Said they were confused kids, that your parents never touched them. Everyone's looking for you. Lots of people think you must be dead."

He stabbed his fork into the gravy-covered trough of fries. "So this is poutine, eh?"

I watched him eat, unable to think clearly or specifically about anything he was telling me.

"Is Dylan Fairbanks here, too? In this country?"

I wasn't about to tell him one way or the other, but my face must have given it away.

"I see. You don't have to answer this next question, but . . . did Dylan kill that boy?"

I opened my mouth, then shut it.

"You know what boy I'm talking about? The boy in Vermont. The half brother."

"Yes, I know who you're talking about."

"Well, it was unsolved for years. The investigation went stale, and no one makes a fuss over a poor country boy. But apparently the youngest brother saw the whole thing. He was only two, and for a decade he thought it was a dream. But now he says it was a memory. He saw a boy drag his brother outside into the night and shoot him in the head."

I could feel all the blood draining from my face.

"You know, I met Dylan one time. It was right after his mother died, before he went into foster care and changed schools. I've been thinking about it a lot lately. It was a very odd meeting. I couldn't get him to share any of his emotions. Of course, teenagers often can't process that kind of extreme loss. I remember he found a grasshopper under my desk, and he held it in his hands the whole time we were talking. I asked him what he was going to do with it, and he said, 'Feed it to my mouse.' And then he reached into his pocket and pulled out a little brown mouse. Right there in my office! I could hardly believe my eyes."

"*She,*" I said. Hearing Gwen referred to as a boy bothered me viscerally, and I needed Mr. Hantz to stop.

His face lit up in surprise. "Oh! So it's true, then? Dylan is a transsexual? There's a big debate about that in the papers. Everyone seems confused on the issue. You've been together this whole time?"

I nodded.

"Amazing." He put his fork down, looking serious. "I don't imagine you're very interested in my life, La—*Jo.* It's been a small, stupid life, for sure. Not like yours."

Not like mine? I wanted to ask what he could possibly mean, but he kept speaking, not giving me the chance.

"But I just want to tell you what's going on in my head right now. Is that okay?"

"Sure, I guess."

"You see"—he pushed his poutine around with his fork—"For a long time I've been falling out of love with my wife. It's been very painful. When we married, I genuinely thought our love was meant to be. Do you believe in soul mates?"

"I don't know. Maybe. It's not provable one way or the other."

"Well, I thought my wife was my soul mate. She was beautiful—she still is, I guess, but I don't see it anymore. Smart, interested in books and foreign movies, all the same pretentious crap as me. The two of us were like a goddamn movie montage. But now everything she does drives me insane. The way she frets over the kids, never letting them consume 'impurities.' This health stuff, it's tremendously self-centered, you know? As if a hot dog will *lower* you."

I sipped my wine, not sure why he was unloading his personal struggles, but relieved to be discussing any subject besides me.

"She dragged me to this macrobiotic 'detox' retreat upstate. All these people yearning to be the purest, the healthiest, to live to a hundred and ten years old. They had a sweat lodge—you heard of those? It's like a sauna made out of branches. Anyway, I go in, supposedly to sweat out my 'toxins,' but really just to get away from everyone. And I'm sitting there in this blazing steam, wondering whether to divorce my wife, and all I can think is why? Why do I deserve to be happy? I'm not dragging my kids through a divorce. I will sit in this marriage and suffer. I will sweat it out, so to speak. This delusion that we all deserve to find our soul mates? Soul mates don't exist. It's an excuse to fuck up your life and sleep around. If you want to be a good person, it's not that complicated, what you have to do. Just decenter yourself and live for others. That's what I decided. And I think I was right, except for one thing."

"What?"

"Soul mates *do* exist. But it's not what we thought it was. It's not about partnership. It's not even about love. It's about something more powerful than that. It's about life. *Survival.* I'm sorry, do I sound crazy right now?"

I could only shrug.

"Let me try to explain it better. *We* are soul mates, you and me. Because of that horrible night. My purpose is to help you survive. That night I failed you, and I think I've hated myself for the last fourteen years. How could I have passed out like that, leaving you alone with all that blood? I never knew blood could be so dark, so *brown* . . ." He shuddered. "I wish I'd been stronger. But now I understand why it happened. It was to create this debt, so that one day—*today*—I could repay you."

I was fixated on how he'd called the blood *brown*. In my memory, it was bright, vivid *red*.

"I don't understand what you mean," I said.

"You need to be *warned*. Back in America, your picture is everywhere, Dylan's, too. It's all blowing up again. What happened to the Satan Daughter? What happened to Dylan Fairbanks? People forgot for years, but now it's bobbing back to the surface. I was placed here—by fate or whatever you want to call it—to warn you."

I shook my head. He had almost lured me in with his weird soul mates concept, but at the end of the day, Mr. Hantz was just a man doing what men do: twisting the story around to cast himself as the hero.

"Americans love driving themselves crazy," I said. "They can whip themselves into a frenzy for all I care. No one gave a shit fourteen years ago. *Now* it's news? *Now*? No. Fuck America. Gwen and I are Canadians. We're not those people."

I wasn't being terribly articulate. But it made me furious, the thought that people were looking for us *now*, that people cared *now*, when fourteen years ago two children—and how many more?—had been allowed to simply disappear.

Mr. Hantz looked incredulous. "I'm sorry, but are you thinking clearly? All it takes is one wrong person. One photo. One piece of bad luck and your 'but I'm Canadian' act is over. Do you not understand that? Do you not understand—"

"I understand," I snapped. "Jesus. Shut up. You don't have to explain it to me. I'm a *lawyer*."

I wasn't breathing right—short gasps of air that made me sound like a coughing old dog.

"It's all right, calm down, shh . . ." Mr. Hantz said. He looked around for the waitress. "Miss? Another glass of wine for my friend?" He grabbed a napkin, dipped it in his water glass, and handed it to me, motioning me to place it on my forehead. Lowering his voice to a whisper, he asked, "Would you ever think about turning yourself in?"

I shook my head. "Absolutely not. I'm never going back."

"But if everyone could see you the way I see you right now, all grown up? People will see that you've changed. And your poor parents must miss you terribly—"

"Stop guidance counseling me," I spat.

"Just think about it," he pressed. "It'll be so much better if you come forward and tell your story. Sandy did it. You can do it, too. You didn't do anything wrong, Jo, except run away, which anyone could understand. You didn't shoot that kid. Dylan should take responsibility for his own actions. Sorry, *her* actions."

My mouth tightened into a line and my eyes flickered around. Incredible that after all this time, I was still a terrible liar.

Mr. Hantz went completely still.

"It *was* Dylan, right? Right?"

I said nothing.

"Oh god," he gasped. "How did it happen? Walk me through it."

I shook my head. "I can't. It was dark, and I don't have a lot of specific memories. I . . . I blacked out a little."

"If you blacked out, then you can't be sure you're the one who did it."

"Yes, I can. This happened to me once before, when I beat that kid to a pulp. You remember it, you were there. It stands to reason . . ." I took another gulp of wine. "It stands to reason that to precipitate that response, I did a similarly violent thing."

"But you can't be sure," he repeated.

"Dylan was there. She watched me do it."

"Of course she would say that, to protect herself!"

"The kid said he saw a *boy*. Dylan didn't look like a boy. Stop trying

294

to pin it on her. She didn't do anything wrong."

Mr. Hantz's mouth opened, then shut. The look on his face wasn't one of horror or condemnation—just awful, total disappointment. A teacher realizing his star student wasn't exceptional after all, that she'd cheated on her tests.

"Oh god, Lacey. Why? *Why?*"

I could have explained everything—that Dodge claimed to be Éclair's killer, that Gwen claimed he would follow us to the ends of the earth. That Mr. Hantz himself had told me the only way to deal with bullies was to make them suffer. But the thought of presenting it all as if it were my opening statement in a bid for clemency made me sick.

"I don't know," I answered dismally. "I think . . . life is unpredictable, and people's souls are tested by random events. Some people learn they're not capable of violence. Some people learn they are, and we're the ones who make life hell for everyone else. We're the ones who ensure society never evolves too far beyond the cave."

I couldn't bear to meet his eyes. As a kid, I'd managed to avoid a lot of the angst that went along with being gay. Thanks to good parenting, I suppose. The shame, the fear, the terror of being outed—it was foreign to me. But I imagined it felt like this: the powerlessness of being defined in another person's eyes by something he found repulsive, something you couldn't help and couldn't change.

Mr. Hantz rubbed his face. I could almost feel his mind working, trying to come up with a way to paint things the way he wished to see them. But it was impossible. He'd outed me as a murderer, and his image of me was destroyed. There was nothing else to say.

He picked at his now cold poutine. "This stuff isn't too great, is it?"

"No," I said.

Eventually the waitress took the plate away. Mr. Hantz paid the full check. I offered him some cash, which he refused.

"I better go," I said, putting the money back in my wallet.

Mr. Hantz took out a small card. "I hope you'll take this. If you need anything, or just someone to talk to . . . I'm here, day or night."

"Thank you. I appreciate that." My voice sounded stiff and formal.

I was about to stand up when Mr. Hantz said, "By any chance, did you hear about Melissa Shears?"

A vision of a rotten girl in a velvet dress flashed through my mind. *Stick out your tongue.* Though I couldn't recall the specific details of her face, the feeling of humiliation was as fresh as ever.

"What about her?" I asked curtly.

"I'm sorry to have to tell you this. She died. She killed herself."

"What?"

"Not long after you ran away. It was awful. She hanged herself."

"No."

"She did. And apparently she botched it or something. It wasn't a clean break, so she just . . . hung on the end of the rope strangling to death. In agony, I imagine." For a moment Mr. Hantz stared at a plop of gravy on the table. Then he shook his head, as if waking himself from a stupor. "God, I'm sorry. I shouldn't have said that. You didn't need to know that part."

"It's all right," I said.

"I really am sorry. I don't know why I said those things."

But I knew. He was punishing me. Just like his wife, I'd failed to be the woman he needed me to be to make his life meaningful.

xxxviii

THE APARTMENT WAS EMPTY WHEN I GOT HOME. I REMEMBERED
Gwen telling me she had a shoot for a lingerie catalog. She'd been nervous. Lingerie shoots could be tricky—having to insist on the privacy
stipulated in her contract, weighing the risk of being labeled "difficult"
versus the risk of the anomalous bulge in her anatomy being spotted
by an unknown enemy. A tiny number of people knew—Bjorn, a few
photographers—each one a link in a chain that could break at any moment. Supposedly the world had changed since Caroline Cossey was
outed and lost everything in the '80s. But no one wanted Gwen to be
the test dummy for that particular crash scenario.

A pile of mail sat atop the radiator. I flipped through the junk offers
and slick sheets of coupons until I came to an envelope with no stamp
or return address on it, just my name. *Jo Scottish.* Inside was a single
sheet of paper, a grainy photocopy of an enlarged black-and-white photograph. It was Marie-Laure, the little girl who'd watched her friends be
eaten by wolves in the woods of Lac-Froid. The photo had been taken by
a local paper just after the tragedy. The girl stared out at nothing, and I
recognized her expression; I had seen it in the mirror a thousand times.
It was the face of a girl who had, ostensibly, survived, but who was internally maimed. I wondered if, in the swirl of legal drama, anyone had
asked her what she thought should happen to the wolves.

I crumpled the paper in my fist. Then I poured myself a glass of
wine, which somehow I knocked over almost immediately. The thick

Oriental rug saved the glass from breaking, and its crimson-and-dark-brown pattern would conceal the spill. I realized I was starving and took some cheese and fruit out of the refrigerator. I didn't enjoy cooking; whenever I tried to make something remotely ambitious, I would get depressed midway through the recipe and end up barely tasting the meal. The flavor of these existential crises was not unlike what Mr. Hantz had described in Poutineville: *Why do I deserve to be happy?* Why do I deserve a rich cassoulet or gnocchi made from scratch? Perhaps he and I were soul mates after all.

If you're a well-adjusted person, you may find it hard to believe that after everything that had just happened, I sat down and had a quiet dinner. Perhaps you want to see me pacing the apartment wildly, calling Gwen's cell phone and leaving hysterical messages, all the while anticipating the FBI agents' knock on the door. But if, like me, you are ranked world class in avoidance, you will understand. All I needed was one excuse not to freak out, and I had it: Mr. Hantz had promised not to tell. He'd *promised*. So everything was fine.

When Gwen came home that night, I calmly explained the situation. She sat frozen on the sofa, an untouched deli sandwich in her lap, her face so blank I wondered if she was in shock. It occurred to me she might be wondering whether Mr. Hantz was lying in a ditch somewhere with a hole in his head.

"I didn't kill him, if that's what you're thinking," I said. "He promised he wouldn't tell. Everything's fine."

Finally, a reaction. She blinked at me, dumbfounded. "Geez, Jo, I wasn't thinking *that*. Sometimes I think you don't know what goes on in my mind at all."

xxxix

MONTHS PASSED, FROM THE GAIETY OF SUMMER TO THE COLD
emptiness of late fall, arguably Montreal's dingiest time. It was the
pause between tourist seasons, after the symphony of fall color but before the Christmas lights went up. The whole city seemed old and gray
and bare.

I had not been able to put my meeting with Mr. Hantz behind me.
My routine now involved daily trips to the public library to scour the
internet for every article and news item about my parents that I could
find. I felt like a person checking in on a television program she'd once
loved but had long ago stopped watching. It was astonishing to discover
that the show had gone on, its small world of drama still turning. After
every computer session I erased the browser history like a novice serial
killer researching ways to dispose of a body.

I kept hearing Mr. Hantz's voice in my head: *All it takes is one wrong
person. One photo.* It's a testament to my broken ability to make threat
assessments that what I chose to trouble myself over during this time
was a photo of me in a 2001 issue of *Canadian Lawyer*, a low-circulation
legal magazine. Meanwhile, Gwen's face was being plastered on actual
billboards across Europe.

Of course, my intuition was weirdly correct; it was a photo of me,
not her, that brought us both down in the end.

Shortly after Sandy Goodwin recanted her testimony, the New
Hampshire Court of Appeals reviewed and dismissed the case against

my parents. Sandy was avoiding the press like the plague, forcing every newspaper to report the same short statement: "What happened was wrong. At the time I was a confused, ashamed, and manipulated young girl. All I can do now is tell the truth and apologize." The statement infuriated me. I didn't want her to apologize. I wanted someone to apologize *to her*.

The judge's ruling was succinct: "In light of the recanted testimony of several key victims and general lack of evidence, we must conclude that the charges brought against Kate and Hugh Bond in 1990 were false and the result of national mania. It is regretful that their lives were upended by these charges, and as of this moment they are free citizens."

Not only were they free from their cells, but they were free, apparently, from each other. They had legally divorced in 1994, a fact that felt more unreal to me than any other aspect of the news stories. Not even their separate prisons and my dad's affair had been enough to disabuse me of my blind, institutional faith in the two of them as *parents*: a man and woman who had created me together and would stay together until the end. The whole thing gave me a feeling of vertigo, as though the law of gravity had been overturned and replaced by a new, dizzying set of physical realities. They were two entirely separate people now.

My father had remarried while in prison. The new Mrs. Bond was (quel scandale!) his former attorney Jeannine Hanson, now Jeannine Hanson Bond. Jeannine had abandoned the practice of law and written a tell-all about her relationship with my father called *Bonds of Love*. The fact that she was using our name, which she was legally entitled to do, made me want to scream a string of obscenities so profane even Éclair would have been impressed.

I bought a copy of the book, with cash, at an English bookstore. Jeannine's ruminations were scattered and self-centered. A flimsy "love conquers all" message strained to bring the whole mess together. That night, I persuaded Gwen to drink a deluge of wine with me and read long passages aloud, which she did in a mocking, faux serious voice, like

Barbie being interviewed by Charlie Rose:

"We made love every night—in my dreams. Unfortunately, in real life, we were able to be intimate only once a month, always in a cold beige room, upon a thin cot covered in the stains of other caged lovers. But Hugh taught me the ways of love during those precious conjugal visits. It was magic whenever he touched me, and our honeymoon never ended, even though it was a honeymoon in a cage. . . .

"My purpose in writing this book is to show the world that love can bloom in the ugliest places. Our two beautiful sons, Wren and Swift, are proof of that. I gave them the names of birds, which symbolize freedom. Society could keep Hugh Bond behind bars, but his heart was never caged. In every way that matters, he never stopped being a free man. It's *love* that makes a man's heart free."

Gwen tossed the book against the wall. It hit the floor with a satisfying *thunk*. "Who is this bitch again?"

"She was our second lawyer. Apparently sleeping with my dad makes her our family historian. She could have at least taken some writing classes first."

"She probably stole most of this crap from a Mormon romance novel."

We spoke little of Mr. Hantz, instead obsessing over Jeannine. Our fight about the cat was all but forgotten as we united against this new enemy. Gwen defaced her simpering author photo on the *Bonds of Love* book jacket and slapped it on the refrigerator with the caption I ♥ CONJUGAL VISITS!, which made me laugh in the same uncontrollable, teenage way I'd once laughed with Éclair.

In one chapter, inanely titled "What Happened," Jeannine blamed Éclair and me for everything that had gone wrong:

> *Sadly, Hugh's daughters inherited their mother's instability.*
> *Without Hugh to guide them with his love and compassion,*
> *they went off the edge. Their mental problems sabotaged every*

step of the trial. Éclair, the elder daughter, made a deal with
the devil. Fame, fortune, and slaggy clothes became more im-
portant to her than her parents' freedom. In the end, it killed
her. She wanted attention, and she got it.

    As for Lacey, she loved being called a witch and took sa-
distic pleasure in frightening people, especially me. It was only
inevitable that on that devastating day, she performed her
bone-chilling Satanic incantation in the middle of the court-
room. Then she disappeared, and we can only assume that she
was consumed by the streets, following her mother's tragic path
of drug abuse. The sisters courted evil, and it claimed them
both in the end.

How could my father have married this woman? How could he let
her say these things about me? About Éclair? Didn't Jeannine know it
was fucking indecorous to speak ill of the dead? She'd never met Éclair,
and it enraged me to think that she might have gotten these ideas about
my sister from our father. "Slaggy" was a British word, the equivalent of
"slutty." Had he told Jeannine that his own daughter was a *slag*?

In the final chapter, "What Now?," Jeannine speculated on the
wonderful impact her book might have on the world:

    I dedicate these words to every woman who ever loved a man
in prison, whether that prison was a literal or a metaphori-
cal one. Stay true to your man and be his shining star in the
darkness. I hope my story can be a guiding light to anyone who
needs help accepting the power of love, perhaps even the other
Bond women. Kate, if you are reading this, I am truly sorry
for any pain that I may have caused you. But love is like a wild
animal. You cannot blame it for what it does. And Lacey, if
you are still alive, I want you to know that I forgive you for
your terrible outburst in court that day. I know you were in

pain. I know it wasn't your fault. I hope that one day we can
embrace each other like sisters.

I found very little information online about my mother since her release from prison. Apparently she was living on a farm in New Hampshire with a co-op of women who, according to one's choice of news source, were either bee farmers or members of a lesbian Wiccan cult. When asked by reporters whether she intended to read *Bonds of Love*, she was quoted as saying, "Sure, right after I finish *The Da Vinci Code*," which made me smile but also disoriented me. Mom knew about *The Da Vinci Code*? In my mind she was forever fixed in the 1980s, griping about yuppies and mail-ordering liquid aminos.

My parents had issued separate statements regarding the mystery of their long-lost daughter. I found the footage on a news website. Though the two interviews took place at the same time and in the same location (the courthouse steps—I could see my dad in the background of my mother's interview and vice versa), they were, decidedly, not together. I couldn't find a single frame where they even appeared to look at each other.

On the slow library internet, each video took five full minutes to load, giving me an uncomfortable amount of time to stare at the still images of my parents' faces. While my father looked much the same (men of his type aged fabulously, even in prison, apparently), my mother had undergone a transformation so startling I hardly recognized her. Yet at the same time, I knew her completely—she looked like me. Her face had lost its porcelain-doll smoothness. Her hair had turned sewer brown. She was unsmiling, uninterested in being attractive to a bunch of strangers. I was sure that, to the average person, she looked very ugly ("Former Beauty Ravaged by Prison" was the headline in *People* magazine). But she possessed a kind of beauty that was more meaningful to me than bouncy hair or pink cheeks: she looked strong.

I watched the video of my father first. When asked about his missing daughter, he said he didn't delude himself that I was still alive. But then he looked straight into the camera and said, "Lacey, if you *are* alive, and you're watching this, I love you and I beg you to come home." His voice sounded different, hoarse, as if out of use. And his British accent seemed less pronounced. Or maybe my memories had exaggerated it. He went on: "It's been a long, rough road, but it's over now, and we can all be together again."

It was ironic that he said this—about us all being together—while keeping a twenty-foot distance from my mother.

When my mother was asked the same question, she didn't look into the camera or even at the reporter, but at a vague spot in the sky. "If Lacey is still alive," she said, "I think she should stay where she is. If she's survived this long, it's because she's doing something right."

It was not a good time to be preoccupied by all this. My workload at the office had doubled, owing to a precipitous decline in Montagne's health. On his behalf, I stopped accepting any cases that required a trial. The times when he couldn't focus on the day's work had grown so frequent that I took responsibility for adjudicating all his casework myself while he read the newspaper or stared foggily out the window. All my clothes were dirty; I never had time to go to the laundromat anymore.

In the end, I wrote the Lac-Froid ruling myself. The most widely quoted section was: "There is nothing more tragic than the death of a child. But it would be a sin to use the law to punish nature for the crimes of human nature. It's time to look in the mirror and acknowledge the true wolf: ourselves." The ruling was noted for its use of a religious term, "sin," and for its apparent lack of affection for the human race. Neither was typical of Montagne, who was dogmatically secular and relentlessly optimistic. But I suppose it wasn't hard to imagine a man becoming both more spiritual and more morose as he approached the end of his life.

Occasionally Montagne expressed confusion as to why I was doing so much work without him. "Ne t'inquiète pas," I told him. "You work so hard, let me share the burden." But it was the entire burden, and I couldn't request an extra law clerk without revealing the extent of Montagne's condition.

I was aware, on some level, that this had gotten out of hand, that I was standing in the way of Montagne getting the full-time care he needed and deserved. I also knew that what I was doing was illegal. Twenty-eight-year-old law clerks weren't supposed to be deciding huge federal cases with billions of dollars and the survival of an entire species at stake. But I didn't care. Control had been up for grabs, and I had taken it. I didn't regret it, and I had every intention of hanging on to it. This was what I did, apparently. When things weren't going well, I took authority into my own hands, in whatever way was available.

One afternoon Narimane knocked on the door of my office, an uncomfortable look on her face.

"Jo? The chief justice just called. She wants to see you right now."

"Madam Durant? Does she want to scold me for smoking in the building again?"

Narimane raised her hands helplessly. I stopped kidding myself; this wasn't about the cigars.

Durant's chambers were much like Montagne's, with beige walls and dark cherrywood furniture. Durant's law clerk, Justin, leaned against the doorframe of his office, eating a sandwich. He grinned at me, chewing an enormous bite. He had a sinister glint in his eye, like a sociopathic young boy excited to watch a beheading. My palms were sweating.

And then I heard her voice:

"She has him under some kind of spell."

It was Patrice, Montagne's daughter. Justice Durant sat behind her desk, with Patrice situated in one of two matching chairs with pastel upholstery. I sat down in the other.

Durant called to her secretary, "Sophie? Can you grab another coffee for Jo?" Then she turned to me and said, indicating her own mug,

"I'm sorry, we ought to have waited for you. How rude of us."

"Pas de problem," I replied.

We waited in awkward silence. Patrice fiddled with her hideous chunky necklace, while Durant pretended to organize a stack of papers on her desk. Both women were in their forties, but their appearances reflected their different priorities in life: Patrice's makeup and hair were flawless; Durant's makeup was askew, her hair a flat, unnatural shade of red suggesting an at-home dye kit.

Sophie arrived with the coffee and handed it to me.

"All right," Durant said, removing her reading glasses. "I want to resolve this matter with as much sensitivity as possible. Patrice, can you tell Jo what you told me?"

Patrice turned to me, folding her hands in her lap like a sorority sister about to recite a poem. "You are a horrible, sneaky, lying, manipulative—"

"Mrs. Tribble, please. We three women are perfectly capable of working this out without name-calling. Perhaps I should begin." Durant turned to me. "Jo, Mrs. Tribble is concerned about her father's health. She believes he is no longer in a mental state to be deciding cases. She believes it's time for him to retire."

I took a sip of coffee, carefully formulating my words before speaking. "I disagree. Mrs. Tribble is not the one working with him every day—I am. Which means I am more qualified to judge the situation than she is."

"'Qualified to judge'! Are you hearing this?" Patrice practically shouted at Durant. "What did I tell you? She thinks she's the judge!"

"Please be civil, madam."

Patrice was fuming. She pointed a manicured finger at me. "But she's a criminal!"

I stiffened. Durant looked as uncomfortable as I did.

"She's a liar and a thief!" Patrice continued. "From the moment I met her I didn't like her. But I said nothing, because I thought the clerkship would just be a year, and then she'd be gone. Only what do I learn? That this snake has finagled a permanent position for herself! Suddenly he's canceling lunches, dinners, weekends. 'I'm doing *this* with Jo. I'm doing *that* with Jo—'"

"I'm sorry your father prefers my company to yours," I said. "But it's really inappropriate for you to be interfering with his work life."

Patrice continued to speak directly to Durant as if I weren't even there. "*She's* the inappropriate one. These queer types—they know how to lie. They know how to live double lives so they can be part of society! So I decided to trust my gut. I hired a private investigator."

"You . . . you had me investigated?"

There was no limit to the kind of shit a professional investigator could have dug up on me. Bill Cosby's grinning face flashed in my mind like the devil, and I froze, bracing for the worst. I'd learned nothing from my past, evidently, and I was being punished for the crime of hubris *again*.

"She runs with a real classy crowd, you know. A bunch of alcoholics and cocaine addicts, very loose people. And that's not all! She assaulted my investigator!"

The bald man, I realized, with his telephoto lenses.

"I thought he was a stalker," I said truthfully.

"This is out of hand," Durant said. "Mrs. Tribble, if you have nothing to state beyond your dislike of Ms. Scottish—"

"What I'm stating is that this girl is bamboozling my father!" Patrice shouted. "He is unwell. Last weekend we were Christmas shopping at Complexe Desjardins. One minute we were looking at presents for the boys, and the next he was nowhere to be found. I discovered him fifteen minutes later standing in the middle of the fountain! He thought he was outdoors! He thought he was at the lake! He barely recognized me! Thank god no one recognized *him*."

The thought of Montagne splashing around in a mall fountain stunned me. I wanted to believe that Patrice was lying, but I couldn't quite convince myself of it.

"He—he has exhibited no such behavior here," I stammered. "Our work is going fine."

"Of course she'd say that!" Patrice said. "Because if my father retires, she'll be out of a job."

I turned on her furiously. "I could have my pick of any law firm in Quebec. I could snap my fingers and have three job offers tomorrow."

"But you don't want another job, do you? Because you're a lazy snake and you're waiting for my father to die so you can get your fat inheritance and spend it partying with your Village lowlifes."

"What inheritance? I don't know what you're talking about."

"He had his will rewritten, as you well know, you little . . . *bitch*!"

"Enough!" Durant slapped her hands on her desk, startling both of us. "Arêttez-vous. Right now."

No one spoke. The buzz of the fluorescent lights above our heads seemed very loud.

"Mrs. Tribble, I've heard what you have to say," Durant said finally. "I'd like a word alone with Jo now."

"But—"

"Mrs. Tribble, I assure you this issue will be resolved. I have all the information I require from you, and I thank you for bringing this to my attention. I invite you to continue your day."

It was obvious that Durant didn't like Patrice any more than I did. Patrice left, clutching her purse furiously.

Thank fucking god, I thought, taking my first full breath since Patrice had mentioned the investigator. It could have been infinitely worse.

Durant sighed, leaning back in her chair. "Mon dieu. That woman is a handful."

"Yes," I agreed. "Dealing with her is not pleasant."

"I'm afraid this conversation won't be pleasant, either. Jo, Justice Montagne needs to retire. If he continues to deteriorate and it becomes public knowledge that he's mentally infirm, motions will be filed left and right to revisit his recent cases. Half his verdicts will be overturned. The Lac-Froid case? They'll try the whole thing over. Northcore has the money to do it, and the next judge may not share your views on the civil rights of wolves." I must have flinched, because she continued: "Yes, Jo. I've grown to recognize your writing."

I squirmed in my chair and picked up the coffee cup, just to have something to do. But my hand was shaking, so I set it back down.

"I want what's best for everyone, Jo, and that means making this all go away, *quietly*. It's what's best for you, too."

I said nothing, staring blankly at a framed photo of Durant's teenage children. Her tone softened.

"I hear things. People don't have the nicest opinions about you, do they? But I think I understand. I know your background. You were one of the Lost Children. I can see how you would latch on to Montagne as a kind of father figure. It's sweet, in a way. But this is a court of law, not a family. You know that."

I took a deep breath and nodded.

"I'm happy to be a reference for you in your job search. I want to see you in a good position, Jo."

"Thank you," I croaked.

"I warn you, this is going to unfold quickly. Patrice already has an apartment reserved for him in a senior living facility with Alzheimer's care."

"Oh god."

"Don't be dramatic. It's a quality community," Durant said, and put her reading glasses back on, which I took as my invitation to leave. As I stood, she added, "This is for the best, Jo. It really is time for everyone to move on."

Before returning to Montagne's floor, I went to the ladies' room. Patrice's claim that Montagne had rewritten his will had barely sunk in. I was sure it was nothing—he'd thrown me a thousand dollars or a painting, most likely, and Patrice was so petty she couldn't let it go.

In the mirror, my face looked dead. I took a dampened paper towel and placed it over my eyes, the way I'd seen Éclair do so many times when the world antagonized her. I imagined her beating Patrice in the face with her purse, but the fantasy of Éclair attacking my enemies didn't bring the same satisfaction it had when I was a kid. Hitting people with purses was not how adults were supposed to behave. It pained me to remember that I was older than Éclair now, that I always would be.

Somehow I dragged myself to the break room. I pulled two mugs and two bags of Earl Grey tea out of the cabinet and stood in a daze while the kettle heated. Then I went into Montagne's office, the smell of bergamot wafting along with me, a smell I would always associate with him.

As I passed by her desk, Narimane could tell by my face exactly what had happened. She didn't ask any questions. I wondered if she'd already put out feelers for a new position.

I pulled up a chair to sit with Montagne by the window. His eyes looked clear and focused for the first time in days, which seemed like a cruel irony.

"Ah, merci," he said, noticing the tea. "Narimane told me Durant called you up. You look like you survived a real beating."

I just nodded.

"No more cigars, I take it?"

"No more cigars."

We sipped our tea and looked out the window. The sky was a dull, uniform gray from end to end, threatening icy snow.

"I've had a truly wonderful life. I'm grateful for every minute," Montagne said.

I was surprised. I wondered if he'd known, this whole time, far more about what was happening behind his back than he'd let on. I felt sadder and even more convinced that this was all wrong.

"I never had to go to war," he went on, "never had to be violent against my fellow man. I'd like to think I did some good. That I left the world a little better than I found it."

"I think you did," I agreed. I could feel myself starting to choke up again.

"You have given me so much," he said. "Gifts I can never repay."

I looked at him, speechless. I knew Montagne had affection for me, maybe even great affection, but he spoke with such profundity I was overwhelmed.

"You saved my life. When you died, I knew I had to live a good life. For you. In your honor."

These words hit me on a level I was not prepared for. I thought about the first time I beheld Montreal's dazzling skyline, how it felt like Éclair had led me there. But then I snapped back to the present. *When I died?* What was Montagne talking about?

I looked at him and saw that his eyes had fogged over.

"Little boys are not taught to say 'je t'aime,' so we never said it to each other. But we're old men now, aren't we?"

"Oui," I answered, my voice barely a whisper.

A fuzzy scene filled my mind: Bridget Fonda and Corey Feldman splitting a Cinnabon in a mall food court. *I hate you. You love me.*

He reached out and took my hand. "I love you, Jacques."

"I love you, Etienne."

As I said it, a tear fell down my cheek. Rather than wipe it away, I left it to evaporate, holding the cup of tea in one hand and Montagne's frail hand in the other. We looked out the window together at the rusty grain elevator. I'd heard they were turning it into a museum.

DURANT WAS RIGHT: IT ALL HAPPENED VERY QUICKLY. MON-
tagne's office was emptied out, the case briefs transferred to other jus-
tices, his books, personal effects, and watercolor paintings of Quebec
landscapes sent to his rooms at the nursing home. I was told I would
retain my salary through the first quarter of 2006, which gave me four
months to find a new job.

Gwen was in Paris promoting her bag, so I was alone. For three
days I barely left the apartment, doing nothing, just lying on the floor
drinking wine, trying to picture myself as an associate at a big corporate
firm. Taking lunches, writing briefs, gobbling up retainers to defend
rich people's money, castigating people for damages, damages, damages.
I was far more interested in criminal law, but I didn't think I had the
mental stamina to deal with people who compulsively fucked up their
own lives.

Maybe I could work for Protecteurs de Prédateurs or some other
conservation group. That way I wouldn't have to work on behalf of people at all.

As my gloom entered another dawn, the phone rang, jolting me
awake. It was four o'clock in the morning.

"A-allô?" I croaked, slammed by the special brand of headache that
occurs precisely between the states of drunk and hungover.

"Jo? Oh my fucking god." A man's voice, speaking in English,
sounding frantic and overcaffeinated. Bjorn, Gwen's manager. "Zach's

been arrested."

"What? What happened?"

"He got busted for coke when he was changing airlines at JFK. I fucking told him to lose that shit before he got to the U.S. The moron was saving a bump for the flight."

"Wait, he's in America?"

"Oh my god, keep up, you fucking alcoholic!"

I turned on the lamp and downed the glass of day-old water standing on the bedside table. "Bjorn, it's four in the morning. Stop cursing at me and give me five seconds to wake up."

"Oh, sorry. I forgot about the time zones."

"Are you still in Paris? Is Gwen with you?"

"Yeah. She's asleep. Our flight isn't till six. Should I get her?"

"No. Let her sleep. She hates being woken up."

"Zach insisted on getting this ghetto-ass flight because it was cheaper, and now he's sitting in jail. You have to help him, Jo! You're the only lawyer I know."

I rubbed my eyes. "He needs an American lawyer. There's nothing I can do. But honestly, you should relax. White people don't go to prison for possession in America. He'll have a shitty week, but he'll be fine—"

"You don't understand," Bjorn interrupted me. "It's not just the coke. It's this whole fucking unbelievable thing. They think he killed someone."

"What?"

"I could barely understand what he was saying, it sounded so crazy. And he was crying, and they made him hang up before he could explain. They think he's some fucking fugitive named, like, Diamond Fair Ass?"

I froze. "Destiny Fairbanks?" I said, and immediately wished I hadn't. For all I knew, my phone was tapped.

"Yes! That was the name. Who the fuck even is that?"

"Okay, listen to me, Bjorn. Are you listening?"

"Of course I'm listening! *I* called *you*, you twat—"

"Shut up! Shut up and listen to me!" I hissed. "You and Gwen, your flights home, do they connect through the U.S.?"

"I think . . ."

I heard papers rustling on the other end of the line.

"Yes," he said. "Through Boston."

"Do not get on that plane. Get a direct flight from Paris to Montreal. Toronto if you have to. I don't care how much it costs. Put it on Gwen's credit card. No matter what, do not get on any plane that connects through America."

"What the fuck is going on?"

"I can't explain over the phone. But I need you to take this very seriously, Bjorn. You cannot let Gwen's feet touch American soil. Do you understand me? If you mess this up, I will hunt you down and cut your dick off slowly."

"Fuck! Jesus! I got it, Jo! You crazy dyke!"

"Okay, okay. Just be calm, come home, and everything will be fine. Call me if there's anything even resembling a problem."

I hung up the phone, feeling adrenaline surge through me. This was it, the moment every professional dreads, the one that tests whether you're actually good at your job. It didn't matter how it had happened (had Mr. Hantz betrayed me? why the fuck was Zach involved?). It had happened, the end. The jig was up.

My first step was to fire up my laptop and give myself a crash course on Canada's process for obtaining political asylum/protected status. I cursed myself for letting months pass without doing any research to build my own legal case. If not for my compulsive avoidance, I could have been ready to face this obviously inevitable moment. But there was no use crying, et cetera.

My second step was to look up the waiting period for obtaining a marriage license in Quebec. It would be deeply ironic if, after all my ambivalence about gay marriage, spousal privilege ended up saving us from incarceration.

Of course, I didn't kid myself that a rushed courthouse affair wouldn't break Gwen's fucking heart. So much for picking out colors and a ridiculously huge cake. But at least no cake meant no psychopath with a gun jumping out of it. Maybe if we could do this quietly, discreetly, fate wouldn't even notice.

The dry cleaner down the street opened at 7:00 A.M.; I gathered my smelly, rumpled suits and shirts and ran them over. What else, what else? What did I need to do? Memories of the summer of 1990 swarmed my brain: me and Éclair and Aaron, trapped in a house with nothing but frozen pizza, tequila sunrises, and chaos. I would not repeat that, I told myself. This time I would be prepared. I thought about my parents, how they'd known the police were coming that June evening and done nothing. Didn't warn me, didn't stock the refrigerator, didn't brace in any way for the blow.

I needed a lawyer beyond myself as soon as possible, but I still had an hour before I could reasonably call anyone on the phone. I would try my friend Alexandrine Sauveterre first. I hadn't seen her since the separatist party in July, but we had a good relationship and she liked me. I knew this ordeal was going to get very personal very quickly.

I sat stiffly at my desk for forty-five minutes, waiting and drinking coffee. At precisely nine o'clock, I called Alexandrine's office at Marion & Martel and made an appointment with her assistant, who offered to set up a lunch.

"Not lunch," I said. "I need . . . closed doors."

"She can see you at ten, is that too soon?"

I realized, stupidly, that I had nothing to wear; my entire wardrobe was at the cleaners. When I opened Gwen's closet, her clothes tumbled out in heaps: a rat king of entangled belts and hair accessories, rhinestones with camouflage, rhinestones with fishnet, pairs of harem pants reminiscent of MC Hammer that I couldn't believe were back in style. Gwen looked amazing in anything, of course, which was the terrible lie of fashion: that beauty was something anyone could buy, rather than something the models had won in a genetic lottery.

I sifted through the mountain of garments and found, hanging in the back of the closet, a red velvet blazer and a white button-down shirt with ruffles down the front. I put it on and looked in the mirror. I looked like Austin Powers.

Alexandrine's office was in the business district, away from the charm of Old Town and the river. I made my way there via Montreal's pedestrian "underground," a word that evoked punk rock and disestablishmentarianism, but was really a system of sparkling clean, bland hallways that connected various office towers to various malls. It was like an endless walk through the corporate headquarters of purgatory. By the time I reached Marion & Martel, I felt so rattled and under-caffeinated that I longed to call a cab and go right back home.

At precisely ten o'clock, Alexandrine appeared to greet me.

"La rebelle! Bonjour! Wow, you look spiffy. Walk of shame?" She winked lasciviously.

"Laundry day," I said unconvincingly.

"I've heard that one before."

Marion & Martel was an all-female firm famous (among men, notorious) for its "girl power" ethos and chatty, casual environment. Alexandrine's office was bigger than Montagne's (for all their eminence, judges were still mere civil servants). The furniture looked expensive, and the windows viewed grandly across the city toward Parc du Mont-Royal.

"I was so sorry to hear about le Justice Montagne," Alexandrine said as we sat down. "What an incredible career. They don't make men like that anymore."

"They certainly don't," I agreed, unnerved by the way she spoke of him like he was already dead.

"So, to what do I owe the pleasure of seeing you this gray morning?"

"It won't be a pleasure, I'm afraid. I need a lawyer."

"Anything for you, Jo. We can keep this one off the books—girl to

316

girl."

"I'm in a very serious situation, Alexandrine. I can't stress how serious it is."

It occurred to me that the two of us had never had a sober conversation before. Our encounters had always occurred at boozy separatist cocktail parties or the occasional old lawyer's funeral.

"Is everything all right? Is it to do with Montagne's will? I heard the daughter's in a wild rage about it, hitting up every law firm in town. I don't really do probate, but I can recommend an excellent—"

"It's not that. It's a criminal matter. It's very complicated."

Alexandrine squinted at me as though seeing me for the first time. "I'm intrigued. What's up?"

I vomited out my story, and Alexandrine listened with a practiced concerned-yet-untroubled expression, nodding occasionally and asking clarifying questions ("When you shot this boy, did you feel that your life was in immediate danger?" "Who initially suggested the homicide, you or Gwen?" "You don't specifically recall pulling the trigger?"). Once it was all out, I felt something that could be generously described as catharsis but was more like empty stillness—relief that the final convulsion had passed and hadn't killed you.

"Let me think," she said. The pause seemed to last an eternity. "So they have this acquaintance of yours, Zach, in custody. And you think it's only a matter of time before the whole thing comes out. Your identity, your location, et cetera."

"Oui," I said.

"You're smart to try and get ahead of it. Does this Zach person know who you really are?"

"No. I have no idea how they linked him with the name Destiny Fairbanks."

"You don't think Gwen told him?"

"She would never. Not in a thousand years."

"Is there anyone else who knows? Anyone at all?"

"I ran into a teacher of mine, back in July. He was here on vacation. But he swore he wouldn't tell anyone, and he doesn't know Zach . . ."

Then I realized, with a sudden, sinking click—

"Wait. Oh god. Montagne's daughter hired a private investigator to dig up dirt and help push me out of the will. It was him, I'd bet my life on it. He nailed me. He must have—he must have followed Mr. Hantz, done a background check on him. I'm sure it's all public record that he was the one who found my sister's body and made the 911 call. And then the P.I. realized I was the girl . . ."

Alexandrine nodded. "All it takes with these things is one loose thread."

"I was thinking Gwen and I should get married as soon as possible, so that if we're extradited they can't split us up and make us testify against each other. You know they'll use my hazy memories as an excuse to paint whatever picture they want."

Alexandrine just stared at me. "Jo."

"What?"

"This crime was committed in America. They have their Defense of Marriage Act. They don't have to acknowledge gay marriage if they don't want to."

"Shit." I dropped my head into my hands. "I'm sorry. I'm not thinking straight."

"It's all right. We will work this out," Alexandrine said. "Let's just . . . Let me get a few things straight. These blackouts—do you still experience them?"

"No, not for years."

"And you were never one of the Lost Children, from that cult in the Eastern Townships?"

"No. I never even met any of them. Well, I did once. There was a girl in one of the children's shelters. They put us together and we pretended to recognize each other. I don't think she was from the cult, either."

It was random, the faces my memory clung to and the ones it threw away. That girl's face I remembered with total clarity. She was Haitian, beautiful but starved-looking. We existed together in the same cramped room for about a week before she moved shelters or ran away—I never learned which. I barely spoke French at that point, and she didn't speak English, but when one of the nuns who ran the shelter presented us to each other, we hugged and acted like old friends. It was ridiculous—old friends who didn't speak the same language? But the shelters were so disorganized that no one could be bothered to be suspicious.

"That whole thing was chaos," Alexandrine said. "I suppose you used that to your advantage."

"You make me sound diabolical. I was just a kid."

"That's not how it's going to be perceived. You know how this works."

"Yes," I said. "I do."

Alexandrine rubbed her temples. "I'm sorry. I just can't believe . . . this whole time . . ." *You were a murderer.* I braced myself for the second half of her sentence. When it came, the blow was more brutal than I expected: "You're not Quebecoise."

My mouth hung open. "I mean, for all intents and purposes—"

"Did you even care about liberation? Or was it just part of your . . . costume?"

"Alexandrine, I care." I was adamant. "I *am* Quebecoise."

She shook her head. "Laisse tomber. So you're saying this boy murdered your sister, motivated by the belief that your family had used the power of Satan to turn Gwen transgender. He had a gun and behaved in a sexually aggressive manner. You felt that killing him was the only option, because he would hunt you both down if you tried to escape."

"It sounds like an insane soap opera, I know."

Alexandrine shrugged gamely. "Actually, it sounds like textbook imperfect self-defense, a murder charge being the worst-case scenario. The extreme circumstances will only validate your state of mind in the eyes of a jury."

I thought of the Menendez brothers case in the early '90s. The two had gunned down their parents in their own home, claiming the father had molested them for years and threatened to kill them if they revealed his secret. Imperfect self-defense hadn't worked out so well for them; after two deadlocked juries, both brothers had been sentenced to life in prison.

"I assume Gwen will corroborate all this?" Alexandrine asked.

"Um . . . sort of."

She frowned. "'Sort of'? These are not my favorite words."

"She . . . she thinks I was a little more motivated by, you know, more in the realm of . . ."

"Spit it out, Jo."

"Emotional purging. You know, 'feel my wrath.' *Revenge*, in a word." I cleared my throat awkwardly.

Alexandrine nodded, her mind no doubt forming an image of me hacking Gwen's brother to pieces and ecstatically drinking his blood. She broke the silence with a brittle laugh.

"Bof, is Gwen aware that 'revenge' is just another word for first-degree murder?"

"I know, it's bad," I said quickly. "But she's not like us. She doesn't think in legal terms. Look, I'll deal with it. We'll get our stories straight."

"Get it straight with yourself first, Jo. If you don't buy it, a judge won't, either. Was it self-defense or not?"

I stared down at the carpet. I had no answer, at least none that a sane person would give. The only guaranteed self-defense was to kill *everyone*, on the 0.01 percent chance any of them might kill you first.

Alexandrine waved a hand in front of my face. "You know what? Never mind. Straighten it out with Gwen and get back to me. That's all I'll say."

Fuck.

Alexandrine gazed pensively out the window. "You know, I remember all that Satan nonsense. What a bizarre thing to live through. I'd just graduated law school. People were scared to leave their kids. And to think it started here, in Canada, in British Columbia. That was the first case, back in the seventies. Some crackpot hypnotist psychiatrist. But you Americans take credit for everything, don't you?"

You Americans. I cringed. Fourteen years of an identity, demolished in the space of a single conversation.

"De toute façon," she said abruptly, "have you googled yourself?"

"Oui, a million times. Go ahead—it's Lacey Bond." I dropped the name like I was referring to a dinner reservation.

"No, I mean *yourself.* Have you googled 'Jo Scottish'?"

"Oh. No. That didn't occur to me. Like I said, I'm not thinking straight—"

"Jo, it's all right. Relax. Let's google you, shall we?" She sounded like a soothing hairdresser. *Let's do honey-blond highlights.*

The was a rap at the door, making me jump. A young, very good-looking man poked his head in. I realized he was Alexandrine's assistant (the word "secretary" was never used to describe men). "Madame Sauveterre? You have your eleven o'clock with—"

"Carl, could you cancel everything I have today? Pass it off to Leslie or Robin. And could you order me—"

"Un sandwich oeuf et crudités et une tasse de minestrone? Bien sûr, madame." He flashed a smile and closed the door.

"I adore him," Alexandrine said with a sigh when he was gone. Then she winked. "Remember *Belle maman*?"

"I remember thinking Vincent Lindon looked older than Catherine Deneuve."

Alexandrine laughed. "French men do age so hideously, don't they? I'd take a Quebecois stallion any day. What were we doing just now? Ah, yes. Jo Scottish."

I sat rigidly in my chair, watching her face as she scanned the results.

"What is it? Is there anything?"

"Oui . . ." She bit her lip.

"Mon dieu. What is it? Tell me."

"Is this your teacher?"

She turned her computer to face me. I saw an article from the *Boston Globe*, accompanied by a photo of Mr. Hantz: candid smile, a waterfall in the background, his family members cut out of the frame.

"Yes," I said. "That's him."

"He's been arrested and charged with misprision of a felony. Concealing knowledge of a criminal act."

"What?" Disbelief muted all other responses: guilt, aggravation, terror.

"And look at this."

She clicked on the website of the *National Enquirer*. Between two tawdry headlines ("Lindsay Lohan Shocker: 'I Nearly Died!'" and "Matt Lauer Saves Crumbling Marriage") were a set of words that made my heart stop: "Long-Lost Satan Daughter and Killer Dylan Fairbanks: DISCOVERED!"

"Oh my god. How long has that been up?"

"Not long. It was posted yesterday. You were brilliant not to waste a single second."

The website showed a photo of me eating dinner with Zach at a restaurant, the two of us seemingly together. The picture was grainy and unbeautiful, a style I associated with trashy gossip magazines. That its subject was *me* and not Angelina Jolie or Tiger Woods was so bizarre it felt like a dream, especially since I didn't even resemble the Jo Scottish on the screen. Her hair was shorter and better styled (I hadn't visited my lesbian barber in the Village in ages). Her clothes were perfect, whereas I looked like I'd rolled out of a donation bin.

In the other half of the photo, Zach looked like a movie star, someone worth stalking. He held a glass of champagne, his handsome face beaming with laughter. Amazingly, the real Dylan Fairbanks had been cropped out of the photo, except for her elbow. She'd been right there, on the other side of me, and they'd deleted her.

"Is this a recent picture?" Alexandrine asked.

"No. It's from months ago. It was the night of the party at the Auberge, actually. Gwen and I went to the Village afterward."

"But how could anyone confuse this Zach person with Gwen?"

"There's a lot of confusion in the U.S. about whether Gwen's male or female. It's all mixed up because Dylan actually disappeared before *I* did. She became Destiny. Here, I'll show you."

I leaned across the desk and googled "Dylan Fairbanks," as I had a hundred times in the last few months. I found the eighth-grade school photo that all the news outlets had been circulating—a dumb-looking, shaggy-haired boy wearing a NASCAR T-shirt—along with a very disturbing digital age progression picture that apparently predicted Dylan would grow up to be a multiple rape suspect/meth addict. Though this imaginary version of Dylan looked nothing like Zach, it looked even less like Gwen.

Alexandrine leaned back in her chair. "Alors. What do you want to do, Jo? The Americans will try to extradite you. If you turn yourself in, it might start the process on a friendlier foot."

"No," I said firmly. "There's no friendly foot. Americans are demonic. They'll string me up."

"Americans are just people, like anyone else. They have to follow legal guidelines. As you said yourself, you were just a child—"

I shook my head. "I'm not a child anymore. I'm twenty-eight years old. You know as well as I do that juvenile courts wouldn't have jurisdiction over this. I'd be tried as an adult for first-degree murder—"

"Voluntary manslaughter," Alexandrine interjected.

"I'm not going back. Quebec is my home. They can't make me leave."

Alexandrine narrowed her eyes. "Actually, Jo, Quebec is not your home. You are a guest here—an uninvited guest. Do you understand that?"

I shrugged defensively.

"Don't shrug at me. This is serious, Jo. You and Gwen will have to answer for your actions—in America. That's unavoidable. Maybe you can come back when it's all over—"

"It won't be over till I'm dead. They'll put me in the electric chair. They'll kill me."

"Jesus, Jo. They will not. You are being incredibly paranoid."

"You don't understand. America is a country of psychopaths. I don't think I met a fully sane person in my life until I moved here. They are bloodthirsty. They don't care about facts. They just want someone's head on a pike and a trip to the mall afterward."

Alexandrine smiled patiently. "I think you had a certain experience that might have colored your views in a certain way—"

"I'm not going back, and neither is Gwen. I want Canada to grant us political asylum."

She balked at me. "On what grounds?"

"Malicious prosecution. Homophobia. I don't know. Just come up with something."

"Well . . . could be interesting. It's the exact sort of pathetic cause the ladies here at Marion & Martel love wasting resources on. No offense."

"None taken."

"Let's try it, and if it doesn't work, well then, there we'll be. This is going to wreck my Christmas holiday, isn't it? Tant pis."

Though her words sounded resolved, she didn't look it. She fiddled with a pen on her desk, avoiding my eyes.

"What?" I demanded.

"It's just . . ." Alexandrine started, then stopped, choosing her words carefully. "You and Gwen don't actually have mutual interests here. They'll try to flip one of you, and the media narrative is that *Gwen* killed this boy. He was her brother, after all. It's not public knowledge that he had anything to do with you."

I replied with a chilly stare.

"I'm not suggesting we throw her under a bus!" Alexandrine was quick to add. "Only that you should each have your own lawyer—"

"No. We're not doing that. Nobody's flipping. Our interests are the same."

She put her hands up in surrender. "D'accord. Now, last things last: *money*. I assume you can't afford me?"

"No," I said. "But Debra Messing will play you in the movie."

This made her laugh, which made me laugh, and for a moment I was convinced that it would all be different this time. I was an adult now—a lawyer!—in a civilized country with other like-minded adults, and together we would settle things in a neighborly manner, because that's all this was, really: a dispute between neighbors, like a scuffle over a property line or the noise of a dog. It would all work out, and I would probably receive a commendation from the Canadian Bar Association.

I'm sure I don't need to tell you how far removed from reality these pleasant fantasies revealed themselves to be, in the end.

xli

2006

"I'M PROUD TO BE GAY! I'M PROUD TO BE PART OF GAY NATION! Because the gay gene—*our* gene—gives zero fucks about national boundaries. Gay is American. Gay is Canadian. Gay is Chinese. Gay is a Hassidic Jew . . ."

The speaker was Maxine Kennedy, a poet from Vancouver, famous for claiming to have given Brigitte Bardot her first orgasm. The party was packed, which was impressive for January. I'd even heard there was a line of people waiting outside in the freezing snow.

"Gay is rich. Gay is poor."

Next to me, my mother muttered under her breath, "Gay is a dog. Gay is straight."

I started laughing, then covered it up with a cough.

"I'm going out for a smoke," she whispered.

I tried to stop her. "Mom, the speech is almost over."

But she was already walking away. She'd been treating me like a distant cousin ever since we'd laid eyes on each other at the train station that afternoon, which was fine with me. I didn't think I could handle much more than that. I'd invited her to Montreal half hoping she wouldn't even come. I hadn't invited my father at all.

I'd had a picture in my mind of what fourteen years in prison did to a person. I'd imagined my mother would be Zen and imperturbable. In reality, she'd grown as mannerless as a teenager, prone to walking off in the middle of conversations if she became remotely uninterested, as if now that she was free, she was also free to be an asshole.

Maxine Kennedy had moved on to introducing the next guest: "Our soul sister, icon, and national treasure—k. d. lang!"

Raucous cheers erupted from every corner of the venue, k. d. lang being the monumental "get" of the evening. Supposedly Mia Kirshner was around, too, but I hadn't seen her.

Marla, the events coordinator, materialized at my side and said, with an air of great secrecy, "We've already raised $170,000. But don't tell anyone. We don't want the well running dry. Do you know where Gwen is?"

"No," I said. I'd lost Gwen at the bar, where she'd been carried away like a piece of driftwood by Bjorn and a wave of fashion people.

"Can you find her? We want to get a picture of k. d. lang with all the refugees, and she has to leave right after the set."

The "refugees" were me, Gwen, and a trio of Russians (two men and one woman) dug up from IRCC to be the faces of homophobic persecution abroad. The Russians had been drunk when the party started an hour ago, and I wondered if at this point they'd be able to stand for a photo without swaying.

"I'll find her," I said.

I left the safety of the corner where my mother and I had been more or less hiding. The venue was all dim lighting, red vintage wallpaper, and art deco nude paintings. A bizarre range of people were in attendance: philanthropists jumping on the latest trendy cause; all the gays, from the bohemian street rats to the power gays of Montreal's advertising and legal firms; fashion bloggers hoping for a glimpse of Gwen; news junkies hoping for a glimpse of me—all stirred together with the gayest celebrities Canada had to offer in a restaurant resembling 1930s Berlin.

Everyone was looking at me as I passed—*gawking*. Word had exploded through half the world that the long-lost Satan Daughter was a random lawyer in Montreal, and the gorgeous model Gwen was "actually" a man. Press vans sat camped outside our apartment twenty-four hours a day, getting covered in snow. We'd been instructed by our publicist to wear sad puppy faces whenever a camera was pointed our way. *Aren't we lovable? Please adopt us, Canada!* I'd convinced myself our loud, grabby campaign for sanctuary wasn't a total sham, as homophobia *had* set off this whole chain of events: if Patrice hadn't hated me enough to sic an investigator on me, Gwen and I might never have been discovered.

After circling the club and finding Gwen nowhere, I looked in the ladies' room, all white marble and black lacquered doors and a sparkling chandelier reflecting in the immense mirror. Bjorn and the Russians were there (Zach remained stuck in America facing his small-time possession charge), and Gwen, too, whipping her head up, mid-motion. If I'd arrived half a second earlier, I could have knocked the silver tray of powder away from her nose.

"Oops," Bjorn said, seeing me. "Nanny's here."

Gwen stared at me blankly, her nostrils twitching. The Russians snickered like naughty children.

"You asshole!" I hissed, not to Gwen but to Bjorn.

"Don't look at me!" Bjorn said. "I'm not her momager!"

I grabbed Gwen's arm and pulled her into the wheelchair-accessible stall. "What are you doing?" I demanded.

She closed her eyes and leaned against the door. She was wearing an outfit Valentino had sent her that resembled a costume from *Oliver!*: a Victorian vest, paired with a baby-blue satin blouse, flouncy bow, and jaunty newsboy cap. It was all part of her gender ambiguous "gamine" makeover, which was Bjorn's idea ("Own or be owned" was his motto lately).

"I'm sorry." Gwen sighed with more than a little petulance. "I'm tired. I can't deal with all this anymore. I'm not like you."

I blinked. "Like *me*? You're the fashion model. You're used to people looking at you. Why are you hiding in the bathroom doing drugs?"

"Alcohol is a drug," she said, eyeing the glass of whiskey in my hand.

"It's not an *illegal* drug. We cannot fuck up here, Gwen!"

"Stop judging me!" she moaned. "Everyone's judging me! Everyone's looking at my face, looking for evidence. My chin, my neck. Everyone's staring."

"No, they're not," I said, but it was a lie. People did look at her differently now, though it was impossible to say whether it was because they thought they were looking at a man or a murderer or both.

"We love you, Gwen!" Bjorn called out.

I heard a group of women stumble into the bathroom, tittering at the unexpected presence of Bjorn, a man in the ladies' room. I felt wildly irritated that at this event of all events, no one had thought to cover the bathrooms with gender neutral signs.

Gwen leaned into my arms, her cap becoming disarranged. I held her for a long moment, with no hint of the self-consciousness I sometimes experienced when we touched. I hadn't felt this close to her in years, not since we were on the streets. I wondered if this was what couples felt like when they returned, after years of marriage, to the tropical island of their honeymoon. We'd fallen in love in a deep fryer; persecution was our Bora Bora.

I kissed the top of her head. "We need to go back in now. We have to hobnob."

"Let me do one more line first."

"Gwen."

"It's not a thing, I promise. I just have to get through this night."

"Fine, but don't let my mother find out. She's finally clean and I don't want her around this crap. Bjorn? Get in here."

Gwen ended up snorting the line off the Russian girl's thigh, like a scene from *Casino*. Then we all poured back into the party. I'd assumed the two Russian men were a couple, but Bjorn was making out with one of them and the other didn't seem to care. Poor Zach had gotten his Canadian visa revoked, and there'd been a lot of breathless talk about

Bjorn running away to New Jersey to be with him. But by Christmas, Bjorn had grown bored with the tragedy and declared himself "single as a kringle," which I gathered was some sort of Norwegian cream puff.

A familiar set of bass guitar notes reverberated through the room. On the stage, k. d. lang was doing a cover of "Walk on the Wild Side." Gwen gave me an airy kiss and fluttered onto the dance floor with Bjorn and the Russians.

I located my mother, who was sitting alone at a table, drinking a glass of white wine. It surprised me that she drank wine despite being in drug recovery; then again, it didn't surprise me at all. My mother had never cared about other people's rules.

We watched Gwen on the dance floor. I loved her style of dancing, which was decidedly strange. She sort of prowled around like a burglar, sneaking up on people. I doubted my mother found it particularly cute, the same way she'd never found Éclair's exhibitionism cute. Having the two of them in the same room made me anxious.

"Gwen seems to be handling this all quite well," she said with a note of disparagement.

"I assure you, Mom, she's just as fucked up about it as I am."

She softened. "Well . . . it's tremendously traumatic to be outed," she allowed. "You were always such a hundred-footer. I knew you were gay when you were two years old. You never had to come out. I guess you don't know how it feels."

"I have an inkling," I said, remembering the way Mr. Hantz had gazed at me over his lukewarm pile of poutine. He'd recently found my email address (as had dozens of internet strangers, who sent me charming death threats on a daily basis) and had written me an impassioned message about how he intended to protect me at all costs. He was prepared to face prison rather than cooperate with the feds.

In my reply, I said only, "Please don't put anything else in writing. My email is probably being surveilled."

Did he realize that if he'd wanted to save me, he'd had the chance that evening in July? If he'd just left me alone, that little bald man with his telephoto lens could never have linked me to the past. If Mr. Hantz had seen me on the train, said nothing, and gone home, it would have been the most heroic thing any man had ever done for me.

The song's sedate chorus filled the room. *Walk on the wild side . . .*

"This is your father's favorite song," my mom said out of the blue.

"No, it's not. His favorite song is 'Nights in White Satin.'"

"That's *my* favorite song."

"Oh."

Suddenly I couldn't wait for "Walk on the Wild Side" to be over. It was overplayed and obvious, and it was annoying that every gay person was required to identify with it.

"He's called me five times tonight," Mom said, taking a silver flip phone out of her handbag and tossing it on the table. "I wish you'd just talk to him so I don't have to."

"I can't believe you have a cell phone. *I* don't have a cell phone."

"I hope you're not freezing him out on my account. I'm over it. I've had fourteen years to get over it. You're being cruel."

"I don't care about the affair," I said. "What I can't forgive is that fucking book. Jeannine *slandered* me and Éclair. How could he let her write that trash about us? Did you read what she said about Éclair's clothes? *'Slaggy'*? She didn't come up with that word by herself."

"He says whatever the person in front of him wants to hear. He's always been like that, you were just too young to notice. Give the man a break, Lacey."

My mother was the only person I allowed to call me Lacey. She was my mother, and she'd been in prison for fourteen years. I wasn't about to tell her how she was required to address me.

The song ended and everybody clapped. Mom swigged the rest of her wine like it was moonshine from a jar. Then she stood up.

"If you don't mind, I'd like to go back to my hotel."

"Of course," I said. "Go relax."

"Call me in the morning. I'd love to see where you live."

"It'll probably be late. Gwen likes to sleep in."

"The afternoon, then."

I walked her to the door. People made room for us as we passed—out of respect or fear, it was hard to say. We kissed each other goodbye in the European style, which felt oddly formal, yet appropriate. It relieved me that she was leaving; her judgment of the party's frivolity was making it even more unpleasant than it needed to be.

Marla the events coordinator corralled me and Gwen and the Russians onto the stage for our photo with k. d. lang. The entire party stared like they expected us to burst into song.

"You in the navy suit, on the left—could you smile? Smile!"

Whatever shadow of a smile I had managed completely disappeared.

"No, that's worse!"

Gwen leapt in front of me like a tiger. "How's this?" She gnashed her teeth in mock ferocity. All the partygoers cheered.

"*Smile,*" the photographer growled.

"Fuck you! This is *my* face! Don't tell me what to do!" Gwen yelled at him. Cocaine always made her tyrannical. I both loved it and couldn't stand it, because it reminded me of Éclair. *She took such joy in provoking people,* I recalled my father saying, as if her death had been an inevitability.

"Gwen, it's fine. Let's just smile," I whispered.

"I wanna hear 'La Vida Loca'!" she was shouting. "Right now!"

"You heard the woman," k. d. lang said, and everyone laughed. Within seconds "Livin' la Vida Loca" was blaring from the speakers.

I decided I was sober enough for another drink. While Gwen and the others spilled from the stage onto the dance floor, I snuck along the wall to the bar.

"Un whisky s'il vous plaît."

I heard a voice behind me: "Some party, huh? I hope you're having a good time."

Turning, I saw a girl, maybe twenty-three years old. Her tight cardigan made her breasts look like torpedoes. She drank her wine through a straw, pursing her pink lips.

"I hope you are, too," I parroted back.

Her face turned abruptly stony. "There are so many amazing LGBT people who deserve a nice home. And a lot of *them*," she added, "didn't shoot an underprivileged child in the head. A lot of *them* don't put their faces on billboards to sell elitist handbags made by child labor. Don't you think there are people who deserve this charity more than you? Don't you think about that?"

"Yes," I said truthfully, taking a swig of my whiskey. I turned to leave, but she stepped in front of me, sticking out her torpedo boobs.

"This party is disgusting," she declared.

"Then why did you come?"

"To tell you it's disgusting."

"Well, mission accomplished. And FYI, plastic straws end up in the ocean and sea turtles choke on them."

"Fuck you." She turned on her heel and walked off.

I glanced around, nervous. Had people overheard? I felt fourteen years old all over again, dreading that anything Éclair and I said or did might end up on the news the next day.

"That looked tense. Ex-girlfriend?"

I whirled around, and there she was, *Diane*, somehow escaped from under the rug where Gwen and I had shoved her. She was perfectly balanced on high heels, wearing a leather pencil skirt that hugged her hips possessively. The fabric of her loose gold blouse spilled over her breasts. Her hallmark burgundy lipstick feathered into the little wrinkles around her mouth.

"I don't have any ex-girlfriends," I said.

"Ah yes, that's right. Gwen's your one and only."

The music changed to a thudding, sultry electronic beat. I pulled at my collar, feeling overheated.

"It's nice to see you, Diane," I managed to say. "Comment ça va?"

"Ça va bien. I can see from your face that you're surprised to see me."

"I am. Who invited you?"

"Alexandrine. We were roommates in college."

We gazed at the dance floor. Gwen and Sveta were dancing exuberantly. Across the room, I could see Marla watching. It was important for us to have a good time, but not *too* good a time. No one wanted the impression that refugees were coming to Canada to have wild parties.

"Gwen looks radiant," Diane said, leaning against the bar. My eyes grazed her unreasonably tight skirt. Leather was a hot material—her cunt was probably sticky with moist sweat. I wanted to slip my hands between her legs and find out. I knew she would let me.

My stomach twisted in a sick knot as I flashed back to Yvonne's office in Concord. Her beige carpet, the steamy windows, the confusion of wanting something while at the same time viscerally not wanting it. Where was she now? I wondered. Did she tense with dread every time she heard my name on the news? Imagining her wasting her life worrying about being outed for statutory rape gave me some satisfaction—but not a lot. All this time later, and I still couldn't bring myself to wish evil upon her. She was the first woman who'd ever found me attractive.

"You know," Diane said casually, "I wasn't so surprised when I read about you in the newspaper. I knew you had some secret."

I asked the bartender for another whiskey. Diane was still staring at Gwen.

"So what's that like?" she asked.

I rolled my eyes. "Whatever could you mean?"

She sipped her drink. "All this commotion over same-sex marriage. Don't you find it rather hilarious? You two could have been married this whole time."

My jaw dropped. Intelligent words escaped me. *You fucking bitch* was all I could think. I raised my hand to slap her, but as I did, Diane lurched forward and collided with me, causing me to trip and fall, sloshing my drink all over myself. Diane was on top of me for a second, our legs awkwardly entangled. Then she picked herself up, sputtering a string of French obscenities.

Gwen was facing her, furious. From my vantage point, she and Diane looked like Godzilla and King Kong, facing off for dominion over all mortals.

Diane reached out her hand to help me up.

"Don't touch her," Gwen ordered. I waved Diane's hand away and turned to apologize to the people we'd bumped into.

Diane was brushing herself off. "Junior high all over again. How fun."

She checked her pocketbook to ensure that nothing had tumbled out, lifted her chin, and walked away, like she'd only come to ask directions to someplace classier. The people around us started chatting and drinking again. I heard someone behind me already revising the story to paint Gwen in a better light ("Did you see that? The old lady called Gwen a tranny, and Gwen smacked her!").

I took Gwen's arm and walked her out of the crowd. She didn't fight me. In the entryway, I grabbed two random coats—half for efficiency and half because I thought Gwen would be less likely to bolt off into the night if she was wearing someone else's coat.

The street was deadly silent, the falling snow muffling all sound. Within five seconds Gwen looked like an ice princess from a fairy tale, snowflakes as perfect as Christmas ornaments resting in her hair.

"How could you invite her?" she demanded, her voice cold.

"I didn't. Alexandrine did. It took me completely by surprise, I swear. I should have walked away, but I wasn't thinking straight. I'd just been accosted by this heinous politically correct girl—"

"The bitch with the Madonna tits? She cornered me, too. She gave me a lecture about how people in Africa were starving while rich white girls spent four thousand dollars on handbags. So I was like, 'You wouldn't be saying that if it were a painting or a sculpture.' And she said, 'Those are works of art,' and I said, *I'm* a work of art.' And she laughed at me."

"Oh, Gwen. Fuck her." I wrapped Gwen in a hug. She smelled different because of the coat—mothballs and peppermint. I'd heard about the oxymoronic phenomenon that the more success a model attained, the more her self-esteem ended up suffering. To the camera lens, Gwen was as much an object as her overpriced handbag. The price of being art was your humanity.

All at once I was on the verge of tears.

"I can't do this anymore," I whispered.

Gwen stepped back. "What's the matter? Can't do what?"

"I can't keep asking people for charity. I should go back to America where I belong, with all the other psychopaths."

She shook my shoulders, hard. "Stop it. You are *not* a psychopath. Psychopaths kill for no reason."

"Psychopaths invent reasons," I said tiredly. "They think their reasons are perfectly legitimate. Just like I thought my reasons were perfectly legitimate."

"They *were*."

My jaw clenched. "That wasn't your attitude the last time we had this discussion. You said I only did it for myself."

It was dangerous to open this line of inquiry. We had not "straightened out our story" as I'd promised Alexandrine we would. No day had seemed like a particularly good one to wind up screaming at each other. If we weren't careful, we'd end up doing it now, to the delight of every vulturelike blogger covering the event.

I waited for Gwen to clap back. She just stared at me.

"You did do it for yourself," she said. "And I think that was legitimate."

For a long moment we stood silently. The snow continued to fall, melting Gwen's makeup and giving her raccoon eyes. Then her phone buzzed.

"Shit. It's Alexandrine."

Gwen flipped the phone open, and I listened as Alexandrine gave her an earful about attacking a guest in the middle of the fundraiser. She'd warned us that we couldn't sustain any more PR disasters. We'd already had about three hundred. It started with the widespread confusion over our ages. I'd been posing as thirty-one and Gwen had been posing as twenty-four, so when people did the math it looked like I'd been seventeen when we'd left the United States and Dylan had been nine, which was kidnapping. Tons of people on the internet still believed my parents were Satanist pedophiles, and this played right into their hands. *See?* they screamed into their computers. *The pedophilic apple doesn't fall far from the pedophilic tree!*

Then there had been an uproar when a model Gwen had worked with in Paris claimed to be traumatized that Gwen had seen her naked in a dressing room. Her name was Cassandra Harris, and she'd given interviews to anyone who would listen, saying, "I can't believe there was a *man* seeing me in those intimate moments. I feel violated!"

Her violation was being taken very seriously by the press. A new era was dawning in which everyone's feelings were "valid." I couldn't imagine Éclair attempting to navigate this trend. One of the last things she'd ever said to me was "Your feelings are stupid and made up."

The morning after the fundraiser, my mother came to the apartment. I was hoping our bohemian digs would temper her undisguised disdain for the fact that I'd escaped our legal hell only to grow up and become a lawyer.

When I opened the door, I saw that she was wearing beige from head to toe, as if she'd spent so long in the drab world of prison that she'd forgotten clothes came in other colors. She was carrying a large jar of honey.

"I brought you this from the farm," she said.

A white label on the jar read, in a Gothic font, KITCHEN WITCH FARMS.

"So it's true?" I asked. "You're living with a bunch of witches?"

"It's a joke. It started as a joke, anyway. But they fly off the table at the farmers market. Times have changed, haven't they? It used to be sex sells this, sex sells that. But now I think horror sells. People get off on being afraid."

"Hmm," I said, unsure how to receive this speech.

Gwen appeared in the doorway of the bedroom, rubbing her eyes. When she saw my mom, she said, "Oh, hi. Is that honey? Awesome."

She took the jar without asking, unscrewed the lid, and dunked her hand inside. She smeared the sticky mess directly onto her face. Mom shot a look at me. *What the hell is she doing?* The whole thing reminded me uncomfortably of my childhood: Mom on one side, Éclair on the other, me in the middle.

I made some tea while Mom poked around the apartment.

"You talk French now?" she asked me idly. *Talk French.* Every once in a while I remembered that my mother was from Indiana and had seen even less of the world than I had.

"It's a bilingual county, but you have to speak French to be part of the community. It's very important."

"Why? If everyone knows English?"

"To save our soul."

"Hmm . . ." She seemed to be analyzing me. But instead of revealing her analysis, she turned to Gwen. "And you speak French, too?"

"Not as well as Jo," Gwen answered shyly. "But I know all the bad words. Can I have some more of that honey? I feel like trash."

"Well, putting food on your face won't help," Mom said.

I watched the two of them anxiously. I'd warned Gwen that my mother was no longer the soothing, spacey hippie from our childhood, that she might make some comment about how hormone injections were a pharmaceutical conspiracy. But so far, she'd said nothing about

Gwen's transition.

She reached out to touch Gwen's sticky, honey-covered cheek. "It's your spirit that feels like trash. *Inside*. There's too much emphasis on the surface."

"Mom," I said loudly from the kitchen. "No one needs your hippie lecture."

My mother ignored me and ordered Gwen to the floor. "Lie down. I'll do your pressure points. We'll unblock the flow of energy through the meridians."

"Okay . . ." Gwen sat down. My mom grabbed her feet and started kneading the webbing of her toes.

"Can we put the TV on?" she asked. "I love hearing the French shows."

"Bien sûr," I said. "That's why they call it la belle langue."

I clicked on the TV and found Ici ARTV. *Mon oncle Antoine* was on. Considered one of Quebec's greatest films, it was about a rural boy in the 1940s helping his drunkard uncle move a casket in a horse-drawn sleigh. The film reflected the contradictions of the Quebecois spirit: nostalgic and bitter, sentimental and existential. Its director had met a grim end. After learning he had Alzheimer's disease, he'd thrown himself into the Saint Lawrence, where his body went undiscovered until the river thawed the following spring.

I sipped my tea while the movie played and my mom messed with Gwen's chakras. I felt relieved we could sit quietly together and not talk—the kind of intimacy reserved strictly for families. But we were haunted people, fitted together by the pieces of us that were missing. Gwen could pretend that my mother was her mother, and my mother and I could pretend she was Éclair, and we could all pretend, for a moment, that we were normal.

Around three o'clock, Alexandrine called, sounding urgent.

"Mon dieu, Jo. We need to talk."

"I can be at your office in half an hour."

"I better come to you. The lobby here is mobbed. Are there reporters at your house?"

I looked out the window. The street was empty except for a pair of parked news vans, their crews presumably shivering inside. "Not really. I think the snow drove them away."

"I'm on my way."

When Alexandrine arrived, she overwhelmed the narrow entryway of the apartment with her abundance of scarves, gloves, and various pieces of outerwear. She shook hands with my mother and tried to engage her in small talk. "How are you enjoying Montreal? Have you tried one of our famous bagels?"

To which my mother replied, "Cities are cities."

I gestured for Alexandrine to sit at the dining table by the window. She plunked down, looking exhausted.

"Can I pour you some wine?" I offered.

"Non, merci. Actually, why not? This is pro bono."

"Let's make it vino bono."

Alexandrine barely laughed—she who laughed at everything—and that's when I understood, without her having to say a word, that the charade was over.

xlii

"I CAN'T PRETEND THIS SITUATION ISN'T DIRE," ALEXANDRINE started. "It was always going to be an uphill battle, but we're being shot at from all directions. I had no idea we'd be taking heat from the *Left*. I thought conservatives had the monopoly on Puritanism. Getting asylum for both of you is looking increasingly unlikely."

Abruptly, my mother stood. "I'm going to see this mountain in the middle of town," she said.

"Mount Royal?" I asked. "You'll have to take a bus. It's too far to walk and there's no metro stop. And it's getting dark."

"That's fine." She was putting on her coat and snow boots.

"Take my bus card and a map at least." I handed them over. Within minutes she was out the door. Alexandrine watched her leave, a look of incredulity on her face.

"Your mother doesn't want to hear this?" she asked once she was gone. "This is your future we're talking about."

"She doesn't like social situations."

"This isn't a 'social situation.' We have to make some incredibly tough choices."

"She's a beekeeper. It's not like she can help. And her train home is tomorrow morning. I'm sure she wants to explore."

I could see from Alexandrine's face that she found the coldness between my mother and me disturbing. I wanted to snap at her, *Go disappear for fifteen years and see how cozy you and your mom are afterward.*

"Alors," she said finally, "here's where we are. We can keep pushing for asylum. But that means months of waiting, and probably neither of you will get it in the end. There's been too much tumult, and the fact is a teenage boy was killed and you are responsible. Now, I don't think the government will kick you out. It's possible that you two could stay here safely for the rest of your lives. You would be illegal aliens, but you would have some rights to employment and public assistance."

Gwen's face lit up. "They'll let us stay?"

"Public assistance?" I echoed.

Alexandrine scowled. "Don't be an ass, Jo. Plenty of undocumented immigrants live perfectly respectable lives here."

I shook my head. "I want my citizenship confirmed. I want to legally change my name to Jo Scottish and take the bar exam again. I want everything to be legal and stable and formalized—"

"Jo, that was a dream! We tried it, and it didn't work. You need to let it go. Your life will never go back to the way it was."

I dropped my head into my hands. Since when was it my greatest dream to have my existence legitimized by the government, anyway?

Alexandrine's tone remained firm. "The time has come for you two to seriously consider turning yourselves over to the FBI. I really believe it will be painless. You'll plead 'not guilty.' The case is fifteen years old, and you were both minors. No one is going to convict you. The trial will be over in a year, and then you'll be free of the whole thing—forever. That's the beauty of American double jeopardy law."

I stared at her, dumbfounded. "Alexandrine, with all respect, you have no idea what you're talking about—"

Alexandrine rolled her eyes. "Oui, oui, they're all out to get you. Americans are killer clowns from outer space. They want to fry you in hot butter and eat you alive."

Gwen watched us argue, her pale eyes darting back and forth between me and Alexandrine.

"Go ahead and think I'm crazy," I said. "But you know that they'll hold Gwen in a male facility. That's a *fact*. American prisons have no procedures for trans inmates, not unless they've undergone complete sexual reassignment surgery."

"The ACLU and every gay rights organization under the sun will be watching this with a microscope, Jo. If one hair on Gwen's head is disturbed—"

"No. No. No. No," I said, knowing I sounded exactly as unhinged as Alexandrine thought I was. "Gwen will not be a test subject for how well the Americans can behave themselves. Fuck no."

A tense silence reigned. I realized, with embarrassment, that Alexandrine and I had been yelling back and forth about Gwen as if she weren't sitting right there. Alexandrine seemed to realize this, too, and turned to her, asking, "Gwen, what do *you* want to do?"

Gwen shrugged. "I just want to see *King Kong* before it leaves the theaters."

A look passed over Alexandrine's face, like she was wondering whether Gwen was mentally handicapped. "Chérie, what we're asking is which *plan* do you think is best? The plan where you stay here, or the plan where you go home?"

"Please don't talk to her like that," I said.

"She seems dazed!"

"I'm not dazed, this is just stupid!" Gwen exclaimed. "Why is everyone so obsessed? Jo did one dramatic thing a million years ago, so what? Why is everyone stuck in the past? Why can't they just *drop it*?"

She gave the table leg a kick.

Now it was Alexandrine's turn to shrug. "People want to understand what happened, chérie. They want the truth to prevail."

Do they? I thought. I recalled the news coverage of my parents' release, how it had focused on Jeannine's insipid book and whether prison had turned my mother into a lesbian. How the only person who'd taken any responsibility at all was Sandy Goodwin, who'd been a *child*.

"Alors, let's take this down a notch, shall we?" Alexandrine said, and sighed. "There is a third option, but I don't recommend it. It's a last resort, and it saves only one of you."

"Which one?" I asked.

"That's up to you. One of you would return to America and take sole responsibility for this kid's death, pleading guilty. It would take the pressure off the government here and make it easier for the other to be officially granted asylum."

"Obviously I'll go, and Gwen will stay," I said.

"I can go—"

"Over my dead body."

"It's a tough choice. It won't be pretty, whoever goes. Jail time is almost guaranteed. If Gwen stays, she'll be stuck in Canada forever. No more flying off to France for modelling jobs."

"Stop trying to scare her," I said. "The French don't extradite. They've been harboring Roman Polanski for thirty years."

Alexandrine threw her hands up. "Vraiment, Jo, I don't know why you asked for my help if you don't intend to listen to a word I say. This is why I hate representing other lawyers." She groaned tiredly. "We're all exhausted and could use some time to reflect on the situation. Let's talk in the morning, shall we?"

"Bon."

She started collecting her various pieces of outerwear, which were scattered around the apartment as if a snowman had barged in and melted, leaving its accessories behind. I showed her out the door, then started putting on my own coat and snow boots.

"Where are you going?" Gwen asked.

"I don't know. I need some air. I need to think."

"Are you coming back?" Her face had gone ashen, the way it always did when she was about to cry.

"Gwen, of course I'm coming back," I said. "Come here."

I pulled her into my arms. She buried her face in my shoulder, and we entered a long, trancelike hug.

"You won't really turn yourself in, will you?" Gwen asked after a while, her voice muffled. "You'll stay here with me, and we'll be illegal aliens, like Alexandrine said."

"Living off Canada's scraps like rats? I did that once. I can't do it again."

"But why should I be the one getting asylum while you go to America to get shit on?"

I sighed. "Because I pulled the trigger."

"But it's not fair. You love it here. You love Quebec so much I feel jealous sometimes. I'm just your dumb girlfriend, and Quebec is your fascinating mistress."

"Quebec is male," I reminded her. "Vive *le* Quebec."

Outside, the cold was bracing. I'd always loved how icy weather gave the mind a reprieve from thoughts, returning the human spirit to a primitive condition: setting one foot in front of the other, just getting through the snow.

Without conscious choice, I found myself on the bus to Parc du Mont-Royal, where my mother had gone. I didn't know if it was the call of trees and snow and silence, or if all the stress had turned me into a child again, a child who wanted her mother.

I didn't expect to actually find her. The park was huge, it was getting dark, and for all I knew, she had already left. I was the only passenger who got off the bus at the top of the mountain (to call it a mountain was generous; its elevation was less than a thousand feet). I trudged through the snow toward the peak, where there was a chalet and a spectacular view of the city that provided the backdrop for many over-the-top wedding proposals between March and October. The overlook was nearly empty now, only a few hardy souls earning the sight of the view at its most beautiful, sparkling with light and snow in the midst of the bitterly cold darkness.

One of them was my mother, standing at the edge.

"Hi," I said, almost saying *bonsoir* but catching myself.

She turned around. "Oh. Hi. I was just about to leave."

We stared at the city together in silence. I was embarrassed by how much I wanted her to compliment the view, to tell me she liked it. But I knew that she didn't. No matter how glamorous a skyline might be, to my mother it was still a concrete-and-steel footprint where there ought to have been a forest.

"Éclair would like this," she said unexpectedly, as if Éclair might come visit one day and see it for herself.

"Yes," I agreed. "Except she never liked the cold."

My mother flinched. By using the past tense, I'd broken the spell.

"Where is she buried?" I asked. I felt ashamed that I didn't know.

She made a face. "We stored the ashes in a temporary vault till we could settle on a place for a family plot. But your father can't make a damn decision, so they're still sitting there."

"Jesus."

"I think that's why all this toxic shit is happening. Nothing was resolved. Her spirit has been restless for fifteen years."

I nodded. It was too much to say out loud that I thought she was right.

"She'd be thirty-six this year, can you imagine that?" I asked.

"Not really, no."

"She'd be some famous artist's muse by now, like Edie Sedgwick," I said.

"Edie Sedgwick died of a drug overdose when she was twenty-eight." My mother shook the snow from her wool hat, then put it back on. "You shouldn't torture yourself, Lacey, imagining Éclair's life would have been all champagne and roses. You know she would have blown every cent of that Lifetime movie money, and then what? Back to Miami. She'd have started up with those gangsters again."

"I know." I sighed. "I know."

We stared at the skyline for a long minute. Then my mother, not seeming particularly eager to hear the answer, asked, "Is everything going to be okay with your legal situation?"

"No," I said. "I think I have to come home."

"Really? It's that serious?"

"Mom, we killed someone. *I* killed someone."

Her brow furrowed as if this were news to her, and I felt a gulf yawn between us. Her legal situation had never involved this level of existential anxiety; she'd had innocence on her side. She could move on, whereas I would always be stuck trying to prove, to quote Aaron Feingold, Esq., that it wasn't all "one big ass-fuck." I woke every morning knowing it was my fault I had this *thing* hanging over my head, because I could have made a different choice that day, the choice *not* to kill someone, the choice 99 percent of people would have made. It wasn't random that I was the one who'd pulled the trigger, not Gwen. She didn't have the heart of a killer. Not even Éclair, who was supposed to be the crazy one—Éclair who had attacked a prison inmate with her purse—not even she would have taken it as far as I had. She would have stopped herself, made some comment about how it wasn't worth breaking a nail.

Me? I'd looked Dodge right in his maniacal face and thought, *I'll have what he's having. Somebody get me a gun.*

My mother gazed at me in the dim light. I could tell from her face that she didn't understand.

"But, Lacey, you were just a child."

"Violent crime peaks during adolescence. It doesn't make me special. Something about the cerebral cortex, apparently . . ."

"Where will you live? It's hard to get a place these days. So many damn forms to fill out. And you can't stay in the old house. Vandals ran amok in it, and half the walls collapsed. The property value's gone to shit. I think it's a conspiracy. The government wants everyone to sell so they can build wind farms."

I sighed, trying not to get impatient. "I'll be in Vermont, Mom. That's where I committed the crime."

"Oh. So you're not really coming home."

"No," I said. "I misspoke."

xliii

IN SHORT ORDER, WE WITHDREW MY APPLICATION FOR POLITI-
cal asylum and called a news conference, at which I gave a brief, unbeautiful statement:

"I'd like to announce my intention to return to Vermont at the request of the FBI. I can no longer trespass upon the hospitality of my ad-
opted country. I am grateful for the support of the LGBT community
here and abroad. Grand merci à mes amis en Quebec. Je me souviens."

Then I stepped aside to allow Alexandrine to speak while I stood
in the background with Gwen. We had been advised not to hold hands
or display affection in front of the cameras. Our relationship was too
confusing for the average evening news viewer to comprehend.

Gwen had also been instructed to look demure and conservative,
words she heeded in her characteristically bizarre way, wearing a barely
there satin dress with something resembling a bra on top. An enormous
spiked belt with sadomasochistic-looking studs completed the outfit. If
worn by Éclair, I'd have assumed the ensemble was specifically designed
to piss everyone off. But I was certain that Gwen actually, endearingly,
believed she was being conservative. The dress was beige, after all.

"Gwen Fairbanks will remain in Canada and will continue to seek
asylum from the persecution of her home government. We fervently
ask that this protection be granted, on the grounds that Dylan's safety
would be endangered by her homeland's corrections system and the
lack of civil protections for transgender individuals under American

law. Lacey Bond, commendably, has agreed to cooperate fully with the investigation into the death of Dodge Roach. The American people will have their appetite for justice satisfied. It would be immoral and beneath us as Canadians to deny Dylan safe harbor in our country. Thank you. No questions. I said no questions!"

My new lawyer's name was Norman J. Wilson, and he was the only one I interviewed over the phone who didn't pitch himself for the job like a salesman. All Mr. Wilson said was "I'd really like to get in on this because my Arnold needs an operation." Arnold, I learned, was a Rottweiler.

I bought a train ticket for myself for February 4 on Amtrak's Adirondack line from Montreal to New York. A pair of FBI agents would meet me on the train and take custody of me as soon as we reached American soil, whereupon I would be escorted to Vermont. Norman would meet me in Montpelier for the arraignment and bail hearing. It all seemed very reasonable and organized, as if everyone knew I was on a hair trigger and it would take only the slightest obstacle for me to say, *Never mind, fuck no, I'm not going.*

Gwen was in denial about the whole thing. She refused to acknowledge that it was happening. It culminated in a fight over—what else?—the damned hypothetical cat.

"I was thinking we could go to the shelter and pick one out before I leave," I said. We were having dinner, cold pita bread and lentil soup. Gwen slopped hers around in the bowl like it was sewage.

"Oh sure, *now* you want to get a cat," she grumbled.

"I don't want you to be alone."

"Then you shouldn't leave. You have so much pride you'd rather abandon me and go to jail than go on public assistance."

"Gwen, I'm not abandoning you. I'm trying to keep you from getting arrested."

"Don't act like you're doing me a favor! If you wanted to be my hero, you would stay."

I dropped my spoon with a clatter. "Look, maybe you can fly off into la-la land about this, but for me, it's always there. It's always in the back of my mind. I can't walk away. Not again. I need it to be resolved."

She folded her arms defiantly.

"What?" I demanded. "Whatever you're thinking, just say it."

"Fine. Maybe if we'd *walked away* from Dodge instead of *resolving* it, none of this would be happening."

I stared at her, speechless. Then I hissed, "I wanted to walk away! I would have loved to walk away! You're the one who said he was going to follow you to the ends of the earth."

She looked confused. "Did I? I don't remember that."

"Yes, you did!" I couldn't believe my ears. She *didn't remember*? As if it were a dim childhood anecdote and not the most fucked-up thing that had ever happened to us.

I barreled on: "You knew all I needed was an excuse. For you, it was just make-believe. You and your *death pit*. But you knew I could take it to the next level."

"Wow." Gwen took a deep breath through her nose. "I'm really trying not to get mad, because I know you're paranoid. But I don't go around *masterminding* people, Jo. That's *you*. You're the one who made us go to therapy. You're the one who makes me feel like I have to hide bridal magazines in the closet."

"Just admit that you said it!"

She threw up her hands. "Maybe I did! I don't remember! Even so, it's not like Dodge was frickin' Jason Bourne. He was just a stupid kid! He couldn't have found us."

"If he was just a stupid kid, maybe I shouldn't have *offed* him!"

"That's not what I meant, Jo! Ugh! You never listen to what I'm saying, so what's the point in talking to you?" She grabbed her bowl and stalked to the living room to sit down in front of the TV.

We'd had almost fifteen years to deal with the fundamental problems of our relationship, and we hadn't done it. I guess we'd always assumed we would get around to it later. But suddenly I was leaving in a week, and no amount of emergency couples counseling could make us ready for the separation in time.

For one shred of closure, I attempted to visit Montagne. The nursing home was a dismal gray building, though I imagined it looked brighter in the spring and summer, with the trees in bloom.

"I'm here to visit someone?" I said uncertainly to the nurse stationed at the front desk. He was a young blond man, reminding me of the smug boys fresh out of law school who'd always annoyed me at the courthouse.

"And who would that be?" he said, exhaling as if already exhausted by me.

"Monsieur le Justice Montagne, s'il vous plaît."

He gave me a quick look up and down, then said, "Visits to le monsieur are restricted to family only."

"I am family."

"No, you're not. I know who you are."

I felt my cheeks go hot with anger. It was my bedrock trigger: strangers thinking they knew me.

"I'm an old friend," I said. "I'm sure that if le monsieur knew I was here, he would want to see me."

"Rules are rules," he said blandly.

"Please, this is important. Look into your soul"—I glanced at his name tag—"Rick. Are you a mindless bureaucrat or are you a human being? This isn't the DMV. This is a place where people are *dying*."

Rick was unmoved by my speech. "I'm sorry, but we can't allow the public to disturb our patients. It can be dangerous. I'm sure you understand. You can write le monsieur a note. That's all I can do for you."

He passed me a ballpoint pen and a mass-produced notepad from the Alzheimer's Society of Canada. I took them and sat down in the waiting area. On the table next to me was a plate of sugar cookies covered by a glass dome, meant to evoke the coziness of Grandma's house but hardly equal to the task. I stared at the notepad, then at my hand, wishing I were a calligraphist. Montagne had always found my handwriting deplorable. I tried to summon the words to say goodbye, but my brain had gone blank. After a moment I gave up and left.

I felt no desire to savor my last night in Montreal. If I could have rustled up some barbiturates, I'd have taken three and blacked out until it was time for my train ride to doom. In the bathroom I found some nighttime cough syrup with about half an inch left in the bottle. I was mid-swig when Gwen poked her head in.

"What are you doing?" she asked, pushing the door open with her foot. "I thought we could stay up all night."

"Why?"

"I dunno. Because you're leaving."

"I thought you were mad at me."

"No, not really."

I put the cough syrup back in the medicine cabinet. "What do you want to do?" I asked.

She looked at the floor. "I want to do a spell. Like, a witch's spell."

I followed her into the living room and realized she meant actual, literal witchcraft. She'd lit every candle we owned and spread a Moroccan shawl in the middle of the floor.

"Come on, Gwen, you know I hate this kind of stuff."

"Don't be mad. It's your goodbye present to me. The only thing I want." She plopped cross-legged on the floor and patted the spot across from her.

Warily, I sat down.

"I want you to do a spell like you did in ninth grade," she said, "when you cursed George Bush to lose reelection and then he did."

"That was a coincidence."

"You cursed Melissa Shears to die a miserable, painful death, and she did."

"Gwen . . ."

"I don't care if you think it's real. *I* think it's real. I want you to do a spell on us, so that we'll stay together no matter what."

"What if I can only do curses?"

"Then curse us."

"Gwen," I said, wanting to speak very carefully. "Don't you ever wonder if you'd be happier with someone else? I've been dragging you down with my issues for a decade and a half. And you . . . you deserve to have everything you want."

She scowled. "Is this about the bridal magazines? I'll light them on fire if you want. I don't care."

"You don't need me as much as you think you do, Gwen. You're going to be fine. You can do anything. You can live a life—a good life."

I can do this, I coached myself. *I can do this. I can let her go.*

I placed my hand on hers. She yanked it away.

"Shut up," she snapped. "I don't want things I don't want. Stop trying to push crap on me to make yourself feel better. I want to be with you."

"Why?"

"Because you're the only person I've ever loved besides my mom. She always liked you, you know. She said you were one of those people— the special people. The ones who're *going places*. You never got trapped in dumb situations the way I did. I knew I would be lucky to be your friend, and I was right. My mom was right."

Mothers weren't prophets. Gwen would have learned that eventually, if her mom hadn't died.

"Come on," she ordered. She opened a jewelry box and dumped its contents on the shawl: an amethyst, some gold chains, a few random rocks. "I didn't know what you would need."

"I don't need anything," I said. "I do it with my thoughts."

"Then do it."

"Fine." I gulped down some wine and took her hands in mine. "Close your eyes. Imagine all the darkness of the universe converging into a ball behind your third eye chakra—that's the spot right between your eyes. It's a swirling black ball of power and pure energy. It's spinning fast, like a baseball in midair. Do you see it?"

"Yes," Gwen answered.

"Harness it with your mind. Control it. Slow it down. Is it slowing down?"

"Yes."

"Slower and slower until it stops. Now, the power of the universe is at your command. Repeat after me: May my love always be with me."

"May my love always be with me," Gwen echoed.

"May she dog my steps."

"May she dog my steps."

"And haunt my dreams."

"And haunt my dreams."

"May I never know freedom."

"May I never know freedom."

"Whether in heaven or hell, may I never be alone."

"Whether in heaven or hell, may I never be alone."

"I curse myself to be with you. For all eternity, I curse myself."

"I curse myself to be with you. For all eternity, I curse myself."

"I curse myself."

"I curse myself."

For a second our voices merged, like in an om, the individual syllables losing their meaning.

It was hitting me, the reality of it. This wasn't like Gwen's trips to Europe. My ticket was, in its overbearing symbolism, one way. And while the whole point was to keep Gwen out of prison, there were other ways for her life to crash and burn. Once I left, there would be little stopping her from wandering off into the streets like a displaced ghost. And I think Gwen knew that, and she hoped it might make a difference if I was there with her in spirit as she faded into that sheer white oblivion.

xliv

VERMONT
2006

THE GOOD NEWS WAS THAT MY LAWYER'S DOG'S HIP REPLACE-
ment surgery went off without a hitch. Norman was so absorbed in
Arnold's recovery it was all he talked about: Arnold's surgical incision,
Arnold's diet, Arnold's closely managed schedule of napping and taking
various pills. After a month I felt like an expert on canine post-operative
care.

Meanwhile Norman had yet to demonstrate much interest in the
details of my case. Which was fine with me, because it meant I could
effectively represent myself. All I needed him to do was show up in his
least rumpled suit and recite the statements I'd written.

I was living in his cellar on a dirty mattress next to a washing machine. The room was damp and moldy, with a faint air of death (I'd
found a dead raccoon in the ceiling and hadn't been able to completely
eradicate the smell). But it was free, which was all I could afford. I'd
emptied half the $20K in Gwen's savings account posting bail, and the
other half I'd forked over to Norman. The "bag money" I'd told Gwen
to keep and spend wisely. It was too soon to tell whether this whole circus had torpedoed her career. It was possible the Bianchi gig would be
the last one she ever got. Even American Psycho had pulled his business
(in terms of silver linings, I'd take it).

Norman lived on a large plot of land that had been a turkey farm
before the government shut it down for violating county land use regulations. In my absence, it seemed Vermont had become the Canada

of America. "It's all regulations and rainbows these days!" Norman enjoyed bellowing.

And he wasn't wrong. My attempt to get a driver's license involved so much paperwork and scurrying between government offices that by the time I finally received the little rectangular card proving my existence and ability to drive—ever linked in the American identity—I felt so disassociated that the Jo Scottish I'd made official might as well have been a cardboard cutout. As for the rainbows, I'd never seen so many gray-haired, Birkenstock-wearing homosexual couples in one place. Norman often said he wished New Hampshire would legalize same-sex marriage, too, so the gays would have someplace else to go.

At night I lay awake on my sagging mattress. For the first time in fifteen years, I was well and truly *alone*. Gwen felt like a phantom limb; I kept having the sensation that she was next to me, only to remember with a start that she was on the other side of a national border.

I'd come away from the curse feeling like I'd tempted fate way too far this time, that what was meant to be a marriage ceremony should have been a divorce. Every day I half expected to hear news of Gwen's gruesome death at the hands of a lunatic stalker or Bill Cosby. Why hadn't I cut the cord when I had the chance?

But now was hardly the time to initiate a painful breakup, not with the FBI probably surveilling my phone calls and emails. Letters were safer, but what was I supposed to do? Write, *Dear Gwen, The universe gave us this chance to make a clean break. I can't do it by myself. I need you to participate,* and wait two weeks for her livid response?

Ultimately, I added "breaking up" to the laundry list of things we'd have to get around to later. I became an expert at filling pages with vacuous, pointless paragraphs. *Dear Gwen, I find myself a stranger in a strange land . . .*

I'd lived in the city so long I'd forgotten how dark and quiet the night could be. As a child, I'd found it peaceful, but now it frightened me. I could feel the trees, the stars, the owls, all of nature, sneering at me. Everything was unfamiliar. New Hampshire's famous Old Man of the Mountain had collapsed while I was away. That craggy face jutting out of Cannon Mountain didn't exist anymore. It was just *gone*.

On March 4, 2006, I pleaded guilty in Vermont Superior Court to charges of voluntary manslaughter—murder's gentler, more emotionally understanding cousin. "Provocation" was the key word now. Dodge Roach had *provoked* my actions by demonstrating unstable and aggressive behavior that night in the Roaches' kitchen. The fact that he'd killed Éclair wouldn't even be brought up, because he'd never been charged with that crime and, according to my plea, it had not factored into my decision to kill him.

I imagined trying to explain to Éclair why she was being completely erased from the situation: *It's just how the law works. Don't take it personally. I'm trying to avoid a murder charge here.* No doubt Éclair would shoot me an eviscerating glare and say, *God, Lacey, when did you become such a fucking worm?*

Manslaughter in Vermont usually got between one and fifteen years in prison, but it looked like this worm might wriggle away with a fine and probation. The prosecutor was Mitchell Porter, Vermont's first openly gay district attorney.

"No one wants to see you go to prison," he'd assured me. "If I could decline to prosecute, I would. We have to go through the motions because of all the media attention. But we're going to make this as painless as possible. The system utterly failed your family, and I promise you, we're not going to fail you again. You turned yourself in. You did the right thing. Now it's our turn to do the same."

They were going to let me go? I nearly fell to my knees like some hysterical person on the Christian Television Network. Of course, I'd be stuck in Vermont until the Canadian government granted me permission to return, but at least it would all be fucking over. In my overwhelming joy, I was tempted to call Alexandrine, to apologize and tell her she was right: America *had* changed—everyone was gay now!

A day later, Norman's phone rang while he was outside supervising Arnold's daily walk. When I picked it up, I could tell immediately that something was off.

"Jo? Is that you?" It was Mitchell Porter.

"What's up?"

"We have a big problem. Can you and Norman meet me at Judge Larson's house in an hour?" His voice had a panicked edge that made me think of Bjorn calling me from Paris at 4:00 A.M. and how the smartest thing I'd ever done was not kid myself, in that moment, that it wasn't all about to go to shit.

AT JUDGE LARSON'S HOUSE, WE ALL SAT DOWN IN THE LIVING room, where Mrs. Larson set out a silver coffeepot and four cups. I was grateful that no one in America seemed to drink tea. If I ever smelled the bergamot of Montagne's Earl Grey, I would choke up with tears.

Judge Larson was a classic, gruff-looking old Vermont judge. Mitchell looked more like a manager of a Zales outlet store than a district attorney. He wore a black turtleneck and had perfectly clean fingernails—unusual for Vermont, where almost everyone got down in the dirt in some way or another. I had a fleeting vision of him as a spokesperson for dish detergent. *Tough on crime, soft on skin!*

Norman and I sat in a pair of leather-backed chairs, with Arnold between us wearing a large and rather ridiculous cone around his head.

"I don't know what to do. I've never encountered a situation like this before," Mitchell was saying. "There's been a change in the witness testimony. From the brother—the little boy who witnessed the death. Well, he's not a little boy anymore. He's seventeen years old."

"What 'change'?" Judge Larson asked.

"He says he remembers it differently now. He says he was wrong about precisely *where* he saw Jo shoot Dodge Roach."

"Oh yeah?" I said dryly. "Did he see it on the moon?"

"He says it was a different tree, about thirty yards from the tree he originally described."

"So what?" Judge Larson asked.

"Thirty yards from the original location is . . ." Mitchell took a gulp of coffee. "Ah! Hot, hot, hot! Sorry. Thirty yards is actually . . ."

"For god's sake, tell us, Mitchell," Norman snapped.

"It's actually . . . the New Hampshire border."

We all froze, like a group of robots short-circuiting. Arnold's eyes looked between us, his cone bobbing. Then Norman, Judge Larson, and I all started talking at once.

"Like hell it is—"

"You can't be serious—"

"This is preposterous—"

Mitchell raised his hands. "Let's stay calm. I'm just telling you what I've been told. I don't know what to do. It's not our jurisdiction anymore. If we want to keep the case in Vermont, the burden of proof is on us. We'd have to *prove* the murder occurred on the Vermont side of the border. Which is impossible. It's your word against the kid's, and you're the murderer."

"He was two and a half years old!" I practically yelled. "You're telling me he remembers a specific area of forest? This is bullshit, Mitchell."

"I know. But New Hampshire wants this, and we can't prove they manipulated the kid to get it. They've got their toughest dog on the case. Have you heard of Zora Grange? Wait, of course you have—"

"Zora Grange? *Zora Grange?* No. No. No." I rubbed my eyes, genuinely praying that I was about to wake up from a nightmare.

Mitchell opened his briefcase, pulled out a piece of paper and handed it to Judge Larson. "Here's the affidavit. I don't think there's anything we can do."

"You have to fight it!" I said, and the desperation I heard in my voice scared me. "This is all a trick! She tricked me! I would never have left Canada—"

Mitchell cut me off. "Jo, it's done. There's nothing I can do. This thing is going to New Hampshire, and you'll have to tough it out."

Norman was furious. "This is really rotten. How am I supposed to try a case in New Hampshire? I have Arnold to think about!"

As I gazed at the sad old Rottweiler in his plastic cone, it did seem, for a moment, that he was the truly aggrieved party in all of this.

And so we started over. After much complaining, Norman agreed to represent me until I found a local lawyer in New Hampshire. I was reindicted, this time for first-degree murder. Zora Grange was going to come for me hard, painting me as a violent maniac operating under the paranoid delusion that Dodge Roach had killed my sister. Éclair would be at the center of everything again, like some inescapable law of physics. I pictured her gloating in the gallery: *You thought you could do this show without moi?*

That night, the local news reported that Mr. Hantz was getting nine months in prison—an extremely harsh sentence for a misdemeanor that usually earned a fine. Norman almost choked on his Sanka when he heard. I felt too numb to react. We watched the clip of Mr. Hantz being led out of the courtroom in cuffs. He looked untroubled, almost Gandhi-like, as his wife and kids cried in an indistinct huddle.

The next day, a thick-set, silent U.S. Marshal named Doug put me in handcuffs and drove me across the Vermont border into New Hampshire. Norman followed in his pickup truck.

My reaction to the handcuffs surprised me. I expected to squirm like a trapped animal, to have a meltdown right there in the back of the car. But I just sat calmly, my cuffed hands in my lap. They were treating me like a far more dangerous person than I was, and it made me feel powerful, at least for a little while.

NEW HAMPSHIRE
2006

THE CONCORD COURTHOUSE LOOKED EXACTLY THE SAME, YET completely different. In my memory, the building loomed large and forbidding as a brutalist Soviet prison. But now, as I was escorted up its steps, I was confused by how provincial and dinky it seemed. The interior had been gutted, the blond woods, tan carpets, and mildly sickening assault of beige replaced by dark burgundy and oak.

Norman kept checking his watch, barely concealing his eagerness to get home to Arnold. I hid my cuffed wrists under the defense table, as if I could somehow fool everyone into thinking that I wasn't a criminal. Anxiety about how I would react when I saw Zora Grange gripped me. What if I started crying like a child? What if I started shaking?

I was about to ask the security guard to escort me to the ladies' room to splash some water on my face when the courtroom doors whooshed open—and there she was. I froze, unable to do anything but watch as she walked down the aisle.

She looked awful. It was as if age had driven her every feature to its ugliest potentiality. She was pale and clammy, too skinny, her neck thin as a twig, her face bloated and puffed like a corpse. If only Éclair could see this, I thought. If only she could be beside me, whispering her bitchiest insults in my ear.

Mrs. Grange didn't so much as glance at me as she set her briefcase down. It was as if we were two strangers about to negotiate a traffic violation. *Look at me, you fucking witch!* I wanted to scream. *You wanted me, you got me. Fucking look at me!*

"All rise!"

The presiding judge was one Roy Hiedler. I'd found little about him on the internet, suggesting a less-than-remarkable career. The most interesting thing about him was his surname, which had originally been *Hitler* and which he'd legally changed in college. I wondered if he would be sympathetic toward me. Surely he, of all people, could understand the temptation to erase the past rather than let it define you.

"Considering the defendant's history of using a false identity to escape her crimes," Mrs. Grange began, "I highly recommend that the court deny bail."

Next to me, Norman squinted at the statement I'd prepared for him, typed in extra-large font on several sheets of paper. "Your Honor, I, uh . . . Sorry, I forgot my glasses."

He fumbled in his pockets, then read from the paper like a fifth grader reciting an assignment: "My client Jo Scottish, formerly known as Lacey Bond, has shown admirable responsibility in turning herself in for the crime she committed as a minor. Despite many opportunities to flee the country again, she has not done so. Judge Larson granted bail in Vermont with no reservations, and I believe the State of New Hampshire should show my client the same good faith. She poses no threat or menace to society. For five years she has been a respected member of the legal community in Canada, and she returned to America of her own volition without having to be extradited. She is obviously not going anywhere. My client Jo Scottish, formerly known as . . ." Norman realized he'd circled back to the beginning of the speech and stopped. "Sorry. That's all."

Mrs. Grange leapt in. "It is by no means 'obvious' to me that Ms. Scottish isn't going anywhere. Due to the severity of the crime, and Ms. Scottish's propensity to flee the country, I must vigorously argue that bail be denied."

Judge Hiedler looked at me for the first time, as if sizing up a horse.

I'd seen my photograph in newspapers enough times to understand my face: the eyebrows that always looked angry, the set of my jaw, which never seemed to relax. I doubted Judge Hiedler would see anything redeeming in me.

But after what seemed like a full minute, he said, "If Ms. Scottish is willing to wear an ankle monitor, I see no reason why bail should be denied."

"Your Honor, with all due respect—"

"That's my final decision. I see you've already posted bail in Vermont, Ms. Scottish, so let's make it simple and have that sum transferred here. Everybody happy?"

Doug the U.S. Marshal immediately informed me that I had sixteen hours to get my crap out of Vermont and produce a New Hampshire address in order to qualify for ankle monitoring. The computer at Norman's house was exasperatingly slow, the little icon of an hourglass turning and turning as the web page of apartment listings loaded. I was on the verge of pulling my hair out when Norman shouted from the living room that some "trollop" on TV was offering me a free place to live.

"What?" I shouted back.

"Get your skinny ass in here!"

There on the screen, saying my name, was Jeannine. She wore a skimpy sundress, even though it was 45 degrees out, reminding me of her too-tight pencil skirts in the courtroom. To Chris Cox, the local news anchor, she was saying, "No, Lacey hasn't reached out to us. I think the whole situation is very emotionally loaded for her, you know what I mean, Chris? But our guest house is always open!"

"There, problem solved," Norman said.

I rolled my eyes. If Jeannine wanted to support me, she would stop talking about me on television.

By this time Norman's computer had crashed, overburdened by its attempt to load a single website. It was 6:30 P.M. and I had ten hours to find somewhere to live or go to jail. I could check into a motel, but I'd have to go into credit card debt to pay for it, an idea that horrified me almost more than imprisonment. I was about to become one of those drowning people you encountered at the public housing authority, beset by some legal or medical difficulty that snowballed into life-consuming debt from which there was no salvation.

Finally I called my mother. I'd avoided contacting her since I got to America, wanting to preserve the image she had of me—or, perhaps, the image I had of myself: a Canadian professional who drank fine wine with her model girlfriend. Not this homeless, friendless, penniless American.

Kitchen Witch Farms was situated about sixty kilometers north of Concord (in my head I still used the metric system). I borrowed Norman's truck and arrived after dark at a white clapboard house with a drooping roof, surrounded by woods. Not far off, illuminated by the headlights, was a bunch of modular beehives. My mom was sitting on the front porch, actually churning butter in a little handheld churn like it was 1840.

I parked on the dirt driveway and got out. My mom looked at me like I was a stray dog she was surprised to find had survived the winter.

"Hi," I said inadequately.

"Hi," she said back, and got up to hug me—a brusque, perfunctory hug in which we barely made contact. "You look good."

"Do I?" I looked down at myself. I was wearing a pair of old jeans and a flannel shirt I'd stolen from Norman's laundry. Though it seems obvious now, it didn't occur to me then that my mother might prefer me this way—not the tie-wearing legal professional, but the rumpled and roughed-up girl who looked like Lacey.

"Sorry I didn't call sooner," I said.

"It's fine. I figured you were busy. I've been busy, too. March is a critical time for bees. The queen is laying eggs, but if the honey stores run low, the worker bees will starve. You wouldn't believe how fragile bee systems are. They can't survive in this world anymore. Not the way we've screwed up the climate."

I sat down in the rocking chair next to her. "So like I was saying on the phone, the trial got moved to New Hampshire."

"I heard."

"I need to borrow some money. I have nothing, and I need a New Hampshire address to qualify for ankle monitoring. I'll pay you back, I swear."

"I don't have a dime," she said. "Lawyers took it all."

"Why haven't you and Dad sued for malicious prosecution and wrongful imprisonment? You could get a million dollars from the state."

She churned her butter. "Sue, sue, sue. As if I'd take a dime of their guilt money."

"It's not guilt money, Mom. The state isn't a person. It doesn't have emotions."

"You weren't so eager to take Canada's handouts."

"That was completely different. This could really help me out, Mom. If you file a suit, Mrs. Grange will have to recuse herself from my case."

She sighed. "Ask your father. He'll do anything you want. But I'm not suing anyone."

I gazed at Norman's truck, dreading the drive back to Vermont. I remembered all the times Mom had told Éclair and me not to feed wild animals: *If you spoil them with handouts, they'll forget how to survive. They'll die.*

I stood up to leave.

"Hold your horses," Mom said. "Why don't you stay with us? There's room in the attic."

My mouth fell open. I felt almost stupefied with gratitude. "Mom, thank you so much," I gushed. "You're sure the other women won't mind? The press will find me. It could be a real shit show."

"It's fine. Everyone's a whore for publicity. It'll be good for the farm stand. Do you know what we charge for a jar of honey? Thirty-two dollars. Can you imagine? What kind of idiot pays thirty-two bucks for a jar of honey?"

It was a pretty lateral move, going from Norman's cellar to my mother's attic, but at least I didn't have to hear the evening news blaring at top volume anymore. The bee farm didn't have a TV. In that one sense, if in no other, it was ideal.

The whole place reeked painfully of my childhood: dried herbs hanging from the ceiling, the overpowering scents of tinctures and teas battling, compost piles on the verge of rot, mud. *And here's the bucket we shit in for fertilizer*, I pointed out to the invisible Éclair, who was becoming a more and more frequent visitor in my head. I could picture the comical look of horror on her face so vividly it was almost worth shitting in a bucket.

Three other women lived in the house: Lynn, Sue, and Rue. Lynn and Sue were older divorcées like my mom. Rue was a lesbian "lifer" with a beautiful mane of auburn hair tinged with gray. I was terrified that she would come on to me; I couldn't think of anything bleaker than fucking my mom's roommate in a bat-infested attic. I avoided eye contact with her and thankfully she did the same, going about her chores as if I were a stray cat too insignificant to be shooed out.

The press outlets found the farm quickly, and they constantly mistook Rue for me, even though she was forty-five years old. Somehow I had been cemented in the public consciousness as middle-aged. Every time I heard the reporters outside barking questions at Rue ("How does it feel to be home?" "Why did you turn yourself in?" "Is it true that Gwen is the real killer?"), I pictured Gwen in Canada, seeing Rue's incredible auburn hair on the TV and wondering if we were having an affair.

My new attorney, plucked from the drab obscurity of the public defender's office, was a twenty-eight-year-old named Matt Brady, who distinguished himself by having the shittiest bedside manner of any lawyer I'd ever met. When he called me to say Mrs. Grange and the DA were prepared to offer me a plea deal of forty years in prison, he sounded so excited I thought I must have misheard him.

"Forty years?" I echoed. "Sorry, I'm at the farm and the connection is terrible. Did you say forty years or *four* years?"

"Forty years! Forty motherfucking years! It's the worst plea deal I've ever heard! And I've represented neo-Nazis!"

I hung up without saying goodbye. *Forty years.* The number roared in my mind, muting all other thoughts. My instinct was to drive straight back to Vermont, with its rolling pastures and gay DA, and beg for my manslaughter charge back. But Vermont was over. It might as well have been Narnia.

"Are you okay?"

I whipped around and saw Rue standing in the middle of the kitchen, holding a dead rabbit by its feet. She was the only one of my mom's roommates who wasn't a vegetarian.

As a ten-year-old, I'd helped our neighbor skin deer and never flinched. Now the sight of the lifeless upside-down rabbit made me ill. The bloody gunshot wound near its eye brought out the red in Rue's hair.

She stepped toward me, looking concerned.

"Stop," I said.

I felt dimly aware of my mother taking me by the arms and leading me out to the front porch. She sat me down in one of the rocking chairs, then produced a bottle of unlabeled wine so dark it was almost black.

"This is delicious. It's blackberry wine. Lynn made it."

I took a sip. It was incredibly sour, with a single, pungent note of blackberry. If I'd served it to my acquaintances in Montreal, they'd have thought it was a practical joke. But at least it contained alcohol.

"You looked like you were about to faint back there," she said. "I guess you forgot what a dead rabbit looks like."

"It's been a while."

The sun was setting in a dull grayish smear. It was not an awe-inspiring sight by any stretch, but I appreciated it anyway, the way I appreciated the crappy prison tattoo on my mom's neck, that crudely deformed outline of a bird: it wasn't asking to be beautiful.

"Are you all right?" Mom said. "You can tell me."

"I don't know. It just feels like my life is hurtling at breakneck speed."

"Don't worry. When you get to prison it all slows waaay down."

I thought of Mr. Hantz serving his nine months at Pondville Correctional, which was a dorm compared with Goffstown, where I was likely headed. Pondville didn't even have a fence. Mr. Hantz was probably guidance counseling his fellow inmates and having the time of his life. Maybe he could finally sleep at night, knowing he'd thrown himself in jail for me, fulfilling his heroic destiny.

"I don't want to go to prison. I really, really don't."

"You'll survive," she said flatly.

"Will you visit me?" I sounded like a mouse. It was too shameful—I'd deserted her for fourteen years, and now I expected her to show up for me?

She gave me a chiding look.

"Of course, dummy," she said. "You don't have to ask. Maybe they'll put you in my old cell. Wouldn't that be funny?"

I genuinely wished I could laugh. I took a long sip of my wine. She did the same. I felt inordinately moved that she was willing to sit and talk to me without her usual multitasking—knitting or churning butter or flipping through *American Bee Journal*.

"Sometimes I look at my life and I have no idea how it came to this."

"I do," my mom said.

"Oh yeah?" I prepared myself for a speech about chakras and the flow of universal energy currents.

"It was Dylan."

I looked at her. "Why would you say that?"

"You forget that I've known Dylan as long as you have. I remember the way he used to look at you, like you were the brightest star in the sky."

"She, Mom."

"*She* figured out the person she needed to be to get your love. And then her crazy brother killed your sister, and you killed him, and that's how it came to this."

"Mom, Gwen's transgender, that's it. Everything else was just bad luck."

"If you say so. But think about how different your life would be if Dylan had never dressed up like a girl."

"You think Gwen transformed her entire identity for *me*? I'd have to be incredibly self-centered to believe that. The idea is just crazy."

"Is it? I would call it romantic. But it had a lot of consequences."

"That's not how it works, Mom."

"I'm not criticizing her. People should do whatever they can to get love. It's a consuming, horrible need."

I gazed at her, uncomfortable with how alike we were. Everything was a conspiracy with us. *Poor Gwen,* I thought, adding it to the list of reasons she would be better off without me.

Mom's cell phone buzzed on the table. She checked the caller ID, then set it back down, not answering. "Speaking of needy people . . ."

"Who is it?"

"Your dad."

I scowled. "Why do you keep letting him call you?"

"Because he's the father of my children."

"Have you ever thought that it was a little weird for a twenty-four-year-old man to shack up with a fourteen-year-old girl and get her pregnant?"

She glared at me. "It was Woodstock, Lacey. No one cared back then. Stop inventing reasons to be mad at him."

"Maybe if you stopped defending him all the time."

"So I should sit back and let you trash a member of my family? Wouldn't that make me as bad as him, according to your oh-so-perfect standards?"

I folded my arms and sank lower in my chair. "What does he want, anyway?"

"To see you, of course. He's beside himself that you're living here. He thinks it's terribly unfair. I told him that you just showed up like a raccoon looking for garbage."

"Thanks for the flattering comparison."

"He thinks I'm planting ideas in your head. I said to him, 'Hugh, I'm too busy to be planting ideas in a grown adult's head. Lacey has her own mind, and I have five hundred thousand bees.' But he thinks you should be with him and Jeannine and Jerk and Twerp or whatever their names are . . . No, I shouldn't say that. They're just kids. They actually seem like nice boys."

"You've met them?" I said, aghast.

"They came to the farmers market. Jeannine made a big deal of buying two hundred dollars' worth of honey products. As if that settled the score."

"What were they like? The boys?" My heart was racing.

"They were . . . boys. They were cute. They looked like your father."

"Never mind," I said quickly. "I don't want to hear this."

The betrayal was too painful. Girls I could have forgiven, but not this. If he'd wanted to replace Éclair and me, why did it have to be with *boys*?

A moment passed, then out of the blue Mom asked, "Is something going on with you and Rue?"

"*No.* Where did that come from? I'm with Gwen. We're a committed couple." The words felt false, like I had a gun to my head.

Mom raised her hands in defense. "I didn't say a word. No need to make a grand statement."

It was a tale as old as time: my mom didn't like my girlfriend. There was even a name for it: the Jocasta complex, named for the mother of Oedipus. It described mothers who fixated sexually on their sons, especially when the son was intelligent and the father was inadequate or gone. There was a reason I remained perversely attracted to the theories of Freud: all families were fucked up in his eyes.

We sat on the porch, watching the sky turn as purplish black as the wine. I downed the rest of my jarful. Maybe I could go to prison for forty years, then start a vineyard when I got out at age sixty-nine. Would that be such a terrible life?

Now that I was a little drunk, I was able to feel almost as blasé about the future as my mother did—almost. She'd reached a level of existentiality that was outside my grasp. She'd served fourteen years for crimes she didn't commit. She'd been a heroin addict. She'd experienced pure, chemically induced heaven, then made the choice to never, ever experience it again. It was a different kind of life sentence. To place all the artificial bliss of life behind you, accepting that from now on it would be all too real.

xlvii

NEW HAMPSHIRE'S DEMOGRAPHICS HAD NOT CHANGED IN MY AB-
sence. As groups of potential jurors streamed in and out of the courtroom, I felt like I had entered a time loop in which only Zora Grange
and I had been permitted to age.

Matt's strategy was to get as many young people on the jury as possible. "The younger they are, the longer fifteen years will feel to them,"
he told me. "No twenty-year-old wants to be held accountable for something they did when they were five."

The problem was that young people were all on the internet. They
knew everything about everything five minutes after it happened. Mrs.
Grange systematically weaseled out prior knowledge of the case and
tossed them out one after another. In the end, our jury consisted of six
white women, five white men, and one Hispanic lady, all between the
ages of forty and sixty-five. It was almost identical to the jury in my
parents' retrial.

We were set to start on April 3. I told my mother not to come and
to tell my dad that if he or Jeannine showed up unannounced, I would
scream. I was being dramatic, yet at the same time, I wasn't. I felt so
tense I genuinely did not know what I would do if I looked over my
shoulder and saw them.

The night before the trial, Lynn gave me a haircut. "Not too dykey,
please," I said, which made no difference. I'd look like Anthony Blanche
regardless.

Matt thought I was making a huge mistake by wearing a suit and tie. He wanted me to wear a dress. "The whole point is to show the jury that you've changed," he said. "We can't do that if you look like the exact same mega-dyke you were as a teenager." He was probably right, but I couldn't bring myself to take the slightest action to increase the odds of my own acquittal.

To Matt's frustration, this included my unwillingness to ask my father to testify as a character witness. He and Jeannine were enjoying immense celebrity because of the bestselling *Bonds of Love*, and he'd even made it on to *People* magazine's list of "2006's Most Intriguing Men." Matt moaned to me repeatedly that I was sealing my own doom. "Ask my mother to testify if you have to," I offered, to which Matt replied, "What, the witchy freak lesbian? That'll help."

The ravages of life had made my father "intriguing" while making my mother a "freak."

Courtrooms always felt like theater sets, with everyone in their place: judge in the middle, the government on the right, the defendant (me) on the left. Always le gauche, a word that means, literally, "bad." I'd thought I was prepared for everything—for the jury to despise me, for Mrs. Grange to be a bitch, for the whole thing to drag me to the lowest rung of my self-esteem, where I would either hang on for dear life or let go and fall into the inviting abyss.

But there was something—some*one*—I'd forgotten. I'd even forgotten his name. Then there he was, on the first day of court: Colt Roach, Gwen's youngest half brother.

The sight of him stunned me. He was beautiful. Though he was twelve years younger than Gwen and shared only half her genes, he could have been her twin. He had the same light blond hair and wide-eyed, slightly vacuous-seeming expression. I'd always assumed Gwen was wholly a product of her mother, fathers having become worthless in my view. But Colt, despite sharing only Gwen's paternal genes, looked just like her.

"You didn't tell me he would be here!" I hissed at Matt.

"I didn't know! He lives three hours away. I didn't expect him to show up till the day of his testimony. Grange obviously thinks the jury will like him. Don't let it rattle you."

It was way too late for that. Before I knew it, Mrs. Grange had stood up and was giving her opening argument.

"Ladies and gentlemen of the jury, I'm here to tell you a sad story. But first, let me warn you, I'm in a certain condition that causes me to require frequent bathroom breaks."

Oh god, I thought. Was she pregnant again?

"I am suffering from *C. diff* related to cancer of the colon. Yes, I have cancer. I am dying. Maybe you think that means I should be in a hospital, or spending time with my family, or carrying out my final wishes. Well, ladies and gentlemen, my final wish is to be in this courtroom with you, bringing a criminal to justice."

Every jury member looked as agog as I felt. Zora Grange was *dying*? And not just dying, but dying miserably? No wonder she looked awful.

"What the hell?" I whispered to Matt. His face had gone white.

"So keep that in mind if I have to run out of the courtroom suddenly. I'm not trying to be rude, it's just my illness. Everybody got that? Good. Now, let's talk about the reason we're all here today. Maybe some of you think that reason is sitting right there." Mrs. Grange pointed to me. I felt myself shrivel as every pair of eyes in the jury box snapped to my face. "But it's not. The reason we're here is sitting right there." This time she pointed to Colt, who looked almost as uncomfortable as me.

"That boy's name is Colt Roach," Mrs. Grange continued. "And fifteen years ago, almost to the day, the woman sitting at that table killed his beloved brother Dodge in cold blood and made it look like a suicide. The defense will claim she did so as an act of 'imperfect' self-defense. But we will prove beyond a shadow of a doubt that Lacey Bond deliberately got Dodge Roach inebriated until he was unconscious, *defenseless*, before dragging him outside and shooting him. She then fled, assumed a false identity, and lived with no consequences in Canada for fourteen years. The defense will try to make you feel sorry for her. They will claim that Dodge Roach killed Lacey Bond's sister, Éclair Bond. My argument . . ." Her scratchy voice gave out. She paused to clear her throat and started again. "My argument is simple. Number one: the fact that Lacey Bond believed Dodge to be her sister's killer does not make it true. Number two: the fact that she did believe it only *proves* she killed Dodge out of malice, not self-defense. She did not seriously believe her life was in immediate danger. She went to that house to exact revenge upon the person she believed was responsible for her sister's death. Full stop. Now, Éclair Bond's murder remains unsolved to this day. There is no hard evidence—let me repeat—*no* hard evidence that Dodge was involved in that crime. Dodge Roach was a kind, good-hearted young boy who had the bad luck of being ensnared in Lacey Bond's web of delusions."

She paused, steadying herself. I could tell it wasn't an act. She was genuinely, literally trying to keep her shit together long enough to get through this speech.

Judge Hiedler broke the silence. "Mrs. Grange? Do you need a moment?"

"No. I'm fine. As I was saying, if Colt hadn't recovered his memories of that night, the killer sitting before you might never have been brought to justice. That thought really scares me. Dodge Roach was fifteen years old when he was killed. That's the same age as my son, Carter. I'm doing this for Colt, but in a way, I'm doing it for Carter, too. I'm dying, and I will proudly spend my final days trying to get one last killer off the streets, to make the world a safer place for my son. For everyone's children."

Next to me, Matt was frantically scribbling notes, obviously trying to revise his opening statement to match the emotional punch of *I'm dying of cancer*.

"I have been moved to tears by the stories Colt has told me about his brother Dodge," Mrs. Grange continued.

I noticed that every time she said Colt's name, he twitched a little, hating the attention. I'd been comparing him with Gwen, but the person he seemed most similar to was . . . me. The girl I'd been at thirteen, hanging on for dear life in the eye of a hurricane created by adults who claimed to have my best interests at heart. I noticed Colt's too-big button-down shirt and his horrid patterned tie. If Mrs. Grange actually cared about him, she'd have gotten him some fucking decent clothes.

"They were a poor family, living a poor, rural life. Sometimes there wasn't enough food to go around. Sometimes their father would abandon them for days. Dodge Roach was an amazing kid who stepped up and filled the vacant parental role in Colt's life. He held Colt when he was scared, cooked his favorite macaroni and cheese, and told him everything would be all right. He was all that Colt had. And then Lacey Bond killed him."

You're crazy, I wanted to scream at them all, especially Colt. *Dodge never made you mac and cheese. He pointed a loaded gun at your head for fun!*

And then, with screeching urgency, I realized what was happening. A tremendous mistake had been made.

"We need to talk," I whispered to Matt. "After she finishes, ask the judge for a recess."

"Are you crazy?" he whispered back. "I can't do that. We haven't even started. I'll look incompetent."

"Matt, it's really, really important."

Our escalating whispers were interrupted by Mrs. Grange, who clutched her stomach and ran out of the courtroom. The room went awkwardly silent.

"Mr. Foxworthy?" Judge Hiedler said finally to Mrs. Grange's cocounsel. "Do you know if Mrs. Grange was finished with her statement?"

"Um, let me send our intern to the ladies' room to check. Marsha?"

A young woman scurried out of the courtroom and returned moments later. "She was finished, but she requests a recess until tomorrow," she reported in a tiny voice.

"I don't think so," Judge Hiedler said, shaking his head. "I admire Mrs. Grange's commitment to the case, but it wouldn't be fair to the defense—"

I kicked Matt under the table. He jumped up. "We have no problem with a recess, Your Honor. We, too, deeply admire Mrs. Grange's commitment, and out of respect for her condition I am happy to present my statement tomorrow."

Judge Hiedler looked surprised, then suspicious, then like he'd stopped giving a damn. "Fine. But, Mr. Foxworthy, we can't do this every day. You and Mrs. Grange need to figure out a system for conducting this trial, is that understood?"

"Of course, Your Honor. We apologize for the holdup."

"All right. We'll start with Mr. Brady in the morning. Court is adjourned."

As everyone started streaming out of the courtroom, Matt turned to me. "You just got unbelievably lucky. What god do you pray to? I'm gonna convert."

"I wouldn't if I were you."

"So what's this big thing you have to tell me?"

I waited until Mr. Foxworthy and Colt were safely out the doors. Then I explained, "All that stuff Mrs. Grange said about Dodge—it's not true. Colt probably doesn't even remember Dodge."

"Then where did all those sappy stories come from? Did Grange have some therapist plant them in his head?"

"No. He didn't make them up. They're real memories. But they're not about who he thinks."

"THIS IS FANTASTIC. I'LL EAT HIM ALIVE."

"Do we have to be that awful? Just let me talk to him." I was picturing Colt's face, which looked so much like Gwen's, crumpling in shame and confusion in front of everyone while Matt ripped him a new one for mistaking his sister for Dodge.

"Even if I thought that was a good idea, Grange wouldn't let you near him," Matt answered. "Come on, stop being a pussy. I thought you were a lawyer."

Back at the bee farm, everything was quiet. The press had mercifully stopped following me home once they realized the only content they were going to get was Lynn or Rue in front of the cameras, extolling the benefits of organic honey products.

Two letters from Gwen sat on the front hall table. I picked them up, gazing at her messy handwriting. She'd gotten the address wrong, and it looked like they'd been rerouted several times. I wondered if there were more letters from her drifting around random post offices in New Hampshire. Perhaps in a hundred years they'd finally be delivered, and the current owner of the farm would read them and wonder what the hell was in the water back then.

I took Gwen's letters to the attic. There was only one power outlet, an extension cord running from Rue's room downstairs, which I reserved for the space heater. I was afraid to risk short-circuiting the whole house by plugging more than one thing into it. So I lit a bunch of candles like I was an impoverished tenant in the 1800s and opened the first letter.

Dear Jo,

    I saw you on the news. You looked really hot. Your dad is old! Why does everyone want to fuck him? I'm doing okay. You would be mad because I'm eating like shit but Bjorn is trying to get me to eat broccoli because he says I'm losing my "glow." So that's great. I really miss you. There's no one to talk to. Everyone wants to talk about MY BODY. No one understands MY MIND. How are you? Some people from L.A. came and they want to do a reality show about me. The idea is that I'm a beautiful, sad girl but also fun-loving and everyone wants to date me, and there's one episode where I decide that I'm finally ready to date and I guess they pick some person for me, and we have a dumb date, and then they kiss me and I realize I only love you, and then I call you in prison and we have this whole beautiful conversation. I was like, "Okay, but Jo's not going to prison, she's coming right back after the trial." And they all looked at me like I was crazy. But then they said that would be fine, too, and the show could just be about me and you hanging out and having drama. Which you would HATE, haha. But I really want to do it. It would be nice to wake up and have all these people watch me put on makeup and whatever. I don't know how to describe it but that idea makes me feel like I'll be okay. So I hope you don't mind if I do it. The show will be called Golden Girl which is fucking STUPID because Golden Girls already exists, but they said it's fine, and they actually want to use the Golden Girls theme song? I don't know what the fuck is going on in these people's minds. But I really want to do it. I also really wish you were here because there are a fuck-ton of

contracts and I think the lawyer is trying to screw me over.
When you were in Vermont did you find out what happened
to Taz?

Gwen

The letter moved and depressed me equally. The fact that she thought to ask after my childhood cat but not her half brothers. That she was obviously being used by these Hollywood people, and yet it went both ways—she was using them, too, to save herself from her horror of being alone.

And deep in my soul I felt an uncomfortable, bitter twinge: the golden girl was supposed to be Éclair. Gwen had taken over the role somehow, like in *Single White Female*, a movie that had starred, of all people, Bridget Fonda. I wondered if the producers were aware of how strange a reality show starring Gwen was going to be. Gwen talking to a stray dog for an hour. Gwen silently supergluing a hundred Swarovski crystals to a beer can. *Éclair* would have known what to do: pick fights with people and shout catchphrases like "This is America!" and "I'm going to be *me*!"

I folded up the first letter and opened the second one.

Dear Jo,
    The reality show people said something really fucking
weird today. They came up with a plotline about how you're a
dangerous killer and how I lie awake thinking about whether
you're going to kill me one day. I was like, "What the fuck???
Jo is the least dangerous person in the world. She saved my
life. I could never be scared of her." And they looked at me
like I was crazy!!! But it made me think, Oh my god, what if
Jo thinks I think of her that way. I mean, you're really stupid
sometimes but you're not THAT stupid, are you? Anyway I
wanted to write you just in case and tell you that I have never

felt that way about you. I know you won't kill anyone else.
You're safe!!! Maybe I yell at you all the time because you did
what you did for revenge and not to do me a favor or what-
ever. But that doesn't mean I'm MAD about it or I think
you're a bad person!!!!!!! I was only mad that you seemed to
be kind of lying to yourself and it was annoying. But maybe
now I understand, because people like these reality show
people are morons and have the worst opinions about people
who ever killed someone, even if it was just one time. So now
maybe I understand, and I'm sorry I ever yelled at you.

Gwen

I read the letter several times over, finding myself on the reality show people's side. It *was* weird that Gwen didn't care that her girlfriend was a murderer.

I found a pen and paper to write her back, but I didn't know what to say. Every time I saw her face in my mind's eye, it morphed into Colt's. I couldn't stop thinking about the way his eyes had darted around the courtroom, frightened by everything they saw.

Before I knew it, I was writing a very different letter.

Dear Colt,

It is with no ill intent that I write you now, only to share
some information that, if I were you, I think I'd want to
know. Your memory has done you a disservice. The person
you have been mourning for fifteen years is not your brother
Dodge but your sister Dylan. She was in your life for only
a little while in the winter and spring of 1991, but you
obviously formed a powerful bond with her. As you probably
know, she is not dead at all but alive in Canada. I took her
with me to a new life. I know how it feels to have a sister
taken away, and I am sorry that I passed on that particular

382

anguish to you. Of all the crimes that I committed in my youth, that is perhaps the only one that had continued consequences for anyone other than myself.

Regarding my more punishable crime—murder— know that no matter how the jury swings, it means nothing. Twelve random people don't have the power to acquit me or condemn me in any real way. I don't know who does. Maybe you, maybe Dylan, maybe only myself. Certainly nobody in this godforsaken legal procedure. But since we may be stuck here, all I can do is write you this message and let you know that the person you've been missing is still alive.

Sincerely,
Jo Scottish

I folded the note and placed it in an envelope. Then I took it back out. Was I being incredibly selfish? Perhaps the truth of the situation was crueler than the fiction Colt and Grange had cobbled together. *Dear Colt,* I might as well have written, *The person you remember is Dylan. I didn't kill her, she just abandoned you and never looked back.* Maybe it would be better if he was allowed to continue believing that the person he'd loved was dead.

I'd been going back and forth for some minutes when I heard a car pull up outside. I looked out the window and saw a sleek silver Prius parked sideways in the driveway. The headlights snapped off, and the driver's-side door opened. A man spilled out like he'd been shot and was on his last legs. I was about to yell for help when I realized he wasn't injured, he was just wasted, and he was my dad.

"Lacey!" I heard him bark, stumbling toward the house. "Lacey!"

The front door slammed open, and I saw my mother stomping toward him. I couldn't hear what she was saying, so I opened the window halfway. A gust of cold air whooshed in, carrying their words.

". . . what the hell you're doing, but you better turn around and get the hell off our property. Are you drunk? Goddamn you, Hugh. I'm calling a cab, and if you think I'm paying for it, you've got another think coming."

"I have to see her! Just let me see her!"

I watched with horror as he tried to evade my mother, who pushed him back. I didn't know what to do, so I just crouched there, terrified that he would look up and see me in the window.

I heard Lynn's voice shouting from somewhere inside the house, asking if everything was okay.

"Shut up, you bloody old woman!" my dad screamed. "Go away! This is our *family* business!"

"We're fine, Lynn! He's leaving!" Mom shouted. "Hugh, go on home and get your head on straight! Lacey doesn't want to see you right now."

"Why? Why? Why?" he moaned, sounding like a man whose house had been struck by lightning and burned to the ground. I'd never seen him like this, but then again, I really didn't know him anymore.

"Because she's angry, Hugh! You let your silly wife write all those terrible things about her and Éclair! Just let her be angry. God forbid someone doesn't love you for five seconds. You're *greedy*, Hugh. You made your choice and you need to go home and live with it. You can't have everybody. We don't need you right now."

"But I need *you*," he croaked. In his drunkenness, his British accent was more pronounced than I'd ever heard it.

Suddenly there was a loud crash, and my mom yelped like a dog. That did it; I ran down the two flights of rickety stairs to the front porch.

Rue and Lynn were already there, shouting at my dad.

"You bastard, you crazy bastard—"

"I'm calling the police, you piece of shit—"

Sue was hunkered on the porch floor with my mom, whose face was covered in blood and some kind of weird, chunky goo. Half-churned butter. My dad had thrown the butter churn at her.

"I'm so sorry. I'm so sorry," he was muttering. Then he saw me. His eyes lit up. He stepped forward, looking stupidly happy, as if it were senior prom and I was encircled by a dreamy spotlight and our song was playing.

"I'm calling the police!" Lynn repeated.

"Don't," my mom said, standing up. "I'm fine. I'm perfectly fine. No police. Lacey doesn't need this bullshit. Lynn, Rue, go inside. We can handle this. Sue, get me a hot washcloth."

For a moment they all stood there, reluctant to leave her, like three butch lesbian bodyguards.

"Go on!" my mother barked, and they obeyed.

Watching them go, I felt numb. Did my dad understand how primitive he'd just become, resorting to violence to get what he wanted? And yet, it had worked, hadn't it? He'd wanted to see me, and here I was, as if the hurled butter churn were a magic wand. Nobody knew better than I did how well violence worked.

"You're so beautiful," he said to me.

"Shut up. No, I'm not. You're being ridiculous. You threw a butter churn at Mom's head. You're such a *man*." I didn't know what to say; I was sputtering vacuously. I willed myself to shut up.

"Lacey, take my hand. I want you to come with me. I want everything to be like it was."

It was such a stupid, simple wish. And the fact that he seemed to think it was in my power to grant it was more depressing than anything that had come before. Within seconds I was crying.

"Goddamn you, Hugh. Look what you've done," Mom scolded him. She placed an arm around me and wiped the tears from my face with her buttery finger. It was the most she'd touched me since I was a child.

"How can you do it?" my dad asked. He was crying, too. "How can you two turn your backs on me? I'm sorry I married her, but you didn't have to leave me. How could you? How could you leave me?"

Even if I'd had an answer, I couldn't speak. I was crying too hard.

"Go home to your kids, Hugh," Mom said, her voice gentler than before.

"They have no bloody idea. They think I'm their bloody hero. I can't stand it. They look at me like I'm . . . like I'm . . . And then they'll grow up and look at me like *that*! Like you!" He stumbled, then sat on the steps, burying his head in his hands. "They'll stop loving me just like you."

"We still love you, Hugh," Mom said.

"Is it true, Lacey?" my dad said, looking up at me meekly. "Do you still love me?"

I blinked back more tears. I hated him for making me do this. He'd be doing it to Éclair, too, if she were still alive. I tried to imagine what she would say. It was probably one of those moments when she would simply stomp off and refuse to participate.

"Yes, Dad." I sighed. "I love you."

He wasn't satisfied. "It's that bloody book, isn't it? I'd burn every copy of it if I could. I never imagined in a million years that you would actually read it—"

"It shouldn't have mattered whether I read it or not," I snapped. "It was a hatchet job on your daughters. If it was just me getting trashed, fine. But she went for Éclair. How could you let her do that? Éclair attacked a jailhouse crackhead just for calling you a fag, Dad. We were all totally embarrassing to her, but she wouldn't hear a single word against any of us. She was *loyal*. And this is how you repay her? Éclair would never—it should make you sick . . ."

My voice was shaking. I heard Éclair's voice in my head, clear as a bell: *Ugh, Lacey, you always do this. Romanticize people after they're gone.* I could faintly recall that I hadn't found her tantrum with the crackhead valiant at the time. I'd found it selfish and downright infuriating, in fact. But now the memory was enshrined in a golden edifice. My father couldn't confront his dopey fucking wife for her? I would have *killed* for her.

And I had.

It was not the way I would have chosen to honor Éclair had I been thinking straight at the time. In the years since, in my zeal to stay out of prison, I'd created an interior prison, one in which I was punished severely for the crime of seeking beauty in the act of murder. There *was* beauty, equal parts sick and sublime. It was artistically perfect: How better to light an eternal flame than with the kerosene of one human soul? It was certainly *dramatic*, to quote Gwen. It was Éclair. But such beauty was erased by my weak and weenie self-defense claim. I had to choose a side; at last, I had to choose the truth.

If only my existence could have faded to black after this blood-soaked performance art piece. In that movie Gwen loved, *The Crow*, our hero floats to the afterlife after his vengeance is complete, off to reunite with his murdered bride. Where was I supposed to go? What was I supposed to do?

Part of me wondered if I should try to locate Sandy Goodwin. Perhaps she held the key to my spiritual release. But the other part of me knew it was useless, that I would only find a mirror. She and I were living two halves of the same purgatory. I doubted a day went by where she didn't relive the moment Angelica had asked her, *Can you see the man's face? Who is he?* and she'd answered, without thinking it through, *Mr. Hugh.* It was the kind of regret that gave lobotomies a certain appeal. Better to have it all wiped clean than to spend the rest of your life defined by one impulsive, destructive decision. One lie. One pull of a trigger.

Looking back, I'd had hundreds of chances to throw Ol' Gunnie in the river and move on with my life, but I hadn't. I was emotionally addicted to it, to knowing the gun was there waiting in a drawer. Waiting for me to play judge, jury, and executioner again. After murder has been introduced as a viable option in life, is it ever fully off the table? Would I do it again, next time with even less of an excuse? My phobia about the psychopath in the wedding cake—it was me, wasn't it? It was always me.

Which brought me to Gwen, weird, oracular Gwen, for whom none of this was of any concern. She didn't care that I'd killed a person. She didn't need me to invent a socially acceptable story about why I'd done it. *I know you won't kill anyone else. You're safe,* she'd written in her letter. How could she possibly be so sure? Was I supposed to just believe her?

I could keep dismissing her as insane—Mrs. Grange had set the precedent, going so far as to formally declare Gwen mentally incompetent. Or I could wake up and try the key that had been dangling before me all along: to see myself through Gwen's eyes.

I know I won't kill anyone else. I'm safe.

I'm safe.

A gust of wind whipped through the pine trees. For the first time since coming home, its familiar sage-like scent didn't make me shudder.

My father shook like a trembling leaf, waiting for me to finish screaming at him. Mom stepped between us.

"Hugh, Lacey, you're both asking way too much of each other right now. Lacey, you need to forgive and forget. Hugh, you need to let Lacey be who she is. She's not the little girl from your memory. And both of you need to slow down. This isn't gonna happen overnight."

I met her eyes. *Thank you.* How strange that she should play the judge in this dispute, she who had never graduated high school and understood nothing about the law.

Sue came out with the hot wet towel for Mom's face.

"I've called a cab," she said. "It should be here in half an hour."

"Thank you, Sue," Mom said.

Sue cast a glare of contempt at the sniffling lump that was my father, then returned inside.

Dad closed his eyes and leaned his head against the porch rail. After a minute, I realized he'd passed out. I snapped my fingers.

"Dad? Hello?"

No response. Everything was silent, from the dark house to the stillness of the night. I knew Lynn, Sue, and Rue were probably all standing at the door, listening to be sure the evil man didn't take another swing at my mother. If only they could have seen how pathetic and helpless he looked, his mouth hanging wide, drool accumulating.

My mom grabbed a pillow from the hammock and placed it behind his head. When our eyes met, she said, "Don't judge him."

"I'm not," I said, and I truly wasn't. I felt sorry for him.

Mom went inside and came back out a minute later, talking into her cell phone. "We've got him here. He's fine. Just drunk as a skunk."

I whispered at her, "Who are you talking to?"

Mom mouthed, *Jeannine*, and I felt my face twitch in surprise. Mom and Jeannine had each other's cell phone numbers? It was so . . . *modern*.

"No, we're gonna send him home in a cab. It's no trouble. You can pick up the car tomorrow." She rolled her eyes at me, and I took it that Jeannine was saying something obnoxious, which wasn't hard to imagine. "Yep. We understand. Like you said, he's a poet. They have to run a little wild to get the creative juices flowing."

It was almost cute, Jeannine's desperation to idealize her husband's bad behavior. I found myself smirking.

When the cab arrived, the driver refused to help us carry Dad into the back seat. In a thick eastern European accent, he told us, "Nah, nah. Not my job. I leave."

"Hold your damn horses," Mom said. "Come on, Lacey."

We each grabbed hold of one of Dad's arms, and for the second time in my life, I found myself dragging a drunk, unconscious male into the darkness.

Mom gave Dad's address in Portsmouth to the driver, plus instructions for how to get there. I stared at his body sprawled in the back seat, half hoping, despite myself, that he would sit up and say something. Say goodbye. But he was out like a light. The cab pulled away and disappeared onto the unlit road.

"That fare's gonna be a motherfucker," Mom said as we watched it go.

We headed back inside, and that was the last time I saw my father. That was four years ago.

xlix

A TENSE MOOD DRIFTED AROUND THE COURTROOM. IT WAS 10:30, and Mrs. Grange had not arrived. I clutched the letter to Colt in my hand, feeling the envelope go damp with sweat. I hadn't decided whether to give it to him. My mind lurched back and forth: *Do it. Don't do it.*

The entire point of trial procedure was that there were *rules.* You didn't just write your feelings down and hand them to the other side. And was it too much, the pressure of being responsible for how this kid understood the truth of his life? What good had the truth ever done me? Or Mr. Hantz's well-meaning interference? It would be great if things were different, but they weren't, and as I'd told Montagne so many months ago, *I don't make wishes. I live in the world.*

At the same time, I could hear Montagne's reply, as clearly as if he were sitting right beside me: *But the world is what we make it, non?*

At 11:15 A.M. Judge Hiedler finally entered ("All rise!") and delivered the news that Mrs. Grange was in the hospital and would likely not be coming out.

"Our thoughts and prayers are with her and her family at this time," he said, then, turning to Mr. Foxworthy, "Mr. Foxworthy, this case is yours. I'll give you today to collect yourself and prepare, but that's it. Tomorrow I want us back on schedule. Is that clear?"

"Yes, Your Honor," Mr. Foxworthy said. "Thank you, Your Honor."

"Court is adjourned."

There was a hubbub as the gallery emptied, and I saw Mr. Foxworthy motion toward Matt. The two of them conferred by the empty jury box, leaving Colt alone behind the defense table. He fiddled with his ugly tie. I clutched the letter even tighter. He was only twelve feet from me, yet the distance felt insurmountable.

The moment stretched out for an eternity, and then it sped up and was gone. Mr. Foxworthy returned and led Colt away.

Wait! I nearly shouted after them. But I didn't. The free-flowing waters of my soul had been diverted over a span of years and years into the fixed, tubelike passages of the legal system, a system that wouldn't be necessary if it were that easy to simply reach out and say *I'm sorry*.

"Foxworthy wants to meet," Matt said, packing up his briefcase. "Right now."

"In judge's chambers?" I asked, shoving the letter deep into my bag.

"No, privately, in his office."

"Do you think . . . ?"

"I do, the son of a bitch."

He was going to offer me another plea deal. It was actually repugnant in a way—Mrs. Grange had been out of the way for less than a day, and already her cocounsel was throwing her crusade in the garbage.

Mr. Foxworthy's office was as bland as it could be: a framed photograph of his two children, a boy and a girl; a plain white coffee mug; a plain pencil cup containing a single pencil.

"We're so sorry to hear about Mrs. Grange," Matt said politely.

"Yes, well, it's unfortunate. It was very brave of her to keep working."

I heard some noise behind me and saw that, across the hall, they were already clearing out her office.

"So, here we are," Mr. Foxworthy began, sitting back down. "Prosecution has fallen to me, and I have to admit I'm not as . . . *passionate* about the case as Mrs. Grange. Make no mistake, I will follow her strategy and see this case through if that's what it comes to. But I'm open to making a deal."

"What's the offer?" Matt asked.

"Fifteen years."

Matt scoffed. "We could get better from the jury."

"You could. Or you could get twenty-five. Or *life*. You know Hiedler's a wild card."

"We have a fantastic strategy. We happen to know a few things about young Mr. Colt Roach that would make you shit yourself."

Mr. Foxworthy sighed. "Ten years. She'll be out in eight."

"Vermont was going to give her a slap on the wrist and probation."

Mr. Foxworthy turned to speak directly to me. "You did it. And it wasn't self-defense. It was premeditated."

When I finally spoke, my voice was shaking. "I was fourteen."

"Well, you're not fourteen anymore. So don't bullshit me. You were never going to take responsibility. You're only sitting here right now because you got caught."

"They had Dodge's photograph. I pointed to his face and said, 'It was him. That's the guy.' And they did *nothing*."

Mr. Foxworthy held up his hands. "You can't know what situation they were dealing with. They were probably building a case."

"For four months?"

"It happens. Sometimes there's not enough evidence to indict, so they wait."

"It was *her*," I said, jabbing my finger in the direction of Mrs. Grange's former office. "She refused to follow the evidence because it implicated *her*. Someone died because of the insane panic *she* stirred up. My sister *died*."

Foxworthy shot back, "That's not an excuse! We don't kill people out of vengeance! We don't act like criminals just because they do. We stand our ground and say, *No, I won't stoop that low*. If you can't feel the slightest remorse, there's no hope for you."

My eyes flickered around as I tried to keep my tears at bay. "I do feel remorse. I'm not good at showing it, but it's the truth. I wish this had never happened to me. I don't believe in violence. We're on the same side."

"Then you understand why I have to put you away. Everybody's gotta pay the piper."

Matt jumped in. "Fuck the piper. Society's no worse off because there's one less cracked-out white boy with a gun running around."

"Jesus, Matt, shut up," I said. I reached into my bag and pulled out the crumpled letter. *To Colt.* I handed it to Mr. Foxworthy. "Can you give this to him?"

Matt looked at me like I was crazy. Foxworthy peered at the envelope.

"What is this?" When I didn't answer, he opened it, saying, "I'm sorry, but I'm not a mailman. If this is evidence, I'm entitled to see it."

I didn't try to stop him. I watched his face as he read it. He was inscrutable. I was sure he'd seen it all in his day. You didn't stay in the DA's office unless you had a weird appetite for watching people self-destruct.

"Gimme that," Matt said, snatching the letter from Foxworthy and reading it himself. He groaned. "Goddamn it, Jo. . . . Wait, this spot here"—he pointed to a particular sentence (*Regarding my more punishable crime—murder*) and shoved a pen into my hand—"Cross that word out and write 'justifiable homicide.' Go on, do it!"

"Jesus, Matt."

"Are you seriously asking your client to tamper with her statement in front of me?" Foxworthy asked.

"It's not a *statement*," Matt spat at him. "It's personal correspondence. My client can write whatever the fuck she wants. And she wants to write 'justifiable homicide.'"

I rubbed my eyes and sighed. "Fine. Whatever." I took the pen, blacked out the word "murder" and squeezed the words "justifiable homicide" in above it. It looked incredibly stupid.

"If we're doing this deal," I said, "I need to make a phone call first. Can I have some privacy?"

Mr. Foxworthy looked reluctant to leave a criminal alone in his office. He pointed across the hall. "Take Grange's office. And it better be collect."

The maintenance men were packing up the last of Mrs. Grange's things into nondescript boxes. Her office was about the size of a prison cell. Without her legal books and framed pictures, it resembled one, too.

How many cumulative hours had Zora Grange spent between these walls? I wondered. She'd dedicated her whole adult life to putting people in prison without ever realizing she was inside one herself.

I picked up the clunky corded phone and dialed collect. Gwen picked up on the fourth ring.

"Allô?" she answered. Her voice sounded exhausted, her French accent as terrible as ever. "Jo? Is it really you?"

"It's me," I said. "I'm in the DA's office. I got your letters."

"I got yours, too."

I twisted the phone cord in my hand, forgetting precisely what I'd meant to say. Gwen spoke first: "Are you calling me because you're going to jail?"

"Yes." I sighed. "It looks like it."

"For how long?"

"I don't know yet. But I plan to behave myself. I'll get paroled. It won't be that bad."

There was a long silence.

"Are you crying?" I asked.

"Yes." Gwen was even better at discreet crying than I was. She didn't make a single sound.

I said, "I've been thinking a lot about that bottle of Le Pin."

"God, don't remind me."

"No, I'm glad it happened. There's no one I'd have rather opened it with."

"Shut up."

"I'm serious, Gwen."

"What about Montagne? He would have appreciated it more."

"I don't need you to appreciate it. I appreciate *you*. Your bracing-ness, your rarity, your authenticity. I'm glad we drank it together, just you and me. I'm glad some sucker will drink a fake version of it one day and never have any clue. Only you and I will ever know."

"And Jean-Luc."

"And Jean-Luc." I had to laugh, though the sound of it was sad. I took a deep breath. "Let's get married, okay? Not while I'm in prison, that's too depressing. When I get out."

There was a long pause. Finally Gwen said, "It would be a good plotline for the show."

We both knew she was protecting herself with this pretense, which was fine. I would prove to her, with time, that she was safe. The same way she'd proved I was safe with her.

"I have to go now," I said. "I'll write you soon."

"I'll write you, too. Bye, Jo."

We hung up. I glanced around the bare office. I couldn't believe I was spending my last moments of freedom sitting in Mrs. Grange's chair, using her telephone, breathing her stale, recycled air.

I went back across the hall and plunked down in the chair beside Matt.

"Okay," I said. "I'm ready."

"What's the bottom line here, Foxworthy?" Matt demanded. "Let's just get it on the table."

"Eight years, take it or leave it. You want to waste all our time with a trial, be my guest." He gestured to a stack of papers piled three feet high in the corner of the office, propped up by a lamp. "If it's not you, Jo Scottish, it's somebody else. I got a list ten miles long. You're all the same to me."

It was like being back in the emotional desert of Germaine House, which I would later learn had been shut down and turned into a bed and breakfast. I thought about all those kids waiting around for someone to save them. I thought about Trisha's car and the petty satisfaction that I'd gotten away with grand theft auto because the statute of limitations for that crime was six years. I recalled the exact moment I'd decided to steal her keys, committing myself to a new creed: never again would I ask anyone's permission for anything. Of all my memories, corrupted to some degree by the rot of time and the perception of others, this one felt as clear and pure as virgin spring water.

"I'll take it," I said. "I can't stand it anymore. I'll take it."

And from there my mind dips out like a spacey heiress declining to play by a vulgar carjacker's rules, simply stepping out of the car and walking away. What was so special about the car, anyway? He could have it, could medicate his fury with that uniquely American activity: a long drive, windows rolled down, through the fields of lupines and oxeye daisies that would be in full bloom as I arrived at the Goffstown women's detention center, less than a year after my mother had been released.

Epilogue

NEW HAMPSHIRE
2010

UNLIKE OTHER PRISONS, WHICH GARB THEIR INMATES IN OR-
ange or gray, we wear stiff cotton drawstring pants and shirts the muddy
color of a red racer snake. The chapters of my life are all color coded: the
brown-and-green flannels of my childhood, the spotless, deep darks of a
lawyer, followed by flat, inescapable inmate red.

I don't know if I will ever be a legitimate lawyer again. I find myself doing legal work for fellow inmates constantly, reviewing their drug
charges, helping shape their appeals. Sometimes a crowd forms around
me in the yard, like it's the playground and, in a strange twist, I'm the
most popular girl. I could take correspondence courses and apply for
the New Hampshire Bar, but to pass the moral character review, the
onus would be on me to prove to the state licensing authority that I am
an ethical person. I somehow suspect this would not be a gainful use of
energy.

I write all this now, I suppose, moved by muscle memory developed
over half a decade of writing rulings for Montagne, adjudicating fates
left and right in that strange amalgam of a voice: Lacey Bond as Jo Scottish as le justice. But it's just me now, my identity laid bare, my fate on
the docket and all the time in the world with which to adjudicate it.

The majority of my existence is conducted in a six-by-eight-foot
cell, three down from the one that contained my mother. I see her every
week during the appointed visitation hours. All the guards remember
her, are nice to her, and allow her to sneak little items to me. When I

requested some French reading material, she brought me a book about French heirloom tomatoes. "*In* French, Mom," I explained. Weeks later, she presented me with a copy of the French translation of *Divine Secrets of the Ya-Ya Sisterhood*.

At first, as I settled into the routine of my new situation, I used my designated computer time to read the online edition of *Le Devoir* every day. Montagne died. His death was convenient for the city, as a controversy had erupted over a park named for a politician who turned out to be a child molester. The park is now being redubbed Parc D'Etienne Montagne. I wonder if I will ever be permitted to set foot in it. Convicted felons are barred entry to Canada without special permission, which it is by no means certain that I will be granted.

Also denied me, forever, is the privilege of voting, which feels like an excessively mean blow. I will always count voting "yes" in the 1995 referendum for Quebec's independence as one of the purer moments of my life.

Montagne left me money: $6 million. Patrice is contesting the will in probate court, so who knows if I'll ever get a dime. Perhaps the amount seems extreme and unsentimental—a vault of cold hard cash when he could have left me his books or one of the valuable paintings from his art collection. But Montagne knew me well enough not to tie me down with things. With money I could do what I wanted.

Chief Justice Durant wrote an affidavit stating that Montagne had been made aware of my status as a convicted felon and was fully compos mentis at the time. He had weeks to change the will afterward, but he didn't, leaving his grandsons virtually nothing. It seems Montagne wished something else for them: salvation from their soft, unearned existence. And in his stupidly endearing, utterly *Montagne* way, he framed it as a gift: the chance for them to be like me.

Many things are incredibly strange about my life behind bars, though perhaps not the things I expected. I got used to the general shittiness quickly: shitty food, shitty shower, shitty conversation; I have yet to meet a single person here who can converse in depth on any subject beyond themselves or Jesus Christ their Lord and Savior. It's the tiny things that continue to dumbfound me—Nicolas Cage's voice on the common room TV as everyone watches *National Treasure*, for instance. I'd only ever seen his movies dubbed in French. Hearing his actual voice makes me feel insane. Had none of it been real? All those years, had I been living the dubbed version of my own life?

The TV is a piece of crap with only twelve channels, so I'm unable to tune in to *Golden Girl* with the rest of America at 9:00 P.M. on Sundays. I know Colt is there, having hiked from Vermont to Canada as if it were a family rite of passage (it couldn't be done this time; the once wild woods of the border are littered with sensors and thermal imaging cameras, and the Mounties intercepted him almost immediately).

He just showed up, so I guess he's going to play my brother, Gwen wrote to me in a letter scribbled on the back of a grocery store receipt that revealed she'd recently purchased five bags of Doritos and a bottle of Mariah Carey brand perfume. *He is your brother,* I wanted to reply but didn't, knowing that by the time the letter made it back to her, the impact of that sentiment would be nil.

I suppose Colt is young enough to be warped into whatever pleasing caricature of a redneck-in-the-big-city the producers need him to be to manufacture more of the nation's number one leading opiate: *great television*. I can't help picturing the look of transparent horror I saw on his face whenever Mrs. Grange urged the jury to look at him—now to be magnified for the consumption of a national audience—and I wonder if all I accomplished in extricating the two of us from that horrible trial was to substitute one set of wolves for another. But at least he's with his sister, and at least he got out of this country.

For *Golden Girl*'s much-anticipated season finale, the second unit crew obtained permission to tape my end of the dramatic phone call that will answer viewers' burning questions (will Gwen go to bed with the handsome tea purveyor from San Francisco? or does her heart still belong to the notorious lesbian felon?).

"I love you, Jo. You're the only one. They can never, ever break us," she said through the shitty phone connection. Then, once the cameras were off, "You wouldn't believe the numbnut they dredged up for my 'date.' He has a tattoo of the word 'infinity' shaped like infinity. I was like, 'You must really like infinity, huh?' And he was like, 'Yeah, it's great.'"

I can say without irony that Gwen is the infinity tattoo on my life, great in its extent, permanence, and triteness—for love *can*, according to it, conquer all. My incomprehension that she could love me is gradually fading. Would I not have loved her if our positions were reversed, making me the benign one and her the one with a heart deformed by violence? Of course I would have. Yet never once had that entered into my thinking. Rarely does the logic of love seem to apply to oneself.

My mother was correct that everything slows down in prison, and while physical space is cramped, there is unlimited room for the mind to wander. What it didn't take me long to realize is that, though I'd spared myself the uncertainty of a trial, there was no escape from the uncertainty of the future. Each day brings me nearer to my parole hearing. Like most prisoners, my fantasies center on the moment of release, that first step beyond the barbed wire fence—purifying, transcendent— without daring to proceed much further.

Doubtless it will be my mother who greets me; Gwen still can't set foot here without risking arrest. Mom will arrive in a borrowed, beat-up truck, and I'll hop in like a kid being picked up from school.

And after that? My mind draws a blank. It will be the first time since I was thirteen years old that the law will have nothing on me. I guess it will be my chance to become the person I was always meant to be, basically my mother: a hardened old farmer, eschewing society in favor of dirt and toil and self-reliance. But somehow, dreadfully, I suspect that I will prove to be my father's child: attached inexorably to my media darling of a wife, on a dizzying carousel of an existence, bewildered and a little dissolute, ever looking backward to determine the precise moment when I agreed to it all.

If you have stuck with me this far, whether out of morbid curiosity or brute commitment to finish what you started, or, in my wildest dreams, a growing (or diminishing) sliver of love for me, I can only imagine your frustration that in the end I stopped fighting and chose this cell over ... what? Letting twelve strangers choose it for me? Or perhaps you feel that getting eight years for taking a teenager's life is hardly the injustice of the century. In any case, here I am. Your tax dollars pay for my food, my clothes, the roof over my head.

And if it weren't me in here, it'd be somebody else, to take Mr. Foxworthy's grimly Zen worldview. We are all interchangeable nobodies, made special only by the brittle chain of love enabling each link to barely hold on to the next: my mother to me, me to Gwen, Gwen (optimistically) to Colt. Somewhere in there is Éclair—beautiful, brilliant Éclair—whose love I still feel even though her link has long disintegrated. She is not coming back, at least not for me. It's up to some Hells Angel to find her now, to be the man who rediscovers the most legendary beauty of the twentieth century.

In jail, it becomes apparent how maladapted our society is to supporting lasting bonds. It's like we're *trying* to destroy love. Smothering it in concrete, deadening it with consumer goods and blitzes of media. We are exceptional—we are the only species that acts directly, consciously, against its self-interest. Over, and over, and over.

At night my mind paces like a caged animal, trying to give a name to what love even *is*. What if my mother was right? What if Gwen anointed me from the beginning, and none of my choices were ever truly my own? Then again, what else could love be, beyond surrendering your life to another person? I've always been obsessed with freedom— the worst obsession, I'm convinced—and in my unending mental labyrinth, I circle back to the question of what that freedom meant to me in the first place. All I can say is that freedom's a feeling I'll never know: to be so beautiful you terrify the world, daring it to annihilate you. Unlike me, whose only hope is to survive.

If there is any poetry in that, it's not for me to write. It's not for my parents, or for Éclair if she were here, or for anyone who loved me as a child. It's for whoever can love me now, nothing to my name but the rugged will to live, which *is* beautiful and horrible—a lone, gnarled tree jutting from the cliffside, exposed, hanging on.

Acknowledgments

TO MY PARENTS, THANK YOU FOR SUPPORTING MY ARTISTIC FREE-dom. Stephen Barr, thank you for your sheer endurance. You can lift twenty times your weight and I regularly ask you to do so. To Genevieve Gange-Hawes, thank you for demonstrating how to interrogate emotions without fear. Thank you to my valiant editor Noah Eaker. You are a true knight in shining armor.

Thank you to Nico Carver, Rachel Wasserman, Erica McGrath, Emily Boyd, Becky Furey, Rachel David, and Skye Thrash. Many thanks to all my readers, and to the teachers and librarians who spend their lives connecting people with books.

About the Author

MAGGIE THRASH is the author of the critically acclaimed graphic memoirs *Honor Girl* (a Los Angeles Times Book Prize nominee) and *Lost Soul, Be at Peace*, as well as two novels for young adults. *Rainbow Black* is her adult debut. Born and raised in Atlanta, she lives in New Hampshire.